DANCE OF THE RAINMAKERS

DANCE OF THE RAINMAKERS

James Coeur

Matador
9 Priory Business Park,
Wistow Road, Kibworth Beauchamp,
Leicestershire. LE8 0RX
Tel: 0116 279 2299
Email: books@troubador.co.uk
Web: www.troubador.co.uk/matador
Twitter: @matadorbooks

ISBN 978 1800463 967

British Library Cataloguing in Publication Data.
A catalogue record for this book is available from the British Library.

Printed and bound in Great Britain by 4edge Limited
Typeset in 11pt Baskerville by Troubador Publishing Ltd, Leicester, UK

Matador is an imprint of Troubador Publishing Ltd

To J. M. with love

Prologue

The girl's voice sounded faint down the phoneline. 'I'm sweating, my head is hurting, and I have a big fever. I can't come in today.'

'Take some paracetamol and go to bed.'

'What else?'

'That's all you can do. You're young, the symptoms should abate after a few days, don't worry.'

'Sorry.'

'That's fine, if you're ill, you're ill. We'll survive. If it does get worse, then call me.'

By the time that Kasia, the health centre's receptionist, had reported sick, the virus already had its talons deep into the village. It would take the discovery, nine days later, of the body of Dr Williams, her boss, for the locals to take the outbreak seriously. And another two years would pass before the fuse lit that March morning would snake its way to what a national newspaper editorial, writing with tinder-brittle hindsight, called "an inevitable explosion of long-suppressed anger". No one at the same paper had chosen beforehand to think about the village, or the hundreds of small communities similarly adrift across the country.

Perhaps, even if they had done, they still wouldn't have been able to predict the actual form the anger would take. Or the many ways the rage would change lives, change maybe even a nation.

However, if truth be told, back then in 2020 the village itself didn't at first quite recognise what was going on. Didn't join the dots, you see. While most of the residents had seen the television pictures, beamed on the evening news from China, bemused at how you could lock down an entire city, but then it was always China, wasn't it? They'd always had these flu scares, hadn't they, and no wonder; you should see where they buy their food from. Val and Chris from up on Cantref Gwaelod Terrace had been on a package trip there a few years back and they said that the markets in that country were disgusting – snakes in fish tanks, pickled scorpions and you name it sitting next to the fruit stalls.

And then Italy went into lockdown, with the Pope taking his Sunday mass online, and soon after there were reports of exhausted Spanish nurses crying at the hopeless tsunami of death that they endured through never-ending nightmare shifts. That captured more attention, and there'd be a slight lowering of the chatter in the pub when the images came up on the corner telly. But that was those countries, wasn't it, not this one. It was just the usual solitary voice of gloom coming from his corner table, malt whisky in hand, which said that this time would be different for everyone. Many eyes were rolled at this pronouncement – hadn't the same voice said that about Brexit, but the sky hadn't fallen on that one – even if a handful of customers nervously swilled their drinks. Surely Britain was an island, and maybe while the virus would indeed fester in a place like London, that city was a long way away from a small seaside resort on the west coast of Wales. They'd be all right, wouldn't they? Get the next one in, Dewi.

It was only about then that the dwindling numbers of local customers at the pub commented on the increase in visitors arriving from across the border. Accents from Manchester, Liverpool and Birmingham blocked the bar, hogged the fruit machine, and took up the regulars' favourite tables, disregarding local custom as carelessly as the summer tourist mob. Around this time, it was remarked that there seemed to be more lights on the holiday cottages on a weekday night – which was quite strange for late winter, when the fleece-cutting wind shrieked in from the Irish Sea. Once-dark off-peak streets were lit by the glow from the windows of prematurely occupied cottages. With them came the boxy Tesco vans, bustling down from Porthmadog, which had quickly become a regular feature on the narrow road down to the harbour area, making food deliveries to those same second homes. Meanwhile, a scattering of muttered complaints was heard in the local shop about the lack of fruit & veg available for sale. This had become a more frequent occurrence, but what could the shop owner do, the holiday crowd were getting there early and buying most of it up, and he had to earn a living, didn't he?

It was true, the waterfront was certainly busier, but many shrugged it off as a welcome bit of money for businesses in what had been a particularly long, wet drag of a low season. Other services in the village were busy, as well. The wife of one of the pub regulars, who happened to be the village policeman, recounted to her friends over a few bottles of discount Chenin Blanc how she had waited near on a whole hour to see her GP. A whole hour, for goodness sake; she had timed it, queuing behind a group of blooming tourists who were registering with the health centre or seeking treatment. Her friends nodded in shared outrage and the next morning those of them who could afford it carried out a bigger shop than usual at the Co-op supermarket in nearby Dolgellau. Just a few more tins of soup, a couple more packets of dried pasta from the low-stocked shelves, a big slab or two of minced beef for the freezer, and an extra nine-pack of loo roll – better safe than sorry.

That same morning, a few days after his receptionist had called in sick, the village doctor himself placed a call to the health authority in Bangor, having diagnosed himself with the Covid-19 virus. With a frail voice, he informed the duty officer that he'd be self-isolating and requested emergency locum cover to be arranged for the community. He tried to read out a list of patients with whom he'd been in contact over the past week, but was tersely told to email them, as everyone in Bangor was flat out and another call was coming through. That email never arrived, an ill-fated omission for two elderly patients in the village who died alone, abandoned by the authorities which were ignorant of their vulnerability. Afterwards it was generally believed that the doctor had been simply too ill to get to his computer to send the list. He was quite old himself anyway, staying on after the normal retirement age as he couldn't recruit a new GP to the village surgery. After a call to the local police sergeant from Dr Williams' worried daughter, who was stranded in Singapore, his body had been found on the floor near his bed. Given the circumstances, no blame could be reasonably attached to anyone, despite the daughter's call for an inquiry. As for locum cover, like elsewhere in the country there were no spare medics, leaving the practice nurse to close the surgery, and then herself enter isolation.

The news about their GP spread fast through the community, and it didn't take long for the villagers to make the connection between the loss of their health cover and the influx of holidaymakers and the second-homes pack. Their mood was not helped by the scenes that weekend, as tourists clustered on the beach and outside the shuttered pubs serving pints from the doorstep. They included a peloton of middle-aged, middle-management cyclists who saw no reason to cancel their regular monthly event after one of them had reported to their WhatsApp group that the virus couldn't spread in fresh air. A graduate student, himself only a village resident since the previous August, draped a bedsheet over a road sign at the entrance to the village, and sprayed the text "Go home, Covid morons – village closed" upon it. That gave an opportunity for one of the peloton to take a selfie where he showed the sign the middle finger, blithely posting it onto Facebook to what turned out to be a brutal online jury.

The following day, the nation went into its first official lockdown, and that we all remember – the otherness it brought, the sense of isolation, and an uncertainty about the future. The police patrols on the border, the tweets from nurses with no protection. Some people hid in their one-storey castles, others acted as if nothing had changed, some partied for the apocalypse. Coming out of the lockdown and trying to make the best of what was left of the season, the baby boomer holidaying couples on the promenade screaming at others to keep their distance; the grain of underlying fear that ran through the spaced tables outside the pub on the square; wearing a mask as a way of life. All the while, more local homes were being sold, becoming lifeboats as the wealthy scrabbled to abandon the cities. Dragging back down into lockdowns as the autumnal and Christmas spikes emerged, the death toll stacking higher, a defining year for generations. When the country finally staggered into the dawn, after the vaccines had been rolled out at quick-slow-quick pace, mass post-traumatic stress disorder didn't cover the half of it. People were learning to live with others again, high streets bore the scars, and the economy was staggering. The desperation for trade deals hadn't gone away, neither had pot-stirring out of the Middle East, and there were the usual ministerial scandals to be spun. So naturally there were higher priority items on Westminster's agenda than a bunch of angry yokels in the backend of beyond. I mean, what did these people expect? For goodness sake, we're working tirelessly here for the good of these same idiots and never a word of gratitude, just endless whining... anyway, we now have "build back better" policy to consider before the next election.

A few months on from the last peak of the virus, a visitor to the village might have observed that the cemetery was marked with a row of fresh graves, missing stone headstones while the soil settled. All those funerals had been presided over by a vicar, dressed like a shabby penguin cast adrift from his colony, corroding in the seaborne winds. Sometimes, with relatives of the deceased still in quarantine, the service would be just him and the gravediggers – those ceremonies could be particularly stark. And to his knowledge there remained a few more bodies in the county's emergency mortuary awaiting delivery back to their former home. It was his spiritual burden, but one which had become one of form rather than belief. In the solitary evenings, encased in the stone tomb that was the vicarage, he'd try to offer up a prayer but find no words coming.

One

It always started in the same way: the first petrol bomb marking a lazy arc in the direction of their van, a pint of fiery reality whirling towards him. Lloyd Parry saw the youths silhouetted against the light of a burning patrol car, its bloodied occupants having staggered to the safety of his support vehicle, now itself under attack.

'Get the window grates down... get them down now!' Sergeant Parry turned his gaze from the shuttered street ahead and looked around at his unit. There were nine of them. But this included the two injured patrol car officers, two WPCs, plus a taut-faced probationer. That made just three other experienced men and him, up against twenty to thirty rioters. He remembered an old saying that his first supervisor would tell him at the end of a beat – how do you get home? Well, you wouldn't start from here...

'Report to gold command, request immediate assistance. We are trapped midway down,' he took a quick look around, trying to find a landmark, but every street in this area with its shabby, soot-stained redbrick seemed alike. Lloyd knew that he should have made a note of the street as they turned into it, but for once he'd been sloppy. The darkened windows of the terrace shed no light, 'Er, midway down Bergen Road I think.' His unit had sped to the area to assist their colleagues, and now found themselves caught up in the same whirlwind.

Lloyd watched the gang strut back and forward across the road about fifty, maybe sixty yards in front of them. He saw their arms being flung out in ancient gestures of pre-fight intimidation, could hear their mouths vent screams of pent-up rage. It caused him to swallow, his breath to quicken. This had been coming for a long time. The white gangs had historically raided Asian territory, but this new generation of local Asians wasn't into deference to white authority like their parents. And if there was one thing which they detested as much as the hated BNP – the organisers of the city centre march earlier that day which had ignited this whole stupid mess – it was the police who kept them down, oppressed, resentful. Tonight was a time to mark out territory and win back self-respect.

Parry looked at the officer standing next to him, who was caressing a baton in his leather-gloved hands. Harris was a local Yorkshire lad, usually calm, but tonight Lloyd could sense the anxiety oozing from him. He wondered whether they were thinking along the same lines. Grainy television pictures of past big-city riots; the camera light blurring from the glare of exploding petrol bombs; scaffolding poles ripped from worksites to be used as lances; lads flinging stones, neckerchiefs hiding their faces; the return fire of tear gas – London and Liverpool in the eighties, Belfast for what seemed eternity, South London again – but tonight it was the turn of Bradford. And here he was, looking after a section of a fag-paper-thin blue line, outnumbered, unarmed and, as far as Lloyd could see, still underfunded by the New Labour government.

‘Have you got through to area command yet?’

‘Sarge, we’re being ordered to withdraw four blocks south to Malvern Row. They don’t have any available tactical support units. The situation is district-wide. Inspector said that we’re way out of position and need to fall back to the new holding line.’

Lloyd glanced back to make an assessment of the situation; the smaller group of rioters that had started to work their way behind their van had grown. To his side, Harris slumped forward, struck by one of the stones now coming at them from all directions. He raised his shield and half-pulled the stumbling officer back to the shelter of the vehicle. ‘Get up, get in the van!’

Lloyd snapped to. Make a decision; don’t passively let it happen, be active, do something. The line of youths to the front was starting to slowly approach them, wrath-filled yet purposeful. Cold fury can be a terrible, wrecking thing. He could see that some of them were armed with broken-off chair legs and baseball bats. Who plays baseball in the county of Yorkshire? More to the point, who bloody-well sells baseball bats in the county of Yorkshire? Then he made out what looked like a hatchet. Just a glimpse, but it was enough to send a chill to his brain. The line was now forty yards away, the gap closing. The chimes of the missile strikes hitting the thin aluminium skin of the police wagon were merging into a continuous percussion, like a crazed mantlepiece clock.

‘Sarge, what do we do?’ It was one of the women officers – he could tell from the jerky movements of her helmet that she was starting to lose control. The stones were striking the van more heavily now and the other two male officers were huddled behind their riot shields. Where the mob got the missiles from bemused him – the council had tarmacked over the Victorian cobbles years ago to save on maintenance bills. 'Right, we're going to reverse out of here. Watson, get ready to go for it, we're not stopping. Punch it straight through their lines. Everyone else in the van…'

The other two officers bundled in, and he jumped onto the front passenger seat. 'Okay, go, go, go!' He felt the van jerk backwards and heard the engine die, the driver had stalled it. 'Come on,' he urged. The woman constable turned the ignition keys once more, but it wouldn't catch. In desperation, again she tried to coax a start, but it was too soon after the previous attempts; the engine had flooded. Staring through the windscreen grill, Lloyd saw a petrol bomb flare straight for him. He heard nothing, just registered the flash of light, the shake and the sharp change of air pressure as the bomb burst like an egg over the bonnet. Their sanctuary was aflame.

Stunned, knowing he was stunned, knowing he should react and get a grip, Lloyd looked about. The crowd was moving forward with confidence now, and as his hearing kicked back in, he could hear the chanting. They were fucked, they were going to die, but if they stayed in the van they were going to roast – suckling pig style. A recent memory popped into his head; watching a cookery programme on the telly, his wife cuddled next to him on their new sofa and the kids playing soldiers out in the garden.

'Right… everyone out. Move yourselves… draw batons!' The occupants scrambled or stumbled over each other and away from the van. Lloyd could feel the heat from the burning paintwork through his face visor. The sergeant scanned the sides of the streets for an alley, some kind of escape route, but there was nothing but flaking brick wall.

Yet there was one house with no curtains drawn and the lights off, looked like a derelict.

'Follow me.' If they could get through the house and the back yard onto the parallel street, it would at least give them a chance and a better one than going hand-to-hand with the large mob.

Lloyd ran to the front door of the property, only then registering the graffitied word "Paki" sprayed across it and smashed it in with two powerful heels from his right boot. 'Through and out the back! Keep moving! Keep moving!' In the corner of his eye, he registered a chink of light through the curtains of the neighbouring house go out. His squad went in, but one of the WPCs remained still, her body shaking, dumbly unresponsive to her sergeant's commands. She was probably going into shock, but they didn't have the time to mess about. Over her shoulder, he could see a bulky figure sprint at them, swinging a length of piping. Lloyd spun round, instinctively stepped in front of the woman officer and felt a blow from the pipe hit the side of his helmet. Slightly dazed, he deployed his baton with an instinctive jab to the attacker's guts, and then a roundhouse strike on his back. The man dropped heavily. In the background there was a sudden flash followed by a wave of heat – their van was now wrapped in flame. Against the light, he could detect movement closing in on him. He pushed the girl through the doorway and followed her inside, throwing his weight back onto the front door to keep it closed, given its lock was now broken, 'Move it Helen!' She seemed to wake up at the shock of the sergeant using her first name and she scrambled in slo-mo for the back exit of the house. Just a few more seconds here to give his guys some distance, he was breathing hard drawing in oxygen to counter his sluggishness. His vision started to close in as the door shuddered with more of the mob arriving to force a way in; but Lloyd, thinking back to his school rugby training, locked his knees to keep his weight on the frame. At that moment he was glad of the gym visits that kept him in shape. Even so, his body was almost bouncing off the door; it felt like the mob was using some kind of a battering ram. He was a lonely legionnaire on the Rhine and the barbarians were flooding over. A window in the room next to the hallway shattered. He was singing 'Men of Harlech' at Rorke's Drift. Was that ten seconds yet? He was holding out against the Taliban as the bullets kicked-up around him.

'We're through Sarge – come on!' Harris screaming at him from the back kitchen.

Lloyd turned his head around, in the process shifting his weight off the door, which, with his counterforce gone, broke open, flinging him onto the hallway floor. One of the rioters fell through the doorway and onto on him, the man's dark eyes inches from his face.

He felt the man straighten up on him and raise his right hand. Spittle from his attacker's mouth splattered Lloyd's visor, screams of hatred drowning out the sounds from the street. He could see a hatchet in the hand. Lloyd couldn't respond, with his eyes fixated on the blade now pausing high above him. He saw the dirty white insulating tape wrapped around the top of the shaft, with its untidy end where someone had bitten off the roll of tape instead of using some scissors. The policeman's limbs had stopped responding, and he could feel liquid spreading where the blow he'd taken outside had landed. He wondered whether his brains would spill out when the mortician removed his helmet. Lloyd heard himself issue a high-pitched whine, a sick dog about to be put down.

A fast movement at the corner of his eyesight, and then the man's face burst into a red mist. Through the red droplets raining upon his vision, he saw a baton strike his attacker's head again before the body collapsed backwards.

'Sarge! Fucking get up!' Harris was standing over him. 'Any more of you fuckers want some? Do you? Do you!' The mob held its position outside the doorway, now leaderless and with their momentum temporarily stalled. Punch-drunk, Lloyd tried to recover himself and staggered foal-like to his feet. 'I'm okay, I'm okay.'

Harris hauled him through the galley kitchen and out into the cobbled yard. They slammed the back door shut and, seeing an old refrigerator rusting in the yard, manhandled it against the door to slow anyone behind. The garden gate of the house opposite was scattered open, indicating the path of the rest of his squad. Lloyd and Harris followed them through, via a side passage leading off the yard and into a quiet street of semi-detached houses signalling a demarcation zone of sorts. They moved off at a trot in the direction of the police holding line, frequently casting glances to their rear to check for any rioters hunting them down. He heard one of the younger men laugh at their escape. A spotlight from above began to sweep across them, guiding them ahead, and they could hear the lumbering rhythm of the police helicopter overhead. Lloyd could feel his own quick, shallow breaths – tasted the acidity in his throat rising up from his stomach. He wanted to stop and be sick, roll into a foetal ball on the street. They made out a large contingent of riot police up ahead and as his squad slowed to a breathless walk with safety in sight,

Lloyd became aware of blood trickling down the side of his face where he'd taken the initial blow. He felt a dampness in his crotch and realised that he'd wet himself.

❧

'Sergeant Parry, we're all done here. Can we go home now? Get off like.'

Lloyd returned from his thoughts to the present scene and turned to face the speaker. Bradford was history – the setting today, as it had been for some time now, was Llanawch, a small Welsh coastal village on the edge of nowhere, possibly even well beyond that boundary. His eyes refocused on the two young men in his line of sight, Emyr and Rhys Jones, the latter of whom was now wiping his paint-stained hands with a dirty piece of what looked like torn pillowcase. He hoped they hadn't cottoned on that he'd been daydreaming. The teenagers, all facial angles, blotchy skin, and simmering resentment, hovered before him.

Lloyd uncrossed his arms and stood up from where he'd been leaning on the bonnet of his police Land Rover and strolled over to examine their work. The colour of the side wall had been restored to its previous pastel yellow shade and the drying paint gleamed under the weak sunlight.

He'd caught the brothers yesterday spraying a Welsh nationalist slogan – "Cofiwch Dryweryn" – on the side of the village bus shelter. Not quite as snappy as "we will overcome", but it did mark the flooding of a village not forty miles away for a reservoir to supply post-war Liverpool. In fact, the whole scheme, as he remembered from school, was steam-rollered through by their city council and local MP without any concern for a bunch of irate Welshies about to lose their home. Greater good and all that. As such, it wasn't that Lloyd disagreed with the sentiment; he just didn't like the law being flouted in his bit of the world. So rather than the inevitable community order and the sheaf of accompanying paperwork, the sergeant had opted to dispense some on-the-spot pragmatic justice, or police-state persecution – depending on which end of it you were on. He'd bundled the brothers into his car, driving them to their home. After the anticipated parental carpeting had occurred, the father quickly agreed to pay for the paint for the boys to make good their damage. The mother was simply relieved that her sons would avoid the criminal record which could blot any job application. Despite all evidence she still held out hope for her boys. As the front door had carefully closed behind him, Lloyd had heard the recriminations starting in earnest. He couldn't understand the language, but the volume had told him all that he needed to know.

Now, the policeman walked slowly around the shelter, tut-tutting here, pausing there, just to emphasise who was in charge. He came to a halt and hooked his thumbs into his equipment belt.

'Well, boys, it's a nice job… a nice job. There's just one thing though…'

'What's that then?'

'You need to do the inside as well,' he nodded at the paint pots. 'Well go on. I haven't got all day here.'

Rhys swore under his breath and chucked the rag at the pots, before picking up his brush with resignation. Emyr gave the sergeant a dark look before slowly complying. Lloyd resumed his position next to the car and, as he watched the boys continue their painting, distractedly patted his belly. It wasn't huge in the scheme of things, not compared to some he saw, and boy, there were some obese monsters to be found amongst the tourists, but he knew that he could do with a little exercise. Perhaps. He looked up at the sky, where a jet's contrail made a steady cut across the satin blue backdrop, the white furrow expanding in width behind it as the plane ploughed westwards. The village was situated right underneath the North American air routes. Lloyd liked to imagine that there'd be a handful of passengers on board about to start a new life amongst all the holidaymakers and businessmen. He doubted that those people would ever gaze down on the village with anything but a cursory glance as it drifted below the wingspan, that is, if they could make it out at all. It must seem so small from up there, set against the expanse of land and sea. Llanawch was a place people passed over.

Below the plane's flight path and across the glistening wavelets of the estuary, the hills squatted in hues of ageless grey and rain-reflected green. They were monuments to Ice Age, the granite sculpted by the powerful retreating glaciers – he'd seen a documentary about it all on the Discovery channel a few years back. Those mountains had formed an impressive barrier to outsiders over centuries, but they were also an intimidating cage to those who lived in their shadow.

Sometimes, in his darker moments, Lloyd would fantasise about a motorway bulldozing a path right through those hills. Anything to vary this unending backdrop of tedium – they were just mountains for God's sake – they didn't do anything, they just stood there, the same as they'd done for aeons. For that, as he all too often mused to himself, was the trouble with this place. Nothing changed, and the locals seemed only too content to keep it that way. The tourists also seemed to like that, but then, they didn't have to live here. He picked out a pair of moving dots edging down the hillside directly across the way. Hikers from the city on the right track, another peak ticked off the list. But at least they were doing something different. How easy it was for a man to drift past his sell-by date when there's bugger all to pick him up off the shelf of life. Not that he wanted too much of a revolution mind, but a little bit of difference in his days now and again would just be fine. A hill top summited here or there, any kind of achievement would do... anything but this big splodgy mass of days. The evening of the riots was now far distant in years, but it still felt near in memory – he couldn't shake it off, it clung to him like a leech, humping his backbone, draining him steadily. Before Bradford he'd had confidence, certainty – now he just put on a show – he'd come down here to recover, and then got comfy. Even the virus had proved a temporary blip, a few months when he felt alive again, people looking to him, being of use. Yet he wasn't about to return up north either; policing the cities was a job for a young man, it would be too hard on him. Perhaps, he reflected, it was stupid to try to make a fresh start at his age...

He could see movement off to his left – a duck was breaking free of the water's surface. Frenetic motions, its great wings straining to pick up speed and generate lift. The bird headed towards him, then at the last second veered away in an arc over the scraggy-nested heads of the brothers, the curve of its flight expanding outwards over the village rooftops, before disappearing from view.

Two

Lloyd awoke with a start, taking a few hazy seconds to become aware of his surroundings. The fingers of dawn reached through the worn curtains as his bedside clock ticked. Catrin, his wife, sighed and rolled away. He rose quietly, so as not to disturb her and to gain a few minutes of solitude for himself before the rest of the house bustled into motion. The dampness on Lloyd's back pinprick-dried in the still cold air, as he tiptoed out of the bedroom, pausing to collect his dressing gown and shorts from the brass hook on the wall. As he slumped his way across the landing, he paused at the door of his younger son's room, hearing the turning of a body in its bed. Down in the kitchen, his feet marking a trail on the cold flagstones, Lloyd turned the radio on to hear the weather forecast and dumped a heaped spoonful of coffee and two of sugar into his usual mug. He scratched himself fully awake and watched from the kitchen window as the tentative wisps of sun became more certain, merging into full daylight.

Lloyd was parked in a lay-by, monitoring the steady flow of early-morning commuter and school-run traffic, when police headquarters in Colwyn Bay radioed him. Instructions to attend to a problem at Glanrhyd Farm – the caller is highly distressed – there is likely to be a casualty involved. Within seconds the sergeant had swung his Land Rover one hundred and eighty degrees around in the direction of the Roberts' place. Their farm was situated about ten minutes away on the coastal side of Llanawch. The radio continued to feed him information: an ambulance was on the way – the district patrol car was en route for back-up. Since the incident down in Cowbridge last year, the procedure now was to cover these situations in pairs.

The sergeant drove at speed towards the farm, his adrenaline levels jolting upwards with every change of the gear stick. He turned his sirens off as he reached the outskirts of his home village and registered Daren Jenkins – double chin slopping into his open-necked shirt, late once more for his job at Arwel's school – sharply brake his car as he spotted the police vehicle travelling towards him. Parry flashed his headlights to let the speeding driver know that he'd been clocked. He maintained a steady pace through Llanawch, dropping down to the square, passing the length of the beach and then climbing again to the coastal road. With the open water of the bay now on the passenger side, he dropped down a gear as the road wound up past the hillside fields strewn with cattle. At the crest of the hill, he slowed to take a right turn by the ivy-encased milk-churn platform which marked the entrance and rumbled up the hardcore track towards the squat pebble-dashed farmhouse. After a hundred yards, he heard the sound of his wheels change tone as they met the concrete surface of the farmyard and let the Land Rover roll to a halt on a patch where a few weeds peeked through the cracked hard-top.

He'd visited Glanrhyd the previous month, to take details of a stolen tractor, the non-recovery of which had turned out to be a big problem for John Roberts. The tractor was second-hand and even then, hi-tech machinery was costly, as his eldest son often reminded him. But the farmer had decided to save pennies, so no insurance, no immobiliser and no tracking device either. Switching the engine off, the policeman listened for a moment as it ticked over and settled. There was no one about to greet him. He removed a tube of mints from the glove compartment, popped one in his mouth and stepped out into the April coolness. Lloyd's nostrils picked up the familiar mixture of sea salt, freshly cut grass and the inevitable stench of cowshit. Even now, he couldn't get used to it. All was quiet apart from the breeze rattling through a faded fertiliser bag covering a broken windowpane in the milking parlour. At this time of the day, a farm should be busy. There was no noise of the machinery in the parlour, no relieved lowing from the herd as their bulging udders were emptied, no shouts from the farmhand.

Turning to face the farmhouse, he walked towards its kitchen door, and without knocking, opened it, and stood at the entrance. 'Marie? It's Lloyd here.' Marie Roberts had called it in, so he'd best let her know he was on the premises. A slight figure, still carrying the shadow of her youthful attractions, appeared in the doorway leading into the heart of the house. A twisted tea towel was grasped in her whitened fists.

'Where is he?'

'Old barn. I didn't want to go in myself. Just heard the noise,' she didn't take her reddened eyes off him. 'I'm glad it's you…'

Lloyd nodded. 'There'll be some others on the way. Best make yourself a hot, sweet drink, okay.'

He closed the door behind him and headed unhurriedly over to the outbuildings, half hoping that the ambulance crew would arrive before he got there and take over. The sheet metal barn door was slightly open, so he slid it fully across to illuminate the interior, all the while keeping his eyes focused away from what he knew he was about to see. Finally, after taking a deep breath he let his vision glide slowly over the manure-stained concrete flooring before picking up a shoe, then leg, coming to rest on the body scattered on the flagstones some five yards inside the entrance.

Lloyd took it in; the still eyes staring up at the leak-speckled roof; the seepage of blood and gristle from the back of the head staining the shoulders of the worn tweed jacket; another stream running down into the muck drainage channel. As his mind processed these initial scattered images, for a few seconds Lloyd was more conscious of the impact of his own shock than the details of the suicide victim in front of him. Then experience reasserted itself, returning him to the situation and procedure. He noted that the nails on both hands were clean; most farmers' skin was tattooed with the dirt and chemical stains of the working day, but it seemed as if John Roberts had made a final effort to ready himself before the traditional ceremony with the twelve-bore.

This was his third dead farmer in the past two years.

Why did they do it? Well, he knew why they did it. But what was the bloody point? What about the missus – didn't he think of that?

He checked himself. Too late to be the nice guy, Lloyd. Too late now to think of Marie, and John her going-to-seed husband, who finally had taken a chance one night in an Aberystwyth pub and landed himself a bride barely out of her teens. Too late now, when you'd felt Marie up against the back wall of the clubhouse at the summer carnival while her old man was inside at the bar in an amateur-drinker stupor with the other farmers. Maybe he'd regret that more if John hadn't treated her like rubbish anyway once they'd lost their child. In love with the farm he was, wanted an heir to take it on and keep the family line going – that's what she meant to him. But now he was dead. He stared at the farmer's corpse as if to provoke some profound thought, but it wasn't forthcoming.

It all seemed pretty straightforward. Lloyd checked his watch for the time and wrote it down in his notebook. Five minutes past nine. It would take a while for the details to fade, but he'd need to provide testimony at the coroner's court. So it would be an open wound for a while, for the wife, for him and the community. He turned away from the body to the sight of Marie Roberts staring at him through her kitchen window. The old beat officer in him grimaced, shook his head and watched as her face disappeared into the internal gloom. Lloyd saw the back-up police car approaching on the coast road, slowing down for the turning to the farm. He retraced his steps to the house, thinking about what to say. Straightening up at the door, he brushed back his hair, replaced his cap. And he needed to remind her that the cows would need milking. Probably ask the next farm to help, that would sort it. He could drop by afterwards. After facing Marie…

Just another April morning, but one where he faced an impossible task, finding the right words. But that, he sighed, was his duty.

Three

Lloyd had spent most of the day dealing with the aftermath of the Roberts suicide. Now he sat at the family table, polishing off his tea of shepherd's pie, chips and peas eaten to a background of *Coronation Street* playing on the TV set in the corner of the kitchen.

'Had a bit of a rough one today.' He put the knife and fork together on his plate.

'Oh yes?' Catrin's addiction to soap opera was a fact of life in the Parry household and she remained engrossed in her programme. Lloyd's eyes flicked from her to the screen and back.

'Where's Arwel?'

'Hmmm?' She turned to face him. 'What's that?'

'I said, where's Arwel?'

'Upstairs. Studying. You were late.' She returned her gaze to the television.

'I had a suicide. But never mind. For whom the bell tolls and so on. All well at the *Rover's Return*?'

She continued to watch. 'Who's that then?'

'Selective hearing this evening.' Lloyd checked himself as he heard the critical tone in his own voice.

‘Old news, I heard all about it already from the postman.’

‘Right.’ He pushed his plate away. ‘It was pretty rough anyway.’

No reply. ‘Well, thanks for the food. I’m off to see our first-born.’

‘I know,’ his wife said.

‘Seems like there isn’t much you don’t know.’

Catrin turned around and stared at him. ‘Sometimes I don’t want to know. But I always seem to find out about it eventually.’

Upstairs the ultra-sensitive volume on Arwel’s stereo edged up a few decibels. Lloyd, his stomach now taut, rose slowly from the table and wordlessly left by the kitchen door. Setting out through the village down to his favoured pub which stood on the harbour, he hoped that she would be asleep by the time he got back – he couldn’t be doing with it tonight.

A tiny fishing fleet still worked out of the village, catching shellfish for distant restaurants, but otherwise it was strictly low-end leisure craft – all blistered varnish, white fibreglass faded to cream, and oxidised chrome. The huge Spanish factory trawlers which used to vacuum the Irish Sea of its fish quotas had put most of the ramshackle local boats out of business. But there was Europe for you – even if the referendum had changed all that it couldn’t bring back the lost business. In Llanawch, like similar villages down the west coast, the harbour and the handsome Georgian houses framing it were the remnants of a once-bustling coastal seaborne trade. The work nurtured many a local man who had gone on to sail the great oceanic shipping routes. The churchyard paid testament to this, studded as it was with the final resting places of clipper captains and able seamen on the early immigrant-adventurer routes to the New World.

On occasion the descendants of these men would return, drawn by the need to understand their past, or simply to examine the church records to fill out their family tree. They were often retired from the professions, often of the golf club variety that Lloyd would aim to avoid in a social setting. Yet around five or so years back an American television crew had swept into the village square. Out of the motorcade appeared a relatively famous Hollywood actor tracing his roots back across the Atlantic for a Christmas network special. The camera crew had stayed an afternoon, captured some atmospheric shots, and interviewed some of the locals for "a little local color". The film star had been unable to resist the temptation of touching the flesh with the fat-asses who'd stayed at home unlike his great-great-grandpappy. He even raised a pint glass in the local pub, taking an ingratiating sip for the cameras, putting down the barely touched drink and leaving with an easy smile, 'Hmmm, real good beer.' That had gone down well in the pub in question which continued to display a photo of the occasion on the wall just inside the entrance.

The actor's blizzard of a smile disguised his disappointment that his ancestors hadn't lived a little further over the sea to the west in the ever-rolling myth of gold, green and Guinness that was Ireland. On camera, Mr Hollywood took a final lingering look at his roots – he wiped away a dry tear. But he wouldn't venture here again, except in every single future promotional interview he would give to the British media. Then he disappeared into the tinted seclusion of the hired Range Rover, vanishing into the folds of dusk, to a London hotel suite and an overnight companion.

There were few people about on the quayside this evening. Though not on duty, Lloyd picked up a chip wrapper skimming along the pavement in the breeze; the lingering trace of vinegar made his mouth water even as he dropped it into a rubbish bin to rest on some crumpled cider cans. He checked his stride to step over the melt from a dropped ice-cream cone, the yellow vanilla colour flecked with sand grains. He strolled past the mounds of pebbles, noting the difference between the foot-cratered dry sand and its sleek neighbour still wet from the tide. Someone was fishing off the short breakwater which hunched in the dark rolling surf, with its foam that looked like the Japanese print in old Judge Heywood's hallway. Bobbing a hundred yards offshore was a small group of sun-faded pink buoys, marking the lobster pots of one of the remaining fishermen.

Time for a pint.

Lloyd had arranged to meet up with a couple of his pals and Hywel, his eldest son, who was presently living with his in-laws and was doubtless panting for an evening on parole. Much like his father, not that Lloyd ever thought about his marriage to Catrin being anything much more than having the same address. There wasn't really a leash to slip anymore. After a brief period of hurried excitements taken in various Yorkshire locations, they'd married and settled down into a life together based on an ability to inhabit the same space without too much discord. Yet, ever since she had given birth to the boys, Lloyd had found himself gradually displaced to a sideshow player in the household, as his wife took centre stage in fulfilling her unshakeable destiny as an official *Welsh Mam*™. He could picture the scene that he'd just left behind. Arwel hunched over his textbooks in his bedroom or more likely his social media. Catrin phoning round her friends for a post-soap opera debrief and a collective moan about their inadequate husbands. He wouldn't be surprised to come home to find a coven of them curled up on the sofa sharing wine and news. Personally, he couldn't see what more there was to talk about: apparently all men were useless, and their wives were so bloody perfect, so what else was news?

The humidity in the pub flung out tentacles of embrace as soon as he stepped onto the worn entrance doormat. It was relatively busy, given most of the younger residents would have mini-bussed it into the local town where there was more action. That's if Goodfellas nite-spot – "Hold your 18th here – free bubblee and cake" – counted as action. A corner table housed a group of pale sixth-formers drinking Irish coffees before following the pack; they huddled closer together for invisibility as they saw Lloyd come in. He made a show of ignoring them while clocking that one of the girls, a friend of Arwel's he recognised, was wearing a very short skirt. Hey, he still had a pulse, even if she was too young for him. Lloyd glanced over at the smattering of family groups in the snug having an end-of-week meal out as a treat, many of whom he knew from the outlying farms and hamlets. One of the things about reality, rather than the fictional version like on television, Lloyd mused, was that villages like Llanawch weren't rammed full of larger-than-life grotesques or harmless eccentrics; people were mostly just average, normal folk. Getting on with their lives without making a big show about it.

His eldest son, ploughing his usual barren furrow with the fruit machine, gestured to him with a shake of the hand to see if his dad wanted a drink. Nodding, Lloyd observed the rugby club crowd – current season statistics: played twenty-three, won five, two games cancelled due to a water-logged pitch – marking their territory at the bar like dogs pissing on lampposts. Around them lay the debris of an earlier round to get them warmed up, scattered salt grains and empty tequila shot glasses. They were well on the way to full-on steaming, which was to kids their age the whole point of the evening. Those lads were caught in the uneasy decade between the teenage years, where life was all fun, sex and excitement, and their thirties, with the horrific realisation that life was boiling down to the Holy Trinity of kids, bills, and finding a cheaper mortgage rate. Drink – whether to celebrate or forget – was the sole common factor.

Lloyd could clearly hear the loudest of them – Gwyn Phillips.

'Your round Sion you total homo, get them in. C'mon Stevie hit us up!' Phillips banged an empty pint glass on the bar to catch the landlord's attention, burped and turned back to his crowd, dreamily fondling his left bicep as he waited for service. 'Shame about old John Roberts.'

Nods and neutral murmurs followed this statement, 'Aye-aye.'

Lloyd turned away to sip the drink Hywel had just brought him, he knew what was coming. One of the wingers piped up, 'What's that then?'

'You know, up at Glanrhyd.'

'What about him?'

'Oh, get with it, Sim. He killed himself.'

'Eh? How's that then?'

'You know, the farmer's favourite. Shotgun in the mouth, close your eyes, think of the overdraft, and goodnight sweet prince.'

'Well, I just saw him last, oh, it would be a week or so ago, walking along the coast road. Seemed all right then.'

'Didn't have his brains splattered all the way to Chester race course then, Sim, did he?' Phillips reached over for one of the newly poured pints settling on the plastic drip tray and took a long draw, his eyes settling on the local law enforcement.

'Sergeant Parry over there found him, didn't you Sergeant.'

Lloyd heard the tone and wearily replaced his pint on the counter. He'd wanted to ignore this overstepping of the line, but the pub chatter had diminished, and he knew that the listening families expected a response from *authority* so that all would be right with the world. It'd become clear to Parry how, over the years, the family men had bit by bit abdicated their responsibilities within the traditional village hierarchy, even in their own families. Now he was expected to keep the younger ones in line. Any trouble right now and it would be just him and Hywel. He couldn't count on anyone else to step in to help.

But he had to pick up the gauntlet. 'Yes, that's right.'

'Big mess was it?'

Lloyd indicated to his son to get a seat away from the bar area.

'How's his missus? Ready to cash in on the insurance I bet,' Phillips chortled, looking round at his gang who returned his smirk.

Lloyd paused in his step and turned around. 'Well, you tell me. She's lost her husband of twenty-five odd years and there's a farm to run, so I wouldn't exactly assume she was only thinking about the insurance money. I suppose she's more thinking about funeral costs right now.' Take a pause, Lloyd, keep your voice deep and slow. He's just your regular small-town idiot. 'What do you reckon then… Gwyn?'

There was an uneasy silence, and Phillips dropped his gaze, closely examining his pint. Lloyd looked around, nodded slowly and followed his son through the parted gang, to a table in the snug. Conversation slowly restarted at the bar, as Phillips attempted to regain his standing. 'Well boys, insurance cheque or not, looks like there'll be some land coming on the market then.'

There was a quickly stifled laugh from one of his pals. 'Yeah, but who wants to buy it now? Doesn't pay anymore, does it?'

'Aye, well, maybe we won't be talking about farming prices for much longer. I heard talk that they're thinking of merging the mart with the one in Machynlleth.'

The group became aware of a large presence watching them from the doorway to the pool room. 'Merging, my arse. Another word for closing it down, like bloody everything else around here.' The figure walked over to the bar. 'There's the bloody government for you – Cardiff Bay or Westminster – all the bloody same. They probably spent money on some effing consultant from London to tell them that as well, excuse my French. And what's our local councillor doing about it? Nothing. As per usual. Too busy getting his expense claims sorted.'

This last statement came from the leader of the pool-room crowd, Meic Davies.

Meic Davies: gym addict, doctorate researcher, and bold speaker of truth about the English client-state that had become Wales. Wales the proud nation that is, and not the so-called "Principality" with all its regal connotations. Charles Windsor, his spawn and the Welsh establishment toadies could stick that up their jacksies.

Meic Davies: student union leader; official big man on Aberystwyth campus; and future president of an independent Welsh Republic.

The man who'd spilt virtual blood on the cyber-streets of Glasgow in support of the Scottish "Yes" campaign, and in the EU referendum where Brussels was a price worth paying for its support of devolution and limitations on the English Government in London. A man who'd gone viral on social media from his relentless shaming of the Covid-19 tourist-spreaders of two years back and in support of Black Lives Matter. For Meic, all those campaigns had shown him that the power of the people wasn't just for the political theory textbooks; technology had given the people the tools to challenge the status quo. If Scotland, even Middle England and the Extinction Rebellion tie-dye circus could man the barricades, then why not Wales? And why not him as its leader? He was the change he sought in the world.

Less than three years ago, Meic had come to live in the village, buying and then renovating an old farmhouse on its fringes. Just another urban Covid-refugee? *No way Iolo* – from day one he'd made clear his family connections to the area, usually about twenty seconds into any conversation. The grocer-shop gossip had him as living off family money or maybe a lottery win because being a perpetual student wasn't a generally recognised route to riches. Meic now pushed confidently through the rugby crew, placed an order for four pints of the locally brewed bitter – Tarw Du Black Bull, 5.2% abv – and turned around to face Gwyn's coterie. Davies knew that his weights sessions made him physically stronger than most of the men in the pub and, given his natural aggression, he could take out any of them one-on-one. The knowledge was mutual; Gwyn Phillips stopped caressing his biceps and tugged his T-shirt sleeve down. He hunched at the bar and stared fixedly at the chiller cabinet displays on the floor behind it.

Meic continued, 'You see, boys, poor old John Roberts was just another victim of the Saes.' He assumed at this point that a few pairs of eyes were starting to roll, one or two mindless smirks forming, but it mattered little, they were going to hear him out regardless. While these boys, like too many for that matter, made a point of ignoring politics, most of them had some patriotic leanings even if it was just belting out the national anthem in the pub during Six Nations matches. He had played upon this sliver of awareness, and in this he'd been supported by the virus crisis and the growing influx of outsiders into the village. Meic had steadily been embedding his worldview into the minds of the rugby squad and as individuals they were gradually coming round, or at least didn't actively oppose him anymore. But in a group with Gwyn as their leader they were less receptive. A situation which would have to be sorted out.

'*Saes* by the way, means the English for any of you who don't speak your own language… Listen, we told them to cull the badgers to cut down bovine TB, but would they listen? No, of course not – too many childhood memories of nanny reading them *The Wind in the Willows* before beddie-byes. So, when our masters say no, it means that farmers like John Roberts lose out when their herds get infected. And it's not just this, is it? Face it, boys, as I keep saying, we've been left up shit creek, all those post Covid investment promises and "Build Back Better" bullshit, where has that gone? The little money that has trickled out of London has gone straight to Manchester and Leeds and Scotland and anywhere but here,' – he looked around at Stevie the barman without breaking polemical stride – 'yes, and can I get three Heinekens as well…'

Meic stared at Gwyn, whose enjoyment of the night was now a fading echo of a few minutes previously. 'How many of you could afford a home around here now? How many of you have to bite your tongue when some dickhead from the Wirral makes a joke to his mates in this very pub about "sheep shagging" or "thick Taffies" or "stupid language"? Think about it, boys, the Scots have been doing something about independence. But in plucky little Wales, we're treated as surplus to requirements, only good for doffing our caps and serving their lordships from over the border when they deign to visit. Now how's that make you feel?'

Gwyn extended a deep sigh. 'And there we were having a nice bit of banter amongst ourselves until you arrived…' Meic always made him feel uncomfortable, with his freaky personality. Each time you thought of a good point, the bastard was ahead of you and would shoot you down, make you look stupid in front of everyone.

'But it's always good to think about something more than coming up with the next bit of laboured banter once in a while, isn't it? Do carry on.' Gwyn's nemesis picked up three of the pints, clasped in a golden triangle between his fingers, and spoke in Welsh, 'Sion, do us a favour and help us bring these over, will you.'

Sion, the slightly built full-back, who'd been on the edge of the group, grimaced but did as he was bid, quietly picking up the pints and following. They left the main bar, heading down the passage to the pool room. Sion dutifully trailed Meic, feeling that telling tremor inside which he tried once more to suppress. He hated himself for it and could only hope that it didn't show – that wouldn't go down well with the boys.

In the snug Hywel looked at his father. 'You were a bit heavier than normal, back there, Dad; everything all right? With Mam?'

Lloyd shrugged his shoulders and continued to tear small pieces from his beer mat. 'That Gwyn Phillips joker is a right piece of work. Big fish in a small pond and those guys hang round him like he was bloody captain of Wales. Still…' Remembering that Hywel has been playing rugby only two seasons ago, he swilled his beer around the sides of the glass and took another swig. 'Any news with the house hunting?'

'No, no luck still. We thought that there might be something going on that new starter-home development out by the playing fields, but even that is priced too high for us. At this rate I'm going to have to win the lottery or something.'

A couple of middle-aged men came over to the table and sat themselves down. Lloyd drained his pint. 'Hello boys. Hywel and I were just talking about our future lottery win. Why don't I send the boy to get a round in, and we can plan which luxury yachts and top-of-the-range supercars we can buy with the money.'

'Oh, come on, Lloyd-boy, we're not having that old chestnut again… mind, I do like the look of that new Jag now…'

Four

Later that evening, having decided on a beachside home in Malibu and a Bentley – less flashy than a Roller – Lloyd walked slowly up the hill to his house. Underneath the glow of a streetlamp, he checked the time, finding it just before eleven. Any meeting of the coven would be long over by now – the women kept "respectable" hours. The village was settling down for the night, just a few stragglers like him, and the distant sound of a shattered pint glass. Later, around two o'clock, there'd be a short burst of slammed car doors and girlish giggles as partygoers returned from their big night out. Some would have got lucky; most would have just got drunk. There wasn't usually any trouble, and in any case, the local town's cop-shop was on duty and picking up calls.

The Roberts suicide had unsettled him. Maybe he should have seen it coming. Only the day before, out on the seafront, he'd broken up a small crowd of people who'd been scuffling over banknotes flung into the air by Marie's husband. He'd managed to retrieve most of the cash, jamming them back into the farmer's baggy jacket pockets, all the while cursing and telling Roberts to take his money home and stop playing silly buggers. Lloyd realised that he might have missed the point of that little scene. Should have taken the farmer for a manly chat instead, found out what was really the problem. But to be honest he'd been bloody annoyed by John's melodrama. The paperchase had led to a sharp bantam-sized exchange with one of the tourists who wouldn't return the notes that he'd scooped up. During his years as a copper, Lloyd had faced much worse than the beer breath of a forty-something male in a too-tight Aston Villa top, and he'd finally recovered the remainder of the cash. Yet all he'd thought about afterwards was that even in Llanawch you couldn't escape the anger that seemed to be everywhere in the country now. He'd barely given John Roberts a second thought as soon as Marie had come to collect him from the station. And not only was that wrong, but it was also stupid of him to miss the obvious like that.

He took a quick look around. All quiet on the Western front. Walking over to a nearby stone wall, Lloyd heaved himself over, and relieved his bladder against it. He gazed up at the stars as the steady trickle of the lager finished its trip through his digestive system. Parry hoped that it wouldn't splash onto his shoes too much, looking down at the splatter he created and then around at the road. There was no one about, and well, it wasn't as if he was in uniform.

A little way behind, cloistered in the shadows, Meic Davies watched – he raised two fingers up in the shape of an imaginary pistol, pointed them at Lloyd and let loose. Two in the back, one in the head at close range to finish. Perhaps another one to blow off the face and send a message to others. Pull his trousers down as a final touch. The younger man smirked as he pictured the fantasy headline – "Local Policeman Found Dead and Exposed in Sex Act Gone Wrong Shock". He waited as the sergeant finished with a middle-aged dribble and zipped himself up. Lloyd, happily unaware of his gangland-style execution, stumbled over the wall and walked on up the hill with only the streetlamps for company.

Meic had other plans tonight, business which he had postponed for far too long. He tracked back to the square and waited in the gloom of the lending library doorway for chucking-out time at the pub across from him. He observed one of the married couples and a few of the old boys leave. Then he saw the rugby crowd spill out, drunkenly pushing each other and laughing. They'd be the last, as usual. The group said their goodbyes – Sion, he noted, walking off alone in one direction, the rest the opposite way, scurrying like a pack of rats to the estate. Gwyn Phillips and Paul, the scrum half, were left and headed for the chippy. Meic pushed back against the door and kept still so as not to attract attention. His targets went into the chip shop, coming out a couple of minutes later, each holding a packet. He'd watched them through the large window, dousing the fried food in salt and vinegar at the counter. What a pair of fat chavs, no wonder they kept losing their matches.

Gwyn and Paul strolled off. Meic hoped that they weren't planning to go back to have a few cans together. That would mean he'd have to sort matters out another day and he felt impatient. He was in the mood now. Meic paced himself about fifty yards behind, just another part of the scenery, move along please, nothing to see here. He could see Paul chain-stuffing chip after chip into his moon-face as Gwyn chatted away. The boys reached a junction and came to a stop. Up the hill lay the flat that Gwyn lived in with his granddad, further along the estuary road was the bakery which Paul lived above with his parents. Their tracker imagined that they'd go their separate ways here.

Meic stopped and huddled down by a green telephone-cable junction box. He saw Gwyn gave his mate a slightly-too-hard punch on the arm and then the two of them parted company, with Paul scrunching up his chip paper before chucking it into someone's front garden.

Meic waited until Paul had rounded the corner, before jogging to the junction. He looked up the incline to see Gwyn labouring his way up the road. With no houses on this section, the route was unlit, the glare of orange sodium dispersed into the quiet darkness. Gwyn was focused on his chips and walking slightly unsteadily. Perfect. Twenty yards now. Meic could hear the crackle of Gwyn's hand rummaging inside the chip packet. The pig couldn't even be bothered to use a wooden fork, but all the better that he had no weapon to hand. Ten yards. He could see the glow of the row of streetlamps at the top of the rise; he'd have to do it immediately. He increased his pace, panted in doing so. Suddenly Gwyn half turned his head, turned back, then stopped, started to turn again.

Now, now, now. Do it now!

Meic hit Gwyn in the face with all the considerable force he could muster. The chips were flung from Gwyn's hand as he staggered backwards before sprawling onto the tarmac. The drink had dulled his responses and his face looked confused as tried to take in what was happening. He wasn't able to react before Meic fell upon him, sitting on his chest and smashing his face with steady, hard punches. As Meic methodically went about his work, he thought back to the work-out sessions in the university's weights room, the clang of steel on steel. The judo training, the bulking out of his meals with whey protein, and all for such sweet moments. He gave Gwyn two more punches, taking care to select his spots to ensure maximum bruising without any head trauma. When the onslaught ceased, Gwyn's vision was blurred, and he could feel his face wet with blood, spittle and mucus. He had failed to land a single blow on his attacker.

Seeing that his job was done, Meic wiped his knuckles on his victim's shirt-front and stood up. He breathed heavily, feeling the exertion and intensity of the attack. Looking down on Gwyn, he felt a twinge of pity, for the worst was yet to come for the rugby club captain. He nudged Gwyn's legs apart before giving him a large kick in the crotch. He looked around as his victim writhed in front of him; his moans turned to coughs as he began to be sick.

'Get on your side, pig-shit,' Meic toed Gwyn in the back, 'we don't want you choking on your own vomit now, do we?'

Gwyn heaved for a minute or two, his face rolling in his own stomach muck and mind rolling in shame. Meic crouched by him. 'Now listen, Gwyn old buddy. None of this need have happened. You do understand, that don't you?' There was little acknowledgement beyond the rolling of his victim's eyes.

'None of this had to happen. But you refused to accept the new reality. From the moment I arrived here things were bound to change.' Meic stood up and pulled out his mobile to record Gwyn's agonies. 'I'm the top dog around here. I'm the alpha male and you *will* recognise that. What do you say, Gwyn Phillips?'

A sob. A nudge with a boot.

'What am I?'

'Top dog,' choked the mess.

'Top dog, that's right. The alpha dog. Pack leader.'

He gave his victim another nudge to the ribs with his shoe. 'Step out of line in future, and not only will you take another beating worse than this one, but your mates will also receive this little home movie. Remember, Gwyn, the camera never lies.'

Meic spat on Gwyn, took a last look around and disappeared through a gap in the hedgerow. He felt exhilarated.

Five

Francesca "Frankie" Pimlott had seen in the New Year in London sipping a glass of champagne while viewing the deeply underwhelming fireworks display taking place above the Thames. Dressed in a dark pantsuit, silk lapels on her comfortable jacket, she ran her hand through her black bobbed hair. From her position framed against the Southbank restaurant's picture windows she'd appraised the other guests. Their upturned faces reflected wonder at the multi-coloured hues of the explosions outside. Civilians, whether in club class here, or those kettled into the drone-zone viewing enclosures across the river, enjoyed this cheap visual crap. The banality of mass entertainment writ large. Frankie snorted back another drop: she gauged that in terms of raw achievement she would quite easily rank within the top decile of those in the room.

Through her newspaper and magazine columns, she'd built up a boutique business with a substantial client list. It teemed with recognised media, business and finance names, plus a smattering of carefully invited celebrities, all paying to tap her "unique lifestyle insight" (*The Independent on Sunday, July 2015*). Frankie's skill consisted of telling people who had finite time and inadequate taste, those types who required a little off-the-shelf individuality, exactly where they needed to shop, dine, and imbibe culture. She could arrange the decoration of her clients' houses (in either off-white or earth shades); she could send them to buy clothes from the same handful of the now not-so-young-or-hot designers she knew at college; and she could send them to whatever restaurant had been reviewed by the food bloggers the week before. Certain types of people bought this happily.

Some mainstream social commentators would have seen Frankie's clients as an early-warning indicator of a civilisation speeding in an over-engineered German SUV straight down the highway to perdition. Others more equitably minded might point out that many generations past, even the revered Victorians, had produced a similar class of the moneyed yet taste-free. Albeit not one so numerous as the contemporary iteration. Frankie's clientele all shared the desire to be seen to be in the vanguard of fashion and trends. For them, being first, being an insider, being in the know and definitely being distinct from others, was how they wished to portray themselves in their own fascinating personal narrative. Life was a journey, no, it was like a round-the-world yacht race, and it was too important to waste on the daily detritus that trapped the less successful, the less hot, the less talented. And appearance was important, since that drove the accumulation of more opportunities, more acclaim and following that, more wealth. This wasn't to be sneered at. Being seen to be a success was a lesson which Frankie had bitterly learned at school, when she experienced how unremarked her – *substantial* – academic achievements had gone compared to the communal fêting of her class mates in the – *very average* –

first hockey eleven. Success needed to be on public display to count.

Tonight's party was organised by her company, Pimlott Associates, for a finance house which was celebrating its annual bonus pool in a safe space. That translated into no media, security on the doors and confidentiality clauses for the waiting staff. Frankie's eyes homed in on one of the city boys who was leaning easily against the long glass bar and chatting rather too closely with her wife, Ruth. This was irritating but necessary, as it was always useful, she thought, to be in with money; even, no, especially with money types – too much cash, little intrinsic style, and easily manipulated egos. She observed Ruth make a wild gesture with her hand, in the process glancing a blow on a large vase of magnolias, so causing it to wobble on the bar top like a drunk trying to catch attention at last orders. Frankie carefully set down her glass and started towards the pair. A smile replaced the tightness on her face as she thought to herself of the road she'd travelled to be here; from just another architectural student in Cambridge to one of the most influential lifestyle experts in London. Not to say a member of the Royal Institute of British Architects. And a Fellow of the Royal Society of Arts, even if all she'd had to do was pay to add those letters to her name. But the honorary Doctor of Letters from the University of East Mercia was real enough. All those letters looked impressive following her name on her business cards – without the East Mercia part obviously.

And as for the London nexus – which was generally a few select postcodes in the centre of town into which (despite everything) still flowed money, people and energy – obviously that went for provincial Britain. And probably still

Europe, even if some of those Berlin outfits had been, of late, increasing their profile in the international press, and London wasn't quite the capital of cool it had been. The wall of investment money buying up the more desirable streets as deposit-box investments and the pestilence of plate-glass developments on the Thames had seen to that.

She was deep in her thoughts as a petite oriental waitress glided across her path, bearing a tray of dim-sum, a thigh-splitting skirt and an enticing perfume, with all three ready to be deployed to advantage. Frankie breathed her in; what a many-splendoured little item she was. What about Shanghai, or Mumbai? The latter were an easier sell, but the Chinese – well now that was the singular great leap forward to going global. She pulled out the latest-model smartphone from her handbag and spoke into it with a reminder to have her personal PR set up some profiling in the Chinese market. *You get in with those guys, and suddenly you're back in the Majors.* She returned to the present as a huge burst from one of the fireworks cast a pale shade of green over the partying crowd. She slid over to her partner's side.

Through eye contact and a quick arm around Ruth's waist she indicated to the master of the universe opposite that his prey was spoken for. The man, initially fazed, briefly excited, then finally disappointed, gave a slight bow and withdrew. No return on his investment of time; but it wasn't worth making a scene in front of his bosses, especially given that he'd wandered into Dykes-ville, Arizona. In any case, there were always the waitresses to hit on. Frankie looked at the banker as he walked away, turned to her partner, and smelt her alcoholic availability – same old, same old.

"New year, new you, yada-yada-yada – pare back your life, pare back your wardrobe, if you haven't worn it in the last twelve months, you never will. Throw it out and free yourself from the mental shackles of clutter!" It was a week or so after she wrote this sentence in her regular newspaper column that Frankie found herself sitting opposite the rag's new features editor. She had speculated on the reasons why she'd been called in 'for a chat'. The editor's glass-walled office was not a positive sign.

She was used to her business with the paper being conducted over the phone or coffee, and if they had an interesting offer for her, then it would surely involve the customary lubricating lunch. The paper had been a pretty traditional gig after all, but change had come recently with new ownership – the rumour was that the money had come out of mainland China and was officially connected. Frankie examined the features of the other person in the room, sitting behind a desk laden with plastic folders. The design guru noted that the desk lacked any personal touches, mirroring the barren office – not following this season's fashions, but much to be expected with the kind of story-less person facing her. The half-empty office itself was unfamiliar, reflecting a move from Canary Wharf to a new development in Battersea near the US embassy. She examined the male editor in front of her: regulation short back and sides haircut, a little Hoxton-fringe, the usual beard, the few lines on his coke-white face possibly derived from chemical experimentation rather than the process of fermentation. Maybe late twenties, more likely early thirties, in a royal-blue slim-cut suit, thick-rimmed glasses and no tie – because that was for the old economy losers. He wasn't of her parish. Yet the greatest source of her concern was that unlike his predecessor he was giving no sign of being intimidated by Frankie. The editor picked up a green file, pulled out the contents and flicked through them, glancing every few seconds out of habit at the information rolling through his laptop screen. Apart from the flow of the air conditioning, the room was silent.

Implying some effort, the editor looked up at Frankie, mechanically raising the corners of his mouth in an approximate simulation of a smile, before returning to his deliberations with the paperwork. He'd seen this in a movie. He pretended to focus on his papers and started the conversation, 'So, you've been writing for us for, about how long now?'

'About nine years. I started just after I won the Wildner Prize for the Ealing project.'

'Ah yes, the "multi-faith, community health cluster",' the editor's bent head rose up. 'Isn't that the one which leaks? Y' know, when it rains, all the patients get wet. Is that the one?' The fake question was accompanied by a genuine sneer.

And at that point, Frankie knew that her writing career was under threat.

'It's being renovated right now – there were some external considerations which weren't commissioned into the design at the time. It happens.'

'I see.'

'Right.'

'I've read some of your stuff.'

'What do you think?'

'Hmmm, Frankie Pimlott on "Why this year's Matisse blockbuster at Tate Modern will change your life",' the younger man clicked his tongue, 'or how about "Scandi-

Noir: Urban-Nordic Interiors Define the Future", and of course the must-read, "My Week by Frankie Pimlott"... yes, the latest column where you refer to having read Marcel Proust. Unabridged. Again. Still makes a change from your usual Joan Didion references.'

'Well, I have read their works. Have you?'

'I studied digital media at uni, not dead poets.'

'Proust wasn't a poet.'

'Neither is the new owner of this newspaper. Boom-boom.'

Frankie shifted in her seat. 'Listen, my column was commissioned by Andrea. She was very supportive.' Frankie rummaged for the most acceptable phrase that would keep the guy onside while not admitting exactly the real reasons her former editor was such a fan. 'Her view was that it was entertaining, informative writing greatly enjoyed by the readership.'

'Yep. But Andrea is no longer on staff here.' The editor looked out of the window.

'Oh really? Nobody said anything.'

'I'm afraid we weren't in a position to divulge her... news.'

'News?' She was already mentally speed-texting her former editor.

He shifted in his seat, searching for a legally neutral phrase. 'Do you still have a licence to practice architecture?'

It had been a decade plus since Frankie had last sat before a blank drafting board, and while she could crank out 500 words an hour on "enduring British designs from the 21st century" for a Sunday colour supplement, it was unlikely that she could now produce any. Ealing had been a lucky commission and was partially based on a recycled design from another member of her degree class. She hadn't done anything of note since then, and in her heart knew that it would be a bit of stretch to do so again.

'No. Why do you ask?'

Languidly, as if he'd recently endured a number of similar conversations, the editor explained, 'You may not have noticed but things have changed recently.'

'I understand that the paper has a new owner.'

'That's one change. Another is that times are hard and paper-based press isn't the wave of the future. Which to google translate for you, our readership is surviving rather than aspiring, and that they increasingly prefer to download rather than take a trip to the corner shop. In case you'd missed it, our readership is British; mostly live outside the M25; and pay their taxes in this great country of ours. We even suspect that most of them voted for Brexit and were pretty pissed-off when their local hospital didn't have enough beds during the Covid thing. That may shock someone like you.'

Frankie made to protest. 'What has that got to do with my column? I don't write for that audience anyway.'

He reddened. 'It takes up space in our paper. To put it bluntly, Ms Pimlott, our readership is fast evolving and the people that we want to attract, the folk who pay the bills, well they don't want some Zone One jockey telling them about how wonderfully cosmopolitan and international London is and where's best in Bolivia to go heli-skiing. It's a turn-off – and they definitely won't pay on demand to read it…' He hadn't taken a breath during this statement and now breathed heavily.

Yes, thought Frankie, *yes, a definite Yorkshire accent – definite* provincial chippiness *in evidence. Probably attended a local ex-*

Poly university up there as well; stint on the local free press; stringer for a few stories of national interest; and then onto the big time. She sighed, 'But it's the capital of the country. Why shouldn't they be interested?'

'Actually, I'm not sure it is the capital of the country any longer. London – your London that is – has become a work of fiction to most people. Like New York in America, it turns out that now it kinda doesn't matter like it once thought it did. All these small-town places, the ones you've ignored in your columns for the past decade, have now got their own closed-down restaurants, empty art centres and crap public services. Tell you what they're interested in: National Lottery, *Strictly Come Dancing*, celeb-sex stories, *Celebrity Love Island...*'

'So, gossip then. Like *Hello* magazine.'

'Oh, they have an interest in the so-called serious stuff. Y' know, welfare cuts, the future of our allegedly world-class NHS, pay for our heroic nurses and doctors – that kind of *little people* stuff. And of course, we like to report on our former European partners and their ongoing travails – provide reassurance to our readership that they voted the right way,' he smirked at this last phrase. 'So sadly, for you, they've lost interest in what is happening in happenin' Shoreditch. Or so our focus groups tell us.'

The editor slotted the papers back into Frankie's file, stood up and walked around his desk and sat on the edge, as he'd seen in a movie. He hadn't meant to get worked up, and needed to defuse the situation, if only in case she sued. 'Look, I imagine that you're upset. Who wouldn't be? So apologies for the faceless corporate brutality, etcetera, but the bottom line is that we have to drop your column. The whole comment section is undergoing a crash diet... we're cutting the society page as well if it makes you feels better. We're trimming some excess, shedding some names and,' he shrugged his shoulders, 'I'm afraid that you're one of them. That's just the way it goes.'

'You're going to have a lot of space to fill.'

'Yep. So we're bringing in some new blood, someone who really gets what's going on out there. Young Oxford graduate, new-wave feminist, about to have a play on at the Royal Court.'

'A woman then?'

He smiled coldly. 'Yes, just like you. So you might want to rethink that industrial tribunal plan that I imagine is brewing in your head right now. Another woman, but modern. From Preston. Tells it like it is. Fresher. Sorry about that.' He gave Frankie a loaded stare. 'But unlike you, she has her finger on the pulse plus according to research she's a positive fit with twenty-three percent of our demographic. Has interesting ideas about our digital product… cheap as well.'

The editor shrugged once more to reinforce his point, then got up from the desk edge, and opened the door, allowing in the sound of clattering keyboards and telephone hubbub. 'We'll be paying you off as per your contract, but for now…'

His visitor swivelled in her chair and realised that both the discussion and her column were at an end.

Six

That afternoon, Frankie sat quite still in her study. She lived with Ruth in a now perfectly formed and well-photographed street in Islington. Once a district in decline, gentrification had transformed the area into a polished rebuke to the exhaust-stained neighbouring boroughs – *you could be like us too… if you tried.* Her area had been hijacked by the fashionistas two decades before and had been the in-place for a season or two, but soon after, the young investment bankers, assorted media kids, and newspaper columnists had moved the artists out and the dinner party circuit in. Yet even if there were no artists, there were still a couple of modern art galleries daringly keeping the flag of bohemia flying on just thirty percent commission.

An invoice from her Harley Street doctor lay beached on the brushed steel desk in front of her like a jaundiced whale. At the consultation, the doctor had said there would be more treatment to follow if Frankie didn't change the way that she lived. She cursed her short-sightedness in not getting private healthcare insurance when she had a chance, another missed detail. She stared out onto the dreary street at those walking past her window, their blank gaze elsewhere. Another day of wage subjugation on their mind or *just two days until the weekend*... dull thoughts that left little room for the more spiritual plane. She couldn't see any children on the street; in school, she supposed, how quickly one forgot term times. Outside, it was just a never-ceasing drone caterpillar of worsted grey and navy wool.

Frankie was aware that she could sometimes be a snob, a "right fucking snob" as an ex-girlfriend had once told her, and that she affected to despise what could be perfectly pleasant ordinary people. She would pigeon-hole them or gracelessly lump them together into one bucket. As a thought exercise, she tried to pick out individuals in her Lowry landscape. A small man in a slim tailored suit, quickly weaving through slower pedestrians – though his eyes were nervous. A middle-aged woman wearing the clothes of a younger version, the make-up thick, but the overall look? Invitation-seeking, ready to yield willingly at the slightest interest – how some women hated themselves, had no confidence. She studied a man in a brown tweed overcoat, straight-backed, as he traversed her laser-line of sight. Tweed in the city, could she sell it as a new trend? Except she then recalled that she'd written a column on the very topic two years ago. What was wrong with her? Frankie sat back in her chair. She felt very tired and very slow. Sometimes when she picked dropped items up from the floor, it was as if she was watching her own elderly father. It was a feeling that had been building since the New Year's party. Looking at the invoice again, she gave an involuntary drawn-out exhalation of the kind which her mother had once remarked upon as instantly recognisable anywhere, then folded the letter and placed it carefully in the top right-hand drawer.

'Fresh air and rest,' was what the doctor had prescribed.

Between this, her column and the contempt of that small-dicked, ageist, misogynist prick on the paper, it had been all told a lousy few days. The columns had paid, not much, but enough, compared to the time she didn't put into them. They had been a form of brand-building for her business – that brought the real cash in. But now, stripped of them, she realised that they meant more than that. It was almost as if without them she had no voice, no longer existed. She had become a non-person, like the drones out on the street. Frankie was about to lock the drawer when she noticed a scribbled note on the back of a postcard – "A View of Llanawch Harbour". How odd to write it down, her iPhone must have been out of juice at the time. She stared at the card for a few moments before making the connection.

Some months previously, just after the end of lockdown, she'd spent a long weekend touring Wales, commissioned by an upmarket travel magazine to write an article reflecting the times: in other words, British holidays were the "New Going Abroad". She'd come across a charmingly old-fashioned workman's cottage in a fifties-era village where they'd stopped for a drink. Sitting outside the pub in the gossamer September sun, she noticed a *for sale* sign outside this harbour-side property, and out of character, she'd scrawled the telephone number of the estate agent handling the sale on a post card she'd meant to send to her office in a fit of retro-communications. It was this same card that she now held in her hands. Opening her lightweight laptop, she searched for the agent and was soon viewing details of the cottage, which remained unsold and had even reduced in price.

As Frankie looked at photos of the house, the idea struck her: weren't places like this very village what the features editor had been talking about? A village like this was as far as one could get from London. And, she pondered, from the way the world was turning, "anti-urban" could become a big trend very easily – it had been fluttering about on the periphery for a while. Indeed, hadn't she just read a feature about the Norfolk Broads in the latest edition of *Wallpaper*? It was almost as if a generation had turned their back on *A Year in Provence* and adventure to nest nearer to home with their childhood nostalgia.

Frankie's mind began to work like a blacksmith facing a lump of hot metal ready on the anvil, and she started to fashion this vague idea into a coherent piece. She knew how it went. Everything today had to be a narrative. People disliked high concepts or challenging ideas – they wanted mummy to tell them a story. The *Jackanory* generation had disposable income. She smiled to herself at the breadth of her cultural database.

Inspiration struck: what if she moved to Wales, tapped that infusion of fresh air, but with the plot twist of leading the village's regeneration and turning it into a vision of seaside perfection? Just imagine, within a year or two she could drag them forward a few decades. The place could have a deli, a New England-style seafood shack with crab and lobster fresh off the fishing boats, a French brasserie, maybe even a decent coffee shop. It could be more: Hebden Bridge was once a small town in the middle of nowhere, and Brighton was once a decaying seaside resort. But look at them now, centres of the LGBT community, beacons of hope in a world of stupidity and self-harm. And she, Frankie Pimlott, would write about it – not the usual "downsized life amongst the yokels" spiel – but her personal crusade to bring civilised modern living for all genders and sexualities to the blighted rural masses. Why should Marylebone and Notting Hill have all the action? Frankie looked up from the house details at the Edwardian lithographs of women at repose in the English countryside pictures she'd hung on the wall one ironic morning. Now she could see them in a different light; maybe, in fact, her subconscious had planned a move to the country all along. Maybe this opportunity had just been waiting for the day that she would finally seize it.

'Ruth, Ruth!' Frankie scrambled out of her study and down the stairs to their Scandinavian-style kitchen with its barren family space leading into the garden ("this summer, take a lead from the Danes and make your backyard an extra hybrid room…"). Her wife – hands deep in a mixing bowl, a half-empty glass of wine bearing floury fingerprints next to it – looked up as Frankie shot through the door.

'Darling, I've had the most amazing idea. Listen to this.' She started pacing up and down the room. Ruth watched her, the little professor about to start another lecture. This wasn't usually a good sign.

'Recall that seaside place in Wales we went to? Yes? Where we had those ghastly soggy chips on the quayside – the ones I was forced to throw away.'

'Uh-huh…'

'Good, do you also remember that fabulous little fishing village in Devon – Bray Head? The new blood there had re-energised the place; they'd started sustainable businesses, got the community going again and all that jazz. Because it was pretty clear to us all wasn't it, that the locals weren't going to do it themselves without a bit of a kick up the proverbial?'

Ruth picked up a spatula and slowly stirred the cake mixture. Oh God, no…

'I've had the most brilliant idea. I am going to personally transfer that sustainable development model from Devon to Wales, and together, we're going to change a whole village. For the better! People are going to love it.'

Ruth banged the spatula on the rim of the bowl. Here she was, baking cakes for other people's kids, displacement activity of course, and in She walks with another of Her big ideas. Ms Frankie but-there's-time-for-children-later-darling Pimlott. Always the big idea.

'Fine. But how are you going to do all that from here?' As if she didn't already know the answer.

'We. Are. Going. To. Move. There.' Frankie looked up at her wife, hands outstretched. 'Just for a while of course. Not permanently. We'll rent this place out – still a lot of expat families out there with corporate housing allowances – and buy a cottage. We can always keep it as a holiday let afterwards… come to think of it, I could put the transaction through the company and save tax.'

Frankie resuming her pacing. 'Now Ruthie, this is clearly a big step, almost a leap into the unknown, but it could just be the thing to give us a second bite at the cherry. After all, the advisory business wouldn't be too much hassle, the girls virtually run it day-to-day in any case,' she sniffed, 'my main job now is merely to sign the cheques and meet a client from time to time.'

Ruth took a long sip of her wine. 'All this because you've lost your column?'

'Absolutely! I'm nearly forty, it's now or never! Think of the possibilities Ruthie… My goodness, one might almost call it a form of public service. Don't you see? This is a new social model in practice. I start with the village, and then maybe I could do a "Jamie", inspiring improvements to backward rural communities all over the country. It might even end up with a trip to Buckingham Palace, or maybe something bigger, like my own Channel 4 series.' She laughed at the sound of her own ambition, visions of hanging out with Sandi Toksvig and Sue Perkins beckoned her. 'Too much already, I know! Even *More4* would be fine.'

Ruth remained unsmiling. 'That's lovely and everything, but have you thought for a moment about how the people who already live there might react to these plans? I mean, if you do all this, you'll affect their lives, and they won't like that.'

She paused in mid-step, staring hard at the reclaimed floorboards a few feet in front of her face. 'Agreed, it might be hard going initially, but it will be the only way they'll survive. They *must* fundamentally realise that at heart. The world had changed over our lifetime, even London and New York have adapted. There is no reason why this place – Lanout, I think it's called – can't do the same. Once they understand, people will soon get onside. I mean what's not to like about having good places to eat and getting to know one's neighbours? Hey, how about this: Welsh street food in the village square. We could get them to convert a Land Rover or have a caravan towed by an old tractor or something. People. Would. Love. It.'

Over the next few minutes, Ruth heard her protests falter, bend, and finally be swept away by the torrent of her partner's enthusiasm. It was not the first time. She had watched Frankie's monomania once she'd alighted on a new "big idea" often; there had been a time when she'd even found her excitement part of the attraction. Resistance was useless in such cases and her inability to even put up a half-decent fight anymore against Frankie's notions, left Ruth feeling slightly disgusted at her own passivity.

'So, we're agreed then. I shall set the wheels in motion.' Frankie made to leave the kitchen, then noticed that Ruth was wearing an apron and had flour on her hands. 'What are you doing?'

'Relearning how to bake a cake.'

'How charmingly Stepford. She paused. 'You know Ruthie, it wouldn't kill you, once in a while to try and sound enthusiastic about my plans. I am doing this for us after all.'

'I know but…' But Frankie had already left the room. Oh fuck it. She grabbed the wine bottle and refilled her glass to near the brim. A big swallow.

Seven

'What a frigging day. Gaaaaaaaarrrrgggggh!' Paul Williams tossed his phone onto the desk, causing his secretary to half-smile at his routine tirade. She hunched on her haunches by the doorway, carefully picking the last slivers of glass out of the carpet.

'Waste of space. For fuck's sake, "our financial situation has changed, and we can no longer go ahead with the house purchase..." What a fucking fuckwit.'

'Who's that?'

'Ty Glas buyers have dropped out.' He etched a thick line through the caller's names on his memo pad, which sported a printed script at the bottom – "Williams & Co, Dolgellau's leading estate agent and land manager since 1993". Only a year previously, the windows had displayed row upon row of properties or "lifestyle dreams" as Paul, the sole partner, would describe them. However, with the banks now having tightened up on lending for holiday-home buying, it was a fantasy which fewer folks could do anything about. Not that he felt it necessary to respond to the problems of the global economy by encouraging vendors to scale down their expectations of instant wealth.

And definitely not when he was on commission. There would always be someone who'd come along bearing a wallet: a cash-rich City guy; some Brummie retiree with a big pension pot who wanted to live the dream and then tell everyone about it. Even if things might be a little slow, perspective was needed. Though he could do without the frigging timewasters.

He looked up from his secretary to catch one of the workmen ogling her backside from the doorway. 'Oi! Have you got that shit off my window yet? No, I thought not, then get on with it.' The man deflated his leer and returned to scrubbing away at the spray-painted words on the display window. Useless buyers and frigging vandals: that would be two bad things already today, and shit usually turned up in a threesome. He'd been taken aback first thing this morning when he'd parked outside the agency only to discover the front-door windowpane shattered and the main window covered with graffiti. What was it again, some Plaid-ist nonsense or something? He read the post-it note where he'd scribbled down the bright red letters now smearing to light pink with the application of cleaning fluid – "Bradwr! Yma ma' Owain ab Edwin yn byw!" Paul turned to his laptop and googled the meaning. Let's see now – "Traitor! Owain ab Edwin lives here!" Now what the hell was that about? Who was Owain ab Edwin? A customer of his? Someone in the area? He did another search. Ah, here we are, end of the 11th century… he sided with the Normans in their failed invasion of North Wales…

Paul leaned back in his seat and smoothed down his silver-coloured silk tie. For fuck's sake. Traitor eh? So that was it. He thought all that estate-agents-are-the-devil shit had died out in the eighties, but clearly not. These people never moved with the times. He'd have to search the database for new buyers for Ty Glas later; this nationalist bollocks needed to be stopped before it started. Ignoring the landline in front of him, Williams reached for his mobile and dialled the number of the town's police station.

A fortnight later, Lloyd was once more scrutinising some property details through the window of Williams & Co. He could still make out a faint pink tinge where the cleaning hadn't quite removed the paint. Carefully, he scanned the photographs, finishing at the bottom right of the display, and once more rescanned from top left in case he'd missed a bargain, grunting when he confirmed that he hadn't. He looked up at his wife, and picked out one description. 'Listen to this: A little bit of seaside bliss. Set in the heart of Wales, the very place for you to get away from the hustle and bustle of city life. Enjoy walks on the golden sands and evenings by the fireside in the many local pubs that the picturesque village of Llanawch offers.' Lloyd raised his eyebrow, before he continued to read out the card, 'This four-bedroom characterful stone cottage has new fitted PVC-double glazing and is served by an oil-fired central heating system. The cosy stylishly updated accommodation includes a lounge, kitchen-diner, and family bathroom. Outside lies a splendid patio garden to the rear for those lazy summer afternoons with a glass of white wine. Parking is to the front. Asking price of £659,500.'

Catrin sighed. 'You do this every time we're in town.'

'I know, but with prices like that how will Hywel and

Sian be able to afford a place? Saving for a deposit will be hard enough, let alone the mortgage payments…' The sentence tapered off into the chill air.

Catrin glanced across the slate-dark street to search for familiar faces. 'They'll simply have to find a way, like we had to in Leeds. Remember?'

Lloyd shrugged at the memory. They came to the butcher's shop, various cuts laid out on platters in the shop window, a review from a national newspaper's food column posted proudly in the glass. 'It's the way of the world nowadays. They'll just have to save up a bit longer that's all.' Catrin didn't want to encourage her husband, he'd been morose ever since the shooting. He was hard work when he was in this kind of gloomy mood. For that matter he had become hard work full stop. Couldn't he just be happy, or just be satisfied with his lot? Nowadays she minimised the time they spent together so she didn't have to put up with the moans and the air of dissatisfaction. Gone to seed, that was his problem. All the wives had the same issue. Her thoughts wandered briefly to the Robert Redford film she'd watched last Sunday, the one with the horses. She felt a pang of disappointment, which she quickly tided away to a far recess of her mind.

Catrin rummaged in her leather shoulder bag for her purse. 'Wait here. Do you want beef or lamb tomorrow?' Not waiting for an answer, she stepped into the shop as Lloyd contemplated some newly laid dog droppings near the phone box. From outside the plate glass, he watched her chatter with the butcher as he wrapped a joint of lamb in white paper. Lloyd briefly visualised the steam rising off his favoured roast beef and Yorkshire pudding that he wouldn't be having for lunch the next day. Arwel preferred lamb.

'Hwyl am rwan Mrs Parry,' the butcher shouted to her back.

'Right, that's the shopping finished. Take these will you,' she handed Lloyd the bags. 'I've just got to nip into Shelia's to see if my book has come in yet.'

'I don't know why you bother; you could get it quicker on Amazon.'

'Amazon doesn't have all the local gossip, does it? See you at the car. I'll only be five minutes.'

He watched her still-defined calves disappear down the street, a contrast to the hips that seemed to get thicker by the year. Reconciled to a half-hour wait, Lloyd headed to the pub for a swift half, the only recourse during such domestic emergencies.

❧

There had been some brief chatter from Catrin repeating what she'd heard from her friend in the shop, mainly about how a local singer who had since become a national name had become a "little too big for his boots" and that his mother didn't think much of the women she saw him hanging out with in the newspapers. After that update, the drive back along the wooded north bank of the estuary had settled into habitual silence.

Lloyd switched on Radio Four. The presenter was talking with an expert about the latest troop movements in Africa: 'of course with all such deployments, it is important to send in force early enough to ensure that the mission target is rapidly achieved without the force becoming bogged down'. At present there were many such experts on the radio and television, just as there had been during the virus. He didn't know where they all came from – maybe there was an expert factory in London churning out these people who at times seemed no more informed than some bloke at the end of a bar. His neighbour's boy had gone out on a tour with the Fusiliers. To think that it had only been a short while ago that he'd been in Hywel's year at school and was coming round the house for tea. He wasn't the first from the village to take this route to the wider world, or indeed feel the desert dust on their skin; it was in the local tradition to join up. Same as the rest of Wales, or Yorkshire or Tyneside for that matter, recruiting country was anywhere with rubbish schools and worse prospects. The war memorial on the high street displayed a solitary carved name below those from the two world wars: a local lad out in the Falklands with the Welsh Guards and killed on the *Sir Galahad*. Like Lloyd, most of the village kept up to date for news about the Fusiliers, it was one way of showing solidarity with the families.

They reached the outskirts of the village and drove past the small promontory where former Judge Goronwy Heywood's retirement home sat overlooking the spread of softly rippling water all the way across to the far bank a mile distant. Each time he passed by Lloyd felt intrigued by the house with its small Victorian clock tower. He'd only visited the place a handful of times but would often bump into the Judge out on his daily walk or having a quiet drink in the pub. After the Heywood residence, the road then curled downwards through the ribbon-development of whitewashed retirement bungalows edging the town, before jinking past the bulging walls of the old town gaol, and finally narrowing to a single lane as it approached the town square facing the bay. Here, for a stretch, the opposing double yellow lines almost intertwined with the strip of pavement barely possessing enough width for a slope-shouldered teenager to shamble down to the bakery located there. During the tourist season, one standing duty for Lloyd and Roy the support constable was to ensure that nobody parked there, for even a quick stop to buy a sandwich loaf could result in a tailback stretching back along the estuary approach.

Lloyd's thoughts turned to Arwel, who'd spent some time with the Judge last summer, acting as a research assistant to Heywood who was in the process of writing his memoirs. The boy was taking his A-levels in a few weeks, and if all went well, then he'd be off to university in Manchester to study law. Catrin had tried to persuade him to apply to Aberystwyth and Bangor "just as a back-up", but his youngest son was adamant – all five choices were to English universities. Lloyd understood, had been relieved even that one of his offspring had the ambition to cross Offa's Dyke. Even so, he wondered what it was going to be like on the boy's first night away from home. He glanced at his wife – she was going to feel it all right when both kids were gone. Arwel's departure was only a few months away. Nothing could slow time, a concept which needed the seeming speeding-up of time with age to fully appreciate. It couldn't have been so long ago that he'd carefully driven Catrin home from the maternity ward. They'd had some great fun when he was a kid, but Arwel had become a little distant of late, as was usual for that age, same as Lloyd had been with his own parents. Anyway, with a degree he'd stand a better chance than his elder brother. Hywel had decided against returning to the Yorkshire where he'd grown up, instead choosing the more laid-back atmosphere in Llanawch, spurning college to get some cash in his pocket as a salesman at the local farm machinery showroom. The local surfing lifestyle had been an attraction, and at least Hywel still kept that interest going when he'd let so much else fall away in favour of pub life. Yet nice as it was to have him nearby, Lloyd often wondered at his older son's decision and whether it was the right one given where farming was heading remained to be seen. It felt that Hywel was just about getting by, but no more.

The engine noise altered as the car scaled the hill road to what had been their home since the move from Leeds. The terrace was lined with rough brown-stone facades, with the burnt umber of a partially collapsed corrugated-iron shed on the bottom corner of the street providing a navigation point. The detached house stood at the crescent of the street strapped in with a handful of others to the rock hillside. From this position, like a medieval lord, they overlooked the village and out to the wild waters of Cardigan Bay. Lloyd's habit at twilight, now mostly alone but in the past often with Catrin, was to sit out with a beer and a pair of binoculars watching the dolphins at motion in the bay. As night pitched down, he would remain out on the deck, viewing the stars canopying over the village in their universal clockwork motion. If he looked long and hard enough, he could sometimes make out the straight-moving diamond dots of satellites passing overhead as if on rails. Funny to think really, they were designed by all these clever engineers and scientists, cost millions, and there they were, orbiting above little old Llanawch. At those moments, with the silence enveloping the house like a fog, the odd clatter or shout drifting up from the village only emphasising the solitude, he felt part of something greater, not just the family and place, but in his time on earth. He knew enough that when he looked up at the stars, he wasn't just looking at a thousand points of light; he was looking back in time. Lloyd wondered whether his ancestors had done the same and whether there was a purpose to this. And then his head would swim; it was all too much to think about, but maybe one day everything would click.

Lloyd Parry would gaze down onto the village as the artificial lights began to intensify against the darkening and feel that this would be the place where all his own roads ended, where he trundled down to nought. This thought slightly depressed him, but this was the existence that he'd chosen... no, the life he'd *needed* then. Now, he felt that maybe he needed a bit of rawness, something hard-edged, different. Didn't have to be a city beat either, he could get back into a large town perhaps, or try for his inspector exams as he once had hoped – he'd even bought the training manuals and they weren't yet out of date. But then again Catrin's life was rooted in concrete here and she wouldn't move for wild horses. Maybe he should just get on with it, stop being a silly dreamer and try to be content.

Lloyd knew that they might have made a packet if they'd put the house up for sale a couple of years ago and moved out of the area. A lot of incomers had been in the market for that kind of rustic coastal life. Enough of them had already bought in the village, and over the past few years, he noticed how the streets had become progressively quieter from each October onwards, how many more unoccupied holiday homes he was asked to check on during his daily beat. There had been much hot air in the local pubs and the council chamber about it, of course, none of which discouraged local-born sellers from the obvious lure of a big payday. The local politicians moaned about incoming buyers, but then they seemed to forget that there had to be a seller on the other side to make it work. If someone knocked on their door offering stupid money, Lloyd would be inclined to take it. He knew he would, and he'd just have to live with the supposed guilt. Catrin was different.

All this deep thinking, it tired a man out. He pulled into the entrance and came to a halt in front of the new garage extension that the builders hadn't yet got around to completing since last summer. 'We're home.'

Eight

City dwellers don't know what darkness is. It's more than just a visual state. Real darkness is like being adrift out on an ocean, everything and nothing happening all at once.

An urbanite can put black-out curtains up to block the neon from the streetlamps outside, but the sound of the city will still seep in. They can then install thick double-glazing to mute the sound, but in their mind will always be the notion that the city and all its horror starts outside a one-inch-thick wooden front door. Outside it can be very, very dark.

In the deep and true countryside when there is no moon, or heavy cloud cover, it is so dark you can't see your hand in front of your face. Maybe if you're lucky you'll see the lights of a farmhouse across the valley to keep you oriented. You'll keep your eyes on that distant light as you stagger-stumble towards it over the uneven ground, occasionally slipping in cow muck or sheep droppings. From time to time you'll catch your unprotected hand on a bramble or high nettle and curse. But otherwise, there is little sound, apart from the rustling of leaf if there is a breeze, maybe the bark of a distant rutting fox. Most of all there is the underlying knowledge that no neighbour is on hand to help or to call the police if you get into trouble. Just those lights you see across the valley that all too slowly draw closer despite all your exertions. You try to hold back the fear. You are isolated and unsighted in the darkness. You can hear your ragged breaths as you stumble. You are living ten thousand years ago. The land is savage, the animals untamed. Danger is out there at the end of a hunting spear. Dawn cannot come quickly enough.

The three men were dressed in black from head to toe. Trainers, cloth overalls, cotton balaclavas. They sought out the hours of darkness as they would a friend, were cloaked by the night as by a favourite tailor. The men stood in front of the closed aluminium doors of a farm storage building. They weren't total troglodytes; they found some light to be useful such as the powerful yet precise pen torches which assisted their work. But not head-torches; they knew from experience that just a little flick of the head, one carelessly directed shine could give the game away. One of the men carried a bolt cutter and lightly gripped the padlock keeping the doors locked in place. Another cupped his hands under the lock as a fielder waiting in the cricket slips.

The third scanned the yard, confirmed its stillness, and whispered, 'Okay. Cut it.'

His companion grunted as he strained for a moment and then the bolt cutter did its work, snipping off the padlock, which dropped into his colleague's hands. The third man tentatively pulled one of the doors open, having already oiled the reachable hinges in order to minimise the chance of the metal screeching an alarm. They were in luck, the door moved quietly, just the wobble of the sheet metal emitting a soft distant thunder.

'Let's see what's inside.'

The men walked into the storage barn and ran their torches over the contents. A mini excavator, a plough attachment for a tractor, a tow hitch assembly, a stack of full fertiliser bags and some plastic sheeting for wrapping the big round bales often seen in the fields towards the end of summer. The leader was pleased, all in all around fifteen grand of gear. Their cut would be around a third of that.

'Good. Let's load it up. And keep it quiet.'

He walked out to their lorry, ramps already down awaiting its fresh load. They'd cased this building out for a few days. It was part of a larger farm complex, but a little distance from the main farmhouse further up the track. A farmworker had a cottage onsite, but another member of the gang had witnessed him imbibe a skinful in the local pub earlier that evening. As was his routine every Friday night. They worked on the assumption that he'd be dead to the world, but there was little point in risking it.

'Hold it.'

The headlight beams of a car passed on the main road which was a hundred yards down the farm track. The men paused in their work, watching carefully as the car's red taillights disappeared into the distance. There was no one else about.

'Okay.'

The third man turned about to see the plough being rolled out of the barn and to the foot of the ramp. He ran over to help give it a push into the lorry. They secured it at the back. Next up was the tow hitch. Then the digger, put into neutral and manhandled aboard the lorry. Around these, the men packed the bags of chemicals, plastic sheeting, and anything else they could find which could be easily resold.

The men closed the barn – an open door might get noticed from the road – and clambered into the lorry. There was still no movement from the cottage.

'Right, let's go. Keep it a sensible speed, we don't want to get noticed. And take the balaclavas off at the bottom.'

The lorry started up and moved away slowly down to the junction, paused and turned right onto the main road. Its headlights cut a narrow swathe along the valley, the engine hum steadily diminished, then disappeared, leaving the darkness once more.

The blackness which deadens your eyes and makes it difficult to see the outline of your own hand. Your ears try to compensate. They pick up the rippling of forest leaf in the breeze, catch the flapping wings of owls, hear a murmur of drunken snoring.

Nine

Even in the dewdrop of early morning, the milder air lapping through the windows of Lloyd's house signalled the arrival of summer. Yet in the Parrys' kitchen hung a clear chill: Arwel was about to sit the first of his A-level exams. If red lights could have flashed and warning klaxons sounded, then this would have been the time. Breakfast witnessed Catrin in maternal overdrive, confident that a concerted display of super-mam-hood over the snap, crackle and pop would propel her son up another grade.

Using her pristine white apron, she wiped the rim of a plate laden with varied pork products and set it proudly before her youngest offspring; 'Look, I've made you a fry-up.'

Arwel, his school trousers shining with wear and an inch short, their respectability lost some time before scraped back a chair and plopped himself down at the table. He mumbled a 'Thanks Mam,' before he started to surgically remove the fat from his unexpected bacon.

His mother fussed over him. 'Would you like some toast?' No answer. 'Lloyd, does the boy want toast?'

Lloyd raised an eyebrow. 'Leave him be. Do *I* get a fry-up?'

'No. It's bad for you.' She banged a bowl of muesli in front of her husband, and switched on the food processor, which like the bacon was making a rare appearance.

After thirty seconds where Lloyd was reminded of the noise of their plane careering down the runway on their holiday flight to Portugal, his wife switched the machine off and poured the glutinous beige concoction into a wine glass. 'Drink this, Arwel, it's a fruit smoothie. I read that it's good for the brain. Help you to think.' Catrin stood next to the table, hands on hips, and watched her son as he self-consciously drank it. Noting that the processor's jug had been emptied, Lloyd decided against asking his wife for one himself. A few minutes later, her men made to leave. Lloyd picked up one of the untouched sausages from the boy's plate and finished it off as they walked out to the car, wiping his hand inside his trouser pocket. Catrin came with them as far as the front door, giving Arwel a kiss on the forehead and an intense hug. She mouthed a *good luck* from the doorstep and stood there, hands clasped tightly at her chest, as Lloyd reversed the patrol car out of the drive. Arwel started to wave back before turning the movement into a sweep of his hair.

The silence was welcome to them both after the intensity of breakfast, doubtless a scene repeated in a number of homes in the locale that morning. Lloyd took a sideways look at his son in the passenger seat, but Arwel was absorbed in his own thoughts. No change there then – the boy was so different to his older brother. As they left the village Lloyd switched off the police radio to let the boy concentrate on the last-minute revision cards he'd pulled out and was flicking through. On the outskirts of Llanawch, they passed a large navy-blue removals van entering the village, and he remembered that another pair of London evacuees who had bought one of the houses facing the harbour, were due to move in today. Using the offer of some of his parents' savings, Hywel had put in an overly hopeful bid for the same property, but it had been predictably blown out of the water. So as far as Lloyd was concerned, this was just more evidence for the importance of his youngest doing well in his exams. Money talked and Arwel wouldn't find any of that lying about the village.

Catrin was the showy one here, forever talking to her friends about Arwel and her ambitions for him. Lloyd sometimes felt that there was more than a hint of trying to beat the neighbours – who in their case actually were called Jones – in this respect, but what he quietly cared about was ensuring that his boy got the hell out of the village and gave himself a chance of a future. He smiled as he recalled the charity hike up Snowdon the two of them had done together soon after they'd arrived in the area. That was a good time, it was a shame that they hadn't done much like it since, but you know…

He dropped off Arwel at the school's bus bay. 'Just don't let yourself down, do your best. We're proud of you…' and felt a hiss of deflation in his inability to find a more original sentiment. He had tried to think of something better the night before, but it was the best he could come up with. Lloyd watched as his son's narrow frame strode across the schoolyard and disappeared into the entrance. If they ever feel like looking back on their years to date, and most don't, children find it difficult to see alternative paths in their lives, as everything they've experienced seems like a natural progression through school classes and years. Life to the young, if they thought about it at all, is like a stick flowing on a stream, they get dropped into the system when a small child and twenty years they later wash up somewhere. But Lloyd always thought of it as a road. It's only later that an adult can look back on their life and see the signposts ignored, the crossroads consigned to oblivion. For Arwel, it had been a conveyer belt from his start at primary school to this day of days which would go a long way to deciding his future. Just one day, a few hours that would be so crucial in deciding the course of his life. Lloyd could only hope that his son had some glimmer of this.

From behind, a car's horn sounded, causing Lloyd to check his mirror to see the father of one of Arwel's friends giving him a thumbs-up. Lloyd returned the hand signal and put the Land Rover into gear for the journey back home. The other parents were surely feeling like this. Going through the same emotions and memories – it seemed only yesterday that he walked the boy to his first day of school back in Leeds, carrying a green plastic *Toy Story* lunchbox for him. Give him a *Buzz Lightyear* DVD today, and he'd turn his nose right up at it. He smiled as the car reached the junction for the estuary road; this nostalgia made Lloyd think about the primary school back in the village. Arwel had gone there for a few years, but it was now under threat of closure. More budget cuts. He'd seen parents standing outside the school gathering signatures for a petition to persuade the council to save it. It was a sad thing indeed. All of them were aware that when the school had gone in other towns and villages, it was soon followed by the remaining bank branches, then the post office. Everyone knew the drill from then on, no school meant no young couples and so no children. And with no children... well... the villagers' collective fears could see the future disappear, and with it, all signs of their past, memories extended by generations of their time on Earth. Each succeeding decade would be a drawn-out end of history for the village, much as when people cry at the funerals of their old friends; part of them cries for the passing of witnesses to their own lives.

He cringed self-consciously at his thoughts. He reprimanded himself as he mused that when it didn't matter, he could suddenly get poetic, but not when he needed a few simple words of encouragement for his son.

A little later, still mulling over that morning's journey, Lloyd patrolled along the seafront on foot. He was meant to be making the rounds of the district in his patrol car, flying the flag of law and order in the outlying hamlets and farms, but today he felt like he needed some sea air. He stepped deftly off the pavement to allow room for a wide-slung tourist couple. The woman had her forearm squeezed into an NHS crutch, and she panted as she toddled past. Her husband displayed a collection of blurring tattoos under an electric blue singlet, and he swigged from a can of Coke. He glared at Lloyd.

'You the local law?'

'I was last time I looked, sir.' He glanced down at his uniform to emphasise the point. 'What's the problem?'

'The problem is that you ought to get this pavement fixed. How's my wife meant to get her mobility scooter down this surface?' He stamped on a loose paving slab.

'Well, that's not my department, but I can pass the message along to the town council if you'd like.'

The man grunted, 'You do that. It's a disgrace. You people charge enough for car parking but can't even make provision for scooters. We pay our taxes you know.'

Parry nodded, watched the man shake his head and catch up with his invalid wife.

Seemed that there were a few fatties in the village today… but then again, the holidaymakers seemed to get larger and more elephant-like with each passing year. Still, there was one upside – they ate and drank more and that was only good for the local economy if not for the national obesity crisis he kept reading about in the papers. Lloyd tightened the muscles in his own stomach – just a bit of exercise and he'd soon get rid of his own little mound of flab. No problem.

It was a funny old roller-coaster of a deal Llanawch had got itself into. It was swamped by tourists over the high season, making life almost intolerable for the locals, but the money and jobs they brought kept the place going over the hard winter months. Well, it wasn't as if Microsoft was going to build an office here and give everyone six-figure jobs and flash sports cars. That would be the day. Lloyd looked out to the vanishing point in the palette of sea and sky, distracted, wondering how they did all that technology stuff. In his day it had been space shuttles and Concorde jets, things you could touch and understand; now all anyone was concerned about was getting the latest smartphone. He used computers easily, not like his first desk sergeant who had handled the station's IBM as if it was a piece of Sunday-best china, but Lloyd had no idea what went on inside these little plastic boxes. Maybe he was showing his age, but he didn't think that the kids had much of a clue either beyond buying the latest games. Hywel and

Arwel definitely hadn't shown any interest in becoming millionaire computer software designers, which Lloyd – as he'd explained to them often – considered a crying shame for his early retirement prospects.

He stopped as he noticed a dog sniffing around the back of the *Mr Whippy* ice–cream van parked at the edge of the harbour. It was a ribcage-thin border collie, head slung low. Lloyd carefully approached the dog, kneeled and gently held out his hand. 'C'mon boy, come here…'

The dog looked at him with suspicion, then slowly padded forward and lowered its black snout to smell the outstretched hand. 'That's right. Have a good sniff.' The collie looked almost out on its paws, its coat matted with sand around the belly and legs shaking. He had a quick feel around the neck, but there was no dog tag to indicate ownership. Abandoned pets, he mused, they all wore that similar look, a cross between disappointment in their former owners, and uncertainty about their next meal. Too often, a day tripper would come to the village, go for walkies, throw their dog a guilt-quenching treat, and then leave the poor creature behind, hoping that it would somehow survive. Lloyd had no time for people like that. They weren't even supposed to have dogs on the beach during the season anyway.

He walked over to his patrol car and opened his lunch box. Removing the ham from his sandwich he threw it to the dog, which didn't need asking twice before gulping it down. He'd phone the local sanctuary tomorrow to come and collect the animal, but for tonight, he decided to take the dog up to the station, feed it properly and give it a bed.

'OK, let's park up here, we'll get some brekkie over at that café, and then we can move the load in.' The foreman opened the cab door of the blue lorry and stepped down, his burgundy T-shirt briefly exposing an abdomen worked flat from humping heaving loads about daily. He stretched from the journey and rubbed his closely shaved head. 'Right bastard of a drive that.'

'When's that rug-muncher arriving with the keys again?' the driver of the lorry asked, as he too hopped down from the cab.

'Jack's rule number one; don't be rude about the customer. She may not be my cup of tea neither, but we want the tip. So, Ms Pimlott to you all right. Got it?'

The two other removals men laughed at their youngest workmate, who adjusted his jeans and scowled. 'All right, all right. But she is though, isn't she?'

'What?'

'A lezza.'

'So is Val in the payroll office, but you're happy to collect your wages from her each week, aren't you? Let's try this place, looks all right...'

'Yeah, but Val's a laugh, isn't she.'

As the men walked toward the café, set on a Full English accompanied by the soccer pages, they took little notice of the young guy lolling in the gloom of the bus shelter, stretched out like a forgotten umbrella. He watched the movers carefully from underneath the rim of his black hoodie, stubbed out his roll-up fag on the bench and reached for his mobile phone.

Ten

Delay was put in a locked chest; inertia banned from the premises; and pipe-dreaming transported to a far-off land.

Days after the initial decision Frankie and Ruth were in Wales viewing the property: the holiday home of a failing small-business owner in need of urgent liquidity. Within an hour Frankie had placed a cash offer. Four months on, with their affairs in London mostly tied up, and a pay-per-story contract signed with a rival to her old paper, here she was, driving the old Audi TT through the hills and valleys of Wales, her wife sitting beside losing the way on the map.

Frankie was driving towards her future and in the bright sunshine the moment felt exciting, almost unreal – she felt the rush of an adrenaline hit. She opened up the accelerator to fifty, fifty-five, sixty and saw the vision-edged blurring of the green verges as they flew by. Traffic was light, and after a series of roundabouts Frankie recognised the coastal road leading to the village, which meant that they were close to their destination. She dropped their speed with a jerk as she noticed a police SUV about two hundred metres in front:

best not to get on the wrong side of the local plods on their first day as residents.

'Nearly there. Excited yet?'

Out of the corner of her eye, she could see her wife close the vintage route map – *suitable for a journey back in time* – and rummage around in her handbag. Probably for her make-up, to prepare herself for the removals crew – she wasn't blind enough to miss the brief appraising look that Ruth had ranged over that young removals Neanderthal back in London. Frankie felt that she would rather ignore what that look meant and tried again not to sift through the other non-career reasons why it made sense for them to leave London with its myriad temptations.

Ruth looked at her partner. 'Do you really think a white linen suit is appropriate? This is Wales after all, not Miami's South Beach.'

Not bad for her. Frankie filed the comment away for later use in a column. 'Well, my darling, I want to make a statement. A splash. Get the locals talking. First impressions and all that. Get them talking to me. Get them wanting to find out more. It's all part of the master plan for success!' Ruth nodded slowly, scanning the lumbering hills on the opposite side of the estuary, her elbow resting on the open window frame. Frankie wished that she could see what her wife's eyes would reveal behind those dark glasses. When she slipped them on, was she erecting a barrier against the sun, or her? 'It's not as if I'm wearing my best suit anyway; in any case I bought these eons ago in LA, it needs an airing.' No response. 'Well, I like it anyway. It's quite Tom Wolfe.'

'Bit of an obscure reference that. Especially for the locals.'

As the car swept into the main square, they saw the removals van dominating the space set against the cobbles and squatness of the cottages. Would they fit everything into their new place? If not no biggie, as Frankie was already negotiating to buy one of the neighbouring cottages from its holiday-home owner – expand laterally behind the facade, give the village an infusion of rural cool, maybe get *World of Interiors* to do a photo shoot. That would certainly put another fifty thousand or more on the combined value.

Frankie rolled to a halt next to the removals van and in the group of men lounging about, sought out the oldest individual, the one sporting the company polo shirt. 'Get here with everything in one piece?' The man nodded. 'Bit of traffic around Coventry, but otherwise…'

'… very good.' Frankie finished the sentence for him. 'I suppose I should unlock the door so you can start.' One of the males who were about to handle her valuable furniture sniggered from behind his red-top tabloid. Frankie felt her cheeks glow. While she'd never use the proud term "working class" in a derogatory sense, white van man was a mystery to her with his comfort-zone mentality, and unwillingness to accept new ideas. I mean, she'd read the *Ragged Trousered Philanthropists* and such when at college, yet the successors of these proud socialist heroes were, in her well-informed opinion, squarely at the root of the country's present difficulty. While there'd always be a need for physical labour, these individuals would doubtless grow fewer in number over time as the information age dominated the economy. But most of all, she disliked the way she didn't command their respect simply because she was different to them, *not better*, *of course*, well better educated anyway. Just different. Did they think she couldn't sense their disdain? Such ignorance on their part. Hadn't they heard of diversity?

'That would be helpful, Ms Pimlott.'

Frankie searched for a trace of sarcasm but couldn't detect it. The foreman continued in matey tones, 'No need for you to do anything, you just sit back with a cup of tea, relax and we'll get it all sorted out for you in a jiffy. I assume that er… Mrs Pimlott will tell us where everything goes.' The foreman glanced for a beat longer than necessary at where her wife with her bare legs were perched against the passenger door of their car.

'No, I'll be supervising the unpacking. It will be more efficient that way.'

The foreman's impassive expression changed so slightly as to be unremarked, but he felt in his bones that it was going to be a long morning. These city-to-country jobs always were, and this woman was a demanding type if ever he'd seen it. Still at least the wife hadn't burst into tears, like one of his customers from last year, when the poor bitch had realised that she was now stuck alone with a half-built barn conversion in the middle of an Exmoor downpour, and miles from nowhere. They'd needed to throw a tarpaulin over the furniture because the roof hadn't been finished.

'Right. I'll get the lads sorted for you, madam.' If he could manage to keep the forelock in a state of tug, he'd get them a bigger tip.

'OK people, let's get this sorted. C'mon, let's be having you.' The cardboard boxes started the final leg of their journey into the cottage, which in the foreman's calculation was looking optimistic given the cottage's square footage compared to all the belongings yet to be unloaded. He was still trying to visualise whether they were going to need to remove a window to get the ten-seater dining table inside when he felt a presence behind him. He turned around to see a young bloke facing him. A few others stood a few yards behind.

Meic Davies introduced himself. 'Beth ydych chi'n meddwl eich bod yn ei wneud?'

The foreman laughed. 'Sorry, I don't speak the language mate.'

The youth looked at him for a few seconds, seeing the middleweight in front of him, then curtly, 'Okay, I'll try again. What do you think you're doing?'

'Eh, what are you on about?'

'I said, what do you think you're doing?' It wasn't subtle; the threatening tone was obvious to the foreman, who didn't try to hide a smirk at being fierced-up by a bunch of yokels, even if their leader seemed well-built.

'What does it look like?'

'Who are the people moving in?'

'Why not ask them yourself. She's over there, that lady in the white suit.' Stony-faced, he nodded over to Frankie, who was instructing a sweating removals man whose storm-cloud demeanour indicated that he didn't have the patience of his gaffer. Not that this was noticed by Frankie, who was pointing animatedly at a sketch of a floorplan. Meic flicked a final belligerent stare at the foreman, and strode over to the short, slight woman with the faux-ruffled haircut. His eyes flicked over to the other woman – a bit of a looker – standing at the entrance to the cottage, and then back to the English woman.

'Oi you.'

Frankie looked up. 'I'm sorry?'

'Where you from?'

'I'm terribly sorry, but do I know you?'

'No. You don't. But I want to know you. Where you from?'

It was then that Frankie caught sight of the gang behind

Meic, all of them staring at her, and she hesitated before replying. 'London,' she broke into an insincere smile. 'I presume that you're from around here?'

'Yes. I'm local. And you're like so not.' Meic nodded over to a thirty-something man on the far side of the harbour carrying some fishing material onto a boat. 'See him over there? That's Gareth the Fish. He and his missus made an offer for this cottage,' Meic lied. 'So did others from round here, but someone knocked them all out of the running by getting out their fat-cat *London* wallet.'

Meic placed himself just a few inches from Frankie and leaned forward until his forehead nearly grazed his target. 'And I reckon that someone was you. That wasn't a good move, like. So, do yourself a favour. Fuck off back to where you came from. Like, now.'

Frankie took a small step back, the staccato delivery impacting on her chest like a boxer's jabbed one-two. She'd anticipated a little trouble, maybe a few words muttered behind her back in the corner shop, but not outright caveman aggression. The youth seemed to have that same unmoving manner as the beggar she'd encountered on the way back from reviewing that Jamaican-Asian fusion restaurant in Brixton. She had been able to make that encounter the main part of the review, adding a neat paragraph about the food at the end, so a silver lining. Perhaps there would be one here also. Frankie smiled at the boy. She tried to remember which pocket she'd put her mobile phone in and how quickly the police out here could respond to a call. She could hear her inner voice quaver as she mustered enough strength to regain the initiative. Right now, she must smooth the situation over; later she could try and win the guy round to her way of thinking. Life was always about the art of the possible. As Dave had once said at a Downing Street reception which she'd attended.

'I understand. Believe me. I recognise that you're looking at me in my nice linen suit and seeing an outsider. I can appreciate where you're coming from.' She paused for effect; the words had given her confidence, and now she felt that the young man was unsure. Probably hadn't come across someone like herself before. 'But I'd like you to know… sorry, what's your name?'

'Meic.'

'I'd like you to know, Meic, that I'm here to help your village, and to help you. I want to be a part, no make that a beneficial part, of your community…'

Frankie dropped as a flour sack through a trap door, finding herself on the cobbles, unaware of the touch of Meic's open hand for several seconds after it had briefly connected with her face and flat-palmed it backwards. A woman's scream peaked out from some carefully buried teenage memory and emerged fully grown from her mouth. She shrieked again, before she could gather herself, work out where she was. Toppled over on her back… in her favourite suit… with dirt and oil stains. The dry cleaners wouldn't get that out. She touched her hand gently to her nose and raised herself to her elbows to see what the other noise was. Around her, she saw a developing melee as the removal men and the local gang drew together. It wasn't that the boys from the lorry cared that much about Frankie whimpering on the floor, but releasing the energy suppressed over a long drive, they ignored the foreman's pleas and gratefully got stuck in. Both sides disregarded Frankie as she crawled out of the ruck like a sodden sheep plopping out of a dip.

Lloyd was telephoned by Mrs Cline-Jones, a retired biology teacher who lived in a flat on the village square. With the passing of her pensionable years, the view from the front room of this flat had progressively become Mrs C-J's sole view of a disturbing, impolite and ever-less-genteel world. The loss of her best friend since school to the virus simply cemented her unwillingness to venture out much beyond a weekly trip to the shop – now there was no one to even share a cup of tea with. In her best received pronunciation – a tone in which she always addressed the lower orders – Mrs Cline-Jones asserted that a fight had broken out, that she had never seen such behaviour in her life, and what she really wanted to know as a responsible citizen was when would the sergeant do his duty and put a stop to it? Lloyd rolled his eyes as she rang off. He had just returned from a call-out about some stolen farm equipment, another one marked up to the crime wave of farm machinery thefts that would doubtless stain his clear-up rates for months to come. With a look of thwarted longing at the just-boiled kettle, he clumped out of the station back to his Land Rover, slamming its door. He drove slowly down to the square. As that first shift sergeant in Leeds had said, don't be so quick to run to a fight, walk and give trouble a chance to take its leave. Lloyd cruised into the centre of the square and watched as Meic Davies and his cronies took on what seemed to be a smaller but harder-looking group of men. Probably the removals men from the van that he'd noted earlier. Lloyd thought about radioing for assistance, but instead switched on his siren for a short blast. A few heads jerked around, seeking the source of the noise, and most of the scuffling petered to a halt as Lloyd hopped out, showily slid his long baton into his belt, and strode towards Meic

Davies, who was gripping the T-shirt of another man, his face distorted in rage.

'Hey, hey, hey! Meic!' He grabbed the youth's rock-hard shoulder and pulled him away. 'Meic, pack it in. Now!'

Meic swung round angrily at the handhold but stopped his swing as he saw Lloyd.

'What's going on now?' He had everyone's attention. 'Do really I need to get back-up here, or shall we keep it between us? Hey you, hands off him.' He signalled to Phil Edwards, a local nut-job, to release one of the removals men from a headlock. 'Right. What's the story? Hey Meic, I'm talking to you.'

Davies got up slowly, panting with the adrenaline of the confrontation. 'We're sticking up for our rights as Welshmen. Seeing as the law won't, Sergeant.'

'And what rights are these then, Meic?'

'The right to live in your own village. The right not to have rich Saes wankers come in here, buying up the place. Those rights for a effing kick-off.'

Lloyd sighed. 'Ho-kay. I think I see.' He turned to the man in the battered white suit who was still slumped against the wall of the house. 'And who are you, sir?'

'Frankie Pimlott. *Ms* Frankie Pimlott.'

He peered a little more closely. 'Oh yes, Ms. Sorry about that. Now what's going on?'

'I want these thugs arrested. Especially him, he actually assaulted me.'

'Actuallaee. I say old bean, actuallaee.' The gang laughed and for some mysterious reason pretended to flap about like penguins. 'Actuallaee, actuallaee…'

Lloyd shot them a warning glance. He looked at the other woman, half-hidden behind the front door. 'And you are?'

'Ruth Pimlott.'

'Now then. Meic, shift yourself out of this lady's garden and wait over there so I can speak with all of you in a minute. Go on, move it! Right, you removals boys, I suggest you carry on and get those boxes off the square. This is a public right of way.' He turned to the couple. 'Um, Mz and Mrs Pimlott, can we go inside? I'd like a quick word, please.'

Frankie looked up from surveying her torn jacket. 'You can't let these thugs get away with it.'

'Yes madam, of course not, madam. Shall we?' He held his arm out so as to guide the couple into their new home. What a welcome to their new home, pretty full-on embarrassing for the village really. He took his cap off as they passed the threshold and set it down on one of the packing boxes. 'How are you feeling?'

'I think he's broken my nose.'

Lloyd moved closer to take a look. 'They all say that, madam. Turn your face to the left, will you… no, I think you're going to live. It's just a bit red, that's all. Now if he'd broken your nose, you'd know it.'

'I need a doctor; I need a doctor right now.' Frankie walked distractedly around the room, snorting air out of her nose to check the damage. 'Where the nearest A&E?'

'That would be in Dolgellau, cottage hospital ten miles down the road, madam. But I don't think it's too serious. I really can't see anything.'

'I think I'll decide what's serious if you don't mind, officer.' Frankie gave a quick glance outside and then looked at her wife. 'So what are you going to do about this? Well? I want that yob locked up for a start.'

Lloyd glanced around the front room. Out of the window he could see Meic's gang lurking on the quayside, giving the removals men dirty looks as they restarted their unloading. He rested his hand on his baton. 'As I see it this is your first day in a new town.'

Frankie began to protest. 'This is not just an assault on me, it is an assault on women. How can you stand by when—'

'No madam, hear me out a minute. That Meic Davies out there, the guy who you say hit you? Well, he can be a right idiot sometimes and there is no way that I'd normally condone this sort of behaviour. I'm not saying that now,' Lloyd scratched just behind his ear. 'But what I am saying is, that if you drop the charges, I'll have word with him, make sure he knows how lucky he is not to be facing a court summons, and you don't start your life here under a cloud. What do you think?'

Frankie studied the policeman, middle-aged, a touch heavy around the jowls, probably a little slow in the head. Clearly more of a town deputy-sheriff type than chief of police. 'So just to clarify the situation you're going to let these thugs get away with breaching the peace?'

Lloyd heard Frankie's wife yield a heavy sigh which made him smile inside. 'No madam. But it seems a bit silly to be making enemies so soon. Usually when people move into a new area, they um, they sort of want to make friends.' He looked for support from the wife now standing near the fireplace. 'What do you think, Mrs Pimlott?'

She removed her sunglasses. 'Frankie, I think the officer is being very sensible. It's probably the best solution for now. We don't want to get into another Islington situation, do we, darling?' She smiled at the policeman, appraising him, wondering what his opinion was of her.

Frankie Pimlott nodded, her breathing becoming

calmer, and appeared to consider her options. 'Very well, diplomacy rules the day, for now. But if that youth tries to intimidate us again, it will be a different story. I won't hesitate to bring charges, serious charges against him. And I will be documenting this incident and emailing a report immediately to my solicitor in London to store as potential future evidence. Please make that clear to him.'

Lloyd picked up his hat. 'Thank you for your understanding, madam. I think that's the best course of action. I'll speak with him right now.' Lloyd looked over at Mrs Pimlott. 'Sorry about the trouble, but in any case, welcome to Llanawch. I'm sure it will get better.'

She watched him leave the room. He was very good, definitely had Frankie down pat straight away, initially coming on humble, and then applying just the right amount of firmness when her partner's well-worn soapbox was dragged out for another appearance.

Lloyd pushed past one of the van men, and walked over to Davies. 'Right boys, you're off the hook. The ladies have agreed not to press charges against any of you.'

'Bloody Saes, lucky for them you were around.'

'Did you hit her, Meic?'

'No, just gave her a shove.'

'Well, I'd better not find out it was more than that.' Lloyd laid a hand on the butt of his baton. 'Listen Meic, they were well within their rights in having you and your text-a-mob arrested and banged up. You could have been looking at fifteen months for affray,' or was it eighteen – he wasn't as hot on sentencing policy as he had been. 'But fortunately, you're not. Just think yourself lucky. And before you get on your high horse, let me tell you that if I so much as hear a whisper of a threat against either of them, you *will* feel my hand on your shoulder and what follows won't be pleasant. I can guarantee that.'

His heart rate had increased, but he steadily held Meic's passive-aggressive stare.

The stand-off was ended by the younger man, who couldn't stop himself from issuing a final sting. 'Come on boys. I don't want to hang around with Saes lackeys. See you… Sergeant.'

He watched the gang swagger off, jostling with each other. They were probably rewriting the fight already. Though he had asserted his control, Lloyd remained uneasy. There was something about this morning, an undercurrent which was new, and he couldn't quite put his finger on but didn't like. There'd been a little barracking at the last removals van which drove into town, Meic and a couple of his gorilla troop, but nothing physical then, nothing violent. This was a step up. He'd need to report it to Dolgellau. He kept post in his Land Rover for a further hour, watching the final boxes being squeezed into the Pimlotts' new home. Parry noted the *wife* of the pair, well that's how it looked anyway from the way they dressed, leave the house and, with her arms folded, walk to the pub. Hmmm, starting early. Nothing else happened in the meantime, apart from Mrs Stanley's dog rabidly chasing an empty plastic bag, which was in its own way an entertaining diversion from the aftermath of the fisticuffs. Lloyd's stomach began to rumble. He started the engine, took a final look at the pub and made his way home for lunch.

Pax Cymru.

Eleven

'*Sarge! Fucking get up!' Harris was standing over him. 'Any more of you fuckers want some? Do you? Do you!'*

He couldn't forget the nightmare.

Months could go by and then it would return, but recently the images had been rolling through his head a little too much for comfort. Sometimes the memory would trigger while on patrol when the gearbox grated under too many revs; or as now, when he was airing his riot overalls at the Llanawch police station, their flame-resistant protective coating crackling in the breeze. Lloyd had once believed the memories would fade. But they hadn't; distance and time hadn't worked their usual magic. Perhaps Dr Gafney, the locum GP, could give him something. He was overdue for a medical in any case, so that would be an excuse to make an appointment. Catrin had long passed the point of interest in his illness; the last time that he'd raised the issue, she told him to stop whinging. He had been waking her up a bit with the shouts and the night sweats, and every well of sympathy runs dry. Still, she was supposed to be his wife, for better or for worse.

Lloyd had been just one of a hundred-odd policemen injured during the nights of rioting. A handful had left the force straight afterwards, but most went back on duty wearing their battle scars with locker-room pride. It was only a few – like Lloyd – who returned to uniform wishing they hadn't. About two months after the disturbances, following the swarm of something-must-be-done visits from cabinet ministers, bishops and imams, long after the media had evaporated away to report on the hunt for a missing child down in Hampshire, and just as the official enquiry laboured into action, he met with his inspector, a letter of resignation in hand.

The letter bookmarked the end of an adventure. He'd left home for Leeds to begin his adult life. Within a couple of years he'd met Catrin and they'd bought a first home together. Both their kids had been born at the local hospital – Jimmy's. Lloyd had gradually seen the city change from its state of resigned depression when he arrived, as the excess cash up from the South began to trickle down, before turning into a river. There were new shops and restaurants opening, modern people wearing smarter clothes, driving their upmarket cars through the centre of town. But the same flows of wealth had bypassed Bradford, leading to resentment and anger. After the riots it would take some time for the city to rebuild what little image it previously enjoyed.

Lloyd hadn't just joined the police because there wasn't anything else for him. He'd chosen to become a policeman – a choice that only in hindsight did he realise might have been a reaction to his teenage life. Of course, he'd heard all the stories from back home about police behaviour during the strike, especially, as his dad's mate Glyn would always say, *the bussed-in bastards* from outside the coalfields. The Met mostly, who brought a hard-man reputation all their own to the picket lines. But he also heard about units from the Midlands, Hampshire, even the West Country constabularies. He'd experienced it all in the Swansea valleys, when everybody had to agree with the decrees of King Arthur Scargill, agree or else you were a traitor to your community and class. And they banged on about it still back home, hadn't moved on from the strike decades later. He bet that none of those clowns at N.U.M. headquarters had gone hungry like the poor buggers outside the colliery gates, who relied on hand-outs to feed their families. He remembered dropping the odd fifty pence or two into his school collection buckets at the time, but this still hadn't stopped him applying to the police, which was about the time his dad finally stopped talking to him altogether. Purposely avoiding the local force, he'd applied to the West Yorkshire mob for no reason other than that he'd supported Leeds United since he was a kid. The thought of duty at Elland Road, getting in to see the match for free, spurred him to fill out the application form and drop it in the post box at the end of his street. Anyhow, who'd want to hang around the industrial mortuary that was South Wales in the late eighties?

And so, with one application he changed the course of his life. But now, after the riot, Lloyd had found that it wasn't the life he wanted anymore. He wasn't sleeping. At work, his hand would exhibit a slight tremor as it buttoned up his uniform tunic before going out on the beat, and he would hear the new uncertainty in his voice on the streets. Once or twice he'd noticed the younger constables exchange glances in the locker room, and soon found that his popularity as a partner in the area patrol car was getting smaller. There were loud whispers, designed to be overheard, that if there was trouble the Sarge might not be a good man in the trenches. The sick days started to tot up. The Yorkshire force, seeking to bring down the cost of possible medical litigation, offered post-traumatic stress counselling. Softly-spoken words, understanding nods, the small box of tissues always to hand, but always unused – *is this going on my record?* – and the calming watercolour landscapes on the walls. Yet all Lloyd wanted to do was get away and quick. It was luck that the opportunity had arisen in Llanawch, his wife's home village. Catrin took a call from her mother and went to work on her husband. Lloyd, looking for a way out and a fresh start, had passively acquiesced. It was an easy decision to move, and one which his bosses in Leeds encouraged. A favour was called in with the North Wales force, who, short on manpower, overlooked Lloyd's lack of bilingualism. They got a good price for their Leeds home from a Bangladeshi businessman adding to his property portfolio, and within four months here he was.

He finished packing the overalls, and replaced them in the locker, along with the newly signed docket stating that he had performed his quarterly check on his civil contingency equipment. Serving in the arse-end of nowhere, he didn't expect to use the kit again outside of the occasional refresher course, but as it was all bought and paid for checking it was slated on the rolling roster of duties.

Lloyd's revived memories made him thirsty. A drink was needed – checking his watch he saw it was coming up to half past five. Pausing to put the portable biochemical sensor on overnight charge, and thus having prepared for the end of civilisation, he left for the short walk down to the pub.

It was quiet, just the Judge in his corner seat nursing his weekly double whisky, small plastic jug of water and a hardback book. They exchanged the respectful nods due from one end of the judicial system to the other, and Lloyd perched himself on a stool at the bar. 'Bit early for you, Lloydie, isn't it?' Stevie the barman, dressed in a checked shirt with sleeves rolled high up his sinewy biceps, had begun pouring him a pint without asking.

'You complaining, then? Got today's paper?' He stretched over the bar top and picked up a copy of *The Mail* lying by the telephone. He ignored the story about the latest EU failure on the front page, and turned to the sports section, slowly letting his eyes wander over the mid-week scores and latest transfer rumours. Lloyd was just drifting into a comfortable lull, the pint slipping down all too easily, when he detected the shadow of a figure across the bar from him. Glancing up, he saw it was the new woman in the harbour cottage – Mz Pimlott.

'Excuse me, but this wine is corked. Could you replace the bottle please?'

Eyebrows raised, Stevie picked up the lightly sipped glass, smiled greasily at Frankie, 'You mind?' He knocked a mouthful back. 'Tastes all right to me.' He replaced the glass on the bar.

'No, no, that won't do. This wine is clearly corked. Don't you know what you sell?' Pimlott had a look of studied disbelief on her face as she spoke to the barman, who was now leaning back against the chiller cabinets, waiting for her next move. 'Well, what do you have to say for yourself?'

With her complaints not making headway, she turned to Lloyd. 'This man should either give me my money back or replace the bottle, don't you agree?'

Lloyd, flushed out from the sanctuary of the horoscopes, took a draft from his pint. 'Not for me to say. I don't do consumer advice.' He looked over Pimlott's shoulder at the wife, who held his gaze. 'And I'm off-duty.' She was wearing one of those tight white tops, where you could just make out the lace of the bra underneath – very nice. She was quite well-proportioned and not uncomfortable about showing it.

Deciding to ignore Lloyd's unhelpful contribution to achieving her rightful redress, Pimlott looked again to the barman, speaking quietly and slowly in the unmistakable tone of the middle classes done wrong, 'So to be clear, you are not going to replace it? Would I be right in thinking that?'

There was a pause, then Stevie held up his hands. 'Look, tell you what, I'll give you half of your money back, but I still think it tastes okay.'

'Oh, good grief.' She gestured to Ruth. 'Very well, we're going. We'll find somewhere that knows how to serve wine. But dwell on this: we could have been good customers and now you won't be enjoying our money in your tills.' Frankie's wife raised her left eyebrow, knocked back her own glass, and, as she followed Frankie out, threw a bright, 'See you tomorrow,' at the barman while covertly weighing up Lloyd.

Leaving the pub, trailing in her partner's slipstream, Ruth reflected on what the policeman must think about her marriage to a person like Frankie – and how it reflected on her. Good God, Frankie, what have you turned into? Or were you always like this and I just ignored it at the time? She thought back on her student days. Her partner's exotic lifestyle had been for Ruth a portal into a different world while she was still a former grammar schoolgirl treading water in a bigger pond, trying to suck life in. She remembered the initial seduction – it still sent a small thrill down her, though much less than it did. Frankie wasn't as... *mannish* then, she still had long hair, still from time to time wore feminine clothes, didn't carry such weight.

Ruth had gone up to Cambridge assuming that she'd get a boyfriend and into a relationship – people always told her how pretty she was – but the couple of experiences she endured in her first term were, well, unsatisfactory was probably the nicest description. It was only later that she would discover that men became less selfish with age. But even when she was with the boys in question, resurfacing from her subconscious were the indications of her true nature though – the unrequited crush on her female drama teacher whom everyone said was *that way*; the way Ruth's eyes sometimes lingered over a classmate in the changing room after hockey practice. So when, over a bottle of a wine her new friend's hand slowly made its way from her knee, circling to Ruth's thigh, and held there while the giggling stopped and a first kiss took place, she passively allowed the hand to complete its journey under her skirt. It had been slow, gentle and intimate in all senses. They had talked, made love, then talked some more. Shared secrets; exchanged desires; Ruth felt an overwhelming need to let it all out and express herself as she had yearned to for so long. And in the glow of the morning as she crept out of Frankie's graduate rooms across the college riverside court to her own room, she decided that was that. She had finally been discovered by someone who made her feel special, who took her to new places and who not only awoke those dormant needs that often burned inside her but understood them completely.

At the time it had been hugely exciting, and she was so proud that this sophisticated woman had chosen her when she could have had anyone. Yet now Frankie's pretensions seemed nothing more than irritating. The sergeant had failed in his attempt to appear neutral in the face of Frankie's tantrum. And, Ruth mused, an extra plus was that quite apart from the policeman's unimpressed demeanour, she'd noted his eyes giving her the once-over. Actually, it seemed to her that he'd done a lot more than give her a quick check out. She smiled to herself, noting the man was quite indiscreet for someone in his position. But, Ruth mused, it shouldn't be surprising that she had piqued his interest for she'd already registered the local women with their salt-crusted faces and their trans-fats bodies. It wasn't being egocentric to think that they couldn't compete with her own gym-honed physique and beauty-spa buffing. She should be allowed that arrogance, after she worked for it. But she would need to focus hard here to keep in shape. Yet even with no competition, Ruth was warmed by just how much the policeman's attention had pleased her. She found it pleased her very much. Maybe this wouldn't be such a dull place after all, even if it looked like an ever more temporary gig given Frankie's inabilities in the how to win friends and influence people department. She marked Lloyd down in the *definite potential* category.

Lloyd and Stevie watched the couple walk across the square to their car.

'Same again?'

'Yeah, go on then,' Lloyd turned over a page and sniffed, 'just make sure that it isn't corked.'

Stevie paused. 'You know, I wouldn't mind so much, but she was drinking wine from a screw-cap.' Without an upward glance, Lloyd stuck his palm in the air and the barman hi-fived him.

The Judge smiled to himself, picked up his jug of water and added a little to his whisky. It brought out the taste, and these days every small pleasure was to be savoured.

Twelve

A month had passed, and Ruth, sitting hunched at the Shaker-style table in the kitchen of her new home, stared at the email printout in front of her. 'So "The Great Thinker" has a mind which turns out to be ever so averagely run of the mill. You can't do anything yourself in the shag department anymore, so instead you have to contact his wife to get your little thrills.'

She watched Frankie's face, bland and impenetrable in even this intimate moment – was she even listening to her? Yet again Ruth sensed that she was being kept at arm's length, placed in a compartment marked "emotional". Frankie still wore her blouses buttoned up to the top, in thrall to the eighties' retro-Edwardian style, just another sign of her being a fish out of water in her partner's eyes. 'Emotionally and sartorially constipated' was how one of her old friends had described this new version of her once-thrilling lover, which had been good advice foolishly ignored. The longer they'd lived together, the less able Frankie seemed to connect with Ruth's emotional state – she misread the cues like the most autistic of men.

'I had to know for sure.' The words left Frankie's mouth under duress.

'Know what? She knew exactly the same as you. I was fucking...'

'Ruth,' Frankie sharply interrupted, anything to stem the flood.

'... fucking her husband.' Ruth felt her triumph slowly deflate as she saw the slight dampening of her partner's eyes but couldn't stop the words. 'You don't like me saying it? I was fucking him, every week. Yum-yum,' smacking her lips in time. 'And he was sticking it in me. It was fabulous. Truly, the sex was fabulous.' She sat back, laid her palms on the table-top either side of the printout and smiled. This last sentence, as erroneous as it was, had been swung at Frankie like a punch daring some, any, kind of response.

Frankie rose from where she sat opposite Ruth, sleep-walked over to the coffee machine and began to prepare a treble shot espresso. Through the window, she stared out at the harbour where a blue-hulled yacht was just motoring out as she listened to the background hiss of the machine. She picked up the mini-projector for her mobile phone, which a magazine had sent her to review, and tried to remember the half-glimpsed thought which had been lurking in her subconscious before Ruth had spoilt the moment with her attention-seeking. The temperature in the room wasn't helping her concentrate: she'd have to take a look at the heating thermostat later. Frankie wished that this particular scene could be played out another time, or perhaps left on the cutting room floor. She had to maintain focus on the bigger picture, for the pair of them. Ruth was sometimes an incapable mess unable to control herself, and now she was speaking again. Couldn't she just let it be?

'But it was already over, so well done, Frankie. You've brought me to the ends of the earth and now ensured that I won't be fucking him again. Mission accomplished I'd say.'

'Ruth, we're here to pursue a new life…' Even she could hear the lecturing tone in her own voice. 'We should put any history behind us and move on.' She knew that she shouldn't, but added, 'That would be the smart move.'

'*The smart move*,' Ruth mimicked. 'Oh really? Seems more like someone exercising her usual control freakery to me.' She snatched up the car keys and let fly. 'I simply can't recall what I saw in you, I just can't. I'm going out now, and if the police come a-calling, it will probably be because I've run over some fucking local banjo player… or jaywalking sheep… or I don't bloody well know. Because there's fuck-all else for entertainment around here. I can't believe you thought that we'd fit in here. Or more to the point that *you* would fit in. But why should I be surprised?'

As she waited for a reaction – not even a raised eyebrow as yet – the memory of Frankie at the college bop returned once more. The way she'd come over and scooped up Ruth's stockinged feet where they were resting on a chair and unasked began to rub the tiredness out of them. Frankie had quietly talked to her, asked what she wanted from this life, and she listened, pleased at how she felt able to share confidences with her like an adult. She'd seemed so enthusiastic about life and so different, and then came the invitation to share that fatal bottle of wine. It was an age ago.

Ruth watched her partner fiddle with the controls of her bloody coffee machine – another shiny little designer toy. She just seemed… detached, worse than back home in

London. The move hadn't healed a damn thing. 'Christ, you've nothing to say…' No response – the coffee finished dripping into the little cup. A matching saucer and biscotti lay waiting for it nearby. 'Oh, fuck this!' Ruth departed, slamming the door behind her. *Control me now, you micro-managing bitch.*

Frankie heard the sound of the TT being over-revved – *Good grief, where would I get that repaired around here?* – and then departing at speed. She downed the espresso in four sips. She knew that she should do something, try and make Ruth understand that this village was a fresh chance for the pair of them, but the woman made it too difficult. Frankie wished that her wife wouldn't create these complications. She didn't know what she really expected from Ruth in their civil partnership. Though Frankie liked to call Ruth her wife, Ruth was holding out on upgrading to marriage, to be like their friends. But a civil partnership would have to suffice for the moment. Still… she let her mind drift back to the taste of the coffee, free-thinking… a finely traced upturn appeared at the left-hand corner of her mouth. With peace settling once more, she regained her train of thought: making connections, linking situations and concepts, devising solutions. Maybe she wasn't born to tie down a woman like Ruth, but harnessing thoughts was something that Frankie excelled at. The idea slowly began to emerge. She paused as the thoughts formed; the older you got the better you were meant to be at making linkages. Better than the young, that's for sure, like that little shit at her old paper. There had to be some compensation for the breast sag and body thickening, right? And now she had made the connection. It would all start with a coffee machine.

❧

The TT felt good as it gripped the uneven road surface. Ruth decided to see where it took her, preferably far away from those residual feelings of guilt about her infidelity, mixed with some anger at its discovery. Though why she felt guilty, having to live 24/7 with *her*, was beyond understanding. Leaving London to come up here had traded one form of oppression for another. At least back home, she had the freedom of the crowd.

Ruth possessed enough self-awareness to realise that Frankie's plan to relocate to the sticks was quite possibly going to be a poor move. It wasn't because she was that opposed to getting out of the city. After all, in many ways, leaving the place would be a release. It was tiring, the relentless strain of life there with the ever-transiting population radiating a mix of energy and edginess. Ruth knew from friends that she wasn't alone in wondering each time she took a tube train whether this would be the day when there would be the euphemistic *incident* and she would choke to death as acrid smoke filled her lungs, or even worse. Or maybe the evening walk home would hold an encounter with a knife gang. Mopeds, once the territory of trainee taxi drivers mapping their way around the city to gain The Knowledge, had become a getaway vehicle for pubescent muggers. In the past year whenever she walked the street, the Doppler sound of an approaching moped would make her shiver. The London of her nightmares was like the delayed reaction to a stab wound; a press of people gulping in buckets of chicken like a near-drowned man gasps for air; a city enveloped in eight million smart-worlds, sexting, swiping, ignoring tomorrow; the merging of Londoners into one uncaring crowd-spilled, victim-trampling dumb mass; a black hole of humanity with the future disappearing into the swirling, overwhelming void. Get a grip… but still.

During the ever-hotter summers, Ruth endured restless nights on damp sheets, marinating in anxiety. If it was bad enough before, the Coronavirus had turned London into an uncertain and difficult place in which to live, and no amount of being by turns, all terribly Blitz-spirit, or globalised-citizen on *Zoom* calls about it, could hide that fact. This had been a city she'd loved, but now she was waiting until their proverbial kids went to college.

When she moved there with Frankie the city had been an oasis, her half-caste colour making no difference, unlike in Cambridge, where she always felt something of an outsider, distinct from the privately educated white girls who had seemed to know each other before they arrived for freshers' week. Perhaps, and this wasn't the first time Ruth had contemplated this, maybe in hindsight there was just the hint of liberal trophy-seeking in Frankie's courting. In retrospect, she'd felt almost on parade through the various women-only dinner parties in Cambridge and then London. Yet at the time she'd set this minor irritation to one side. She'd been overwhelmed by excitement, lust and tenderness, enough for her to dizzily accept Frankie's offer on the day of her graduation to move in together. It took a little time afterwards before things started to progressively fall off – where freshness became stale, where endearing foibles became irritants, and where sexual adventures bedded down into straight-couple roles.

Ruth slowed down approaching a tight corner, leaning into the bend with her shoulders as the Audi swept round it, accelerating out of the turn, shaking dew droplets from the long-grassed verge. As for the affair referenced in the letter, well, doubtless like so many, it had started in the weeks following the vaccine. At a conference, sipping a cup of coffee from under her long eyelashes, craving the attention of any one of the white – *always white, what's going on there, Ruthie, kicking against something?* – middle-aged suits, just someone to make her feel connected to life. Then one of them did, and primed, she accepted. She had to admit that when she had crossed the threshold in that first hotel room, the idea had flitted through her mind that she might as well be shacked up with a real man rather than a pseudo-one. The other same-sex couples they knew – and at times it seemed as if Frankie had signed a contract to socialise only with lesbians – seemed to have much more of a sharing, equal dynamic. But her partner just didn't think that way, and it seemed that from the very start she'd been treated as the junior in the relationship, the acquiescent one.

For Ruth, it being the first time that she'd slept with a male since college – definitely the first time she'd slept with a grown man rather than a boy fresh out of sixth form – didn't feel like cheating. If it had been with a woman other than Frankie then that would have felt different, more complicated, a richer connection, but all the more dangerous for that. But with a man she'd managed to slot it into a little compartment and felt easy doing so – because she knew that's how the men she met handled their own indiscretions. While that first time was the hardest, the affairs afterwards were much easier. She was careful – never picked up anyone not already attached, always a man with something to lose who would be as discreet as she was. But she must have become careless if even the self-absorbed Frankie had detected that something was amiss.

At first the affair had been a stimulating diversion, but that phase ran its course, and within weeks it had stagnated to routine rutting. At this point she realised that the thrill had been mostly in her head. A Travelodge in Bayswater, the same weekday, at the same time. All the signs of a once-attentive lover settling into a by-the-numbers shag – she knew, she knew. No more evening meals at quiet little restaurants or overnight "client business" in Edinburgh. The weekly 'Physio – knee treatment' entry in her work diary, once the source of all-consuming sexual anticipation, now felt more like the habitual lancing of a boil. Even if it was a boil she needed to scratch. Step one, hike her skirt; step two, bend over bed; step three, five-minute trip to low-earth orbit; step four, listen as Andreas talked about how demanding his job in debt capital markets was. Step five, with biological needs met, press reset to mainstream lesbian in a partnership. *I wonder if my mother was like me? I think she might have been, maybe it was a genetic thing.* She felt a minor shudder of distaste when she thought about her need to give herself to such a banal little banker-turd. But Ruth also felt her body warm as she remembered the liaison, once again startled by how easily she could slip into arousal in lieu of a better offer.

Streams of light filtering through the trees presented a strobe effect across her vision as she shot along the estuary road, and it returned her to the present. To her city-attuned eyes used to an immediate street-level skyline, the sky seemed vast here, emphasised by the lazy spread of the estuary, the subtle moorland browns and woodland greens on the opposite bank following the curve of the river. There was a beauty here which she hadn't expected. There might not be any boutiques to while away a weekend, but the landscape did provide a magnificent drive. She imagined herself on the far riverbank watching the Audi speed along the road, hearing its distant solo roar. Strapped into a powerful car, the engine's horsepower in the small of her back, as it responded only to her touch… oh Christ, she was at it again. Come on Ruthie, think *Robin from Human Resources*, anti-passion guaranteed. She dropped down into third gear to take a steep incline. Ruth knew that she was a far better driver than Frankie, though of course her partner refused to acknowledge it. Driving itself didn't seem to really interest her; for Frankie it was the cultural signal that a particular car provided that was important. Ruth was a better navigator, too, but irritating her neurotic partner by showing ditzy confusion over any map was a minor pleasure which she'd never grown out of. The petrol gauge showed three-quarters, so as her friend Becky used to say, put the pedal to the metal girl. She concentrated on the feel of the road through the sports-set suspension, passing unnoticed the small cluster of dead flowers bunched at the base of a newly rebuilt section of stone wall.

Lloyd recognised the car as it sped past the lay-by where he'd parked to savour his mid-morning tea break undisturbed. He glimpsed a flash of black hair: it was the wife from the harbour front, driving like an absolute maniac. He started his engine and moved into her slipstream. He thought of how he'd administer a warning about the dangers of speeding. The gap between them was increasing, so the Sergeant turned on the blue lights and flashed her to pull over. After both cars had come to a rolling halt, he strolled over to the driver's side window. He could see her face in the side mirror watching his approach.

Ruth slipped on a look of feminine bewilderment, *why goodness me, what have I done officer?* 'Hello sergeant, how can I help you?'

'Morning Mrs Pimlott. Um, you were driving a little fast back there.'

'Really? Was I?' She smiled sweetly at him and felt a slight twinge inside. Her initial instinct had been right; there was a certain something about him, he wasn't the usual billiard-ball head scowling from behind a stab-proof vest. Nevertheless, she didn't want more points on her licence, so time to play the game.

'I think you know you were.' Lloyd leaned down and placed a hand on the window-frame to steady himself. He tried on a smile. 'We've had quite a few accidents on this stretch of road, mainly local lads on a night out, but you know. There are some nasty bends just back there and you probably don't know the road all that well. So, all I'm saying is take care now.'

'Sorry officer. I've just had an argument with my partner… she can be so… well I'm sure you understand…' *Jesus Ruth, why tell him about the argument?*

The policeman raised his eyebrows but continued to smile. 'Right… Yes, I guess that I can imagine that.'

'I'll take it slowly in future.' She tucked a loose strand of hair behind her right ear and saw Lloyd was turning to leave. 'I should have thanked you for when we moved in, by the way.'

He turned back. 'What's that, you mean the boys in the square?'

'Yes. I thought it was getting rather nasty, and my

partner is um… unused to that kind of thing.' She stroked her pendant and caught his eyes flicker involuntary downwards to where it lay between her breasts. Business as usual there – men really were unable to help themselves.

Aware of her gaze, Lloyd looked away down the road in the direction of the village. 'That's my job. But if you'd like some free advice, I'd try to keep quite a low profile, at first anyway. Some of those boys need a bit of time to get used to incomers to the village, if you catch my drift.'

'You mean English people? Or lesbians?' She saw him redden. 'Are they going to burn down our home? Isn't there a law against that? Or do you mean something else?' She looked directly into his eyes, holding the stare for several beats. *From where did that little flirtation arise?* She felt herself purposefully letting her control slip, in fact the very thought of being unable to control herself only fed her fast-distancing responsibility. So, let it feed itself…

'Something else?' His eyes narrowed. 'No, no, no. It's just that… I think I meant that most of these boys have lived here all their lives like, so they will need to get to know you both.' He reddened. 'No, you know what I mean. Yes, get used to you being around. Simple as that really. I suppose, come to think about it, that you're getting used to us as well. Or maybe not.'

Ruth felt a certain calmness descend as she listened to the rich timbre of his voice – luxuriated in his tone, swam lazy backstrokes in his words. Beyond it, she could pick out notes of birdsong from the woods.

Lloyd gathered himself a little. 'And, while we're talking, you might make Ms Pimlott aware that it probably isn't too clever to order wine in the local pub and then complain about it. Like she did a few weeks back. Reputations get around fast.'

'Hmmm, I'll tell my partner, but well,' she leaned closer to him, 'she's a bit clueless at times. Doesn't really understand how things work outside of Zone One. I'm sure you've come across the type many times.'

'Zone One?'

'You know, on the Tube map. Up in London.'

'Oh yes. Right. The Tube. We don't have that up here, you may have noticed.'

'Yes… I've picked up on that.' She laughed softly.

'But that thing about the wine the other day – Stevie the barman couldn't stop talking about it. Now I know that the pub isn't exactly the Ritz, but it works for locals, and if you don't mind me saying so, you seem to think that place is okay. I've seen in you in there a few times without your, er, other half.'

Ruth played mischievous. 'Looking out for me, were you? Now why would that be?'

Lloyd didn't know what to say next, he looked at his watch, inadvertently transferred his gaze to her chest, then quickly back to his watch. That was stupid, all it would take would be an email to his inspector in Dolgellau and he'd be on a charge. He ought to be getting back to the village station anyway. He had to allocate investigation numbers to those farm robberies for the insurance claims, even if he didn't really feel like breaking off the conversation. 'Well, Mrs Pimlott, I'm sure I'll see you around. Just mind those bends now.'

Dark as they were, he wondered whether he saw a weakness come into her eyes, perhaps an invitation… he became aware that he might be showing and was grateful that his lower body was hidden by the car door.

'I certainly will. My name's Ruth by the way. What's

yours?' She played with her necklace. *Look down again. Go on, take another peek.*

'Er, Lloyd.' He could smell her scent.

She watched his eyes glance downwards once more – three times meant a confirmation. 'Hope to see you around, Lloyd. You don't mind me calling you that, do you?'

'Um… no.'

My God, she delighted, *he was almost panting*. 'Perhaps you can show me the local ropes.' Another tempting smile and she pulled away, giving him a quick wave in the mirror. Lloyd found himself waving back, like the schoolboy thirty years earlier saying goodnight to the first girl who'd let him kiss her.

He stared at the back of the woman's head as the car moved away, until it disappeared, and the sunlight overwhelmed him.

Thirteen

The twelfth-century church was sited at the foot of the mountain where it began its slow rise to the cloud base above, erected there – or so local myth had it – in order to be that much closer to heaven. Stone-walled, its long uneven roof of lichen-splattered slate buttressed an imposing stone tower, once used as a lookout point for raiders. It achieved a look of rustic divinity, showcasing its former life as a monastery and a place of holy pilgrimage from as far afield as Northumbria and Wessex. Because of this status, most of the stained-glass windows had been donated by the wealthier merchant-pilgrims as a means of – they hoped – securing their place in the hereafter. One length of the church flanked the sea, with a series of lichen-stained gravestones dropping away to a low wall topped with slate offcuts, and beyond that, the ragged edge of the clifftop. A modest Celtic cross was positioned at its entrance.

Inside, the Reverend Midwinter, bearing a new haircut, and a freshly laundered set of garments, creaked up the wooden steps to his pulpit to give his Sunday morning sermon. He basked in the presence of a sizeable congregation. Eighty? One hundred? More? He doubted the dark wooden pews had seated such a flock since VE Day. Just a month ago he'd been preaching to a scattering of dutiful pensioners and a small yet unblinkingly intense band of students from the local university. Evangelical types whom he suspected would have become quickly disappointed enough with his service to form their own breakaway sect. In any case, he was grateful now to avoid running through the intellectual contortions of the lengthy theological debates in which this "hallelujah squad" seemed determined to engage him. Midwinter had in the past felt relief that his once-steady progress up the ranks of the clergy had stumbled into this cul-de-sac reserved for those who had plateaued in their ambition and faith. Indeed, he'd be the first to admit that once there had been a certain comfort in fulfilling low expectations. Yet how soon things could change, for today he was about to preach before more of his parishioners than ever before. All of whom awaited his word – and that of God, of course, one shouldn't forget – even young Gwyn Phillips and the village rugby team. It might, Midwinter mooted, be a sign from above. It could even reinstall his belief, though in the wake of the plague that might be too much to ask. It had been a hard time for him, a black time indeed, and it had taken some effort to get over it.

Sitting in the front pew, arms crossed and back straight, was the man responsible for getting his parishioners back into the church, Meic Davies. A compromise had been reached, which perhaps might not be well received in the environs of the Bishop's Palace in St. Asaph, but whatever arrangement he had made was certainly broadly speaking in the spirit of the new strategy that the church was adopting to address its future in the country. The Reverend glanced at the two middle-aged men sitting near to Meic, wearing tight grey suits and a look of boredom. Their ruddy faces seemed familiar, but he couldn't quite place them.

It had been a mixed blessing, perhaps, when Meic had arrived at the front door of the vicarage just four weeks ago. The young man was an unexpected conduit for a wonderful idea, or it could just be that this was the Lord moving in mysterious ways. He had noted the young man on a number of occasions around the village but they had barely exchanged two words. But he had seen that Meic was often to be found at the harbour-front pub, a place which the Reverend occasionally visited, spending just long enough to sip a couple of halves of bitter shandy. It was a vague effort to take his ministry beyond those of the institutionally devoted and one encouraged by higher powers. The diocese had recently become very keen, adamant even, on what it called "outreach", visiting schools, community groups and the like. However, the children at the local primary school had proven quite unreceptive, with shockingly little knowledge of the scripture. As for the community at large, he was usually left with the impression that his visits made people uneasy. Sensitive as he was, Midwinter had noticed after several visits that the pub's drinkers tended to cluster at the bar and away from his table by the fireplace. He'd never thought to join them there; surely they'd come to chat, if they had any interest.

He thought back to when he had opened his front door.

'May I come in, Vicar?'

He was surprised to see Meic. The Reverend hadn't realised that the boy might be curious about religious matters, and certainly not of the mainstream variety. 'Yes, I suppose. How can I help you?' The Vicar was aware that the tone of his question might be misinterpreted as brusque, and he should be more gracious. 'Would you like some tea? Or a sherry?' But Meic didn't appear to respond.

'Um, I may still have a can of beer in the pantry left over from the Christmas party? Would you like that?' He vaguely recalled seeing the boy drink beer from a pint glass.

'Tea would be fine.' Meic smiled warmly. 'I thought that we should have a chat.'

With the housekeeper on her afternoon off, Midwinter prepared a pot for two. The boy was wearing a jacket: that must be the difference he thought; he'd never seen him in one before.

'What would you like to discuss?'

Meic examined the man standing meekly in front of him. Bit of a scruffy-looking article, dirty cuffs on the shirt, lank hair. He seemed pleasant enough, but carried an out-of-place air, much like a once-favoured board game discarded at the back of a cupboard. The younger man watched as the Vicar searched through a cupboard for a bag of sugar to go in the empty bowl. He was probably lonely, for there had been no Mrs Vicar or even a sexually harassed parishioner on the scene since Meic had been around. Maybe Midwinter had more in common with some of his brothers in the Catholic priesthood than he let on, but he couldn't feel any vibes there either. Just a pervading sense of settled dust. Meic wasn't unsympathetic about this, he could appreciate what prolonged loneliness could do to a man's psyche, but still – needed a bit of effort. Best be direct.

'Tell me, Vicar. If you believed in life after death, would you choose death?'

The Reverend looked down at the faded blue linoleum, and considered the question, which he found ever so slightly disconcerting. He remained silent as he tried to recall his answer to a question on a similar theme that had come up in his final year theology exam. But, no, it was beyond his memory.

'Bit strange a priest not taking the bait on that? I thought that was something which you would have spent a great deal of time considering.' In the silence, Meic could see a slight reddening of Midwinter's cheeks, but the eyes remained evasive. 'Look. I wouldn't be worried, Reverend, so don't fret. I'm not here to make you feel uncomfortable. I've actually visited to offer you a helping hand. Help everyone in the village eventually. Help all of your flock.'

Midwinter's face fought an inconclusive emotional skirmish. 'I rather thought that was my job.'

'Yes, you're right and it can be once again... Listen, you've been here, how long now?'

'Just over seven years.' This was most strange. He should have felt anger at the insult of *once again*, but anger over what? The truth? He picked up the Chinese-patterned teapot. 'Shall I be mother?'

Meic smiled and let the Vicar pour two cups. 'And in that time, I imagine that your congregations have shrunk. If I'm wrong, tell me otherwise.'

The teapot paused, and then resumed its delivery. As did Meic. 'I know that it's hard for the church today. People just don't seem to believe anymore, do they? But you see I think that they just need something to believe in. The thing is, Reverend, I have a proposition for you. A way of putting you back at the centre of village life, where you should be. Don't you think?'

Midwinter felt that this was his point to respond. 'Well, yes. I suppose...'

'Good, I'm glad that you agree. It is the Welsh way after all, a strong church means a strong people.' Holding his thumb and forefinger slightly apart Meic block-wrote the headline in the air while trying to sound sincere. 'And if I can get people into your services, all I'd like to ask of you is that I have a chance to speak to your congregation afterwards… maybe about the primary school closing and one or two other things.'

'I'm not sure I understand. Would you like some milk?'

Meic didn't answer. 'Are you interested?'

Midwinter stared at the willow pattern, looking at the little figures perpetually hurrying across the bridge – hives of activity, so unlike himself. Passionless: that's what the last woman that he'd harboured a glimmer of love for had said. But that was many years ago now. He knew his time here could not be counted as a success; a record of failure continued from his two previous parishes. Not that those issues were entirely his fault. The speed at which a trivial misunderstanding could grow into a petition for his removal had taken him aback. And of course, it was deeply unfair. Yet it was clear from the unspoken words at the meeting with the Bishop that his appointment to Llanawch was the end of the line unless things changed for the better. He was effectively being put out to grass, pending early retirement and the purgatory of non-being.

'Are you interested?'

He had so loved the years of his theological studies when he had felt at the centre of his group, but today he was one of the lost boys. He hadn't felt the calling for a long time, had accepted his fate. And now this unlikely messenger was ready to help him. Perhaps it was divine intervention. Or more likely, it was a change of luck long overdue. Sometimes, God willing, chances would come around in the cycle of life.

'Yes, I'm interested.'

❧

Paul Williams hammered up the sign at the entrance to the Roberts' farm: "Ar werth – For sale – By Auction" in big red letters. Just one of the little jobs he liked to do himself, likening it to launching a ship – so let the good Glanrhyd sail a swift passage on the open market to the port of cash buyers.

He stepped back to check that the post was vertical. It had been clever business attending the wake after the farmer's funeral; bent over to offer his condolences he'd slipped his card into the widow's numbed hand. It wasn't taking advantage see, it was offering a service, making it easy for them. Williams had sold a number of these worn-out farms in the past few years and would have been surprised to discover the similarities between his business strategy and those of the eighties Wall Street corporate raiders. It was all about taking something big which had worked together as a whole, splitting it up into smaller pieces and selling those individually on for more cash than you'd get for the combined entity. It was very easy to break up established estates such as Glanrhyd, what with the price of agricultural land rising. Auction off the machinery and equipment; offer parcels of farmland in another; then hint at how easily planning permission could be obtained to convert any outhouses to pull in developers; and finally offload the farmhouse. If it was no longer needed as a family home, it invariably would go to an incomer. They just paid more. The kids hardly ever wanted to carry on farming and why should they? Say all you want about the recent rise in lamb prices, and the need for more domestic food production but it was a mug's game – his office manager probably earned more than the average hill farmer for a lot less hours. And she had a nicer arse, that's for frigging sure.

Satisfied with the erectness of his sign, he dropped the hammer into the boot of his BMW and put his well-waxed jacket back on. He'd place the property on his website, small ad in *Country Life*, email the details to the usual professional home-search firms in the big cities; encourage the initial viewings, and then auction the rest of the assorted crap off to the trade market. Of course, things nowadays weren't as good as they had been, but an auction meant his commission would be paid faster than a conventional sale. He appraised a car slowing down as it passed, the driver taking a long look at the newly erected sign. Maybe some interest already? He surveyed the state of the car, an old model: that meant it was just a local so wouldn't be a goer. He would email his England contacts this afternoon.

Lloyd grunted as he took the weight of a box of what sounded like crockery from his car and hiked up the narrow staircase to the top-floor flat. Today, his eldest, Hywel, and Sian were moving into rented accommodation, deposit covered by Bank of Lloyd rather than the High Street almost-namesake. He entered the one-bedroom flat where his son was struggling to assemble a flat-pack coffee table. 'Not too bad, is it Dad?'

Lloyd glanced around him. 'No, it's all right. It will do for you two as a starter home like.' It was the first time he'd seen the place, but Catrin had told him it was nicely laid out, modern and to sign the cheque. What she hadn't told him was that cat-swinging was out of the question. Was this all they could now manage? He tentatively touched the doorframe and saw the indentation made by his fingertips. 'Just been decorated?'

'Yeah, the landlords have just done up the whole block, we're the second tenants in. One of the teachers from the comprehensive lives downstairs.'

'So who's the landlord?'

'Dunno, some big law firm in Manchester – probably some company behind that. We just deal with the managing agents.'

Lloyd nodded and walked over to the window. 'Great view though. You can see Cader Idris from here. Do you remember climbing it after we first moved down here?' In the distance he could see the slow rolling summit, the slabs of dark rock streaking through the tufting hillside green. In winter the mountains would darken as if they'd sucked the colour from the surrounding landscape into their depths. Those were the days of dreariness – the sea, the people, the air itself, all spirits placed in hibernation.

'Off with the fairies again, Lloyd?' Catrin teetered into the room with her daughter-in-law, unsurprised to find her husband staring at another far horizon. He was doing it all too often, out on that deck at all hours, just gazing out to sea. Such a dreamer, anyone would think he wanted to be somewhere else, other than with his family. But then weren't all men like that at times. She glanced downwards at his shoes and saw a patch of dirt on them which he'd clearly missed that morning with his polishing cloth. That wasn't the only area he was getting sloppy in either.

She clapped her hands to attract his attention. 'Now then, aren't you supposed to be helping to move the boxes? There's an awful heavy suitcase down there which I couldn't manage, would you be a dear?' She swivelled on her heels away from him, ready to direct more important matters.

He returned with the luggage to find Catrin opening a screw-top bottle of white wine. 'Rachel up at the hotel recommended this to me. I thought it would be a nice way to christen the flat.' She served the wine into the plastic cups which she'd taken from her shoulder bag. 'Well, there we are then, congratulations then you two – your first home together…'

'No wine for Sian, mother.'

'Eh? Don't you feel well?' Lloyd turned to his daughter-in-law.

The young woman gave her husband a complicit look. 'No, it isn't that. I just won't be drinking for the next few months.' She glanced and stroked her abdomen.

Lloyd stayed up late on the sundeck that evening, facing the blustery wind coming in from the awakening sea, his feet stretched out in front of him, with a bottle of beer in his hand. As she occasionally would – less so nowadays – Catrin had joined him outside earlier on, but now she was back in her womb in the company of a recorded episode of *Emmerdale*. The movement of the sea made him feel reflective; he thought about when he recalled unexpected memories from the past. Events which at the time seemed unremarkable, just part of the normal fabric of the day, had become lodged in his head. A walk to the shops with his grandmother when he was seven; a particular game of toy soldiers amongst hundreds of miniature battles; a training run one spring evening when he was playing junior rugby. But other moments in life, even as they are taking place, you know that you'll always remember them. Today was one of those days. He was going to be a grandfather. It was amazing news, it brought back the time when Catrin had told him over tea that she was pregnant with Hywel. But... my God, it felt just like yesterday when he left Swansea, and now he was already a granddad. Or about to be anyhow. So that was it then. He took another swig and watched the white-water wave crests slashing haphazardly across the ocean.

Fourteen

Meic watched as his two associates plopped themselves into the mid-range silver Mercedes: the slicker-than-thou car of upwardly mobile thugs, but also the workhorse of the Eastern European taxi drivers whom these guys resembled. The pair bore severe haircuts and the veteran moustaches – the well-hard, hard-won relics of their past. He imagined them clambering out at the other end, the backs of their jackets concertinaed, the trousers flecked with service-station pasty crumbs. Not that it would make much of a difference to their overall appearance. The suits were horrible. The lack of vents in the jacket, the industrial weight of the cloth, the cut-price boxiness – it broadcast that you were about to stray into the orbit of a style-free planet. Meic despised the Pimlott bitch, but at least she had a sense of dress, a touch of flair, which was more than could be said for these hoods. It was as if they took pride in dressing like tosspots.

Meic still remembered being taken to Gieves & Hawkes by his old man to be fitted for a college interview suit, which at the time awoke feelings of guilt – particularly as he'd been going through his *Socialist Worker* phase. His own father might have originated from this area, but in his adult life as a London lawyer Meic had never remembered him as anything other than immaculately tailored. Just as the son had cloaked himself in a new persona when moving to the village from London, so had the father decades earlier on the reverse journey. Observing his new legal colleagues draped in smart suits and languid drawls, he'd blown his first month's salary on a trip to Savile Row, slipping on a new accent at the same time. Thus camouflaged, he'd moved steadily upwards to an eventual partnership in the firm. However, a few years into his tenure, his airport-transfer taxi went off the side of an Austrian mountain road while returning from a skiing weekend. That did for him, his secretary and the taxi driver trying to text on his mobile. Meic had been in his fresher year at Aberystwyth and inherited two important legacies – part of a large life insurance payout, and an even deeper emotional connection to his father's roots. His mother sold the house and went off to Spain to drown her husband's infidelity in rioja and pool boys. She called her only child from time to time when she felt lonely or guilty.

Meic felt that he was completing the circle that his father had begun with his return to the area. He certainly wasn't here to be another West London trustafarian chillaxing in the provinces and Instagramming back their poverty tourism – *'check out this country pub/cute village shop/field of real cows!'* Meic was of that breed and yet he wasn't, he was an insider-outsider. And that duality would help his countrymen make a new beginning… and all that "New Wales" kind of stuff he'd need to keep trotting out. There he went again, even his subconscious mutated into a political party broadcast.

All these thoughts spun around his head as he set his smile to rictus and threw a wave as the car disappeared down the lane to start its journey to the Vale of Glamorgan, the tyres churning up small clouds of dust in its wake. Reflecting on the past hour with his associates, he felt pleased with how things had turned out. It had gone almost to plan, the single deviation being when the quieter – and therefore potentially more dangerous – of his two guests had randomly selected one of his old texts on Marx from the living room bookcase. Upon opening the front cover, he chuckled, 'So, it's "Michael K. S. Davies of Lower Sixth, St. Paul's School" is it? I see. Don't worry, we can keep a secret if you can,' giving Meic a complicit wink. The man knew that their partner had political aspirations, but it was all the better to give their business arrangements cover.

Meic had put his name forward for nomination to the Plaid regional list for the forthcoming Senedd elections. With a history of activism in Aber student politics, it was a well-trodden path and in theory he should be in with a strong chance. But he was a realist: it was important to tone down the past, because if it came out that he was the English-born son of privilege it would not endear him to any selection committee. Especially in these times of diversity triumphing over rationality, where he'd have to bare-knuckle it out with assorted less qualified but box-ticking minorities in order to secure his slot. Leaving that book on the shelf was a careless oversight, and now he'd have to go through his collection to remove any other evidence of private schooling. The family photo taken on the slopes at Aspen when he was fourteen had been another, but that had been locked away in his desk drawer after Sion had picked it up off his desk one day and examined it with a puzzled look. Not that exotic holidays were unknown in these parts, but well… it was the accumulation of evidence that could end in a rejection by the committee. He'd have to play it safe, and he was sure his father would understand if he was still here.

Yet it was one thing to play the defensive game of airbrushing his history, another to have something extra to mark him out from all the other student politicos and "community activists" applying for the chance to represent the working masses for seventy thousand per annum. Most pertinently, he needed something that would put him on the fast track as soon as he reached Cardiff Bay. Spray-painting a government office was fine as far as it went, but it wasn't really in the Michael Collins league. Meic knew that he had to make a big splash, build a broader base of influence and thus ensure that the play-it-safe leadership couldn't afford to ignore him. He had no wish to waste his greatest years just being voting fodder for the limp party elders. A national reputation forged before any election would put him in line for quick promotion to the leadership team and then, then he could really do something with his career.

In the doorway of his home hearing the song of birds, the buzz of insects in the flowerbeds, he scanned the sloping field opposite where the long grass tossed about in the breeze, flickering its silvery underside. A farmer on a quad bike was rounding up a scattered flock of sheep with his dogs. Quad bikes… now there was a thought – plenty of them around here. He didn't know about Poland, but Slovakia and the Balkans were pretty mountainous. Meic walked back into the house, withdrew the offending textbook from the bookshelf, took a quick look at the inside cover for old times' sake, and put it in the bottom drawer of his desk with all the other baggage.

Frankie walked past the workmen repainting her cottage radiant white – for authenticity just as in Georgian times – and paced though Llanawch's main street. She had been told by the postman earlier that morning the pastel-colour cottages were a tourist draw, but that just showed that the village was attracting the wrong type of middle-brow tourist. She could barely conceal her pungent reaction to the red-dragon-sticker-on-a-slate-coaster style souvenir outlets which made up an upsetting proportion of the street's numerous independent retail outlets of nine shops. Or ten if you included the small Boots the chemist next to the doctor's surgery. It saddened her – these shopkeepers would all have to face up to the decision to change for the better or close. Because if it wasn't her, it would surely be someone else telling them – someone without her sensitivity.

Maintaining an outpost of fish and chip tourism didn't figure in Frankie's plans, unless it involved a particular breed of fish shop using the best locally sourced organic ingredients, cooked to order by a trained chef. Rick Stein. Nathan Outlaw. Padstow. That was the template. Not chicken wings in a basket at the local excuse for a sailing club – Cowes they were not. She'd already pencilled in the closed-down bank branch on the corner as the site of a potential new restaurant in her draft redevelopment plan. Nevertheless, she'd found a diamond – or rather a lower quality gemstone – in the rough as she rather liked the town's main hotel, refurbished several years ago with the European money that was no longer coming. Another outsider with a bit of vision had seen the opportunity: laying stone floors, introducing light wood fittings, and installing adventurous young waitresses from the poorer reaches of the continent. Spanish house fizz sold by the glass with a big jar of Italian olives behind the bar providing lip-smacking salty snacks. Far better, she imagined, than the inevitable Australian chardonnay and the bag of crisps that would have been served by the old Welsh management. While the Hungarians, Romanians and Spanish had mostly moved on since the vote, there were still jobs to be filled by their surly British versions.

The clientele turned out to be mostly tourists with a smattering of businesspeople. The manager had answered her questioning with a resigned air, remarking that the locals felt that it was a bit pricey, and the portions were too small. In other words, it wasn't bog-standard pub grub. No surprise there, that attitude was to be expected from those who didn't know better, but Frankie felt the manager should, because the place still lacked real authenticity in its kitchen. The ability to sear a passable scallop, iron your tablecloths and have those ubiquitous dark leather sofas in a bar, doth not a Michelin rosette make. Perhaps she should sit down with the owner and discuss how, together, they could improve things. Still, her aim for today was a tad more prosaic, namely, to bring a touch of civilisation to this Jurassic café.

Frankie paused outside the entrance, perusing the menu printed on gaudy lime-green card in the windowpane. My goodness – people still use this style of cardboard? She hadn't seen anything like this since visiting Ruth's hometown, and that must have been over a decade ago. “Full Welsh breakfast” was the promise but doubtless it was just another artery-attacking fry-up, no different to something to be found in a greasy spoon café when London still hosted them. The menu didn’t note the provenance of the ingredients. That was just lazy, but then, as Frankie mused, would anyone want to advertise that the sausage came from a faceless warehouse rather than a local farm? What was that quote again, the two things you shouldn’t want to see made: laws, and sausages. She scanned the menu: toasted sandwiches, filled baguettes, with… ham & cheddar, coronation chicken, egg & cress. It was worse than she feared. Still, fortune favours the brave. Showing the courage of a true pioneer, Frankie stepped inside.

The land of pine furnishings awaited her: chairs, tables, counter, everything decked out as if it was a set from a seventies-era sitcom. Behind the counter stood a glass fronted fridge, with cartons of banana and chocolate milkshakes, *long-life* orange juice and other horrors. The theme continued; next to it stood a middle-aged woman in a red butcher’s stripe pinafore. Rosy pocked-marked cheeks, a futile attempt at make-up, wavy straw for hair tied back by… was that a red elastic band, like the ones the postmen around here used? The woman also looked at Frankie, taking in the rolled-up jeans, plimsolls and French fisherman’s vest.

‘What can I get you, love?’

What would be the least unhealthy option here? ‘Um, can I get an espresso.’

‘An ex-press-so?’ The woman appeared slightly flustered by the order.

‘It’s a small strong coffee,’ a thick midlands accent

shouted from behind the plastic beaded curtain, which she presumed contained the kitchen. The accent stuck his head through the doorway. Dumpy, hair flattened by kitchen-sweat, with matching stains under the hefty armpits of his grey T-shirt. 'We don't do that here.'

'I see, well how about a black coffee?'

'Oh yes, we can do you that,' the woman moved towards an industrial-sized can of Nescafe sitting on the counter and put a heaped spoonful into a blue-checked mug. She smiled and added another spoonful. 'There we go. Extra strong for you. Anything else love?' The cook continued to appraise Frankie.

'Do you have a croissant, or a pain au chocolat?' She tossed that last one in just for kicks, feeling a long-forgotten memory resurfacing as she did so – the voice of her Latin teacher at school noting that no one liked a smart alec.

The cook spoke slowly. 'I tell you what, how about some toast instead.'

Frankie nodded compliantly, being entirely unsurprised when she wasn't offered a choice of breads. She chose a seat as far away as possible from the incest-case sitting in the corner nearing what appeared to be a climax as he chewed deeper into a bacon roll in a series of mechanical bites. The counterwoman brought over the coffee and white sliced toast. It was already buttered, its thick glop turning translucent and dripping over the crust like quick-drying cement. Either that or phlegm. Hmmm.

Yet, it was perfect, like being given a blank canvas and a selection of oils.

The place was crying out for help, and she was the woman on the white charger. With a few minor tweaks, the village would soon have a café to be proud of. It would need to be affordable initially, of course, to keep the locals onside and so forth, but it could be the acorn from which the oak of her regeneration project would grow. After a gulp of retro coffee and a gingerly-taken bite of margarine-for-goodness'-sake-Christ-is-this-actually-the-third-world-infused toast, she returned to the counter.

'How long have you been here?'

The woman looked affronted. 'Since sixty-thirty this morning, same as every day.'

'Running the business, I mean. When did you open?' *Nicely handled, as always.*

'Oh sorry. Didn't get you. We've owned this place for oh, twenty, twenty-odd years now. Twenty-five years nearly, isn't it, Geoff?'

The cook came into the front section. 'That's right, twenty-four years. Just after Princess Di was murdered.'

'You must be very proud of it.'

The counter woman answered, 'Yeah, we used to come here for our holidays. Then one year, we saw this place was for sale. And only a few weeks after there was a round of redundancies at Geoff's factory.'

The cook intervened, 'Made machine tools – best in Daventry.'

His wife continued, 'It was too much of a coincidence, wasn't it, Geoff?' He grunted. 'Well, we decided to take the redundancy, sell up and buy this place. And we haven't looked back. You could say that we're living the dream. In fact, I had a customer in yesterday who said just that!'

Frankie feigned interest and waited for the practiced routine to finish. She smiled. 'Wonderful. Living the dream. My name's Frankie Pimlott, by the way. Just moved into the area.'

The cook answered, 'We guessed.' The woman gave a short bark, too late covering her mouth with the back of her hand to hide the smirk.

'I'd like to give you a gift, which could help you to improve your little dream. Would you like a coffee machine? To let you make Americanos, cappuccinos… you know, frothy coffee.'

'I know, we had *Sex and the City* on the box here as well,' the woman deadpanned. The cook folded his arms. 'Let's get this straight; you're going to give us a coffee machine? Why's that then? Goodness of your heart is it?'

Frankie leant onto the counter, conspiratorially. 'There're many reasons, but most of all it would allow me to come here every day and enjoy a nice espresso. It's my favourite. And of course, I'm sure it would help business…' She left the idea hanging in the air.

'Oh. You're some kind of expert then, are you?'

Frankie stood up and let them bask in her winning smile. 'Well as a matter of fact, I am. I've advised a number of leading London independent coffee shops about their market positioning.'

They looked at her blankly.

'Well, have a think about it, the offer is on the counter, so to speak.' And with a little rat-a-tat on the counter-top – *quite a Dickensian touch* – she left.

Dusk was draining the light from the room, settling like a blanket on the fields outside the window, creating stillness.

'Did you enjoy it?'

'Yes… you?'

'Yes.'

Near silence. Just the breeze rattling through the trees, the echo of metal on metal in the distance.

'What are you thinking?'

'Nothing in particular… surprise, I guess.'

'Why surprise?'

'Well, you know.'

'My circumstances?'

'Yes, your circumstances.'

'We all have them.'

A finger tracing a line on a chest, a hand thrown behind a head, pressed against a pillow.

'We need to get moving.'

'Just another five minutes…'

Fifteen

A month later, carrying out his morning beat on the harbour front, Lloyd smiled as he walked by the single-man shack advertising the "Legendary Number One Cardigan Bay experience" together with sailing times. A sandwich board displayed pictures of bottle-nosed dolphins and a joyful family, actually that of the owner, enjoying their quality bonding time through the sun-kissed delights of near-shore fishing. Within five yards, pre-trip sustenance was available from an ice-cream van, its bilingual price list less a political gesture than a sales technique. And a short sea-legged stagger away was the chip shop, a couple of doors along from the most tourist-oriented of the village pubs. You could have a big day out in these few square yards. Lloyd turned the corner and patrolled by the rows of small pebble-dashed fishermen's cottages. He paused to talk with Evan from the service station, busy painting his front door.

'All right Evan, doing a bit of DIY?'

The man turned around, rested his brush on the lip of the paint tin and wiped the front of his battered overalls. 'Yep, thought it would make a change.' He swigged from a pint-glass of squash as he took a breather from his efforts.

'Doesn't look too bad, take care now.' Lloyd continued his patrol, the radio-battery swinging from his hip, walking down the street past a series of fluttering curtains. Sad, reflective eyes watched him pass, logging his movements. He felt the gaze but was used to it; in a village there was little privacy, his patrol might be the highlight of the day for some of the street's lonelier residents. The sergeant glanced at the front doors as he clumped past, starting to sense a pattern. By the time he reached the main road, he'd counted nine red-painted doors. When had they all been repainted? It seemed odd, that so many people were using exactly the same colour. Then again, perhaps it was a new fashion. About a decade ago, a number of harbour-side houses had adopted pastel shades for their fronts – mostly the holiday homes in an attempt to persuade potential renters that they were situated on the calm waters of the Mediterranean rather than the rigours of the Irish Sea. Probably just another fad, but still… Across the street from him Rob Reynolds, seeing Lloyd's glance, quickened his pace, eyes fixed on the pavement. This time tomorrow, Rob was due up at the station on his weekly visit to sign-in following the court order. It was a little discussed secret in the village after the local paper had run a story on the habits of the former council officer. But Reynolds had kept a lower profile since, curtailing his other favourite habit of soap-box raging in the pub, and so into history he passed.

Funny though, Lloyd thought, a number of other villagers apart from Reynolds seemed to be having difficulty making eye contact with their local beat officer at the moment. The front door of one of the cottages opened and Meic Davies stepped out directly into the Sergeant's path.

His head was turned as he spoke to the unseen resident. 'So we'll be in touch then, about the next meeting. Thanks very much for your time. Hope your roses improve!'

'Morning Meic, didn't know you knew the Johns.'

Meic wheeled about startled but soon recovered. 'Oh, I know lots of people, Sergeant. Getting to know more by the day. How about you?' He gave Lloyd a wink and brushed past him before knocking on a door a few houses up the street. The policeman shook his head and continued on his beat. Davies could be such a snide little turd at times. No, make that all the bloody time. He heard a low rumble emanating from the square and looked towards it. A few seconds later, he watched as a column of motorbikers lung-roared down the high street. The touring bikes gleamed to within a ratchet of blinding polish, their owners all sporting black open-faced helmets, Ray-Ban sunglasses and neatly trimmed greying beards. On one pinion, a well-moisturised biker-chick looked at him, adjusted her leather trousers and gave him a beaming grin. Lloyd appreciated the gesture and tapped his cap for her. The bikers cruised past him and despite the sound and fury Parry felt unthreatened. No power on earth would stop this mean gang of rebels and hell-raisers from doing whatever pleased them, apart from a surprise visit from the tax inspectors to their respective graphic design businesses, or perhaps tickets to a Rod Stewart concert. They were mean, not so lean and very polite in the chip shop, where they always stopped for lunch on their monthly route through the village. The chapter had even made a donation of books to the local school last Christmas.

Welcome visitors, quite unlike the idiots from Chester who had surrounded a couple of the local boys the other night, after an argument over a girl, and put the Welsh pair into A&E. At least Lloyd had managed to track down one of the assailants, who was now charged. He broke his rounds within five minutes to pop into the local Spar to pick up a carton of milk. The house had run out that morning, and with Catrin away today meeting with her tutor about taking some more evening classes he felt that he'd better take care of the chore, otherwise there'd be no cereal for his breakfast tomorrow.

'Hi-yah, did you see this? We're in the news!' Rich Hughes the shopkeeper was waving a copy of *The Daily Gazette* at him.

'What's that?' Lloyd picked up another copy from a stack on the bottom shelf.

'Middle section, just by the letters page. Take a look at that. Who'd have thought we had a celebrity in our midst?'

Lloyd licked his thumb, flicking the pages of the paper, until he came to the article.

Frankie Pimlott's brilliant new weekend column only in your Daily Gazette

Stuck in the Middle (of Nowhere) With You

It has been over a month since we made the life-renewing move to the green hills and valleys of deepest – and darkest – Wales. After an initial series of incidents worthy of Anthony Powell at his drollest (more of which later), The Handbag Queen and I have settled into an enriching daily routine. Imagine: life without work deadlines, cancelled trains, without the press of people in the West End, the incessant drone of the congestion-charged car, or the smell of fast food on public transport. Truly, we feel ourselves lucky to be enjoying this seaside paradise or perhaps I should say, para-dai-ise.

But cracker-level punning aside, we also feel very humble. For so many of the necessities that we were accustomed to as chichi city dwellers are simply not available to our Celtic cousins. And this is both a shame and a cause for concern. Why should the pleasures of civilised life be denied, just because one is two hours hard driving from the nearest urban conurbation? That's why I'm making it my personal project to bring the benefits of city – in my own modest way – to my new friends in the country.

A few days ago, I started with a small but practical step, donating a state-of-the-art coffee machine to the local café, run by two extraordinarily brave individuals. Change demands courage on the part of those who embrace it, and this couple was ready to move with the times. The look of delight on their faces as they pondered the pleasures of skinny cappuccino and double mocha twist was a joy possibly on a par with how their Edwardian predecessors would have received the coming of the automobile.

If one of my favourite poets – Dylan Thomas – was alive today, I'm sure he'd start the day with a double espresso, not least to banish the demons of the night before. Fourteen straight whiskies anyone?

It could be the start of 'Café Culture Cymru' – indeed the possibilities bring to mind a vision of a certain Dublin circa 2000. And despite the

> financial crisis, look what's happened to that 'Dirty Old Town' since…
>
> Over the next months I hope to tell you more about the inhabitants of this picturesque Welsh village by the sea, and how they enjoy some of the new experiences I introduce to them. Until then, as they say in these parts – *Bore Dah*. At least I think that's how they spell it, maybe I've missed out a vowel of two while deciphering the local lingo!

Lloyd replaced the paper on its pile. 'That's very clever, university education there to see. She'll make some friends with that…' He turned to Hughes. 'Anyone else buying this paper today?'

The shopkeeper shook his head. 'Just the usual deliveries and a few tourists.' He sniffed. 'Mind you, that Meic Davies came in about half an hour ago and bought some copies. Don't know why anyone would want more than one paper mind.' Despite the world being delivered to his doorstep each morning, Rich Hughes read only the *Gazette*, which he kept open on the counter through the day as a break from tidying up the pic 'n mix assortment.

Typical. Lloyd bit his lip and replaced his cap on his head. 'Okay then, have a good one.' He made his way down to the square, popping a mint in his mouth as he walked, but there was no sign of the Audi TT, or of Meic's cronies either. And sod it, he'd forgotten the milk, he'd have to swing by the shop later. Lloyd couldn't imagine that Meic would let Frankie Pimlott get away with that article. He'd see it as a provocation. How could Pimlott be so dense? Maybe he should have a word with Meic, try and defuse the situation. And sooner rather than later. He felt the tightening in his stomach again as he walked over to Pimlotts' home to check for trouble. He could see problems coming down the pipeline and that was the one thing he didn't want to happen, not here in the village. Preserving the peace outweighed his natural inertia, which meant that he had to nip this one in the bud. Couldn't these people just think before they acted? He paused to smooth down his hair and then rang the doorbell. He could hear the light pad of footsteps on the other side approach the door. He glanced around the square once more; no one there to notice him.

Another week passed before the letters started dropping through the doors of the more desirable residences in Llanawch. Catrin opened theirs as Lloyd munched on his muesli – his wife had put him on a diet last autumn after one of the characters in *Eastenders* had experienced a heart attack. Though the same character was now fully recovered and in the midst of a passionate affair with the new (and secretly pregnant with his child) barmaid, Lloyd's breakfast purgatory remained.

'Oh, that's odd.' Catrin turned the letter over to look at the back. 'We've never had one of these before. A letter from the estate agents in town. They want to know if our house is for sale.'

'Why should it be for sale? Let's have a look,' he scanned the note. It was as Catrin had said, the letter stating that the agents had received *a number of enquiries from buyers keen to purchase homes in your area.*

'I wonder how many other houses have received these.'

'It looks like a circular, so I'd imagine that it's gone to quite a few.' Lloyd wondered whether he should give Paul Williams a quick call. 'Do you think it might be worth having the place valued? They'd do it for free and it might be interesting to know just how much the house is worth.'

'But we're not moving, are we? I mean Arwel's only just left school, and he'll be coming back from university regularly. All his friends are here, aren't they?'

'Yes, but he'll make new friends at uni, move on from there.'

'Well, all my friends are here then. Hywel, Sian and our grandchild. I want to be close for them.'

'I wasn't saying that we should move, but…'

'And your job as well… and your friends, I suppose. Why would we want to sell?' Catrin was aware that she'd pushed the return to her home village, and her husband had always felt a little out of place here. But he hadn't helped himself, had he? Lloyd hadn't made any real effort to learn the language even though he'd promised that he would. At least her youngest spoke good Welsh. She hoped he would keep it going after he moved away – maybe find a nice Welsh girl. Catrin busied herself about the kitchen. She hadn't really thought about it before; it struck her that news of Arwel's results wasn't that far away, and then he'd be off to university within weeks. She wouldn't be able to take care of him when he was sick; worse, she wouldn't even know if he was sick or not. The thought upset her. She knew that it was the way of life, but it had all happened so quickly, and she didn't feel ready for this. She turned on the tap to fill the kettle, mechanically placing her index finger into the flow to check the temperature.

'But it would be nice to know in any case, wouldn't

it?' Lloyd rose from the table with a sigh and pulled on his police jersey.

'And where are you off?'

'To the station.'

'It's a Saturday, I thought Roy was on duty today?'

'Yes well you know what he's like, as much use as a fart in a gale. Anyway, I've got paperwork to catch up with, I've let it stack up a bit.'

'I hope that you're getting overtime for this,' she shouted after him.

He wasn't.

And neither was Ruth Pimlott.

Meic was reading the same letter over his own breakfast, the spoon in his hand dripping low-fat yoghurt as it hovered mid-air. It had been one of those late nights, but his tiredness was fast being replaced by rage. 'Fucking bastard. Fucking traitor. Have you seen what that money-grabbing scumbag Paul Williams is up to now?'

Across the kitchen from him, Kerry – a fellow student with whom he'd developed a friends-with-benefits relationship – picked up her car keys. 'Who's Paul Williams?'

'Local estate-agent pond-life, that's who.'

'What's he been up to?'

'He's asking us to sell up, sell off our heritage to anyone coming along with a bag of cash, that's all.' Meic crumpled the letter in his fist. Soon there wouldn't be any locals left to defend their birthright, just another possession that the English had bought cheap, or simply stolen. 'Right, that bastard. This is the final straw. I'm going to the Glanrhyd auction today and I'm going to fuck that bastard up once and for all.'

Kerry was a Celtic Studies student, with little interest in anything that happened after 1921, and now she'd had her itch scratched was ready to return to her Aberystwyth digs and work on her dissertation. He looked up at her. 'You off?'

'Guess so. Got to start on the next chapter.'

'Yeah. Well mind how you go. Next week?'

She nodded, might be something to look forward to after finishing a new block of 5,000 words. 'Sure. WhatsApp me.'

Meic picked up his mobile, hearing her car's engine fade away. He'd really given it to her last night, he'd felt so pent-up, excited after his late-evening excursion into the village. Kerry had accepted his excess energy more than willingly. He loved it when good girls turned bad.

'Sion?'

'I'm heading over to the auction today. Which starts at three according to the paper. We're going to have a little bit of fun.'

Sion felt the excitement once more at Meic's voice; he wanted to extend the call. 'So, er, you going alone, or do you want the boys there?'

Meic paused for a beat. 'The boys as well, I think. Just to be sure. Round them up, will you? Tell them that there'll be some proper action this time. They should be up for that. Tell them it'll be pints on me afterwards.'

Sion laughed. 'That should do the trick.'

'I'll meet you there.' Meic glanced at his watch. Opening time in fifteen minutes. 'I have to pay someone a visit. So see you up at the farm at three, okay. And don't fuck it up.' Meic smirked, then left for the village centre.

'Okay then, see you then…' but Sion found himself speaking to a broken connection. He felt a stab of irritation.

Earlier that morning outside the café, Janice and Geoff found they had no need of their keys when they arrived to open for the day. The door had been crowbarred. 'Did you bank the money? Did you bank the money?' Geoff pushed the door slowly open and carefully entered.

'Yes, I put it in the safe place at home. Like always. Oh no, look…'

On the counter, their brand-new coffee machine lay smashed. Someone had taken a sledgehammer to it, the outcome requiring less a visit to the repair shop, than burial at the scrap yard. 'Well, I suppose we still have that tub of Nescafe left in the kitchen, eh Janice.'

Now, in late morning across the street, Meic surveyed the scene with satisfaction. All he now needed was for that English fucker on the square to turn up, so she could get the picture, too. Of course, it was a shame that the innocent had to get hurt – he saw where the café's owners had posted a pathetic, "Still open for business!" sign in English – but casualties of war and all that. In another era, another country, they would've been branded as collaborators and Janice would have had her hair shorn in the village square – Geoff taken to a quiet yard and given a punishment beating. Meic stuck his hand into his trouser pocket and absent-mindedly started to fiddle with his keys. He waited a few more minutes until he caught a glimpse of police car, then strolled back home, whistling to himself. He saw the Vicar on his bike and gave a cheery greeting. Reaching his own driveway, Meic's face hardened as he thought of this afternoon's auction; there was more business to attend to on this day. The idea of what he had had set in motion made him feel almost overwhelmed with bliss. He was on his way.

Paul Williams revelled in the theatrics of the auction room – the initial calm before he spoke, those attending simultaneously the audience and the actors, the sly gestures from participants, the quickening of bids, of pulses, as the auction neared its conclusion – and then finally the sound of the gavel.

'For the third time, am I bid any advance on five hundred and twenty thousand pounds?' he scanned the last two bidders in the room. No reaction from either of them, 'Going once. Going twice.' His voice built, a pause to emphasise the moment, 'Gone! To the gentleman on the phone from Sevenoaks.' Auctions meant extra commission and charges, and this meant around nine grand in the bank. Paul moved onto the next item, the eastern parcel of land.

Meic, observing from the back of the room, nodded to himself. Sevenoaks – sounded like more wealthy property developers looking to have a holiday home for a fortnight a year and renting it out to others like them for the rest of the summer. Or another bunch of privately educated eco-warriors looking for green nirvana. Or another corporate high-flier, tired and looking for a more spiritual mid-life where they could settle down and commune with their investment portfolio. They all came here looking for the rural magic and helped to corrode that same life from the moment they moved in. He could feel the bile rise as he slipped out to join his gang outside, who were standing by the auctioneer's BMW parked at the side of a cattle shed. 'Let's get it done.'

An hour later, with the auction over and bidders dispersed, a puce-faced Paul Williams drove his heavily scratched car down the farm lane to join the main road. At the junction he found a group blocking his way. One of the yobs lent down to his smashed side window. 'Think that you'll be wanting this, Paul.' The youth gestured to another member of the gang, who threw the "For Sale" sign, snapped in two, through the window onto the back seat.

Williams pulled up the handbrake with venom. 'You little bastards, did you do this to my car? I'll frigging well have you for this. Do you realise how much it will cost to get resprayed? Well, do you? No frigging idea as usual, bloody millennials.' He started to fiddle with his seat belt clip, in order to get out.

Meic looked around for witnesses, and seeing none, pulled out a Stanley knife, judging the weight of it in his palm before leaning in close. 'Did we do this to your car? What if we did? It's only what any true Welshman would have done.' Seeing Paul freeze at the sight of the knife, Meic grabbed the estate agent's tie which held in its wearer's jowls, and sliced it clean off. Holding the stub in his hand, he turned it over to examine the label. 'Debenhams? I would have expected more from you, given all those pieces of silver you've been earning from selling out our country. Isn't that right, Paul Williams of Number Six Llanyfi View Drive, Dolgellau? See, we know where you live. So, I don't think you'll be *frigging having* anyone.' Meic stepped back to assess the other man. 'You can fuck off now, Paul.' He banged the roof, laughing as the car lurched forward in a clutch-stabbing panic and finally accelerated away.

Meic turned to face his gang. 'And this, people, is how the story begins.' Too late, he checked himself, as his suppressed accent slipped out in his excitement, 'As the Saes say.'

John from the estate cut in, 'Did you see that twat's face when you took the knife out? I thought he was going to shit his knickers. Are we going to do that English dyke and her black bitch, then?'

Meic rounded on him. 'Hey, we'll have none of that. No discrimination here.'

'All right, Meic, just saying like. Not being racist like.'

Meic relaxed his stance. 'We dislike all the English equally,' he laughed. 'Frankie Pimlott's time will come... Tell you what boys, it's been a good day's work for our country. Let's go down the pub, first pint's on me.'

The gang beat Sergeant Parry to the pub by three fast-downed rounds. But the policeman had reasons other than Meic for stopping by – partly hoping that the smell of wood-smoke and beer would disguise the more telling scents that might now be on him. The bar seemed busy tonight and basking at the centre of the hubbub was Meic Davies, now fully emerged from the back room and holding bilingual court in the main bar. As soon as Lloyd appeared through the door, Stevie was pouring his usual order. 'Heard about the café? And the auction? It's all happening here, my friend!'

Lloyd shook his head, perched at the bar and soaked up the day's local news, feeling slightly sicker with each new twist: he would have known all about this if he'd really been at the station. There was that tight feeling again, just after the moment Meic Davies purposefully caught his eye. The look of triumph on the lad's face told Lloyd all he needed to know. Hostilities had commenced.

Sixteen

The vivid blue of a big summer sky shorn of springtime cloud presided over the High Season on the streets below. Another month of sun and fun, bring your families, treat your best guy or gal, feel the welcome in the hillsides, buy the cheap booze and take in the glorious views. These were the precious days when the village traders made enough profit to enable them to cast their own blight on some foreign resort for a fortnight later in the autumn.

A man walks into a pub. Walks in, that is, within five minutes of opening time, as he did every Monday, and Tuesdays, and Wednesdays to Sundays (inclusive). Stevie set up the drinks. 'Quiet down the marina today, Merv?' The answer, as most days, 'Yeah, as the graves. Huw can handle it if there's a rush…' But there never was.

On occasion Lloyd would pop his head round the door and ask Merv the Boats to shift his badly parked ancient green Jaguar where it didn't bloody interfere with the traffic flow. Today wasn't one of those days.

For Frankie, the refurbished hotel Plas y Morwr – which, she had been told translated as Seaman's Lodge – showed what could be achieved. The hotel overlooked the harbour from several streets higher up the hill. People sat in chairs on its terrace, turned to face the sunlight pouring onto them as if in a Hopper painting. The building's slate-paved entrance was framed by locally sourced woods as contrast. Traditionally patterned woollen blankets had been thrown over the dark leather sofas. A scattering of paintings by local artists enlivened the tastefully off-white walls and were offered for sale. Someone had spent a little money on interior designers, and they'd made an acceptable fist of it. What one would call, "regional boho-cool".

With Ruth off on another of her drives, Frankie had decided to take a promenade about the village, topped off with a modest lunch for one. Despite the recent upset over the coffee machine, the past fortnight had generally left her in a positive frame of mind. As her doctor had suggested, time away from the city had been exactly what was required. It had been a gradual transformation, but her previous sense of tiredness had been replaced by a certain lightness of spirit. She could feel it in her thoughts, in the faster pace of her stride, and in the fact that not everything that Ruth did irritated her. Perhaps this was because of the sea air and peacefulness of the surrounding countryside. She might write about this – maybe a book proposal in the making – she wondered if she could tag on something about mindfulness, but perhaps that was a little too 2017 for publishers. She had always meant to knock off one of those books which seemingly came from nowhere, broke out of their niche and dominated the best seller lists – perhaps now was her chance, they couldn't be that hard to write. As

Frankie waited at the restaurant entrance to be seated, her mental jottings were interrupted by a conversation between the manager and one of his staff.

'Oh and change the name of the ham on the menu, to "Ceredigion Ham".'

'But it came from the cash & carry, they didn't say where it was from.'

'Doesn't matter, bach, putting any place-name before the product – makes it sell like hot Welsh cakes! The tourists loves it, don't they? And put another pound on the price while you're at it.'

The speaker was Alex, who looked up to see Frankie waiting, blushed at being caught in the act and, trailing a slight scent of unwashed clothing, showed her to a table. The restaurant was about two-thirds full. Lots of powder-blue cashmere knits and pressed stone chinos. Perfect, or should she say, *parfait*? The Islington refugee slipped easily into gastronomy mode as she perused the menu. From her requested corner table, she looked out of the expanse of picture window at the activity on the harbour square below. Above the usual murmur and clinking of cutlery on china, several tables behind her she could hear an American couple discussing their meal. With an intuitive feeling for good column copy, Frankie placed her small notebook on the table and tuned in.

'I woulda thought that the lamb would've been good with all those sheeps around here. What's your steak like?'

A moment or two passed and then the nasal tones of his wife pronounced, 'It's a little lousy. American steak is much better.'

'Yeah, only steak better than American is that Jap beef. I wanted to order you Angus, that's a Scotch breed, but they only had that. Didn't have any American wines on the list either. And everyone knows that Oregon Pinots are the best in the world. Yep, the best in the world. Famous for it.'

'Why did we come here?'

'All the books said the food was good, but where do these guide-book people eat, garbage cans? I don't think this guy is a chef at all.'

'Where's the service, there's only like ten tables. Are they like hiding from us or what?'

Frankie had already noted that the older waiter – showing all the signs of anticipatory Alzheimer's – hadn't even offered her an aperitif. A local. She'd obviously have to raise this up with the owners, as they were missing an opportunity to up-sell there. She removed a pen from her jacket and began to discreetly take notes. The American couple's mutual delight at their disappointment had reached its pinnacle over the main course, and now with the end of their meal in sight they had moved onto post-climax dissatisfaction about the size of the bed in their room. Again, not as good as Oregon.

They would soon have something else to complain about. The clear skies which had bathed Llanawch for several weeks now had been invaded by a front of dark cloud. This was fast blowing in from the sea and, after colliding with the conifer-draped hills surrounding the village, was unloading a fine drizzle onto the holidaymakers. A Mexican wave of pac-a-macs appeared from shoulder bags. Frankie watched the geriatric evacuation of the bowling green, their slow movements unnoticed by the teenagers who continued their frenetic tennis match on the hard court behind, the change in weather only adding to their fun, indicated by the increased volume of their shouts. Meanwhile, on the seafront, the daily two o'clock coach party was heading directly from their transport into the café for a cup of tea. Rain and tea – for the retired widows, it was custom that was important. She felt a sympathetic pang as she thought of her own aged mother – whom she should remember to ring more often. Of course, there must be a place for the elderly – after all, one day she'd number among them – but that shouldn't impede progress on upgrading the main offering.

She wondered what some of her friends were doing in London right now, what they'd be doing this evening – the theatre, a late exhibition, a restaurant perhaps? And certainly, nobody would be raising an eyebrow at the sight of two women on a date. That was the downside, here she was marked as different. Even Ruth seemed embarrassed at times when Frankie insisted on holding hands in public. She never used to, but then again, she never used to turn every civilised conversation into some kind of guerrilla skirmish.

A little later, with the brief storm abated and the sun once more prominent, Arwel and his mates sat outside a pub, enjoying their post-exam fantasy that they were surfer dudes taking in the rays on Manly Beach in Australia. He was relaxed; being with his friends made him feel less out of sorts and less nervous. He'd set aside the thought that someone sitting in a little back bedroom on the other side of the country might be marking his exam papers right now and deciding on his future. He was trying to leave that reality to results day in mid-August, but it kept nagging away at him. At a table nearby, a tourist slammed down his bottle of Czech lager with a sigh and answered his vibrating mobile phone, pushing back his chair to the white-washed wall behind, his legs automatically spreading. 'Howard, what's the story?'

Arwel, along with the other customers in the beer garden, had little choice but to submit to the raised voice. Just who was this bloke? The clipped responses to whomever he was speaking provided few clues, and now the call seemed to be finishing. Arwel took a sip of pear cider and pretended to listen to what his friends were saying about Sarah D, who hung out at the Sportsman's Inn, and how far she was willing to go depended on how many Bailey's and ice she'd been bought. As they were speaking to each other in Welsh, knowing that the surrounding tables of visitors couldn't understand, his friends – including the girls – were coming up with even more depraved suggestions.

To think that in five years' time, that could be Arwel on the phone. He'd be a graduate, and if he did well at Manchester, on the fast track with one of those bachelor apartments overlooking the city, a wardrobe of smart suits, and a group of friends who were more like him. Friends he'd picked himself, rather than those he just went to the same school with. That was the most important thing. The thought motivated him more than any near-term prospect from the village, like Sarah D. She wasn't even going to the local FE college, let alone uni. She would be okay for a quick snog and a bit of a feel, but he wanted a clever girl, someone into the same books and music. Beautiful as well. And not Welsh. He looked at his mates – did they understand that this was going to be their last summer together? Laughing along with the tail-end of a joke, he wondered where they'd all be in a year. He'd take bets that one of the gang would be married by then, probably with a kid on the way. It wasn't unknown around here – all it took were lousy grades and you were toast.

A quartet of young Chinese women in facemasks, probably students at the university, walked past the pub, carrying tubs piled with unnatural shades of ice-cream, stopped to take selfies. His friends quietened down temporarily as they watched the girls, before switching fantasies from Sarah D to what Asian women were like, the tone growing ever more urgent as they talked about those possibilities. Under-achievers in search of the unachievable.

❧

His elder brother Hywel, meanwhile, had taken another early day and was beating a path to the harbour, humming a few bars from a tune which had been in his head since hearing it on the breakfast radio show. Having parked at his parents' place, Hywel strolled down the high road towards his favoured local, looking forward to the first pint of the day. Coming uphill towards him was a middle-aged couple, both in tan hiking trousers, colourful polo shirts, and carrying small backpacks. The man hailed him. 'Do you know if there's a pub up that way?'

Hywel paused, taken aback to think that anyone would believe that a pub would be situated up a mountainside. 'Er... no.'

'Is that you don't know, or that there isn't a pub?' the man demanded, in the punchy tone of an office bully, used to receiving prompt answers.

Hywel nodded slowly, ruminating. 'Yes, yes, now I come to think of it, there's one, oh a mile or two further on up the hill… You just need to keep going. Past some bramble bushes.' He watched the man and his taut-faced wife stride off. He felt no guilt, especially when he passed the silver Range Rover with a Henley-upon-Thames car dealer's sticker parked fifty yards further down the road. That'll learn them.

Seventeen

Down in the village centre, a red-faced couple, husband kitted out in standard Boden checked shirt accessorised with Wayfarer shades, his wife dressed head to toe in lifestyle-by-Cath Kidson, wearily dragged their trolley bags up a narrow alley towards a pebble-dashed cottage smoothed by onion-layers of pink masonry paint. The bag wheels sounded an uneven tattoo on the cobblestones which echoed off the stone passageway walls. The man looked at the details on his smartphone. 'This is it, I think. Number two, Mariner's View.'

'Nice windows,' his wife huffed a reply as she recovered from the exertion. 'Fabulous shade of duck blue. They have something like it in Farrow & Ball.'

'Uh-huh. I'll give the letting agent another call.' The husband concentrated on the phone's screen as he struggled to find the number in his call history list. 'She was supposed to be here with the keys, waiting for us. Even the taxi driver didn't know where this place was. Incredible.'

'Hey, you!'

A man dressed in black shorts and a taut T-shirt was homing in on them like a laser-guided missile. He sported a stud earring and spoke with a Lancashire accent overlaid with Estuary English attitude. 'You staying here?'

'Er, yes, we've just arrived. Are you from the agency?'

'No, I'm not. You need to take in your wheelie bin, it's been left out for a day.'

The husband responded slowly; this was supposed to be a holiday, not a reprise of his harassed working life. 'As I said, we've just arrived.'

'Well, it needs to be moved.'

'Do you expect me to do it now?'

'Do what you like. I'm a resident here, you know, unlike you lot. I'm off to the gym. It's too much!' The man glared at the couple, adjusted his backpack and strode off, grunting as he brushed past a young woman strolling up the alleyway towards them. She turned round to look at his fast-retreating back and shook her head.

She smiled gently at the couple. 'Mr and Mrs Acheson?'

'Yes, that's right.'

'I'm Eleri. I believe we spoke on the phone at lunchtime? I've got your keys.' She dangled a small key chain and started to unlock the front door of the cottage. 'I see you met Raymond Henshall, then.'

The wife frowned. 'He didn't seem very happy. I hope he isn't normally like that.'

'Oh no, don't worry about him!' Eleri opened the door. 'Bark worse than his bite.'

'He said that he was a resident?'

The agent laughed. 'Resident but not local. From Manchester way he is, bought a weekend cottage a couple of doors down from you six months ago. He's a bit territorial if you know what I mean, like a little growling puppy dog. It's his first season here, not yet used to change-over day I suppose. Now, enough of him. I've left you a nice home-baked cake on the kitchen table and there's some tea and coffee in the cupboard… the weather forecast is nice and dry for the weekend… need a hand with those bags?'

Eleri kept it to herself in front of the grockles, but she was sick of Raymond bloody Henshall and his ilk. They acted as if they expected the village to be some kind of private playground especially for them. They got annoyed when things changed, but they were the ones who changed things. And how were people supposed to make money? It was all right for them, coming in here with their fat pensions and cash-bags from selling their homes in the city. The rest of the village, the true locals that was, not the incomers playing at it, had to get by after all.

The businesses in the village had noticed a new kind of tourist money arriving after the virus, as people turned their back on foreign holidays. Among the usual regional accents from the Midlands and North – often working-class families staying in the massed caravan parks that encrusted the north-east coastline like barnacles – there now mingled the understated tones of the Home Counties brigade with their black BMW X-5s and Range Rovers lined up on the quayside like an affluent army of occupation. Their self-assured chatter subdued even the former top dogs from the Cheshire set.

Two bob-haired women in pink Zara tops and Jackie O-style glasses deploying their privately educated accents like a stiletto knife: 'I bought some Welsh cheese.'

'Oh, you can get some of that now at Waitrose in Cobham. They were running a promotion on it. I bought some to get us in the mood for this trip. It wasn't bad.'

Sprawled beside them, their husbands pleasured themselves over an upmarket travel brochure.

'You know you can even hire a private jet quite cheaply now? Even cheaper if we split it four ways. Imagine going to the Reykjavik jazz festival in that.'

'That is outrageously tempting. Fuck the kid's inheritance, we're going to spend it all!'

'Good job your parents didn't think like that, matey.'

'Yeah, but still – you've got to make your own way in this world, and in any case, inheritance was the norm for our generation. The kids don't expect to get anything, and I've already told them words to that effect.'

A Paul Smith-clad man to his sun-dressed wife: 'It's all terribly charming for a break and so forth, but could you imagine growing up here? Must be such a limited life for kids. Leander will become much more rounded back home with all those opportunities – and I'm sure Charterhouse can sort him out an outward-bound course or something up here for a week if it's needed.'

A small boy dressed head to toe in Kids Gap scrambling for the batteries which have fallen out of his electronic game: 'I love batteries, batteries are my friends.'

A pair of London lawyers and their wives: 'What do you fancy tonight? I saw a Thai place in one of the towns we drove through. Or shall we pluck up our courage and go Welsh? I could do with some more soggy chips and mushy green beans…' A short communal laugh follows.

A couple pushing a three-wheeled uber-pram, laden down with offspring and enough baby accessories to cover every eventuality bar nuclear fallout, note, 'We'll have to lose the nappies somewhere, the stench in the car is becoming a touch overpowering.'

'Perhaps we can find a bin around here?'

'Just dump them over by that wall, no one will notice.'

A group of friends in their early thirties, on a university reunion lounging in Quicksilver T-shirts and three-quarters cargo pants, having dragged together all three small cast-iron tables outside the harbour pub in order to hold their drinks and extend their territory – move them if you dare – their noise level rising with the tide and the pints: 'Yes, yes, I've already given to the Red Cross, but now I'm sponsoring a child in Sri Lanka.'

'For sure, I've already sponsored a poor little child in Uganda, but for my next birthday, I'm thinking of asking people to go to this site to sponsor some farm animals and equipment for a Kenyan community which I stumbled across on holiday. Remember? When I climbed Kilimanjaro?'

'Oh yes, so you did. I thought of the farm animals thing, but have now decided to buy some books, for a village school in Greenland. The Inuits, y' know, authentic with their nature and kayaks and history stuff. I can make a bigger difference there. We'll plan to visit it next year and maybe climb one of the peaks. This company I discovered runs helicopter eco-hiking tours up there. I'm setting up a Facebook page… I'll send you the link.'

The friends were quite evenly matched in talking across one another, but there would never come the day when one of them would donate a moral victory to the other.

'I can't believe these people. Have you seen all these EU flags on the road improvement signs? And then they vote for Brexit. So now they expect us to subsidise them for the billions they've lost.'

'I know, they're either hypocrites or just plain thick. I know what I'd put my money on.'

A laugh greets these words, which is stifled as the pair

of IT consultants from Ealing earwig the conversation at the neighbouring table between a family from Leicester…

'I tell you, if some of these politicians lived in these places, with those people, we'd see some big changes pretty quick. Mark my words. Some of them are all right though, but the ones on benefits get my goat. We're paying for them as well; they must think we're right mugs.'

The technical pair exchange looks, quickly finish their bottles of lager and move on.

And so the tourist chatter in the village continued into the early evening. Matters under debate included whether to wear baseball caps inside; why wave shapes are different across the world's oceans; the cheapness of the beer; premier league prospects for the next season; and various other social lubricants.

There was talk of a different kind at Hywel's destination pub, where some of the younger agricultural workers hung out. 'I wish bloody Cardiff would make up its mind. A few years back they were telling us to diversify the business. So then, I converted the old labourer's house into a holiday cottage. Then we had to go organic, so I did that and started supplying some of the supermarkets direct with my lamb. Then they were pushing us to set aside land for biofuels and for wind turbines for this climate change business. But then they removed the subsidies, so we were buggered. Then they tell us to go upmarket, so I considered breeding those Kobe beef cattle. Just like Lee Morgan did over at Ferry View. He was telling me that there were big start-up costs but it's all the rage in these top restaurants now.'

'Yes, I heard that.'

'You could even export it to France... well, that had been the plan for Lee anyway. Maybe not now. Anyway, this morning I get this letter from the Welsh Government about returning as much land as possible to mass production again. 'Food security' they say. Can you believe it? Bloody load of idiots they are. Have they seen beef prices recently? Bastard trade deals. Did I tell you that I met the bloody Director for Agriculture from Cardiff once – some English woman from Hampshire fuck's sake. Spouting more shit than Lee's bull she was. "Our top priority to increase diversity in farming," he mimicked a woman's voice. 'I mean totally clueless like. Just shows our own government isn't even run by us, they'd rather bring outsiders in to lord it over us.'

One of the members chipped in, 'I'll tell you something else, boys. I was down Trawsfynydd way the other day.'

'They still haven't cleaned that place up. Everyone knows it. Bloody scandal it is.'

'Anyways I was down there, filling up on diesel, and the guy at the counter tells me that the government are going to reopen it as a research plant for these biological weapons.'

'No way, why's that?'

'Because the place is already fucked isn't it. The lake and everything are all radioactive, so they don't need special permission or anything.' He scratched his balls as if to emphasise the point.

'Welsh Government going to do that?'

'No, not those jokers. The English Government, they own it. I wouldn't trust the Cardiff mob to organise a piss-up in here on a Friday night.'

'Yes, at least with London they do a fuck-up properly. Nice and professional like.'

The speaker was long-haired and bearded in the New Celtic fashion. No London hipster individualist-by-rote look here, these farming boys wouldn't have looked out of place fighting the Romans on the shores of the Menai Straits. Hywel recognised him as a client of one of the other salesmen at his firm. He let his eyes take a wander over the bottles of spirits on the shelves behind the bar – his mother would have a fit if she could see the dust on some of them – and continued to listen in to the guys' chat for a bit of distraction. The talk had moved on.

'But leaving is just making things worse just when we don't need it.'

'Yeah, short term maybe, but we'll be stronger for it in the long term.'

'What about the September subsidy payments? What about money? We get subsidised, everyone knows that.'

'Oh yes, that's one argument. If we relied on the farming alone, we'd be in the poorhouse.'

'You can say that again.'

'You know where my money used to come from? Bloody Europe Common Agricultural Policy and what did people get for that? A bit of lamb for the Sunday table and a nice-looking "sustainable" hillside. And then this "rewilding" bull. I tell you we were treated like landscape gardeners. So this subsidy argument doesn't wash with me.'

'Yeah, but the money…'

'Fuck it, I just want to be a farmer again and farm my land how I see fit. No interference anymore. This is a chance for us to stand on our own two feet! Stop being children waiting for a handout from the parents. That's what Meic says anyway and I for one—'

'That Meic is popping up all over the place. He was down the rugby club the other day.'

'Well, likes his soapbox all right, but he says some good things…'

One of the group turned back to the bar, to order another round.

'… he was saying that English pensioners living in Wales swung the vote, otherwise we wouldn't have voted to leave. He said that English pensioners like those up on the estate didn't really give a stuff about us or about anything other than sticking two fingers up to someone.'

'Eh? But you just said that Brexit was a good thing.'

'Yeah, in some ways, but you know, it'll work out in the end.'

The conversation switched into Welsh for a couple of minutes as one of them went to the gents. This made it harder for Hywel to follow, even interspersed as it was with a smattering of modern English phrases, but as the friend rejoined them it instantly switched back into English. The group had moved on to discussing an actor. 'Yeah, he's okay, but he just does Tony Blair impressions. Not bad, mind, and my daughter says he does this vampire thing now as well. And Hopkins was all right in that cannibal picture, I'll give you that, but give me Richard Burton any day. He was brilliant, saw him on the telly the other night, what was it now…

'*Where Eagles Dare*?'

'That's the boy. You know, where they shoot up that Nazi castle, with Clint Eastwood in it too. "Broadsword calling Danny Boy, Broadsword calling Danny Boy…" He's good and all. Yes, and he was a big drinker, mind you. Burton. *Big* drinker. Bottle of vodka before lunch drinker.'

‘Well, no one’s going to last long doing that, are they now?’

‘No. We all have our moments like, but a shame really. Good he was. Bit of a waste in the end. Perils of drinking.’ He swilled the last of his pint and then drained it with a satisfied burp. ‘Pardon me. Another one?’

Scratching his face and smiling, having just seen the film also, Hywel rummaged in his jeans for some Golden Virginia and Rizla papers and, with his pint of bitter sat before him, proceeded to roll a couple of fags, for the satisfaction of creation rather than to light them.

‘Excuse me.’

Hywel looked up. A man in a – Quins wasn’t it? – rugby jersey was staring at him.

‘Excuse me, but I hope you’re not thinking of lighting it. The sign says no smoking.’ The man gave him a stern look.

‘Just rolling up, friend. For later.’ Hywel licked the edge of paper and placed the cigarette in his tobacco tin – he’d done a nice job. There was a raised voice from over his shoulder. ‘Hey, buddy. The man can do what he wants here. Roll it, smoke it, wipe his arse on it. This is a locals’ pub.’ The Richard Burton fan stood up to his full height at the bar and stared at Hywel’s questioner.

The pub quietened. The Harlequin shirt parried, ‘I’m not looking for trouble.’

‘Well bugger off then. This is *our* place. Bloody idiot.’

The Englishman took a defiant sip of his pint, placed it carefully back on the bar and then left with a head-shaking grimace. Hywel raised his eyebrows and nodded to the farmer. But he’d already turned back to his friends and was explaining with some restraint why he fucking hated

English fucking rugby and its fucking posh fucking hooray henry fucking poof fans fucking calling Twickenham "HQ" my fucking arse haven't they been to the Millennium or fucking Auckland stadiums those fucking RFU know-nothing twats.

❧

With the beach crowd thinning, Lloyd took a final promenade before clocking off for the day. He passed a father whose son had just run into his embrace, the boy seemed to have been scared by something or other and was seeking refuge. The man looked contented and Lloyd felt a stab of envy at the sight. He hadn't touched Arwel beyond a quick pat on the back since the boy had slipped into his teens.

The place looked pretty different from the shoreline. He spent his days patrolling its – Lloyd couldn't help but chuckle to himself – its mean streets, and as many an evening, he observed, as the world of Llanawch shifted a little with the onset of dusk. Changing tones of light appeared from the horizon of the western sea – casts of orange, red and purple over the waterfront buildings, longer shadows drawing slowly into the blackness stealing in from the east. He sighed with contentment, looking back at his tracks, the footprints in the sand winding their way to where his size nines stood now. The tide was coming in and those prints would be covered within the hour, wiped from the surface. When he was young, his dad would sometimes take him to Rhossili Beach on the Gower of an evening. Not often, but enough for them to make a deal of it. They'd park by the pub on the headland, drop down to the beach, and walk a thirty-minute loop back to the pub. Then they'd perch on the picnic tables outside and he'd have a coke while his dad sank a pint. Bitter wasn't it, was it Felinfoel Double Dragon or Brains Special? He couldn't remember what they'd served, probably all Budweiser and Fosters now. Looking at the village he tried to log all the details: where the flickering lampposts were, the broken kerbstones, the surf shop's window display. If they sold the house, if he and Catrin left, all those memories would eventually desert him, be cleaned away, just like they'd painted over the faded woodland mural on the side of the primary school last week, preparing the building ahead of the closure. A lot of parents upset about that decision and he couldn't blame them.

Odd that. He hadn't thought about leaving the village since they'd arrived. And now that's all he could think about. He stared out to sea for another few minutes, and turned back for the station, allowing himself to drift onto a route which would take him past his local. Maybe just a quick half.

Eighteen

Screened by the surrounding hills until the last minute, the sharp rays of morning slid over the ridge and skimmed across the village, resuscitating the hunched streets, liberating the shadows to shades of rose. It was going to be another hot one.

The light reflected off the estuary's surface, intensifying it. Those usually out and about at that hour, such as Pete the milkman, found themselves shielding their eyes as they adjusted. From May to September, the seafront would see a flotilla of weekend artists already out at dawn, brushes at the ready, set on capturing the vast Turneresque canopy, ignoring or including the flotsam of human life on the beach as they saw fit for their masterpiece. The mums embarrassed at the tightness of their new swimsuits, hoping that nobody would notice – unless the guy was hot – the dads sighing at the thought of cleaning the sand out of the car upholstery after they got home, and distracting themselves with the sight of the other wives. The kids, blood-rushed when faced with the heat-shimmered expanse of possibilities. Dropped ice-creams, smashed sandcastles, hearts drawn in sand, splashing in the surf, all lay ahead of them.

Up at the Parrys', the daily routine was underway with Lloyd in the shower sniffing uncertainly at the new lavender fragrance shower gel his wife had bought. He squeezed a gloop into his palm and carried on – he'd just have to smell like a bloody florists' parlour through the day. The water flushed away the accumulations of the last twenty-four hours as he washed off the lather. Every so often the shower would be a place where Lloyd's thoughts would turn to his urges – a glimpse of intimate flesh while on duty, the scent of warm perfume on a craning neck evoked – and his brain would begin to lustfully poach. For him, women possessed that peaceful aura, but then again, as he'd worked out over time and through his many mistakes, they needed a man to appreciate them. Well, maybe...

Lloyd Parry knew that he could be a bad boy at times. In Leeds, he'd stuck to the odd available WPC and the occasional female witness who had a thing for uniforms, but down here, he'd been more selective out of necessity. It wasn't that he was a womaniser, but gossip got around fast, and his wife was plugged right into that particular little grapevine with its network of human surveillance systems. Sometimes it felt as if Catrin actually manned their switchboard and heard everything that went on in the place. Thus, while Lloyd appreciated the need to be careful, he'd just broken the rule about shitting on his own doorstep and that might be a worry. In the past his wife might have turned an old-fashioned blind eye; after all she was quite traditional, and her dad had been a bit of a randy old goat himself in his day. So maybe, just maybe, Catrin thought it was normal that the bloke would stray. Maybe she didn't. It wasn't a subject her husband had wanted to raise, given that boat-rocking generally wasn't a good idea. Of course,

Lloyd could quite understand the father, especially given his touchy mother-in-law. Having a new woman, the way they made you take them, well, it made a man feel as if he had achieved something, that he'd hunted his prey and was still alive. He loved that feeling.

The sergeant stepped out of the shower and stared at his own hazy image in the misted bathroom mirror above the sink; it reflected the muddle of his mind. His dreams were filled with the future, about what he could do or be, and then he had woken to reality – another day of routine. Lloyd dried himself off and saw that as the steam retreated to the edges of the mirror it brought his reflection into focus. A week ago he'd felt empty, but now this was the person that Ruth Pimlott had chosen, that she had given herself to. His body stirred at the thought of her, the meeting at Glanrhyd two evenings ago. Her idea, not his, but which admittedly he hadn't fought. In the empty farm kitchen, she'd wanted to do it right there on the bare table. She had simply hiked her skirt, slid her knickers to one side, and pulled him in. Surprising in a way, given that she was supposed to be married to another woman, but Lloyd had sensed an undercurrent from the off. Ruth felt like velvet, tasted like golden syrup and went like a woman possessed. He hadn't felt shame at doing it up there, more a sense of release, as he hadn't visited the farm since the inquest. Lloyd looked down at the bulge now showing under the waist towel. It was no good, he'd have to arrange another meeting quickly; he needed it badly.

Downstairs in the kitchen, his wife prepared breakfast for their son. She efficiently whisked the butter, eggs and milk and gently heated the pan. She'd talked briefly this morning to Lloyd about going away in the autumn, once Arwel was off, but… well first he'd answered that Madrid would be too boring, and then Amsterdam too cold. Such a stick-in-the-mud. But what about her art appreciation studies? It was a case in point; whenever she became excited about something, a meal or book or just an idea, her husband seemed unable to respond. He would stiffen at the thought of leaving his comfy rut – avoiding anything different or new. Not like her. She poured the egg mix into the saucepan and stirred the thickening mass. That business with the estate agent circular had left a seed in her head which was growing. What if it hadn't been such a good idea to return home in the first place? She'd witnessed how Lloyd had gradually gone downhill in her opinion. When they'd first started courting it had been so exciting; like her, he was Welsh in a foreign city, but yet he wasn't quite the boy next door. Then, when she became pregnant with Hywel, she knew that their life together would change – only women truly understand the reality of a new child. But now that Arwel was about to leave, it was back to the two of them again and she felt it was time for them to make a new start. She ground a little black pepper into the pan and made a mental note to buy some dried pasta for supper. Except that Lloyd just wouldn't respond to her, not in bed, not anywhere. He wasn't climbing the peaks anymore, it was like he was freewheeling down a hill on a bike into middle age, and it was all she could do sometimes to grit her teeth and not give him a few home truths. He'd have a bloody shock if he knew the half of it, how she'd come to see him. A lot of the men in the village would have a shock for that matter if their wives came clean. Right useless lumps they could be, clutter you had to work around.

The scrambled eggs were ready. Catrin turned off the heat, dropped two slices of granary bread into the toaster, and went to the doorway to call up to her son, still in his bedroom. His father might be turning to seed, but she wasn't having Arwel waste his final few weeks before university spending all day lazy boning. It was lovely to have the gift of grandchildren on the way, thanks to her eldest son, but she couldn't quite escape the feeling that her hopes were most bound up with her youngest, always had been. Arwel was a bright boy, much like his grandfather, and he had the opportunity to make something more of his life. His birthday was coming up and she'd been saving to buy him one of those Interrail tickets. She knew that his dreams went beyond Llanawch, so as painful as it was for her to see him leave home, she was going to help him nurture them.

Lloyd took up a position at the thickly painted iron gates as parents dropped off their children at the primary school for the last time. It was end of term. It was also the end of an era. The council had closed the school and some workmen were ready to move in to start stripping the school of its books and equipment. Except that they first had to make their way through a huddle of protesting mothers holding home-made placards. And not many workmen want to push aside a mother, especially if their wife was among the protest group.

The women provided the backdrop to a portly councillor being interviewed by a BBC Wales news crew. The female reporter, in her well-styled hair and pale-raspberry top, looked out of place against the backdrop of the local mothers in their hardwearing home clothes.

'I'm joined here today by Councillor Madoc, who chairs the education committee at the county council. Councillor, with the closure of the school, what do you have to say to the parents who will now have to transport their children to school many miles away?'

Her interviewee displayed a greying moustache setting off a face already reddening in the sunlight. 'Of course, we didn't want to close Llanawch, but we were faced with some very difficult decisions.'

'You mean close Llanawch school, not Llanawch itself.'

A thin smile recognised the cheap remark, typical of a Cardiff media-luvvie. His voice dropped a half-octave. 'As I said, a very difficult decision. But we are engaged in a reorganisation of our primary school provision and this was an unfortunate but unavoidable outcome. We have to change because the world has changed.'

'In what way?'

'In this county, in Gwynedd, we are facing a reduction of nearly sixteen per cent in children of primary school age over the next decade. At the same time, our teachers face hugely increased workloads – mainly as a result of Whitehall intervention, you see. And as a result, we have difficulty recruiting suitable candidates to headteacher posts.'

'But what about those who say these closures are simply about cutting expenditure, and that's all the council cares about because they impact fewer people than, say, cutting everyone's rubbish collection?'

'That just isn't true. We've cut collections as well.' His forehead tightened as realised his error. 'What I mean to say is, in this day and age, we do have to cut our suit according to the cloth available. And we all know that the cloth available is shrinking. And it is not helped by the billions the Welsh taxpayer had to spend on bailing out the London banks a few years back or more; obviously

Covid emergency spending, that money had to come from somewhere. We didn't get our train line electrified you know – unlike Cardiff. But people should rest assured that we in the council are working night and day, night and day, to ensure that we minimise the impact of the cuts on hard-working people.'

As he spoke, he wondered whether they could use the school as storage for some of that unusable protective equipment they'd bought from Mexico a few years back. Fat chance of selling the site anyway.

The reporter thought about how in hell she could edit these ramblings down to a couple of ten-second sound bites for the evening report. 'But it's not just the fault of the government and the bankers, is it? What about the auditor's report on expense and budget mismanagement at the council, which was delivered to you last week? When will it be made public, or will the BBC need to use the Freedom of Information Act again?'

Madoc shook his head at the reporter's lack of manners. 'We are digesting the report and will take appropriate action. But as I say, I came here today to talk about how hard we are working in this county to ensure a fair education and good opportunities for all. This is not about cuts, it is about better, more efficient services for the whole public.'

'Councillor, thank you very much. So, another school closes, and what people here are asking today, is how many more will follow? This is Sarah Thomas, back to you in the studio.' The interviewer maintained a fixed smile until her cameraman signalled that he'd stopped filming.

Rhys Madoc stepped closer and looked down at the journalist. 'There was no need to bring that report up.'

Sarah stepped back, repulsed by the close proximity.

'Oh, you got off lightly, barely a scratch.' She fiddled with the microphone.

'Still, you'd better tread carefully up here. They're not all as nice as me.'

Sarah glanced up and just about managed to raise a half-smile. 'No – I can see that Councillor Madoc… Oh look, your fan club.' The reporter inclined her head in the direction of the approaching gaggle of mothers, at full steam and line abreast.

'Ah, ladies.' Madoc put on his most ingratiating smile. Even if the women weren't living in his electoral ward, he recognised that the camera nearby had now swung from him around to the new scene. In fact, out of the corner of his eye he could see the journalist bitch's head swivel toward the group.

The leading woman, filling out her worn jeans and wearing a pink fleece, shot back in Welsh, 'Don't you *ladies* us, you patronising waste of space. What about our children? We want the school reopened.'

'And what's your name then?' The Councillor switched language and looked at her blowsy face.

'Bethan Evans—' She made to continue, but Madoc cut in quickly, 'Well, Bethan, as you no doubt overheard, there are good reasons why we sadly can't do that. You should have all received an individual communication from the education department about arrangements in September for your child.'

'We got the letters all right from some jobsworth in your office – but it's the first time you've bothered to set foot here. Perhaps we should have booked a TV camera to get you down here? You seem to like them.'

'Well, pressure of work. I can assure you that you

were in our thoughts, but you're not the only school under review... hey what's that!' One of the women had approached him from behind, pulled out an egg from her pocket and slammed it into the back of his head, wiping her hand on the back of his jacket.

'What in God's name... what did you do that for!' Another egg hit him, this time on the front, and then a bag of flour burst over him. The women surrounded him, heckling, jabbing him in the chest, grabbing him by the arm.

'What about our children? What about our school? What about our village!'

Perched on the school's brick front wall, dangling his legs, Meic Davies watched as Lloyd strode over to break-up the melee. This was perfect, he didn't even have to intervene now that the women were so pumped-up about the school after his talk at the church last Sunday. He saw Lloyd grab the councillor by the shoulders and start to bundle him towards the police car, in the process taking a hit of egg himself. Meic smiled from behind his shades; even better, Sergeant Plod could barely control his own people. What was that saying about making omelettes again?

Lloyd pushed the councillor into the passenger seat, slammed the door on him and pushed through the women to reach the driver's side. 'You've made your point, Bethan, now go home!'

'What are you protecting the likes of him for, Lloyd?'

'He's a councillor.

'What kind of councillor? He doesn't give a shit about us.'

'Listen, any more from you and there'll be consequences. Now out of my way, please.'

The woman sneered at him, her blue Nordic eyes

sparkling. 'Going to put the handcuffs on me, are you? You'd like that, wouldn't you? Bet I wouldn't be the first to have them on either...'

There was something in the laughter of the other women that made Lloyd stop and turn. He instructed in a low voice, 'Just go home, all right.'

'It will take more than that, Lloyd.' Bethan slid through a gap in the group and yanked open the passenger door and spat at Madoc.

'Right! I told you,' Lloyd pulled her arms firmly behind her back to cuff her. 'For God's sake, Bethan.' To the rest of the group he shouted, 'Out of my way, everyone, now! Move!' He frog-marched her to the tailgate door of the Land Rover and banged her down on the bench inside like a gavel.

The crowd were silent as he got into the driver's seat and started the engine. They parted to let him drive off. One woman shouted 'Mochen' – *pig* in Welsh – and they were slowly on their way. Behind him, the remaining women, playing to the camera which had started rolling again, chanted, 'What do we want?'

'OUR SCHOOL!'

'When do we want it?'

'NOW!'

The sound of their shouting diminished. Next to him the councillor methodically dabbed the egg off his hair and spittle off his jacket. 'Do you call that protection, Sergeant? Because I don't. I'm a democratically elected official, and you stood by while those people... those women,' he hissed, 'assaulted me.'

'No one would have seen that coming, Councillor. I'll take you to the station and you can get a taxi from there.'

'The least you can do. You should expect to be hearing

from your Chief Constable shortly. You may not be aware that I'm on the Police Authority Committee as well. I'll tell you something for nothing, I will not stand for such an amateur performance. I mean, what do we pay you for?'

Lloyd slowed to turn up the road that led to the station and the small rough-grassed green in front. 'That is your right, of course, sir. But I did all I could. Bethan was down in London on the Extinction Rebellion protests a year or two back.' He raised his voice through the grill, 'Weren't you, Bethan?'

The voice sneered from behind the cage partition, 'So what if I was?'

'No problem for me, Bethan, wasn't my patch.' He glanced over at Madoc. 'But well, there you go. What I'm saying, Councillor, is that it could have been worse. She might have super-glued herself to you. That would have been a lot more awkward.'

'And you don't think that was awkward? In front of the television camera and that reporter? Good God, Sergeant, you're a bloody disgrace to the uniform. I want this woman charged and locked up.'

Lloyd hunched over the wheel and gritted his teeth. 'I'm here to enforce the law and do my job, that's all.'

From behind him, perched on the back seat, Bethan muttered, 'So we all saw. You've shown your true colours now, haven't you.'

❦

That afternoon, several hundred miles away, in their chrome and glass Mayfair offices near Berkeley Square, the employees of Hythe and Brent – "Agents of premier countryside property" – were struggling to get into their computer systems. The managing partner walked through the door, having returned from her lunchtime spin class, and noticed the sales staff wasting time huddled around one desk looking at its computer screen when they should have been hunting down buyers on the phones. 'What's going on?'

Her colleague banged his fingers on the keyboard uselessly. 'The system isn't responding, none of us can get into our files.'

'Why not?'

'Don't know, I don't understand it. Website is down as well, Julian just tried it on his iPad. It is usually fixed by now.'

'Have you called IT support?'

'Yes, but they're swamped. I don't think they've seen this issue before…'

'Well, call them again, otherwise this is going to lose us money. Tell them that if they don't respond, we'll cancel their contract and outsource elsewhere. I knew we should have gone with that Indian supplier.'

Two blocks away, on Park Lane, another firm of agents was also struggling with a system crash. Their in-house technical guy was already on the case. 'Looks like a virus.'

'How long will it take to fix it?'

'I… I don't know.' He entered a line of code, but the screen remained unchanged. 'It looks pretty complex. I'll have to run some hunter-killer software, but I'll need to take the whole system offline to do that.'

A shout from one of the other desks caught the manager's attention. 'Peter, I've called round the regional offices – it's just us and Chester who are down. The others seem to be okay.'

'Funny.' He turned back to face his tech-support. 'Dafydd, has this happened before? Just two offices going down?'

'No, but anything's possible.' Dafydd put on a worried look. 'It'll take me a few hours at the least to sort it out. This looks complicated – you're lucky that you have a specialist here.'

'Two hours? Well, get cracking then.'

A few hours later, the phone rang at Meic Davies' home. When he picked up a quiet Welsh voice informed him, 'It is done. All of the targets have caught a cold. I fixed my office, but the others will be sitting in their stew at least overnight, probably a bit longer.'

Dafydd replaced the receiver in the call box just off Oxford Street and pulled out some hand gel to cleanse his hands. Not wanting his mobile traced, he'd used a public line, maybe he'd said too much or was on too long. But they'd kept to the code as agreed beforehand. Just like being a secret agent. He felt satisfied, he'd struck a blow for Wales, which Meic and he had long talked about in the chat room. But now those posh arseholes in the office would see how much they should value him, with their competitor's networks still smouldering. He'd be suggesting a pay rise in the morning, or maybe later in the week.

At the other end of the line, Meic wondered why he felt slightly tired rather than elated. The situation, after all, was moving in his direction – it would just need one more flashpoint. Yet all this leadership during the day and the business to transact at night could be wearing, and he could only hope that it would eventually pay off at election time. That's if he was selected, but surely that would soon become a formality… He dropped onto his sofa and switched on the television with the worn remote. Flick, news: all about London. Flick, food programme from England. Flick, teenage soap opera. Then S4C – Welsh music with the statutory audience bussed in from the survivors of the local care home.

He was about to surf to BBC4, but he decided to stick with the Welsh talent; he'd need people like the ones in the audience to vote for him shortly and all that. His thoughts danced away from the dark-haired harpist who was currently playing, to a vision of what his Senedd office would look like in Cardiff Bay – "Meic Davies MS" on the door. A research assistant who looked like that cute harpist outside ready to do his bidding – he rather liked the thought of that. And Cardiff it did have to be for him, not one of the sell-outs standing for Westminster and thinking that the Senedd was second-best. Wales was better than that, different to England, whether it was our culture, language, society, or the relationship its countrymen had with each other. How could the Old Etonians who run our country out of their panelled London offices have any conception of what it means to be Welsh, or for that matter Cornish or Scottish, or Irish? He shook his head with disgust and flicked onto a documentary about Roman fort construction.

Across the village in the police station, Lloyd completed the incident report form for the farm machinery theft he'd just attended and signed his name at the bottom. This time two quad bikes had been stolen. Normally that wouldn't be so bad, because it was a manageable loss, but the same farm had been done over eight months ago, a bailing machine that time, so their insurance premiums would be shooting up even further now. He leaned back in his chair, balancing it on the rear legs. There were a few too many of these thefts occurring. There must be a gang operating in the area. But who? He hadn't noticed any strangers apart from the usual tourist crowd and in truth the thefts had been going on for a while – out of season as well. Knowing that he was due at headquarters the day after next, he decided that he'd take the opportunity to catch up with a friend in the CID office there. It could be that this was happening elsewhere in the region so it would be useful to check. Proper police work at last.

He chucked his biro onto the desk and surveyed the empty cell. As soon as Councillor Madoc had been tenderly escorted to his taxi – still huffing and puffing – Lloyd had released Bethan with an informal caution.

'Right, now you've cooled off you can be on your way.'

Bethan pulled a face. 'Are you going to charge me?'

'No, just don't do it again.' He opened the front door of the station and gestured to her to leave.

'People won't forget this, Lloyd.'

'You don't need to thank me.'

She snorted, 'Oh no. No, that's not what I meant at all. Not at all.'

Nineteen

Lloyd had a date with a two-day training course at the police headquarters in Colwyn Bay and had booked himself into a small B&B for the overnight stay. He left the village in the hands of Roy with instructions to call for back-up if there were any more issues involving the school or the café. It didn't take Sherlock Holmes to sense the way the atmosphere in the community had darkened over the last few weeks. As his deputy needed to use their only police car in his absence, Lloyd was en route to HQ using the family Mazda. The journey usually took about an hour but would probably take more given the time of year.

The road verges trammelled his vision as he hit the north road. These high verges fell into two main categories: earth packed into a metal mesh with a handful grass seed chucked in to bind it, care of the council's roadbuilders. This design signalled that recent work had taken place on the road – widening or even a new section. But mostly the roads were ribboned with dry stone walls, often topped with discarded slate from the local quarries, sometimes with rusty War Office-surplus barbed wire. And, Lloyd mused, there was a definitely beauty to them, how they seemed to fit the country. The new walls were to be found on the main roads with heavy traffic usage, the latter on the by-lanes of life. The road borders' muddy green hues were broken up at regular intervals of several miles by the bright yellow plastic bins filled with grit in anticipation of the annual freeze. Some of these had cracked open and spilled their guts, with an occasional tuft of hardy weeds sprouting from them. Yet however modern, wide and well-prepared these arterial roads were for the normal business of the area, during the summer months passage would invariably be slowed. It was often caused by a slow-moving tractor driven by a hunched-up farmer who had little interest in the Highways Department's strategic masterplan for shorter transit times. Behind him, for farming remained an almost uniformly male occupation, the tailback would include spotless 4x4s driven by aspirational housewives from the executive homes set, and their cheaper beaten-up Japanese cousins driven by other local farmers who had practical requirements beyond a mobile throne.

If the tractors didn't slow a driver, then the herds of cattle coming in for milking would; or the Caravan Clubbers; or the continuous roadworks with their automatic traffic lights – take your pick. Nevertheless, inside the new plate-glass council offices the planners continued to stick pins into maps with visions of broad, flat and straight road connecting people to as-yet-unidentified "value-added" jobs – even if the cash from Brussels paying for road improvements had evaporated with no replacement. However, none of this could disguise the fundamental poverty of a region totally dependent on tourism and the public sector for employment. Farming and quarrying, two historic generators of income, had long become minor industries. The range of supermarkets which the tourists used themselves told a story: the Home Counties comforts of Waitrose and Sainsbury's were nowhere to be found. A basic scattering of Tescos brought some everyman delight for the middle classes, but the cut-priced Aldi and Lidl chains were now the destinations of choice. For those without a car, most large villages boasted a Spar with its bright blue and green cans of own-brand lager lined up on the metal shelving waiting for their Friday night destiny. Those few upmarket food stores or delicatessens situated in the market towns had just one customer segment in mind – incomers, whether they were tourists or affluent retirees. The locals weren't interested in paying over the odds no matter how hand-crafted, local or organic the food. After all, they produced the stuff, not consumed it.

Most of the towns and villages hosted shops which served the outlying area and stuck to selling useful items which people needed. However, the growth of the retired population in the area had spurred the development of villages which now seemed solely devoted to leisure. This could be lifestyle businesses run by incomers – the art gallery, the tea shop, the nautical wear boutique – or cafés and restaurants which were aimed at the incomers. All these services provided short-terms jobs, but with longer-term costs. For many locals the Welsh heartbeat of the area was becoming ever fainter, and the place which they recollected from childhood no longer existed. It was as if their lives had been packaged and merchandised.

Lloyd knew what category – local or incomer – he fell into. He might be officially more active in the village, but it was Catrin's home and in her blood, while he was still the Swansea Jack at heart. Not that he wanted to return down south, mind. All that rust-belt comradeship and golden-age-of-coal memories which were apparent in the local pub every bloody time he revisited the place. Even as a teen, Lloyd had felt it backward-looking bullshit and it rang no truer now he had become middle-aged. He refocused on the road ahead, glancing down at the speedometer and seeing that he'd driven four miles without noticing. Lloyd found himself stuck behind a navy-blue Volvo estate and his thoughts turned to Ruth. He didn't know how he'd found the nerve to start the affair with her in the first place. Maybe it wasn't courage, as the decision had been taken out of his hands, perhaps it was fate.

Fate?

Good grief, this isn't bloody *Mills and Boon*, get a grip. Desperation for a bit of action between the sheets was more like it. Catrin hadn't exactly been an attentive wife in bed for quite some time now – the gaps between *special* nights had become longer and longer. No wonder he strayed. He was a man after all.

He slowed for a roundabout and took the first turn left, watching the blue car peel away to continue onto the expressway in the direction of Caernarfon. A few hundred metres on, down an avenue marked by lampposts and flower beds, the police headquarters finally came into view. Lloyd smiled as he thought of a past chief constable who had taken it on himself to break into the building in order to demonstrate to his subordinates just how poor the security was. Bonkers he was. Mind you, same guy had plastered the area with speed cameras as well – quite a few colleagues hadn't liked the employment implications of that, and soon after the early retirements began and had continued since. Lloyd parked within view of a close-circuit camera, flicked two fingers at it to see if the duty security was awake, and carrying his folder of pre-course reading, entered the building to sign in for the class.

The man standing before them with menaces was in his mid-thirties, just under five-eleven, in good shape, brown eyes, dark vampiric hairline, and wearing a black leather jacket, navy polo neck with dark jeans. The sun blazed outside. Perhaps, Lloyd wondered, he particularly felt the cold. The man spun a set of keys around his forefinger. 'My name is DS Blunt. I'm on secondment to your force from the Greater Manchester Special Branch team. I'm a specialist in the National Domestic Extremism Unit and one of my duties is to teach you guys about dealing with the terrorist threat in your area.' He paused for effect. 'Lucky, lucky me.'

Blunt sized up the class, the keys ceased their arc. 'You, what's so funny, what's your name?'

He looked at one of the fifteen or so officers seated facing him in the seminar room. Lloyd recognised the target of Blunt's ire as a sergeant from the Pwllheli nick – bit of a know-it-all type. The officer reddened and tried to hide his half-smile – but mentally he was back in the first year of school again. Blunt sighed before resuming.

'The UK is under terrorist attack on a daily basis. Islamic radicals. Anti-abortion activists. Animal rights brigade. Our old friends, the Irish Republicans are reactivating. Nationalist movements, I'd guess you'd know about some of that up here. The radical wing of the reformed BNP. Bio-radicals. And other assorted nutters. You should see some of the reports that I get across my desk, it would make your so-called crime waves look like a… well… crap anyway.'

Having lost his train of thought, Blunt looked down to

the speaking notes he'd placed on the desk. 'You guys may think that up here where the air is clear is a long way from the action of London and Manchester, but the threat *here* is just as real as *there*. You aren't bobbies on the beat. That's all old-school rubbish. You're part of the *national* security team to combat and neutralise threats to the public and to maintain order. The rule of law – remember that? And you *will* play your position in the team. Think about this small town. Think about your own smaller towns. Far from the mad crowd eh? Well people, just look at this little lot.'

Blunt pressed a button on his laptop and a series of bullet points slid across the television screen behind him. Lloyd heard a yawn being stifled behind him. 'Point one: this force has to cover a long coastline and we all know how the IRA in the eighties used the coast down in Pembrokeshire to infiltrate the UK. Point two: you cover one of the UK's category three ports – Holyhead – an entry point which received a red-flagged warning by the Home Office in its last security review. Point three: Wylfa nuclear power station, with the possible new reactor building. Enough said, that should be obvious. But just think for a moment how much damage was caused by that plant in Japan flooding. Point four: training camps. We've uncovered terrorist cell training sites in various parts of Wales, and we know that this activity is ongoing in Snowdonia. Yeah, terrorists need team-bonding too…'

He paused. 'That's a joke people. You have permission to laugh.'

One of the women attendees ventured an ironic titter. Blunt looked on unimpressed. 'So in this session we're going to cover how to spot and undertake basic surveillance of these camps. Point five: safe houses. The cities are on high alert, so imagine that you're a terrorist and you're planning the next atrocity. Now you're hardly going to camp out in front of Scotland Yard, are you? You're going to hide out where you think the local plods aren't on their game. Hide somewhere like here. And finally, point six: VIPs. In the next twelve months, another important individual will be based in the area and requiring protection. We all know about Prince William when he was up at RAF Valley, but this VIP will be at Bangor University and is an important non-UK national from an ally state. The North Wales Police will again assume primary support in their protection, as coordinated by your friendly Special Branch team, of course.'

Blunt folded his arms. 'So, a lot going on. Just because this is the sticks, it doesn't mean that you shouldn't be ready to act swiftly and decisively to intervene in any terrorist action. That's why I'm here. Questions?'

'Who's the new VIP?'

'Middle Eastern; you won't have heard of him, but the Diplomatic Protection Unit is already crawling all over us on this. He'll travel with bodyguards, but as I said, the officers on this force will provide support under my command. Some of you may even be chosen for that… if your marksmanship is up to scratch. So, we'll be having a firearms session for those licensed at 3pm. Consider it an informal trial ahead of official selection. Right. Open your folders to page one. Let's start.'

'One more question, Sarge – will we get paid overtime?'

After the course had finished for the day, Lloyd spent ten prickly minutes in the office of the inspector in charge of personnel. It was clear that Councillor Madoc had extracted his revenge and the word had come down from high to give Lloyd a slap on the wrist. He was left in no doubt that his end-of-year review would not be favourable.

'Hey, someone said that you were about. Pissing off our political masters and all, I heard?' Detective Inspector Danny Collins looked up from his desktop upon seeing his mate standing in the doorway of the CID office.

Lloyd grinned. 'Fancy a pint?'

'You know me, Lloydie-boy, always up for a few cold bevvies on a warm evening. Know just the place as well, they do a great Thai curry in the back room.' He collected his jacket and slung it over his shoulder.

They walked a few streets to Danny's local.

'How's the course going then?'

Lloyd sniffed. 'Okay. Some new stuff, some pretty straightforward.'

'What do you reckon of that Blunt from the Specials then?'

He gave a smile. 'Bit intense, isn't he. Loves his guns as well. You should have seen him on the firing range this afternoon. At one point, I was thinking, Bodie and Doyle.'

'Yeah, he just needs a bloody white Ford Capri, and it would be perfect.' Danny took out his mobile and distractedly checked email. 'You know the story there, don't you?'

'No. What story?'

'They kicked him out of the Manchester mob. He's on probation here until they decide what to do with him. Bet he didn't tell you that.'

Lloyd looked quizzical. 'Now how would you know that?'

'Got a mate on the Merseyside force that's seeing to one of the seccies in Manc HQ. She told him that Blunt had been for interview; they didn't want him but passed him onto us. We're the waiting office while they decide what to do with him… Hang on, here we are.' They walked into the pub and Lloyd ordered the opening round.

'What's wrong with him then?'

'Can't say for certain. But about a month before Blunt and his sovereign ring showed up there was a Specials raid in the Somali district in Manchester. One of the suspects was beaten up in the van back to the nick and made a complaint. Put two and two together.'

'Yes. I could believe that. Believe it quite easily.'

'Just saying, watch him, that's all. A few of the guys took him out for a bevvie when he arrived. Once was enough for them.' Danny took a pull on his bottle of beer. 'So enough about old psycho-knickers, what's this email you sent about these farm thefts then?'

Lloyd unfolded a sheet of paper from his jacket pocket and laid it on the table in front of them. 'Take a look at this spreadsheet. I've sorted it by date, location, and stolen item. About thirty incidents, started off with portable stuff, you know, stuff you could chuck into a van. See here, fertiliser bags, small generators, power tools and the like. But over the past eight months, the thieves have started taking big machinery, towable equipment like ploughs, quad bikes, even tractors.'

'A tractor?'

'Four of them. Now you can't just drive a tractor away without someone noticing, all the farmers know who owns what in the area. And you can't hitch a bailing machine to a pick-up, so I reckon that whoever's behind all this, has a flat-loader lorry to transport this stuff out.'

'Out. You think it's going elsewhere?'

'Stands to reason doesn't it? You can't sell it in the area where it would be recognised, so it would have to be sold in another part of the country where it wouldn't be. They'd have to change plates, maybe repaint the vehicles, all easily done.'

'Makes sense.'

Lloyd continued, 'But I'm thinking, what if it isn't for another part of the country? What if it's being shipped overseas?'

Danny saw that Lloyd's pint glass was empty. 'You've run dry, hold that thought and I'll get another in.' He eased up to the bar, and shortly returned with their drinks. 'Okay. Overseas…'

'Right. I did some research on the internet, and I came across the same thing in a few English counties – Devon, Suffolk, Yorkshire. They had a similar M.O. And guess where the local boys thought it was going?'

'Let me guess. Poland. Romania. Russia.'

Lloyd's face fell. 'You knew…'

The D.I. laughed. 'It's not just your district that's having these thefts, mate. We've logged them all the way up the coast and inland as far as Bala. And the national database has incidences of these farm machinery thefts right across the country like a rash. We spoke to criminal intelligence in London, and they say that there's a pipeline of these goods all the way to Eastern Europe where there's a ready black market. The guy there told me that the insurance companies have kicked a right fuss up about it. There's a task force forming up. We're even thinking about issuing bodycams or webcams to farmers. No shit.'

'Seems I'm a bit behind then.'

His mate shook his head. 'Nah, I wouldn't say that; you worked it out in the end. But what I need you to do now is keep an eye open, look out for odd movements at night, things being stored where they shouldn't be. You know the score.' Danny twisted in his seat to face Lloyd. 'You ever think about applying for CID?'

'Come off it.'

'I'm serious. I know you; I know what you can do. Aren't you bored down in Llanawch? Don't you fancy a change of pace?'

'What, in the glittering metropolis that is Colwyn Bay?'

'It's all relative, mate. Listen, have a think about it. We've got a few slots coming up at year-end. I could put in a word for you with the DCI. What do you think?'

Lloyd shrugged his shoulders. Possibly a change wouldn't be so bad, maybe he could commute in; it was just an hour each way after all. 'Yeah, why not.' He looked around. 'Anyway, the seal is officially broken. Where's the gents?'

'Over there, door behind the bar, on the left.'

Danny studied the sheet of paper as he swigged his drink, not bad work. He glanced up as his mate returned. 'Sorted?'

'All present and correct,' Lloyd replied. 'We've been here before, haven't we? I recognise the bogs. Bloody health hazard they are.'

'Er, yeah, I think a couple of years ago when we had that session. Remember that Cathy Wilmore? You seemed to get on pretty well with her if I remember. Very well indeed.'

'Christ yes. She's not still around, is she?'

'Nah, she went on maternity and never came back. Par for the course.'

Lloyd shrugged. 'Who can blame them? It can be a shit job for a woman.'

'Jesus, when did you become Mr Open University then?'

'What? Don't be daft. I'm just saying that's all. Would you want to be a woman working around twats like Blunt? Old Spice man.'

'Yeah, guess I know what you mean.' Danny paused and emptied the last drops of beer from his bottle. 'Still. Anyhow, you up for a bit of Thai? On me.'

'What's that for? I can pay you know.'

'Nah, just some thanks for your support last year. With my dad passing and that.'

'There's no need for that Danny, anyone would have done the same. We're friends aren't we?'

'Still… let's eat.'

The next morning, Lloyd was sat in the front room of his B&B happily shovelling in a fry-up; a glass of orange juice was at hand to ease his conscience. The morning paper was propped up in front of him on the sauce bottles, he turned the page. Oh God – not again.

Stuck in the Middle (of Nowhere) With You

Frankie Pimlott's witty column only in The Daily Gazette

I re-read Proust several weeks ago and I was struck by how his memories are revived by the simple act of biting into a Madeleine cake. I enjoyed a similar experience last week. I set out from our newly expanded cottages here on the village square to take a constitutional along the harbour front. Once this was a great port for the fishing fleets of the Irish Sea, but now only a few boats remain, and I was able to purchase a – very reasonably priced – lobster straight off the boat (how jealous my friends at *Scotts*, perhaps London's finest fish restaurant, would have been). I cooked it myself, a little organic seasoning from a local farm shop, and served it with the home-made mayonnaise that has, after much practice, recently become the speciality of Chez Pimlott. One bite and a veritable flood of memories – from pretty Norman fishing villages (Proust resurfaces once more as he has a tendency to), to seafood platters consumed overlooking the waterfront at Hoi An in Vietnam.

After eating such delicious fare, I approached the fisherman and we talked about many things, not least our shared passion for my beloved Arsenal FC. But how often from incongruous beginnings stem exciting ideas, and thus we ended our conversation having brainstormed the possibility of opening a shack on the harbour which would prepare and sell his freshly-caught catch – much as they do in New England fishing communities. After all, why should the best produce be placed in an insulating crate and sent away to London and Paris? Sorry, *Scotts*, but surely together, my fisherman friend and I can tempt some of the locals off their addiction to lamb chops! Though despite an invitation, I'm yet to venture out to sea in his boat – and those of you who recall my experience with the aforementioned New England fishermen, for my infamous piece on the author Sebastian Junger several years ago, will know why.

In my next column, I'll write more about my plans to nurture a "Social Enterprise Centre" which can help villagers to run sustainable businesses. By a stroke of fortune, the perfect premises for such a centre may just have become available through the closure of a local school. From the ashes arises a phoenix. I feel so strongly about empowering people through such enterprise, and in my way, I suggest that I am creating my own *perfect storm* right here in this pretty-as-a-picture Welsh village. Until the next time, "Dai awn diolch"!

As if triggered by his newly churning stomach, Lloyd's mobile rang. It was Roy, his constable.

'Hello. I'm eating breakfast. What's up?'

'Er, Lloyd. Sorry to disturb you like. But there's a bit of a problem at my end.'

He sighed. 'What kind of problem?'

'Well, more just outside the village really. Um, you know Glanrhyd?'

'Go on.'

'The new people are moving in today. Thing is, a gang of boys have hijacked the removals van. And—'

Lloyd put down the piece of sausage he'd just forked. 'You what?'

'Hijacked. Like taken it over.'

'Well, have you called it in to Dolgellau?'

'That's not all. The van...well they've kind of set fire to it.'

'What! What about the men in the van?'

'Don't know.'

Lloyd started cramming the remainder of his breakfast onto a slice of white bread to make an impromptu sandwich. 'And who did this?'

'Not sure.'

'Haven't you investigated?'

'Not yet. I'm up at the station and just got a call. Anonymous it was… so I thought I'd better call you first.'

'Well get up there and call in a report. I'm on my way.'

Lloyd put the phone in his pocket and folded over the bread before taking a large bite. A thought struck him. He called Roy back. 'Hey, it's me. Tell me now. You have called the fire brigade, haven't you?'

A silence at the other end. 'I'll do it right away.'

Roy – a few months off retirement after thirty-five years patrolling his boyhood village and almost as useful as a work experience student on their first day. Lloyd shook his head and returned to his room to pack. This didn't sound too good. He'd have to get back there sharpish. He sent a text to Danny, settled his bill and started on the drive home.

Twenty

Ruth Pimlott watched from the windows in her front room as Lloyd crossed the village square to the waiting patrol car. Her partner stood at the back of the room. 'What's happening now?'

'Nothing, just the policeman and the other one talking.'

'Should we talk to them about that letter?'

Ruth sighed. 'No. I think that they've probably got more on their plate than a poison pen letter.'

'But it was rather explicit. It was talking about gang rape.'

'Yes Frankie. But of you not me, so I don't think I've got much to be worried about. I'm just the village whore according to the writer and I think that's a rung or two above serial sodomy.'

'I think you should tell him.'

'Who?'

'You know…'

Ruth tensed. 'Why me?'

Frankie aired the suggestion with faux casualness, 'You seem to know him better, that's my observation anyway.'

'If you've got something to say, say it. Otherwise keep your paranoia to yourself. I'm going upstairs to read my book.' Ruth brushed past her partner, noting from the hallway clock that it being after noon she could reasonably have her first gin and tonic of the day. *That was becoming a recent habit.* She shouted back at Frankie, 'And I'd keep a low profile if I was you, I noticed that that big lug from the rugby club giving you a serious eye-up the other day.'

Outside in the square, Lloyd and Roy had a short confab in the Land Rover.

'Right… just to check, the van is on the main road to Glanrhyd. The fire's been extinguished, and you've put warning signs around it.'

Roy nodded, anxious that he hadn't missed something on the checklist.

'Okay. What we'll do now is that I'll drop you back at the station. You hold the fort there. I'll call this in and have a drive around to see if anything is stirring… seems pretty quiet for this time of day, doesn't it.' Lloyd noticed that the pub door was still closed. 'Past opening time as well. Not like Stevie to miss some custom.'

The sergeant looked around the square; a few people milled about at the harbour end, but no one local that he could pick out. After he deposited Roy at the station house, he decided to take a slow patrol of the village. He passed a couple of supermarket delivery vans doing the rounds of the village. A large Spar articulated lorry was unloading a big old order at the shop, it looked like a few people must be clean out of supplies. But few people on the streets. It could just be the drizzle that was keeping them indoors. He picked up his police radio. 'Llanawch mobile calling HQ, Llanawch mobile calling HQ. Come in HQ.'

The speaker crackled, 'Come in Llanawch – we've been wondering where you are. We have someone for you here.' A pause as the microphone was handled over. 'Lloyd, its Danny. Listen, Harlech police have just found four guys in a bunker on the golf course, tied and gagged.'

'Are they okay?'

'Fine really, only a few bruised egos. They're removals men from Maidenhead and they say that a large group ambushed their vehicle just outside Llanawch and kidnapped them. The men were masked. Do you know anything about this?'

'Yes, my deputy called me this morning to tell me that a removals van was on fire. I've only just got back here.'

'Lloyd, shouldn't this have been called in first?'

He slowed down and pulled the car onto the side of the road. 'Yes I know, I know. I just thought that I'd take a look at the situation myself. I told Roy not to report it until I got back here. He called out the fire brigade to deal with the burning van, and I'm now on my way to the scene.'

'Do you need back-up?'

'Let's wait on that. I'll take a look first and assess the situation.'

'Lloyd, call in within thirty minutes, otherwise we'll have to get involved at this end.'

'Okay, will do.'

He replaced the handset and continued on his way. He smelt the trouble before he saw the vehicle's smouldering carcass halfway up a hill, a cascade of damaged furniture strewn down the road, ashes floating on the breeze. On another day he might have noticed the charred painting, the set of chairs with their seatbacks still bound together by canvas straps, but with their legs fractured; the damp cardboard box upended on a mound of smashed china. But it was the smell of burnt rubber which assailed him, the exposed seared ribs of the lorry, the darkened and shattered glass. Bradford memories came quickly at the stink. He parked in front of the incident scene and walked around it, checking for forensics. On the scorched road, someone had sprayed a crude red dragon. For sure there was one clear suspect now – Meic Davies.

Lloyd ran back to his car, slammed the door, rammed it into gear, and took off towards the Davies house. This time he was going to have it out with that boy. It was a three-minute drive, up the rutted gravel driveway and past the large stone barn adjacent to the main residence. But he found no one in. He took a walk around the house and peered in the back windows; hands cupped around his eyes for better visibility. Tried the kitchen door, locked. Not even a toilet window left ajar which could allow him to gain entry. He walked over to the barn and rattled its doors in hope, but they were secured with a large shiny padlock; yellowed newspaper inserts in the slit windows blocked any view into its interior.

What now? Where would that little shit be hanging out? And for that matter, where was everyone? On the way up he'd vaguely clocked that apart from the Spar grocery, many of the shops were closed; it was only now, though, that he processed the information. Lloyd drove back through the village, seeing the closed door and even fewer signs of life than an hour previously. The red doors were noticeable now, more of them, reflecting the sunlight off their freshly glossed surfaces. And then he rolled up to the wooden gate, black and glossy, which marked the entrance to the church. The gate was open, and from its small roof flew a new Welsh flag. Having parked, Lloyd now passed underneath this, and walked through the graveyard, his right hand gripping the baton-top for comfort. The rain had been eagerly soaked up by the now verdant greenery, and Lloyd could hear the leaves shaking off some of the excess rainfall from the vibrations of the birds in their branches. He could also hear a voice – *that voice?* – from within the church. The sergeant stealthily approached its main door with its large cast-iron hinges. He leaned closer to a crack in the door panels to listen to the speaker – and his suspicions were confirmed.

'... so that is where we find ourselves on the plan. Now, we've come a long way together over the past few months. We had a few of these meetings as a community, with a lot of discussion about our village and what we want to achieve here. And I know that some of you were sceptical at first. I know that initially some of you thought that it was futile to fight the system, that our problems weren't going be sorted. But the trouble is, if not us, then who? Because over the next few weeks, however tough things get, we have to remember that we've been abandoned by those who were supposed to help us. Our farms have been systemically closed down by those, like the supermarkets, that wouldn't pay an honest price for the fruits of our hard labour. And what has been planted on those once fertile fields? Wind turbines, that's what. I spoke earlier about the planning application for Glanrhyd which has just been lodged with the council. I'll say it again: eight turbines one hundred metres high, destroying the natural beauty of our land and towering over our fragile little community. And why? Because the new landowner cares about the environment? Of course not. Because they'll make millions in selling energy over the next decade. And guess what? We taxpayers will be paying for it, subsidising their desecration of our land, so they can treat themselves to the latest Aston Martin sports car and luxury villas in the sun. These turbine-magnates aren't entrepreneurs or decent businessmen. They are pirates who pillage our land. And don't you believe for one minute that a petition or a protest march will stop these scumbags – speak to any village in the land, and their rights have been trampled on by money.'

During this speech Lloyd unlocked the door and slipped into the vestibule, where he could view some of the congregation, while being hidden from Meic who appeared to be preaching from the pulpit.

'And while we're talking about money and our community, let's think about the second-homeowners. *These people* can afford far more than any of us, so they push out young families and then leave them vacant fifty weeks of the year. *These people* who have the arrogance to come into our home and tell us how we should live. Tell us that our lives aren't good enough by their fancy London standards, and that *we* are the ones who need to change. The same outsiders who can't be bothered to learn even a few simple words of the language of our community. These are the people who are contributing to the death of the Welsh language and the desecration of the Welsh culture. I won't mention any names. We're above that. But you know who I'm talking about.'

Sion in the audience shouted out a *yeah!* 'And these same parasites, when the crisis came, all scuttled here, carrying the Covid virus with them. But did they care? Did they think about us? No, all they cared about was themselves. They are ones who infected our old doctor and swamped our health services – the services which you all paid for with your taxes, but they all used. Because these people won't even pay local taxes – they use their fancy lawyers to get them out of that. And I'll tell you something else – there hasn't been one word of apology from those people, not one. They just think it is business as usual – but we're the ones who have paid. English scumbags, that's what they are!'

A cheer from parts of the audience went up, but Phillip Harries had taken his to his feet. 'Now that is not on, I won't have it.' He looked around. 'You all know me. I've been working at the cottage hospital in town for nearly fifteen years, and living here, which is a lot longer than you, young man. And I may not be Welsh, but I thought that this was about the good of the village, not some racist crusade…'

Another member of the congregation screeched out, 'Don't you call us racialists, you bloody snob. You're all the same, you English look down on us!' She was joined by a male voice at the back. 'I don't think Dr Harries is with us. I think that it's best for all, if he either clears off, or sits down and shuts up. Or he'll have the rest of us to deal with.'

Meic gestured with his palms held out, fluttering downwards, to calm the people in the church. 'Now, now. We don't want any violence here. And you, Dr Harries, don't take this as some anti-English crusade, or even an anti-incomer vendetta. We are merely opposing those who are taking over our community, whether it's to change the way we live, or to keep us the same, like some folk museum exhibit. But you have to concede that many of these people are indeed English, no?'

Harries' cheeks flushed, as Meic continued, 'Now we're not talking about people like you, who put down roots here and contribute to the area. But you're a man of science, so here's a hard fact for you: 8.7% of homes in this county are now given over to second home-owners. That's this county as a whole, so we can assume that many of those homes are in coastal villages like ours. Outsiders satisfy their own dreams by destroying the dreams of young families in this community who can't now afford to live in their own homeland. So can't you see why we've reached a point of no return here can't you? You get that surely? So Dr Harries, as much as we all respect your work in the community and all that you did with Covid, you still have a decision to make. Are you with us or not?'

Always force the issue, don't give them room to think... Davies smiled benignly as Harries shook his head, and shuffled past his neighbours in the pew. The doctor left to agitated murmurs from the crowd. As he made his way out one of the rugby boys stepped into the pew, causing Lloyd to quickly duck behind the entrance pillar, and waved Harries out with a cheery whisper. 'You can eff-off doc. We don't want to be seeing you around here from now on. Get the message?'

The doctor turned around and gave the youth a dismissive up and down. 'Do pass my regards to your mother. She's booked into the hospital outpatients on Tuesday.' As the medic left Lloyd noted the grimace on his downcast face.

Buoyed by the show, Meic continued his speech. 'A great pity, but some people, and I'm not saying that the doctor is one of those, well they just want things to be the same as they always were. Those are the kind of people who have benefited from the system – who hold the best jobs and lift the ladder up after themselves, who travel the world and forget about where they came from. Some might call them morally corrupt. And speaking of corruption, you know our councillors as well as I do. You know how it works. The planning for those turbines will be rubber-stamped, no doubt in return for a back-hander, or for some pittance of a sponsorship of a sports team in the councillor's ward. The same councillors on the planning committee, as you know, who voted to close our village school and who put our children's futures at risk. Who put the future of this community at risk!'

'Too right! That's the issue here, the school!' Bethan shouted from a middle pew, causing her neighbours to clap.

'Yes, the school is vital. But there's something bigger at stake. We all know that London is always banging on about "subsidising" the rest of the nation – but who steals our water? And who took our coal? We are one of the last colonies of London's empire. And our protest will gain attention; they'll have to think about us at last, fix our problems if only to make us go away. Just look at Scotland, look at the heartlands of Brexit – London was forced to buy them all off in the end. Well, we want a little attention. We want a little slice of the cake. And now is the time to demand it, not ask nicely, but shout for our share!'

More cheers, but just as Meic was about to continue, Bethan's voice once again was heard. 'All this protest, yeah, fine. But what do we actually want out of this? Independence for Wales? I don't care about that, because it's just another political game and we'll never win. But getting our school back – now that is achievable. That is what we should be demanding.'

It didn't pass Meic's notice that a lot of the women applauded her words, their necks craned round to see her. 'Yes and getting the school back will be *one* of our aims, don't you worry. But what I am saying is that all of us have been ignored, bruised and sold out by these people and it is time for us to fight back. And that fight has now begun!'

He dropped down to what he hoped was a measured, more statesmanlike tone. 'By now you'll know that we've had to take some difficult actions this morning. We were left with no choice. We didn't like doing it, but it had to be done. In the past, we've tried sit-ins and peaceful protests – and you've all seen how useless that has been in changing things. We've even had our own national party, Plaid Cymru, in government. And they've done some good work – but they haven't been able to influence the powers that be in Westminster. As a result, we as a community face a slow lingering death. Nothing, no one, has saved us so far. So now is the time for direct action!'

Meic looked at the Reverend Midwinter, sitting on the front pew, the blue light from the stained-glass window bathing his upturned face. 'And in case some of you think otherwise, nobody here is advocating a Northern Irish solution. Nobody wants violence and nobody in this house of God would advocate that.' He raised his arms upwards. 'But enough is enough. Scotland got it right. It's time to look to our future; to preserve our precious language; and to take control of our community. So, all of us together, now need to take a stand. Not just for Wales, but for each other.'

Midwinter gave a small cough as he ruminated over the words – it seemed, to a weak-blooded Englishman such as he, that the much-fabled "Celtic brotherhood" disappeared with the push for Scottish independence, that's if it had existed in the first place. The Scots had been successful, but at the expense of Cardiff and Belfast, certainly to the detriment of places like Newcastle and Sheffield. As the

Vicar recalled, it had been a distinctly un-Christian "we're wealthy and we're leaving" attitude coming out of the SNP campaign. So why Meic should refer to them seemed a trifle disingenuous. But who was he to intervene; if people felt angry enough to shout down a doctor, then what would they do to some priest that many of them barely knew? In any case, Midwinter owed the young man speaking from the pulpit. For the first time in many years, he felt wanted, as if he had a purpose.

Meic continued, 'I feel that the time is coming very close when the plans we've discussed today will need to become real. The days ahead will be difficult, but we need to be strong, and together we can be. But together, we can stand proud and tall and get what we deserve. So I urge each and every one of you to be strong over the coming days. Together Llanawch will fight for a better future!'

A roar of appreciation greeted these final words. Lloyd took a deep breath and stepped into the aisle, facing Meic. The noise died down as row upon row of familiar faces turned to stare at him. It felt like the entire village was on one side, and he was on the opposite. He looked for Catrin but couldn't pick her out. Lloyd didn't know what to do. His knuckles showed white as they gripped the baton handle. At the far end of full church, Meic Davies looked down and greeted him with a sneer. 'Good morning, Sergeant. I hope you enjoyed my little speech; for your benefit I switched into English when they told me that you were outside. I understand that the language classes didn't go that well for you.' That raised a cutting laugh from the front rows.

Lloyd walked down the aisle. Two hundred pairs of eyes followed him silently. 'Sorry Meic, I grew up in a time when learning Welsh was because you wanted to, it was an option, not because you had to climb the career ladder… or to become a politician.'

'Learning Welsh has never been optional – not for any true Welshman. But people like you will never understand that. Your sort actively help the outsiders to destroy our culture. And that is the worst thing any Welshman can do.'

Lloyd came to a halt. He'd noted that Gwyn and his rugby club posse, the only other people apart from him and Meic standing, were grouped at the door to the belltower. Turning back to the pulpit he retorted, 'I've just seen your handiwork on the coast road.'

'Yes, I'm led to understand that a removals van from the Home Counties was intercepted and direct action was taken against it earlier. What a great, great shame. Don't know who could have done it.' The boys all laughed at that, what a chuckle this was.

Having reached the front, Lloyd turned to face the villagers, scanning their faces to see any signs of support. 'I speak to you all – not just Davies and that mob over there. The law has been broken today about a hundred different ways. If anyone here knows anything about this, then it is their duty as law-abiding citizens to report it to the police.' But if he could hear the uncertainty in his own voice, then his audience surely must.

From behind him Meic questioned, 'The police… that's you right?'

'That's right, Davies.' Lloyd hooked his thumbs into his equipment belt.

'Don't think so, Sergeant. Not our law. Not any longer.' Meic surveyed his congregation slowly, and then in a low voice, continued speaking to his adversary's back. 'But there is something you can do for us.'

As he spoke, his cronies moved to take positions around the church, cutting off Lloyd's retreat. 'You've been behaving like a little bit of a turncoat monkey recently, carrying out your monkey business for the Saes. So, my simian friend, we want you to take a message back to your organ grinder. A message from the people of Llanawch – and it is this: we don't want to harm anyone, but we in this community have drawn the line today. No more incomers. No more Londoners, no more English, no more anyone, okay. If they want to come here on holiday, fine. Come and spend money, behave themselves, treat us with respect, then be our guests. But this village is for the villagers. So today we have collectively taken the decision, that no one else will be allowed to move here unless we, the people of this village, consent. And if the council don't like it, they can, to quote one of our fellow residents here just before you entered – *Bog off.*'

Lloyd faced Davies, began to speak, but the younger man roared at him, 'That's all, Sergeant Traitor. Right now, you're not one of us – you're one of *them*. But for your wife's sake, a proper Welsh-speaking local, we'll let you stay on. Well now you have our message – go and give it to your superiors. You are now dismissed.' Meic gestured to two of his men standing by the door. 'Let him out.'

Bar the creaking of the wooden pews as bodyweight shifted on seats, the church was silent. Then the bells rang out, rising into a glorious peel, echoing through the rafters and outwards across the village, across the estuary to the country beyond. Isolated no more, the Reverend Midwinter was finally in his element. Now it was Lloyd who felt alone, and out of place, Lloyd who couldn't think of anything to say. He replaced his cap on his head. 'Don't push it.' *Christ, was that the best he could come up with?*

As he walked out past Meic's goon squad, he heard their leader proclaim, 'And if you didn't know, ladies and gentlemen, that was the law! The English law, that is.' The sniggers which followed Lloyd were acidic.

Twenty-One

Back at the police station, Lloyd sat with Roy as they stared into their mugs of tea, mutual incomprehension reigning. Lloyd had called in a report to headquarters immediately after the church and now they awaited a visit from their commanding officer. Roy repeated his mantra of the last thirty minutes, 'I tell you; I didn't know anything about it… it's a total shock to me as well. Total shock I tell you.' He took a swig from his *World's Number One Grandad* mug.

They heard the sound of a car pull up outside. Roy looked up through the window. 'Its Charlie Melrose from Dolgellau… and he looks on the warpath to me.'

The door swung inwards, and the fair-haired police inspector entered, rat-a-tatting, 'Sergeant Parry, I'm hearing bad things from Colwyn Bay, very bad things. They tell me that there is a crime wave in my own district: kidnappings, arson, citizens taking the law into their own hands. We're talking about Llanawch, I tell the Superintendent, not Sicily. But no, he says, why haven't you reported this to us, Inspector Melrose? What kind of shop are you running in Dolgellau, Melrose? Don't you know what's going on in your own backyard? The Superintendent himself, Parry!'

'Yes, morning sir, but—'

'So let me paraphrase the Superintendent; what kind of shop exactly are you running here?'

Lloyd stood up. 'It's complicated.'

'Of course it is.'

'Okay, well it seems that the villagers have taken it upon themselves to put a ban on any incomers moving here. First I heard of it was this morning.'

'The villagers? The whole village? Don't be ridiculous, man.'

'That's how it seems to me. They were all gathered together, up in the church.'

'Like a public meeting?'

'Kind of.'

'There must be a leader? Someone to talk to? Someone who knows what the *hell* is going on here?'

Lloyd mutely nodded.

They stood in the church graveyard, watching the villagers file past. Outside the doorway where Lloyd had earlier crouched, Meic Davies and the Reverend stood side by side, shaking the hands of all who came out, as if following an uneventful Sunday morning service. Lloyd gratefully noticed a few of the older villagers throwing him small lifelines: a swift glance, one or two thin smiles even. Stevie the barman made the sign of a drink with his hand, but the majority, people whom he'd lived amongst and served for years, wouldn't even meet his eye. *I see, it was like that was it?* As the crowd dwindled, the Inspector straightened up, five foot seven inches of Hereford backbone. 'Stay here Parry, I'm going to have a word with the lad.'

'Sir, before you go, remember that he is a bit volatile. I'd take it easy.'

'Dealt with worse before, Sergeant. He's just a kid.'

Lloyd watched his Inspector stride towards Meic, and added in a low voice, 'And he really doesn't like English policemen.'

Meic turned to face Melrose. In his notebook afterwards Lloyd would write: 'There was an exchange of words which grew in volume, until both parties were shouting at each other. The Vicar began to intervene but Meic Davies ordered him to step back. The Inspector attempted to restrain the suspect by placing his left hand on Davies' right forearm. Davies resisted, shouting, "Fuck off Inspector Morse, we're in charge here." The suspect threw a punch at the Inspector and then forcefully pushed him away. By this time, a crowd of approximately seven to eight youths had gathered and started chanting obscenities. Davies walked away, accompanied by the Vicar. I drove the Inspector back to the station.'

Lloyd stood upright by the driver's window of the Inspector's car.

'This is a disgrace. Why do you think we spend money on these outstations? Do you know how much they cost us? To gather intelligence, to understand what is going on. It is clear to me that you don't have any clue as to what's been happening in your own patch. No wonder we're reconfiguring the service.'

'Reconfiguring, sir?'

'You'll be told in due course. For now, this is not good enough. I'm asking headquarters to send specialist assistance later today. You are to support them as they see fit. Do you understand?'

'Yes sir.'

'In the meantime, while you still have a station, try not to balls anything else up.'

The Inspector drove off. Lloyd wandered back into the station where Roy was waiting. He looked at the untouched pile of admin still in his in-tray.

'Looks like the cavalry is on its way. Best stick the kettle on.'

Twenty-Two

The four officers got out of the squad car and stood on the village square. Lloyd, Roy, a detective constable from Colwyn Bay and leading them, DS Blunt. The latter was, as he phrased it, 'in no mood to take any dicking around by these fucking civilians.'

Reconnoitring the area behind his wraparound sunglasses, Blunt continued, 'What you have here is an agent provocateur, a right troublemaker. Simple solution gentlemen: take out the ringleader and you remove the problem. So you need to visually ID him for me, Sergeant. And when you have, wait for my command, and then we move fast and hard. Evans and I will arrest him. You two control the crowd. We then move as a unit of four back to the car. Evans will drive, you in the back with me, suspect in the middle and deliver him to HQ.'

'I think it might be best if we try and do this with as little force as possible. Everyone seems a little bit hot under the collar today.'

'Sergeant, while I appreciate that your job is community policing and that you probably don't want to rock any boats in your locale, my job is to sort out difficult problems. Right, tell you what, why don't you let me decide how to perform the surgery, and then you can be the nice nurse giving the aftercare and kissing it better. Got it?'

Blunt was sick of dealing with these local beat cops. They were almost as bad as the pen-pushers back in Manchester, the idiots who'd never experienced Moss Side on a Saturday night, but who thought that they had the right to suspend a high-performing officer like him from duties. A year ago, he'd been on the fast track and it was looking like a sure-fire transfer to the Met's anti-terrorist squad, but that was gone after the inquiry into the incident with the Somali bomb-maker. Those bastards had been plotting to kill. In Manchester. The fucking Muslims again. And it could have been anyone who copped it. His parents. The Inquiry Board's kids. Anyone. He just did what any decent copper would have done and gave them a little civics lesson in the back of the police van. They would have had far worse back home in Africa. Yet out of the three of them he was scapegoated, and now here he was propping up these dozy bumpkin plods for penance.

He smoothed his hands on his leather jacket. But today could be his lucky day. He knew that the nationalists were the toerags who'd tried it on with the Royals before, and with this Arab prince coming to Bangor they might again, so collaring one of the morons right now might get him back to Manchester where he should be. And then later, maybe the Met.

'DS?' Lloyd's voice interrupted his thoughts. 'DS, the guy you want is walking towards us right now.'

'Which one?' There were a group of about fifteen guys. Some of them appeared pretty hefty and he wondered whether he might have overplayed his hand. Nah, short sharp shock got them every time, just like the SAS. He'd love to slot some of these twats right now between the eyes. Bang. Bang. Bang. Fucking magic that would be.

'Meic Davies is in the white T-shirt with the red dragon.'

'Right, wait for it. On my command.'

The group sauntered up to the policemen and spread out. The guy identified as Davies spoke. 'What's this, Parry? Some more of your piggy chums?'

Blunt smiled thinly, felt his body loosen up, ready to move fast.

'You see Sergeant Traitor, I thought that I told Inspector Morse that I wasn't interested in talking to little piggies anymore. Didn't he get the message?'

'Meic, I think that you've stepped over the line this time. I'm going to have to ask you to come with us.'

Blunt snapped his head round to stare at Lloyd. The Welsh prat, that's the element of surprise fucked right there! From the corner of his eye, he saw Meic reacting, taking a step back into the gang, they'd need to be quick. 'Right snatch squad – go, go, go!'

Blunt grabbed Meic's right arm and started to force him into a shoulder lock, feeling resistance build after the initial shock. Strong lad. The other Special Branch officer, Evans, made a grab for Meic's left arm. Two on one. 'Start walking him back!' They started to drag Davies out of his gang, some of whom were starting to respond. Blunt could see Lloyd move between him and the crowd, then lost sight of him as a large forearm smothered his face. He felt his sunglasses clawed off. His own shoulders pulled by other arms. 'Fall back to the car,' he shouted at nobody. He could feel Meic's strength wearing him down as he struggled, so he put in another big effort, using his body as a lever to twist Meic off balance. But the lad's weight brought them both down, with Meic underneath. In his peripheral vision he saw Evans being dragged off by some of the lads. Blunt reached behind for the handcuffs on his belt, but felt his own arm being pulled into a lock. To get out of it, he had to release the suspect. A punch flew in and Blunt kicked out into his attacker's groin, feeling his shoe connect.

Meanwhile, Meic had scrambled out from underneath the copper and had risen to his knees. Blunt swivelled around to see Lloyd attempt to reach him but then be driven back into the bus shelter by the weight of three men. Now Blunt himself attempted to get to his feet, but felt a boot going into his stomach; he rolled onto his back and caught a glimpse of Davies standing above him. Another boot went into his kidneys and he groaned with the pain. He heard a shout, 'Meic, that's enough! Meic!' It was Lloyd Parry's voice. The kicking paused. Blunt knew he had two options: to curl up and take the blows or try and scramble away. They wouldn't get Meic now. He rolled off to his right to a patch clear of legs and used the momentum to push himself onto his knees. He saw Meic look at him, threatening further action. Blunt reached into his deep left pocket and pulled out a canister which he pointed at his attacker. 'Want some pepper spray, do you? Want some of this, you fucker?'

Meic eased back, put up his hands and laughed. 'That the best you can do?'

Slowly, still holding the spray out in front of him, Blunt got to his feet. The blows he'd taken were just starting to throb. He felt a trickle of blood down his cheek. The bastard. 'Get back. Go on, fuck off back!'

Meic held his arms out by his side. 'Okay boys, let them go.'

Blunt started moving carefully backwards in the direction of the squad car. His Special Branch colleague got up off the floor, his face showing a few knocks, his shirt torn and hanging out. He pushed through the gang of lads, passive-aggressively standing in his way. He saw Lloyd released from where he had been pinned against a wall. The other local cop was already at the car. Not a fucking scratch on him.

'You've just made a big mistake, sonny.'

'I'm not the one walking away with his tail between his legs,' retorted Meic.

'You've got one big fucking lesson coming your way, pal.'

'We've made our point. Safe journey, oh and er, don't come back soon.' Meic looked him up and down, then walked back through his gang, who were giving the snatch squad the bird, before following their leader.

Blunt waited until they'd disappeared into the pub, and then opened the door of the squad car. He wiped his face as he stood there and, looking over at Lloyd, said, 'You were fucking hopeless. What did I say about going in dead on my command?'

'I warned you to keep it low key, but you wouldn't listen.'

'Fuck you, pal. I'm in command here. What I say, goes. I'm going back to HQ and coming back locked and loaded. No more Mr Fucking Nice Guy.'

'So what are you going to do?'

'None of your fucking business. You've just blown the operation. Now, I don't know whether that was intentional, or just shite police-work, but I'm not taking the risk.' He motioned to his constable to start the car's engine. 'Shame, I thought that you were pretty handy on the range yesterday. But it's my op, my neck, and I'm not taking the chance on you, nor on your comedy sidekick.' He turned to Roy, 'And you're a fucking amateur.'

'Now there's no need to be like that…'

'Oh, fuck off, plod.' Blunt slammed his car door. If he had taken a quick glance in his rear-view mirror, he would have seen Lloyd and Roy standing uneasily, staring at the ground.

'Heard about what's going on in Llanawch up in North Wales? You were looking for a story, get your sweet little arse up there and you'll find one…'

Lexy Donoghue listened once more to the message on her mobile, replaced it in her handbag, gave her mouth a slash of designed-to-devastate lipstick, and stepped into the pub on the square. As her eyes adjusted to the dimmer light, she surveyed the scene. The bar was relatively busy; clumps of people marking out their territory, a number of red rugby tops and ill-fitting jeans in view; the local set looked the same in all these provincial pubs, no matter where. But locals usually meant plenty of potential leads. She always kept an ear open in bars for any interesting snippets of conversation. It was a habit she'd acquired from her editor at one of her early jobs on a regional title, a good journo should never be off-duty. After she'd graduated to being a cub reporter on local politics, she'd even followed councillors after meetings to pubs and bars on the off-chance that they'd drop some inside gossip or scandal into the conversations with their cronies. It'd led to a few stories, and her final exclusive, on the leader of the council visiting a massage parlour notorious for *specialist* activities, had led to a trial at a national in Wapping.

What would her old boss have thought about the business today? The internet had made it easy for her trade; any racist, homophobic or sexist fool sitting at the end of a bar could now showcase his – nearly always *his* – views to millions via Twitter or Facebook. And it all provided Lexy and her colleagues in the media with a constant stream of stories. Even better, the same idiots bought the same papers to read, so perpetuating the cycle. But it wasn't as satisfying as digging out a new story and making it your own.

She looked round for a place to sit down to make some notes, but there was nothing available. On the table nearest the door, a thirty-something guy caught her eye; shoulder-length, streaked-blond hair, weathered tan, blue eyes, but sadly surrounded by a coterie of adoring young women. Lexy marked him down as a bit of a player straight away, indeed, knew the type well. She judged him as an extreme-sports guy, the less death-defying end of the x-sports spectrum that is – probably ran a water sports business. If experience was anything to go by, he'd imagine that he was a true, rugged, individualist – ignoring the reality that he was just another small businessman milking the holiday fantasies of city dwellers. She continued with her fictional exercise: well-worn stories about his youthful travels – the backpacker trail in Asia, and the time he was a surf bum in Australia. Given enough time, the yarns and shoulder-length hair might open the legs of any easily impressed girl on holiday, looking for a small sexual adventure, but would cut no ice with the adult population. Unless they felt really turned on and drunk on ouzo, that was. Lexy thought back to Mr Blond-Mane's counterpart in Greece just two years ago and felt a slight warmth rise in her cheeks. She gave him a knowing smile as he checked her out but headed for the bar and perched on a stool there.

'What you'll be having, then?'

She looked at the barman staring at her. Unshaven, he wore a faded blue polo shirt with a logo of a polo player on the left breast. The pallor of his wispy arms suggested that it had been some time since he'd been near a polo field, if ever.

Lexy smiled. 'White wine.'

'We've a choice – Chardonnay or house white?'

'Hmmm, Chardonnay would be great, thanks.' She continued to scan the room, looking for someone who might have a talkative side, but the barman would be a good place to start; they usually heard all the gossip. 'That would be three pound eighty.'

Though aware she had the right change in her purse, Alex handed over a tenner, and carefully watched him as he hunched over the till, his lips actually moving as he counted her change. He did a double-take as he pulled out some coins, dropping one then two back in before returning to the counter, placing a crumpled five-pound note and the remaining coins in her outstretched palm. 'There you go. We mostly use cards nowadays see.' He turned to look for other customers.

She pulled him back to her. 'So how's business?'

'Oh, you know, not bad like.'

She took a sip of the wine. Awful. 'Very good,' she smiled at him.

He blinked. 'Glad you like it.'

'So, I hear there's been some interesting things happening around here of late.'

Stevie was pleasantly surprised that this woman wanted to continue talking to him. She looked pretty nice, well turned out, not quite his usual league, but you never know, worth a shot like. 'Well, er, yes, a bit of trouble. Things that go bump in the night. You know how it is.' The woman continued to smile at him, nodding. There was a silence, and Stevie wasn't quite sure what else he should say, but after an awkward pause, added, 'Bit more than that though. Mind you, there'll be some trouble brewing if you ask me.'

Lexy played with her hair. 'What kind of trouble? Everything seems *so* quiet.'

Stevie checked that Meic hadn't just come in, and then leaned on the bar opposite the woman. Nice perfume, nice lips. Didn't look like police. He whispered, 'Well, I shouldn't tell tales out of school, but there was this removals van which got arsoned-up at the top of the village.'

'No, really?'

'Oh yes. They tied the moving men up and everything and set fire to it. The van that is.'

'My goodness... anything else?' She ran her finger around the rim of the glass.

Stevie watched her red-nailed finger make its navigation once, twice around the rim. 'Well, not really... but sort of. We've all decided that we're going to stop people moving here. Not on holiday or the like. Some of my best customers are holidaymakers. That's all good. But more like the people who want to buy holiday homes and stuff here.'

Lexy leaned closer, she could smell the beer-coffee bitterness on his breath. 'So how are you going to manage that? You can't stop people from coming... or can you?'

'You wouldn't think so, but we've got a plan to do it.'

'You have a plan? Oh, do tell.'

'Well, I don't have a plan. But I know a man who does.' Stevie stood up and chuckled. 'I guess it won't do any harm. Name's Meic Davies. Lives up the road in Ty'r Barcud Coch. Interesting fella.'

'Tee what?'

'Tea Bar-cud Cor-ch,' he emphasised the pronunciation for the visitor. 'It means Red Kite House.'

'Oh yes, Welsh. Sorry, I should have guessed.' Lexy leaned back and took another sip from her wine, office party standard, and she checked the start of a grimace. 'Thanks. You've been very interesting yourself. Know if this Davies character will be at home now?'

'You can but try. Either there or the church.' The woman hopped off her stool.

'Do you want another? On the house? Free?'

'I'm done, but perhaps another time. What's your name by the way?'

'Stevie.'

'Well Stevie, perhaps I'll be back for another little chat shortly.'

Lexy left the bar, feeling Stevie's longing look on her back, and walked over to a map of the village posted on the side of the bus shelter that she'd seen earlier. Its glass covering was cracked in a couple of places, but not enough that she couldn't make out a route to Meic's house, that's if she got the spelling right. Starting her car, she felt pleased at what could be a sellable story. There was a whiff of something else interesting here, beyond the burning of this lorry; this ban on home buyers from outside, for instance. As a newspaper stringer she had contacts. She'd try the London dailies first, with the no-welcome-in-the-hillsides angle, and the local titles using the Wales-under-siege theme. Probably a couple of columns worth of story, maybe a feature article – and if she got her skates on with Davies then she might be able to catch editorial for the Thursday editions. The gearbox crunched – *Jesus, it was always doing that, only a man would design such an awkward machine* – but this story could have legs, you never quite knew.

❧

At police headquarters in Colwyn Bay, the Deputy Chief Constable fidgeted on his swivel chair, looking across his desk at two of his subordinates, who were in the process of giving him an unwelcome report. As they'd talked, the DCC glanced frequently at his computer screen. Another load of emails had arrived in the course of this briefing: the work never ceased. Maybe if his chief was more interested in management and less interested in appearing on the television, he wouldn't be lumbered with practically running the entire force. Still, another year and the old boy would be retired, and then…

'So, tell me once more. Because I'm finding it hard to believe that this is the same one-horse town where I took my kids to the beach last year.'

Blunt spoke up, 'You wouldn't think it. It's just another crappy little shi… small village. But we've identified an agent provocateur there, and he's stirred it right up.'

'Looks like a nationalist type, sir,' Inspector Melrose interjected.

The DCC nodded slowly. 'Yes, we had some problems with them in West Wales back in the nineties. You think they're Meibion Glyndŵr?'

'The Sons of Glyndŵr? I don't think so. They've been

quiet since devolution. We could pursue some intelligence gathering though. Put the word about.'

Blunt pursed his lips; what did a uniform like Melrose know about criminal intelligence? He spoke slowly and clearly. 'That would be in Special Branch's remit, sir. I can make the arrangements to see if there is a link. But I think that we have a more pressing issue.'

'Which is?'

Which is that we need to grind this Meic Davies bastard into the fucking ground. 'Which is that the law has been flouted and four of your officers attacked by a gang. You will recall the recent Home Office circular, that we are to be active in responding to any civil disturbances as early as possible, particularly since the London unrest. Not to add that this could be seen by my superiors in Manchester as a potential terrorist problem.'

'Terrorism, you really think so?' The DCC frowned, but Blunt saw that he was engaged.

'Potentially sir. The ringleader is a guy called Meic Davies. My team has already run a check. No criminal record, a mature student at Aberystwyth University. He's written quite a bit of nationalist propaganda on the internet. Independence for Wales and the like.'

'That doesn't make him a terrorist. Just go into any student union and you'll hear worse.' The DCC sat up and placed his elbows on the desk.

'Perhaps. But there was one article from a year or so back.' Blunt extracted a printout from the slim folder in his lap and handed it to his superior. 'You can see there, sir, in black and white, that he states that the Principality should consider breaking away from the UK, and that politics may not be the only method by which this is done. He cites Sinn Féin, final paragraph… if you read between the lines.'

The older man finished reading the article and placed it on the desk. 'Yes, yes. People do say silly things from time to time… but I agree that this is potentially concerning. Nevertheless, my main issue here is that we cannot stand for officers being attacked. We enforce the law in the region, and no one takes the law into their own hands on my watch.' He leaned back into his chair. 'Suggestions please.'

Inspector Melrose spoke, a tone of annoyance entering his voice. 'We might have picked up on this earlier, but the local beat officers have been off the ball. I suggest that we reinforce those two officers with a patrol car. All we're doing is bringing forward the time when we'll cover the village via a car anyway. If it all dies down, then we can close the station as planned by the end of the year.'

Blunt snorted. 'Sir, with all due respect, the Inspector's plan doesn't address the problem. At best we have a civil disobedience situation in progress, at worst a terrorist cell emerging, and no way of knowing where this will lead. Another patrol car is not going to solve that. And even if we have more people on station, I would remind you that earlier today, with four officers attempting an arrest, we were outgunned.'

'You mean outnumbered?' Melrose tossed the knife in.

'Outnumbered, right. So my recommendation, having dealt with these situations before, is that we go in hard and fast with the right resources. In other words, we arrest Meic Davies and charge him with as much as we can lay our hands on. Remove him from the equation. We then launch intelligence gathering in the community to see just how far this situation has gone and respond to that as needed. But the most important thing is to act right now with Davies before our authority is completely undermined.' Blunt stared hard at the DCC. 'I don't think we can respond with anything less, otherwise Manchester, and our friends in London, will want to know why.'

The DCC drummed his fingers on the desk; he'd never enjoyed any dealings with Special Branch. They always thought that they ruled the roost and their answer to any problem invariably resulted in depleted contingency budgets. But with the chief's post coming up, he couldn't afford to let anything slip that a future promotions board might query.

'Very well. I agree with your recommendation. What will you need?'

Blunt grinned.

Twenty-Three

The three police vans took a right turn at the Dolgellau roundabout and in convoy drove along the estuary road. The day was failing, the light losing its hold on the day, flickering unsteadily into night. On-board the vans as they swayed through the corners, fifteen officers, led by Blunt, made final preparations for the operation. They were sweating slightly, dressed in what little riot gear they'd been able to cobble together at short notice, given that most of the kit and the officers trained to use it were on duty policing a pre-season football friendly in Wrexham. Some officers just wore their bright yellow raincoats and flat caps. In an ideal world, Blunt thought, he would have liked a few hours more to prepare, to be able to select a harder group of officers, rather than the odds and sods available. But it was important, as he'd told the DCC, that they returned that same day. Call it a show of force, but Davies' thugs would soon get the message not to mess with the police, and more particularly, not to mess with Jason Blunt. He noted a road sign – "Llanawch, 1½". They'd be there in five minutes, another ten minutes to locate the nationalist bastard, then five minutes to arrest, five minutes to extract, tops. Thirty minutes and they'd be passing this point with Meic in custody in the back, heading for a police cell. Blunt patted the small bulge on his right hip, hidden by his leather jacket. Better safe than sorry, that being he was safe and those terrorist scumbags sorry.

Lloyd's day had started badly, and it was ending worse. Breakfast in Colwyn Bay felt like an eternity ago, and bar a few cups of tea and a half-packet of mints he'd found in his glove compartment, he hadn't eaten since. He was looking forward to supper and had just signalled for the left turn up the hill to his home, when he saw the police convoy driving towards him. He slowed down, leaning over the wheel to get a better view. The vans passed him at speed, their lights flashing. This was news to him. He picked up the handset, 'Llanawch mobile calling HQ, Llanawch mobile calling HQ.'

'Go ahead Llanawch mobile.'

They were fast tonight. 'I've just seen three of our units driving into Llanawch, where are they heading for?'

A pause. 'Llanawch mobile, stand by.' Another pause. 'Arrest being made in Llanawch. DS Blunt is officer on scene.'

'What? This is my patch. Nobody told me about this.'

Another pause. 'Duty officer suggests you clock off for night. This is a special operation. Other mobile units will cover you overnight.'

Lloyd lobbed the mic onto the passenger seat, swung the Land Rover round one hundred and eighty, and accelerated after the convoy. 'Bollocks to that boy. Bollocks to you Blunt.'

Meanwhile, the police vans coasted quietly into the village square and to a halt. Blunt wound down the window to listen, all was calm. He could hear some muted chatter and laughter from the pub, but other than that, nothing. Not even a man and a dog. He could hear some duck noise echoing from further up the estuary. 'Okay, let's do it.'

The officers got out of the vans; a couple of the older ones grunted with knee ache as they jumped down. Blunt gestured to one squad. 'Right, you guys check the pub for the target. Rest of you spread out here.' He folded his arms and watched as five of his men clumped across the square and entered the pub, a sudden burst of noise released with the opened door. He heard the sound of a 4x4 behind him, approaching quickly, and a door slamming. That would be the local plod; he'd heard the exchange on the van radio.

Lloyd walked quickly up to Blunt. 'What are you doing?'

Blunt inclined his head, not moving his focus from the pub door. 'Your job for you, son. Search and arrest of the suspect Meic Davies.' He looked at Lloyd. 'You shouldn't even be here. Weren't you just told to bugger off home?'

'This is my patch. You can't come on my patch without telling me.'

'I'm Special Branch, pal. I can do what I sodding well like. Now fuck off.'

They heard the sound of breaking glasses, followed by shouts. The search team hadn't reappeared. Blunt pointed at the nearest constable. 'You. Go and find out what's happening. Quickly.'

The officer jogged towards the open doorway, but halted as he saw his colleagues stumble out, three of them dragging out a thrashing body between them, the fourth giving them cover, swinging his extended baton towards the doorway as he backed out into the square. Some of the group that had been fought that afternoon followed them out, keeping just out of the baton's range, a larger group of pub customers trailing them in turn.

Blunt turned to the rest of his men. 'Start van one, we get Davies in there, and the other two vans will provide cover… the rest of you, follow me!'

He ran towards the arresting officers; the target's face was hidden by a hood. Blunt grabbed the hood and pulled it down. 'Right Davies, you're nicked…'

But the youth in the hoodie wasn't Meic. He let go of the grey fleece material and took a step back. 'You've nicked the wrong man, you stupid fuckers.'

He could make out the fluorescent jackets of the rest of his unit, as they held their flanking positions, but his eyes remained focused on the large crowd standing twenty yards directly to his front. The village was waking from its slumber, and from several directions he heard the sound of car doors being slammed, engines being started, and horns blaring to each other like a flock of sparrows warning of an approaching hawk. Shouts rolled in from the upper streets, soon drowned out by the distinct tone of a larger industrial engine. Blunt sensed an atmospheric change, the crackling light was yielding to evening, yet the air vibrated, humming into life like a power transformer being switched on. The last time he'd had this feeling was the raid in Manchester, the start of his problems.

Then all hell broke loose. Birds scattered from the square's trees.

To his right, a blue Toyota pick-up truck raced into the square, five or six lads leapt out of its open back, and just as Blunt subconsciously registered that they looked like big lads, he noticed that the crowd were walking slowly towards him, the shouts gaining in volume.

'English monkeys!'

'Piggie traitors. Oink, oink!'

'Get out of our village!'

He saw a few of the gang from earlier in the afternoon, faces lodged in his memory, but now they were carrying baseball bats or cuts of timber and had pushed their way to the front of the crowd. Some of Blunt's men turned round to look at him; he realised that they were waiting for orders. 'Deploy batons!' Working with *these* people was like babysitting. Didn't the fuckers get trained, the bloody amateurs. He knew that he had to regain the initiative, but what was the best way?

Then he heard a voice, different in tone to the others, controlled. 'Yes, Mr Jason Blunt, why don't you take your boys and leave.' He turned in the direction of the voice; it was Meic Davies, but how did the bastard know his name?

Meic made eye contact. He smirked. He wrinkled his nose. 'Before anyone gets hurt.'

Blunt didn't take in that the crowd was growing by the minute, he didn't hear the sound of the large diesel engine getting closer, nor feel its accompanying rumble underfoot. He was wrapped up in his duel with Meic, and Lloyd knew it. He pulled at Blunt's arm. 'Don't rise to it. He wants that. We've got to cool the situation down. Take the heat out of it, man.'

'Fuck you, I know my job,' Blunt snarled. 'And it's to take that fucking scrote down.'

He tore his arm from Lloyd's grasp. 'Snatch squad. Snatch squad!' The officers in front of him responded. 'Listen up. See that bastard over there, guy in the light blue top? That's the target. Take him!' The squad looked uncertain.

Lloyd made a last effort. 'Don't be stupid, move your men back before we're surrounded.'

Blunt ignored him. 'Get in there! Do it! Do it! Do it!'

The men moved purposefully towards Meic, all of them waving their batons to keep the pressing crowd back. But Blunt felt something thud against his head, his legs seemed to weaken, and he staggered backwards. He found himself on his knees. Something wet was running into his right eye, so he raised his hand to check, and looking at his red fingertips, found that for the second time in a day he was shedding blood. He wiped them on his jacket. His own blood. The sight of it, coupled with the disgrace of a second defeat, promoted a violent rage within. He looked up. The crowd were screaming, no, not screaming, they were laughing at him. Meic Davies was laughing at him. His men were useless, they hadn't got anywhere near Davies. He saw them try and fend off blows from the baseball bats, from the clubs. Like chocolate cops, melting in the heat. He was the heat. He was Special Branch. Something hit the ground near him and exploded. He rolled away, but the bottle contained wine, not petrol. For some reason, it seemed important to read the script on the label – "Bushman Hills Chardonnay, 2021, Product of Australia". He stood upright and reached inside the right of his jacket.

Lloyd had witnessed the final second of the stone's arc as it homed in on Blunt, but it was too late to shout a warning. He watched as his fellow officer staggered backwards under its impact and fell to his knees. It was Bradford all over again. The crowd… did he see flames, were there machetes around? He knew that he should act, but he couldn't make his limbs move. It was all flooding back. The door being battered in, the spittle upon his face, the madness in the eyes. His shaming helplessness. He turned back to his stricken colleague, who had now regained his feet and was fiddling with his jacket. Then he pulled out something black, glinting, metallic from underneath. No, surely not, a pistol. He saw Blunt point the gun in the air, as if starting a race.

The first shot was a shock, but when some of the crowd didn't respond, the second confirmed the first, imposing a rapid stillness. 'Armed police! Now get back you fuckers!' Blunt started to drop his arm, the pistol's aim falling towards Meic Davies. Lloyd grabbed the arm with both hands and held it up, pointing harmlessly into the air.

'What do you think you're doing? Put it away, for God's sake.'

'Let go, you stupid fucker, I'm in charge here.'

Blunt struggled to wrest his arm free, but Lloyd held firm, before in unison they became aware of the deep shuddering growl of a large diesel engine, now close. They looked at the source of the noise: a tractor, and it was heading towards their police vans.

Blunt's squad didn't need any encouragement; seeing their retreat about to be cut off, they broke lines and scrambled for the vans. The sharper among them headed straight for the van with its engine already running; its once-anticipated cargo of Meic Davies was now directing the movements of the crowd unhindered. The others watched as one van was flipped over on its side by the tractor's raised blade, its windows cracking as it hit the ground. The machine backed off and rotated towards a second van. This had just been started, and with its back doors swinging wildly open, it attempted to escape. The officer inside, more used to manning a front desk, rammed his foot down on the accelerator, but looking up and seeing a small group of women run into his path, sharply swung the steering wheel hard right.

This caused the next casualties of war, as the now out of control police van jump-mounted the low kerb, crashed through the sea fishing shack, smashed the litter bin aside, and skidded to a halt just a yard from the harbour's edge. The driver slammed the gear into reverse and the van drunkenly lurched back over the debris, a piece of hardboard caught in one of its wheel arches. The first police van, police officers sliding over each other inside like freshly caught mackerel, started to move off under a hail of cobbles. Blunt, seeing this, finally freed his arm, shoved Lloyd away and sprinted for the back doors of the second. He looked over his shoulder at the crowd running after him. He turned and brought his weapon to bear just above their heads. This slowed the mob down, causing a slight smile to trace his lips. He walked slowly backwards and started to re-holster the gun, but before he could fully do so, one of the officers grabbed him sharply by his arm to pull him into the van. The gun barrel caught on the lip of the holster and before Blunt knew it, the weapon had fallen to the cobbles, slithering away across them, and he was lying face down on the vehicle's floor as the battered van made an ungainly retreat from the square.

Less than ten minutes had passed from when the police vans had arrived outside the pub, but now the villagers watched as the two vans, their blue lights still going, withdrew along the coast road with their heavy loads. Lloyd turned around. The crowd was slowly dispersing, some back into the bar, others home. Meic and a couple of his gang had entered the upturned police van. No one took any notice of Lloyd. Even a threat or a shaken fist would have been something, but he found himself an irrelevance. Ignored and humiliated. Which was probably what Meic Davies had hoped for all along.

From a darkened window overlooking the square, Ruth watched Lloyd as he stared at the ground for a minute, then with a shake of the head, walk slowly back to his police Land Rover. She saw him check the car for damage and, finding nothing, get into the driver's seat. He sat there for another minute, looking straight ahead, before driving on, picking his way amid the aftermath. She found that her eyes had dampened.

'What's happening now?' Frankie asked from her position, crouched awkwardly behind the far side of the bed. 'What are they up to?'

'Nothing. It's gone quiet.' She let the net curtains fall together.

'So it seems the world will end with a bang *and* then a whimper.'

'You should put that in your blog. Meanwhile, I'm going for a walk.'

'Don't go out there, Ruth, it's dangerous.' Frankie made a weak grab at her arm.

'It's our home as well, isn't it?'

She gabbled, 'But they're not like us, they don't think like us, you don't know these people.'

'No, I suppose I don't. But neither do you.' She examined her partner standing there like a nervous child – but she didn't feel like playing nanny today. Ruth slipped her feet into the nearest pair of flat-soled pumps and padded downstairs. Frankie stayed in the darkened room. She edged closer to the windows to see in which direction her wife was going to walk, while trying to remain in the shadows.

Ruth heard a small voice from above. 'Have we got enough food in?'

She looked at the hallway mirror, then closed the front door behind her and quietly followed the shadow line of buildings out of the square. The mob didn't frighten her, but then again there was no need to draw attention to herself.

Twenty-Four

Lloyd parked outside the station and rested his forehead on the steering wheel. With a drawn-out sigh, he got out of the car and entered the police station, bolting the door behind him. He pulled the blinds down over the front window and slumped in his chair, wondering what would come next. After a minute, he fired up the police network radio and listened in to the chatter about the aborted arrest. The desk telephone rang, which he left unanswered, instead turning to the sheaf of paperwork resting in his in-tray. Parry leafed through it looking for a document that he remembered from about a month back... ah... yes here it was: *Consultation on the Reconfiguration of Physical Locations – North Wales Police.* He scanned down the bullet points on the summary page, which set out the plan to consolidate policing into district hubs, including a list of potential police outstation closures, noting Llanawch, and concluded with – *Potentially affected officers should lodge any concerns by 5pm, 15th July*. Ah.

So that's what Inspector Melrose had been talking about. But Lloyd had missed his chance; he'd been too lazy to read the document, assuming it was just more admin he could ignore. The deadline had passed, and he cursed his own slipshod ways, which would suit the hatchet men in human resources at headquarters. Catrin would go ballistic when she found out, and there was little chance that she'd agree to move away because of his job. She wouldn't see that he'd been shafted by his own colleagues. He could picture the conversation now, likely she'd bring it back to the kids, the grandchild on the way and how Lloyd was letting them all down. He picked up his mobile to call home but paused and then slowly replaced it on the desk.

What about calling headquarters? He looked at the landline sitting there expectantly. But no. Sod them. Sod them all. What he really needed was a drink, but the pub would be out of the question tonight.

His uniform shirt was soaked in sweat, so he yanked off his tie and used the sink in the toilet to throw some cooling water over his face. Through the open top window he could hear the random drone of engines drift up from the village. Best not to think what was going on down there. Lloyd padded his face dry and looked at himself in the mirror, noting the redness in his cheeks and the dark rings under his eyes. What he really needed was to stop being such a soft bastard, curled up in his own shell and afraid of the world.

He stood in front of the mirror for a few more seconds and made eye contact. Then he threw down the towel.

Right, nothing more to be done here tonight, the village obviously didn't need him. It was time to go home and get something to eat and tomorrow would be another day. Lloyd switched off all the station lights, including the blue lamp, and locked the door behind him. He took a quick look around the station's perimeter before setting off for home. The heat of the day was subsiding as it dissipated from the road surface into the starlit night.

It occurred to him that the more he tried to change, the more he undermined his existing life. But that didn't mean he should stop trying, though. He knew that he'd given up on his ambitions too easily, had let the shock of Bradford overwhelm him and hadn't fought it. So if they were going to close down the station, then so what – the enforced change would help to kick his backside into gear. It might be just what he needed. He could apply for a transfer to detective work, as Danny had suggested the previous day. He certainly had enough experience under his belt, and he'd passed the exams for it back in Yorkshire. That result might still count for something; he'd done it once and could do it again, he'd just need to get his head down. If it hadn't been for Bradford, he might have made D.I. by now. Sure, he'd have to work out of the towns – Caernarfon, Bangor, Holyhead – but the distance shouldn't be a problem. Just anything but an area car out of Dolgellau, the same old beat, the same old faces, serving a community that as events had made plain, didn't have an ounce of respect for him. He wouldn't miss having to clear up their mess either.

With a new-found bounce in his stride, Lloyd cut diagonally across a front lawn, skirting the gnomes on fish duty around an algae-ridden pond, and onto the next street. The law didn't seem to apply in the village tonight, so why should he stick to it? Lots of freshly painted red doors on this street. He mulled over these doors, his walking pace slowing to a dead stop. *So that was it.* It had taken him a while to cotton on, but finally he realised the link between the house names and the colour of the door: those with a red door had Welsh names, those without were mostly holiday homes.

He resumed his journey and passed the light blue door of the next house, *Care Less*, seeing that a red line had been painted through the nameplate. The old name for the house had been *Ty Glas*, but it had been renamed by its new English owner. At the time, even Lloyd had thought it a bit of a provocative gesture, having seen the guy tutting at Welsh being spoken in the local Spar – 'they do it just to annoy us, why should I bother to learn their dead language, sounds like someone having a stroke, I spend good money at this shop, so speak with me in a proper language'. He'd sat – bored shitless as he recalled – at the back during the village council meeting last November where agitated discussion about the name-change had dominated the agenda. Meic had been there as well, and vocal. The outcome of that waste of time had been an impotent letter sent to County Hall asking for an official review into maintaining traditional house names in the region. County Hall would doubtless need to confer first with Cardiff. And Cardiff would need to check with London. Whether London would then need to seek permission from Washington was unclear. But Lloyd saw now that there'd been all these little signals that he'd missed – he berated himself and Meic Davies in the same breath. All right sunshine, have it your way, burn the bloody place to the ground and see where it gets you.

The family home loomed ahead, its curtains undrawn and the lights off. In the hallway he removed his boots in case he'd picked up some muck from the square. He walked through to the kitchen and turned the light on – no one there.

'Catrin?' No response.

'Arwel?' All he could hear was the hum of the fridge. He opened the door, pulled out a hunk of cheese and some cherry tomatoes. He began to make himself a doorstep sandwich to fill the gap before his wife returned and could make him a proper supper.

As he munched through it, he was aware of the stillness of his home. Unlike her not to be home. He wondered, for the first time that evening, whether she had been caught up in the village disruption earlier on… that was probably it. Lloyd picked up his mobile, scanned through the missed calls register to see if she had tried to contact him… no, just Melrose. Which was odd because she would normally be on his case for being late. He dialled her mobile. It rang and went through to voicemail. He dialled again.

Catrin answered at the third ring. 'Lloyd.'

'Hi, I've just got home. You're not here.'

'No Lloyd, I'm not.'

'Well, where are you?'

'I'm over at Julie's. I'm staying overnight.'

He paused. 'Why's that?' And then optimistically, 'Julie, um, unwell, is she?'

'No Lloyd. I think you know why I'm here.'

'Well, er…'

'Don't try to lie, Lloyd, let's be grown-up about this.'

He mumbled, 'Okay.'

'A little birdie told me something today, something that I already sort of knew. You've been seen.'

Lloyd got up from his seat, walked into the hallway and up the stairs. 'I see.'

'It's not the first time I had to find out about these *goings-on*, but I've chosen to ignore it before now.'

He didn't say anything.

'And your silence now has just told me that I wasn't wrong.'

'I don't want to hurt you, or the kids.'

At the other end of the line, he could hear Catrin's voice catch. 'It's too late for that. You've broken my heart, Lloyd. You broke it a long time ago, and every time it comes close to mending, you break it again. You just never learn, do you? You're just like a bad little boy. But the charm has worn off of late.'

He had reached the doors to her wardrobe in their bedroom. 'Perhaps we should sleep on it. Talk in the morning?'

'No, I'm not staying around here. This is what I'm going to do. I'm going away to my sister's for a few days to have a think and Arwel is coming with me. We'll be back in time for his A-level results next week.'

He opened the wardrobe doors, noting the gap on the top shelf where a suitcase should have been. 'So you've packed.'

'I don't want you contacting me, Lloyd. I need some time on my own to decide what to do. Do you understand?'

'Yes, I think I do.' He felt relieved. He just couldn't face a big scene tonight.

'Our children have left the home now. There's no need for us to stay together if this is going to keep happening. If you're going to treat our marriage like a joke. I'm not going to hang around to cook your dinner while you have your… your affairs!'

'You're not serious.'

A new tone came into her voice. 'I'm deadly serious, Lloyd. You've made a right fool out of me and in my home village to boot, the place where I grew up. Someone else had to tell me and I bet you everyone knows about it. About you and that English slut. The fool that you've made me look.' She was building a head of steam. 'And I'll tell you something for nothing, buster. I won't have it. Over my dead body you're going to treat us this way.'

'Catrin, listen to me. I'm really sorry. I can't tell you how sorry I am.'

There was silence at the other end of the line. 'We're all sorry, Lloyd. But only one of us should feel guilty.'

He swallowed. 'I know, I know.'

'Just leave us be for the moment. Don't try to call me or come around. I can't cope with anything else.'

Lloyd stumbled over a response, but the line had gone dead.

He closed the doors to her wardrobe and walked numbly to Arwel's room. Lloyd sat on his son's bed and gazed at the scattering of posters on the wall: a David Hockney exhibition poster from that trip to London, Gwenno, and Roger Federer. In a way, they seemed reassuringly alien to him. He thought back to the decoration on his own teenage bedroom walls: Sam Fox in a one-piece swimsuit, the Terminator, and a Leeds United official pre-season team line-up.

Of course, the boys wouldn't like this business, and he'd expect them to give him a rough ride, but then they'd always been their mother's children, even Hywel. There had been times when he wondered whether they'd actually come from his own loins. He was five foot ten, but they both were over six foot – even young Arwel had surpassed him during the course of the sixth form. They looked much healthier than he ever had at that age. Then again, they grew up in fresh sea air, rather than the justice downwind of Port Talbot steelworks and his dad's chain smoking. They'd eaten much better, no beans and corned beef on a Sunday for those lads, and all those vitamins that Catrin had obsessively poured into them since birth must have helped. Lloyd patted the pillow. He hoped that they'd forgive him. But he sensed that would be down to him; it wouldn't come naturally.

As he returned to the kitchen to find a beer, he saw an unsettling vision of how it could end: him sitting in a clock-ticking parlour alone, pulling his regrets apart. He'd been a selfish bastard, but what was the alternative? That voice inside his head which told him he needed to get out had become too strong to suppress. It felt like this need, where he had to make something happen today and not wait for some future which might never happen, which was really driving him away from Catrin.

His beer quickly polished off, Lloyd dimmed the kitchen lights and once again climbed the stairs. He turned right on the landing for the spare room. As he lay back on the bed a thought struck him. All this in one day – the fighting, the job, the thing with Catrin – should mean he was totally up shit creek. But yet he was still here.

He was still alive.

A few streets away, Ruth knocked on the door of the empty police station. After she'd watched the scene playing out on the square earlier, she'd felt compelled to seek out Lloyd, to find out if he was okay. To her eye, he'd appeared out of sorts on the square, a little lost. After looking around to check for any unwelcome onlookers, she wrote a short note on a tissue she'd found in her pocket using an eyebrow pencil, being careful not to rip the thin paper, and pushed it through the station's letterbox. Ruth turned to make her way home, then halted and frowned as she realised that Lloyd might take it for rubbish and throw it away without seeing the writing. Or, she pondered, the other policeman might read it before Lloyd got there. Jesus, how hard did all this have to be? She found an old receipt in her other pocket and scribbled 'The note on the tissue is for Sgt Parry's eyes only.' She pushed the second note through the letterbox. That hopefully would do it.

Twenty-Five

It was eight-thirty in the morning at police headquarters in Colwyn Bay. The sun was climbing outside, but the air conditioning in the conference room could only add to an already chilly atmosphere. The Deputy Chief Constable sat at the table with an array of officers who waited on his first words to see where the meeting would head.

'So, what's the status at the moment?'

Superintendent 'Lew' Lewlowicz ran a gentle hand through his receding blond hair and glanced once more at the sheet of paper in front of him. He wished that he hadn't agreed to cover his colleague for a family wedding, because now he was lumbered with this little lot. 'We haven't attempted to re-enter the village since yesterday evening. We have cars posted a mile or so from the village boundary on both exit roads, and we're turning back traffic.'

The Chief nodded. 'Injuries to officers?'

An inspector piped up from the end of the table, 'Just a few minor cuts and bruises. One of the constables has been signed off for a few days – his existing back injury flared up during the scuffle.'

'Very convenient. What about our people in the village? What have we got there?'

'Just a sergeant – Parry – and a part-time constable. Not our finest officers to be sure, a pretty pedestrian pair. We were unable to make contact overnight via the radio. We also tried Sergeant Parry's mobile and home numbers. Both rang but were unanswered.' Inspector Melrose pursed his lips.

'I read the Special Branch report about yesterday's operation. This Sergeant Parry – is he reliable?' The DCC looked around the room for witnesses. 'Because it appears from where I'm sitting that he's lost grip on the situation.'

Melrose was blunt. 'From what I personally saw, I wasn't impressed by his handling of the lead suspect in the matter. It was obvious to me that this problem has been festering for a while, yet the first we hear of it has been just in the last few days.'

The comment hung for a moment. 'So we should write him off?'

Inspector Melrose was about to speak again, when Danny Collins interrupted, 'No, I wouldn't say that we should do that. He's a good officer and knows his duty. It seems to me that—'

Melrose started to speak over him. 'Sir, the Detective Inspector here does not have direct line management of the officer in question. I do.'

Danny looked at the DCC. 'May I be given a chance to finish, sir?'

His superior officer nodded.

'It seems to me that right now we need all the local intelligence we can gather, and Lloyd Parry can give us that. You have the report from Special Branch, but I talked to a few of the officers involved. I think that if anyone lost control of the situation it was Sergeant Blunt. It appears like there was a serious lack of planning in last night's op and a fair amount of… ah, inappropriate force.'

'Thank-you for your views, Collins. But the last thing we need today is finger-pointing. That goes for you as well, Melrose.' The DCC rubbed his chin and looked in the direction of the Superintendent. 'Lew, what I'd also like to know is how in God's name did Blunt get hold of a firearm? It wasn't even signed out.'

'No sir, it appears that er, in this case, there was some laxity in the firearms control process.'

'You can say that again. We've let things get too slack.' He tapped his fingers on the edge of the desk. 'How many bullets did he discharge?'

'Between three and four, sir.'

'Well, is it three or is it four? We have to be accurate, think of the inquiry Yes, gentlemen, you can count on one of those coming down the track, no question about that. And where is this firearm now?'

The room tensed. 'It seems that the weapon was lost in the course of the operation.'

'That's what I heard. To summarise, we have a police firearm signed out illegally, discharged at civilians, then lost in the village, and in unknown hands? A lethal weapon. Would I be right? Don't bother to answer that.'

The DCC pulled himself up in his chair. 'Well, this is perfect, isn't it? That we have an outbreak of civil disobedience is bad enough, that we don't even know what's behind it. But it also appears that we have no proper control over access to firearms, right here in this station.' The DCC slammed his forefinger repeatedly on the tabletop. 'And now we have a police handgun in potentially hostile hands. Good God, what is going on here? How is this going to look when word gets out? What about our annual performance measures? We'll be a laughing-stock. No one in this room is going to come out of this pile of manure smelling of roses. It's your careers on the line as well, think on that!'

There was a small cough from the press liaison manager, followed by a louder one when no one responded to its predecessor. 'Um, excuse me for interrupting, but I believe that word is already out. It appears that a video was posted on YouTube overnight. It shows smartphone footage from the disturbance.'

All eyes were on the DCC who uttered a sigh. 'Tell me it can't get worse.'

'You can hear the shots going off, and see our vans exiting the scene. It is quite vivid actually, pretty good composition for an amateur. Um, I can forward you all the link if you want,' the press manager finished weakly.

The DCC threw her a sharp look. 'But this doesn't mean that it's widespread knowledge. We could get the Home Office to force them to pull the video, couldn't we?'

The press manager looked at her intertwined fingers resting on the tabletop. 'Just one or two things, sir. It's YouTube so it will be difficult to force them into removing the posting quick enough.'

'And the second?'

'Um, it may be too late. It's going viral.' She refreshed the page on her phone. 'It's hit several hundred more views just since we've been sitting here – they must be distributing the link all over the web.'

The DCC pictured his chance of promotion the following summer rapidly diminishing unless he took decisive action. 'Very well. We are unofficially buggered. But officially, our aim now is to regain control of the village and enforce Her Majesty's law. We can deal with the consequences later. But be in no doubt, ladies and gentlemen, that heads will roll over this shambles.' He closed his file and stood up. 'I'm now going to brief the Chief Constable and the Police & Crime Commissioner on the situation and our response plan. Lew, I want you to put together a large squad ready to handle hostile public disorder. Full riot kit, shields, long batons. No skimping on kit or boots on the ground, call in our best guys – I'll authorise overtime as appropriate.'

'Anything else, sir?'

'Leave the paperwork on the missing weapon to me for the moment. We ah, may be able to recover it relatively quickly.'

'Understood.'

'Be ready to move within two hours. You should also have a tactical firearms unit in attendance. Oh, and Lew…'

'Yes sir?'

'Keep Special Branch out of it, especially that fool Blunt. This is our turf, and we can handle it ourselves.'

Around the same time as the meeting ended, Lloyd was approaching his station house. It had been another lousy, disturbed night for him. He'd woken-up in the early hours sweating again, but this time the nightmare had changed. As usual he was in the police van in Bradford, watching the mob then tracing the arc of the firebomb as it zeroed in on them. But this time, no one else escaped, the flames enveloped the van, ripping through its walls to the terrified souls inside. Lloyd was the only one to get out, running down the terraced street, yet now the flames leapt in his wake, chasing him down. The faster he ran the quicker they swept towards him, until he launched himself down an alleyway which had never been present before. And at this point, the city was gone and now he saw a lane from his childhood, dead-ended with the same garage wall against which as a kid he'd endlessly kicked a ball. But there was no football to be seen in this fresh night-terror landscape. In his dream, Lloyd halted and turned around, to see the flames deliberate and menacing, as they began to encircle him, carefully, hypnotically, until he could see into the heart of the firestorm. The intensity of the heat upon his face forced him to step back, only for the wall to have vanished, and in its place is a flight of steps, leading down to a river far below. But Lloyd lost balance and tumbled down… which is when he awoke with a start.

He'd drunk a solitary cup of tea afterwards in his kitchen, reflecting on the visions. Then after listening to *Farming Today* on the radio, he'd flopped back to bed for another sleepless hour. And now, back on the job – there was an A4 piece of paper nailed to the door of the station. He peered at it.

TO AN ENEMY OF THE PEOPLE

You – Sergeant Lloyd Parry of the occupying English Stasi – are accused of betraying the people of Wales.

You enforce the English empire's laws and act against the interests of what was once your own blood and flesh. You help displace true-born Welsh men, women and children from their own homes. You protect those who steal our lands and natural resources. You collaborate with their agents and support their illegal oppression of Welsh people.

So-called Welshmen like you believe you're the voice of realism, but all you desire is the continuation of the handful of privileges that your English rulers allow you like a dog thrown a bone by its master. These rewards are taken on the backs of the hard toil, the sweat and the freedom of the Welsh nation. But the day of independence is coming when united as one we will throw off the shackles of London's dead hand. History is on our side.

You are a traitor and stand accused by the community in which you practise your abhorrent deeds. As your first punishment we choose to send you into exile. Unless you change your ways, more punishments will follow.

Signed,

The United People of Llanawch.

For the first time in a day, Lloyd laughed – what was this, the bloody French revolution or something? How up its own arse. And this independence talk? Lloyd didn't necessarily agree with it, but if that's what people wanted then fine. But there'd be a price and it seemed that Meic was telling the people that they could have it both ways. That was just plain wrong, and Davies could stuff his rabble-rousing *legal documents* right up his arse. Good God, he was just a police officer trying to do his job, not some Nazi overlord. The sergeant took a photo of the notice with his mobile before removing it.

After unlocking the front door, he gingerly checked the letterbox. Nothing, not even the dog excrement he'd half-anticipated, just a tissue and an old receipt. He studied the words inscribed on the tissue, then carefully folded it and placed it in the top pocket of his tunic. He picked up the phone and dialled his deputy's number.

'Roy… yes, I'm at the station. I need you on duty here… no, avoid the square. Just plain clothes for you today…Yes, I'm calling them now.'

He glanced at the kettle before switching on the radio. He picked up the handset. 'This is Llanawch Station checking in for instructions.'

'We read you Llanawch. Stand by please.'

Lloyd stood up and looked over the front desk through the window. Just one of Meic's mob standing on the far side of the road fiddling with their phone. No surprise there, he'd imagined that they'd keep tabs on him. That's what he would have done in their shoes.

'Lloyd, it's Danny here.'

'Morning Danny.'

'Where the hell have you been? We've been trying to contact you.'

'Well, I'm here now, aren't I. What's happening at your end?'

'You should prepare for the heavy mob down there by eleven-thirty. The cavalry is on its way.'

'I think we need to play this one cool, Danny. I'm going to email you a photo of a letter I found nailed to the station door this morning. Just sending it now, check your inbox… got it?'

'Hang on… yep. Give me a sec…' Collins scanned the photo. 'Looks like a nationalist job.'

'Yeah, your guys would be pouring petrol on a fire here. You've got to tell them, don't stir it up. This needs a softer touch.'

'It's a bit late for that. Those are the orders and straight from the top.'

Lloyd grimaced. 'Right. Do you want me to form a reception party?'

'Affirmative. Meet them on the Dolgellau Road by… er, Henllan Reach. You know that place? Make sense to you?'

'Yes. I've got it. Do you need me to scout around, get back to you?'

'Yep, affirmative. Any update you can give us would be seen as helpful, if you know what I mean.'

'Oh yes. Danny, one thing… tell me, am I being led to the scaffold?'

His friend considered this for a moment. 'You're on the way, but I'm sure people will forget about it if things turn out okay. I suggest you look sharp today; that won't harm your case – there are a lot of people counting on you.'

'Wilco – Sergeant Lloyd Parry signing off.'

There was a knock on the front door. Lloyd unlocked it to see his deputy looking even more sheepish than usual.

'Sorry Lloydie, that I didn't come and help out last night.'

'Don't worry about it. It's what we do now that counts.'

Roy, in mufti shirt and jeans, looked the boss up and down. 'Bit hot for a full tunic today, isn't it?'

'Ah, I thought it worth dressing up as it's a special occasion, see.' He gave the other man a wink. 'Now I'm going to take a drive around, find out what all that noise last night was about. You stay here and man the station.

And lock the door behind me. They may try a raid and I don't want any of this kit getting ransacked. Let's not make it easy for them, eh?'

The other man looked uncertain. 'Right-oh then. All a bit nasty this.'

Lloyd paused at the door. 'It is. One last thing, Roy – if they do come for the station and get in, don't resist, just leave it and go home. You're too close to retirement. That's my orders now. Understand?'

'Sure thing. Thanks Lloyd.'

'Don't worry – it will turn out okay.' And with that, he was gone.

Staying in second gear, Lloyd motored down to the village square, checking for any new signs of disturbance. There was a smattering of people about, but no one interfered with him. No one said hello either, but whether that was down to Catrin or to Meic who could tell. He parked next to the crumpled police van and crouched by the shattered windscreen to examine the interior. Someone had gone to town on the instrument panel, it was totally smashed, with the wiring ripped apart. The roof of the van, now lying on its side sported a red spray-painted 'Cymru am Byth'. He stood up and looked at the open doors of his local, which had a crude red cross sprayed onto white cloth and hung over the pub's railings. His eyes quickly skimmed over to the Pimlotts' home. One of the net curtains parted to show Ruth's face. Lloyd waved a quick hand and smiled with what he hoped was nonchalance – he received a smile in return. He'd have to sit down and have a long talk with her after all this was over. The Sergeant walked over and held the red cross sign in his hand. It reminded him of the treatment tent that they'd put up outside the health centre during Covid.

Back in his Land Rover, he tapped the steering wheel as he considered his next move. Setting the car into gear, he headed for the estuary road towards Dolgellau to meet the reinforcements. He followed the same route as the two police vans had taken the previous evening, up the harbour road, slowing past the kink in the street by the shops and on past the estate with its terraces of retirement bungalows. Through the car's open window, he could smell the heat of the grass stubble in the fields as it baked to straw. Coming up was Heywood's estuary-side residence and it was here by its gates that Lloyd pulled up sharply. Some seventy yards beyond the broad expanse of the retired judge's front lawn, a barricade had been thrown across the main road. Work was still ongoing, with a tractor bearing a tree trunk clutched between its mechanical jaws, dropping the load onto a barrier of earth, rock and timber, already around five feet high. It was a well-chosen spot; on the left-hand side of the road was a cliff about ten metres high where the road had been blasted through a few decades back in order to widen it. On the right was a narrow verge braided with the grooves of wheel churls. It framed the estuary's shoreline; you wouldn't be able to get a car through the space without it sliding down into the water.

A battered old Toyota pick-up was parked nearby and Meic Davies stood talking to a group of around forty people, occasionally pointing to a map spread out on the open tailgate. Some of the group carried pickaxe handles or bats and Lloyd made out a small pile of rubber dustbin lids nearby. Another man perched on the cab of the pick-up, looking through binoculars up the coast road.

Lloyd reversed his vehicle back into Heywood's driveway, from where he could just see Meic's position through the boundary trees. He picked up his handset. 'This is Llanawch mobile calling. Come in please.'

'We read you Llanawch mobile. What is your status?'

'I'm on the approach road but cannot make the rendezvous.'

'State your reasons, Llanawch mobile.'

'There is a large barricade blocking the road and a significant number of... rioters, people, whatever, manning it... do you copy me? Over.'

'Affirmative, we copy. How many civilians?'

'Ah, twenty plus, maybe more. Over.'

'Duty Superintendent asks whether there is any sign of firearms.'

'Negative. I can't see everything from my position. I'm observing them from some distance away. Do you want me to make contact? Over.' Lloyd noticed Meic Davies look up and scan around until he was looking directly at him.

'Negative Llanawch mobile. Stay back. Expect support as planned at eleven-thirty hours.'

'Wilco. I think that I've just been spotted. Llanawch mobile, over and out.'

There was a tap on his window. Startled, Lloyd turned around and saw that it was the Judge.

'I presume that you've taken note of all this, Sergeant?'

'Yes. You okay, had any bother? Assuming that you didn't know about this.'

'Yes, I suspected something might be in train, but not this

as such. No, I've been left alone, barring a nasty little note posted through my door this morning, telling me to mind my own business. Who would have thought that I was born in this village? More seriously they kept me awake all night long while they constructed this damn thing. Can you believe it?'

Lloyd stepped out of the car. 'Yeah, I could hear them on the other side of the town as well. Looks like they're expecting trouble.'

'So, are they going to get it?'

'Riot squad's on the way. HQ have taken over. But keep that to yourself.'

'I see. Seems what I would have expected.' Heywood rubbed his chin. 'Of course, one wonders what this Meic Davies character hopes to achieve in practical terms.'

'Perhaps he's up for a bit of trouble, likes aggro maybe. Like those weekend football yobs – software sales manager during the week, knife-wielding thug at weekends.'

'Oh, do come on, Sergeant, don't try and underplay it with me. Just a yob? With most of the village behind him? This looks rather too well-planned to my mind to be a spur of the moment occasion. I don't underestimate him; Davies has always struck me as an intelligent man, but I doubt that he could pull this off alone. My instinct is that there's something or someone else at play here.'

Lloyd nodded. 'Well, we'll know soon enough. Here we are now then.'

They watched a line of around ten police vans slowly approach the barricades, drawing to a halt a short distance before it. The vans disgorged a large squad of helmeted riot officers.

'Judge, do you mind my staying here for the moment? I just want to keep a closer eye on things.'

Twenty-Six

Lloyd jogged to the end of the drive, feeling his belly wobble as he did and, coming to a halt at the wrought-iron gates, watched Meic Davies direct the other villagers as they manned the barricade. The younger protestors looked burnished by the sun, a far cry from their pallid winter versions, and sported facemasks, goggles and red construction helmets. The sergeant nodded in appreciation; someone had obviously been studying some of the other protests around the world. Again, lots of rugby shirts in evidence and other red clothing – bandanas, T-shirts. Most of all it felt like the people were moving with purpose, they seemed to hold themselves better, less of the pork chops about them. If last night seemed like a scramble, this barricade, the gear and the preparations made it look a lot more professional, much in line with the Judge's comments.

Meic would also have agreed with the conclusion – he'd shelled out quite a bit of cash to buy in the protective equipment, carefully placing lots of small orders so as not to raise the suspicions of anyone monitoring such purchases. Unaware of the attention from his nemesis, Meic went about his business, making a short call on his mobile before clambering onto the back of the pick-up truck in order to gain a better view of the scene. Arrayed in front of him the police had formed into several lines spanning the width of the road, with the front line positioning behind full-length riot shields. It wouldn't be long now. He called over to one of his lieutenants, 'Phil, have a check for any tattoos which are showing on the guys – forearms, neck, whatever and get them covered up.'

'Eh? Why's that?'

'The pigs will be taking video footage and tattoos can be used to identify people in court afterwards… if it comes to that.'

'Oh right, makes sense.' Phil headed over to the barricade.

Meic looked down at Sion, who had been hanging around the truck all morning like a useless part. 'And you, are the webcams set up?'

'Yeah, we've just started broadcasting live on our own sites and via Wikileaks.'

Good, between Wiki and the clone sites, any censorship would be slowed down long enough for others to see – hopefully they'd get picked up by other overseas activists eager to keep the anti-London feeds going. Meic would use all channels, whether Silicon Valley or even those closer to Moscow and Tehran, to get the word out. And why not, he wasn't going to be squeamish about applying all means necessary. He had no doubt that the English state would be ruthless in its response to their protest, any reading of history told him that. He wondered if the police had realised that the word was out – the various social media accounts Dafydd in London and his group had set up were already receiving many messages of support. What had the Umbrella Movement protestors said, 'Be shapeless like water'? They were so right, stay moving, keep adapting and the authorities wouldn't know what hit them.

He looked over at the barricades. 'Sion, make sure those banners are draped properly so that the TV cameras can see them.' Another little masterstroke, align with protest movements around the world and watch the tweets of support come flooding in. Though he'd held back on the Free Hong Kong flag – risking the ire of China's cyber-warriors was not a smart move.

Meic twisted around. 'Ms Donoghue, why don't you come and join me up here. We've got a wifi booster here and cam set up for you to file your live stream.'

Lexy took his hand, which she noted lingered on hers, and let Meic pull her up onto the truck. Taking up a position directly behind the cab she laid her laptop on its roof. It had been a risk to meet Meic; she'd worried that the direct approach would put him off, but it had worked out to their mutual benefit. She knew within a few seconds that he was attracted to her, and wanted her close, which meant that she got access. It was a basic trade-off; she imagined that if she'd been fat and ugly, he'd have likely given her the cold shoulder and there'd be no story. She shrugged it off. The ethical conflicts of a fourth wave feminist were never easy, but she did what she had to do, setting aside her discordant inner voice and striking a deal with Meic over a bourbon shot. So here she was with exclusive coverage for the first few hours of the siege, in return for connecting the protest leadership, well Meic, with the London media and some of her other useful contacts. Lexy opened her laptop, clicked on her live-stream application, with its direct feeds to the news agencies, and began typing.

❧

Llanawch Siege Live!

Reporting by Lexy Donoghue

11.42: Good morning everyone, my name is Lexy Donoghue and I'm reporting from the frontline of an extraordinary moment for the Welsh coastal village of Llanawch. A few days ago, this was just another seaside resort going about the business of making holiday-makers happy. But yesterday there were two unsuccessful police raids on the village which led to violence and great anger among residents.

11.44: In response, earlier this morning local leaders have taken the unprecedented decision to shut off access to the community in an act of defiance against the authorities. I'm standing on one of the two roadblocks which the locals have constructed overnight which have effectively physically sealed the village off from the outside world.

11.48: The authorities have reacted quickly and ordered in a sizeable police presence. I can count around sixty to seventy officers dressed in full riot equipment including shields and long batons who greatly outnumber the thirty or so community protestors manning the roadblocks.

11.58: A small convoy of cars has just come up from the village, and there are more villagers arriving at the barricades. Many more women here now including a few older ones.

12.01: Draped over one section is a *#MeToo* banner, next to it a *Black Lives Matter* banner and by that a rainbow flag, which must represent the LGBTQ+ community in the village – so we can see a real coalition of interests here today.

12.07: No movement from the police as yet, but there are considerably more people behind the barricades now which has made things a little more even.

12.16: I just had a chat with couple of the women on the barrier. One of them – Rebecca – was a veteran of the Greenham Common protests. Those of you who were around in the 80s might remember that. I asked her whether she was worried about facing the police, and she told me that if they could face down the Parachute Regiment back in 1983, then she wasn't too worried about what she called "a bunch of bum-fluff bobbies". Well, there we have it, a bit of grit from one of the older generations on the barricades.

12.24: Now another policeman has walked up but this time from the village side. He's not clad in riot gear.

12.25: I've just been told that he's the local village police officer. He's conferring with Meic Davies, who has been appointed the leader of the protest. I'll try and get some views from both of them shortly.

12.27: Correction to my post at 12.16, the name of the lady I chatted to is actually "Rebeca" which I've just been told is the proper Welsh spelling. Apologies all round.

12.32: It is becoming a pretty hot day here in Llanawch, temperatures up to the mid-twenties and barely a cloud in the sky. It must be quite warm for the police to be standing there in their full black kit. The protestors meanwhile have distributed water bottles to everyone on their side of the barricade, they even have set up a tea tent nearby.

12.38: This is interesting, two squad cars have arrived, and they appear to be carrying armed officers. I saw two rifles and machine pistols being unloaded from the cars' boots. I don't understand why armed police are needed for what the villagers have repeatedly told me is a peaceful protest. While some of the villagers are holding thick sticks or bats, I have seen absolutely no evidence of firearms in the village.

12.42: The armed police have taken up positions behind a wall on the landward side of the road. If I can see their rifles, then so can the protestors. This is very concerning, and it feels quite intimidating, almost like using a sledgehammer to crack a nut.

12.46: More on that firearms deployment by the police. I've just been informed that an armed police officer fired several shots in the village square last night during an attempted arrest. Luckily no one was hurt. Why would a firearms unit be deployed here? I've reported on armed police raids from the ganglands of Manchester, Nottingham and London, but seeing police officers wielding automatic weapons in a small, apparently harmless Welsh village seems a curious decision.

12.50: No word about the deployment from North Wales Police yet, nor have we heard from the government. Maybe no one has told them about what is starting to look like a significant police operation here on the West Wales coast today.

12.55: Sky News have messaged me to say that they are now broadcasting this live feed and webcam on their website, a big welcome to those joining me via Sky – it's great to have you with us.

13.07: Welcome to those of you joining us from the BBC News website.

13.10: To recap, we are in the Welsh fishing village of Llanawch, where a stand-off has developed between a large armed police contingent and unarmed local villagers. This follows incidents in the same village yesterday where it is alleged a police officer fired several shots in a crowded street.

13.15: I've just received a press statement put out by the North Wales Police, it reads: "Following a serious assault on a senior police officer, four officers were sent to arrest the suspect in question. They were also physically assaulted. Another group of police officers entered Llanawch last night, to make a lawful arrest, but they were attacked without provocation by a large group. A police van was destroyed by protestors and another van sustained damage. Acting in self-defence, and fearing for the safety of a fellow officer, the sergeant leading the operation fired two warning shots into the air. His swift action resulted in no serious injury being sustained to his fellow officers. As is normal when a police firearm is discharged, a full official enquiry will be held into this incident. North Wales Police are resolved to ensure that this on-going incident comes to a peaceable end but must balance this with the need to uphold the law and open public rights of way."

13.20: FYI, that's a direct copy from Reuters. The police admit to firing live rounds. Across the barricade I can make out that a one or two of the riot police have removed their helmets. They look drenched in sweat.

13.25: The response from the protestors' spokesman to that police press release? "A complete distortion of events. The police have been the ones who behaved provocatively in all the incidents."

13.31: The mood behind the roadblock is upbeat, people are chatting and laughing with each other. I can see at least one card game in play. A few of the protestors are taking selfies and other photos of the riot police on their phones.

13.33: That favour is now being repaid. Police officers with telephoto lens and hand-held video cams are now taking photos of individual protestors. *If you are also at the protests, or are affected by them, tweet me @LexysLaw.*

13.35: You can also do this via the Sky, BBC News, ITN, CNN or RT news channels – all of which are carrying this live feed. Welcome to one and all.

13.46: A statement just out from the Home Office in response to a media enquiry, they say that they are "monitoring the situation closely."

13.50: Welcome to subscribers from The Guardian Live, Bloombergs and Politico news sites.

13.55: There is still no action here on the frontline. Speaking to a few of the protestors, it seems as if this situation has been a pressure cooker waiting to explode. There is a great deal of criticism around politicians, many saying that the village has been betrayed by successive governments. Housing worries, lack of jobs and the local school closure seem to be common complaints.

14.10: Two police officers, still wearing their helmets, are striding towards the roadblock. I assume that they are in charge of the operation this afternoon.

14.11: The protest leader, Meic Davies, and the village bobby have met them on the police side of the barrier.

14.12: I can see lots of hand movements from Meic Davies. It looks like they are having a lively discussion over there.

14.14: The village bobby, a Sergeant Parry I'm told, is now standing between the protest leader and the two riot officers. He seems to be calming things down.

14.16: Now the taller riot officer is poking the protest leader in the chest. He must be making a strong point.

14.18: Well, that's all over. The meeting broke up quite abruptly from what I could see.

14.22: Meic Davies is back behind the roadblock and he told us that the police asked him to give himself up for arrest or else they'd move in with force. I heard a very strong response from the villagers in support of their leader, so he stays out of custody for the moment.

14.30: I can see activity behind police lines. And now a riot officer is speaking to us through a loudhailer. The police are ordering the protestors to disperse at once and stop causing a public disturbance.

14.32: The police have issued a second warning. A few choice phrases have been shouted back from the roadblock. *If you are also at the protests, or are affected by them, tweet me @LexysLaw.*

14.35: Here we go. I can see the front two lines of riot police are now moving towards the barricade. A few smaller groups of officers have formed looser squads behind these lines.

14.36: Standing here on the frontline, watching the riot police march forward, is an intimidating feeling.

14.37: This is incredible. A number of the women protestors have linked arms and sat down directly in front of the barrier. These women are showing great courage. The men of the village are standing behind them on the barricade, ready to move down and support them. #WomenFirst

14.38: The first police line has stopped dead, around five metres from the sitting women.

14.39: One of the women is leading the chanting at the police, that they are a disgrace to their mothers. The former Greenham Common protest lady I spoke to earlier is among them.

14.41: The police look dumbfounded; I don't think they expected to face women. Some of these women look probably old enough to be their grandmothers.

14.42: A snatch squad has moved in and has grabbed two of the women. Three of the younger men have jumped down from the barricade and are wrestling with the police.

14.43: There was a scream from inside the trouble. I heard it clearly. The squad have moved back a few metres, but they don't appear to have arrested anyone.

14.44: It looks like the woman the police were trying to take has been badly injured.

14.45: The village policeman has jumped the barricade and he is signalling to the riot police. Looks like he's calling for medical attention.

14.46: Two medics have run through the police lines and are giving the woman emergency treatment.

14.50: Extraordinary scenes here. The police lines have split apart to allow an ambulance to gain access to the injured woman. She's now been laid on a stretcher. I can see blood has been streaming from her head and she looks unconscious.

14.52: The ambulance is making a five-point turn, and is setting off down the road, with lights flashing and a motorcycle escort.

14.55: The police lines have completely broken up now. Some of the police are walking back to the vans, trailing their shields. Others are still on the road, unsure what to do.

14.58: The person who I think is the senior officer on the scene and was speaking with Meic Davies just thirty minutes ago, is talking with his men. He looks angry from here. Many of the police are now removing their helmets.

15.04: Sergeant Parry, the village policeman has been talking to the women in front of the roadblock, and now they are getting up and climbing back behind it.

15.14: I don't think we'll see any more activity for the moment. The police seem in not a little disarray and seem unready to do anything else for the moment.

15.20: I have never witnessed anything before like the past thirty minutes on mainland Britain.

15.25: I couldn't see exactly what happened, but with two women, one of whom was injured, up against a squad of baton-wielding male policemen, I'll leave you to draw your own conclusions.

15.40: Now the Welsh Government in Cardiff has released a statement that they too are "closely monitoring the situation". Nothing more from them yet, but I'll keep abreast of developments here and will continue to post on this live feed as events unfold.

Superintendent Lewlowicz was furious. He'd flipped up his helmet visor and was berating Inspector Melrose as their officers drifted past their control post located in the lead van.

'What the hell happened there? I gave you orders to remove the women and then clear the barricade of protestors. You couldn't even do the first thing.'

Melrose shrugged. 'The squad bungled it; someone whacked that woman in the heat of the moment. There was a lot of blood that's all, she'll be okay.' He wiped his face with a cloth. 'Not my fault.'

'You are trained to remove casualties away from the scene quickly, not freeze and lose the initiative. I'm disappointed, Charles, very disappointed.'

'She was an old woman. Most of them were. It threw our guys. We didn't expect them to use the women as a human shield. They're just cowards.'

The Superintendent saw a couple of the officers removing their riot overalls and laughing. He banged the bonnet of the van with his fist. 'You men! What have you got to smile about after that performance? You should be ashamed. Call yourself a police service?'

The two men instantly dropped the laughter. 'Sorry sir.'

Then under his breath one muttered to the other, 'I don't think clubbing a granny is anything to do with policing.'

'What was that?' Lewlowicz had overheard the remark and was advancing towards them.

'Nothing sir.'

'No, come on, let's hear what you just said.'

The man stared directly at his superior with an unconcealed look of disgust. 'I said, sir, that putting a defenceless old woman in hospital, sir, doesn't seem like good community policing to me. With respect. Sir.'

'That's what you think, is it?'

'Yes sir. And I bet that I'm not the only one who is wondering why we were ordered to do that. In our own country. Sir.'

The Superintendent looked him up and down. 'What do you mean by that? If that's a reference to my surname, you should be aware that my grandfather fought for this *country* during the war. Royal Air Force.'

'Sorry sir, I didn't mean anything by it.' The officer's face was by now a shade of well-barbecued lobster.

'I'll let it pass this time, but I think I've heard enough *feedback* for today. You two get back to your squad van immediately. I hope those orders are acceptable to you both.' He smiled thinly. After forty-eight years, still the jibes about his heritage.

Melrose shouted over to him, 'Sir, the DCC is on the line. He wants to know why the operation has stalled.'

Lewlowicz looked down at the road surface. 'Oh good,' he intoned, but picked up the handset all the same. 'Sir? No, we didn't… They put a human shield up… The men didn't respond well… No, that won't be possible, I don't think I could rouse them for another go… No, sir I don't think they'd respond to anyone right now… I suggest we hold position and reassess options… The Met? Well, I'd like to keep it under local command if possible… Home Office, I see… Yes sir. I'll do that.'

He handed the handset back to Melrose. 'We'll be hosting some advisors from the Metropolitan Police. How fortunate we are. They won't be arriving until tonight, so we're to maintain a holding watch on the barricade. Operations to resume tomorrow.'

'The Met sir? That bad?'

'Yes, Charles, that bad.'

'What about the men? We can't keep them all here overnight.'

'Keep ten officers on scene. Organise a roster – reliable men only, not the ones who can't complete a simple job. Have the armed unit bed down in Dolgellau in case we need them quickly. Get someone to organise food for them as well,' he looked at Melrose, 'and water for that matter.'

'Right sir.' The command radio buzzed. 'Melrose here, what is it? Wait, I'll put you on speaker.'

'Constable Llewellyn at the Hellan checkpoint, sir. I have a television news crew from the BBC here. They're demanding access to the scene. Shall we let them through?'

The Superintendent sniffed the air. He had no orders about a media presence, and it could be very embarrassing. It wouldn't look good. Probably best to wait until they could reconstitute a proper force. 'No, tell them that all media is to be kept beyond the checkpoint until further notice. Tell them that it is for safety reasons – their safety.'

Melrose relayed the orders. There was a pause and the speaker crackled again. 'They're not very happy about this, sir. The lead reporter says that if she can report from war-torn Syria, she can handle downtown Gwynedd. Says that she'll get a court order if we don't let them through.'

'I don't care if they get a letter from the Queen, they're not coming through! Tell them,' he paused, looking to the estuary for inspiration, 'tell them prevention of terrorism provisions or something.'

And with that, the senior officer walked over to his clipboard and started to draft operational orders for the next day. Melrose looked at his back. That was a bad move with the media, but after the bawling out he'd just received, he wasn't going to say one sodding thing.

Over on the other side of the barricade, Meic was shouting at the leader of the women who'd halted the police, 'What did you and your female flying squad think you were doing? I had the situation under control.'

Bethan wiped a tear from her eye, which had been caught in the scuffle. 'Just fuck off, Meic. We stopped them, didn't we? Got some good publicity *for the cause*.'

'Listen, I'm running this show, and this wasn't in the plan.'

She looked up. 'And who put you in charge? Why does a man automatically think that he's the leader? Why do we even need a leader?'

Meic put his hand on his hips and leaned closer to her face. 'Because otherwise we're just individuals without a clue, that's why. Because I'm the one stumping up the cash for all this and the one coming up with the plan!'

'And I guess my role and that of the other women is to make the tea, stand by our men, eh? Butter some bread while you and your rugby pals go off on your big crusade. It's just another boy's club isn't it, this whole thing. Well, this is our village as well, so if you men want our support, you can bloody well lump it, Meic Davies.'

Some of the women watching nearby gave a cheer. 'Go on Bethan, tell him!'

Meic took a deep breath. 'Okay, have it your way. But I tell you, we need to stick to the plan. That's how we'll get what we want.'

Twenty-Seven

Late afternoon had slipped into early evening, the background cries of seagulls diminishing with the setting of the sun in the western sky. Their cacophony had been supplanted by the rising drone of an approaching speedboat as it powered up the coast and reached its destination. The bow wave from the low-slung craft toppled forward as the craft slowed to enter Llanawch harbour. Waiting on the quay, Meic watched it manoeuvre towards him and felt some anticipation; this could be the breakthrough moment for his protest. Harry Caudwell, blond locks galloping in the breeze, stood in his cargo pants and pale linen shirt in the prow of the boat, ensuring that the cameraman in the back seat could capture this framing shot for the viewing public. He gave an arm-aloft salute to those awaiting him as the boat nudged into the rubber tyres slung alongside the slime-ridden quay wall. Meic Davies reached down with a helping hand, for it to be brushed aside, as the BBC presenter scaled the metal ladder two rungs at a time. Harry slapped Meic on the shoulder and called down to his camera crew, 'Did you get that?'

'Yeah, all good.'

'Okay, now you come up here and we'll do a shot of me entering the harbour.'

Meic looked on as the cameraman humped the equipment and himself up, Sion grabbing onto him as he slipped near the top. Harry turned to Meic. 'Apologies, I have to do this for the show, bloody reign of terror from my producer otherwise. I'm sure that you understand.' With that he dropped back down into the boat which then returned to just outside the entrance to repeat the performance.

'Action!' Caudwell entered the harbour like a relieving naval force, leapt up the metal ladder and gave Meic an iron handshake.

'Okay boss, that was good.' The cameraman moved to set up the next shot, as Harry turned on the charm.

'Well, well, you must be Meic Davies. Thanks awfully for responding to my message. Probably seemed a bit random, but I was in the area filming for my new series and put two and two together; thought that it was time for Harry Caudwell to seize the day!'

'We appreciate your efforts. Sorry you had to come by sea, but we had to close both entrance roads.'

'No problem, I've got a mate who has a summer house down here and this is his boat.'

Meic looked impassive. 'We did have your colleague Sarah Thomas from BBC News lined up to interview me, but the police wouldn't let her through.'

'I did see that. Perhaps she should have applied some lateral thinking like me. But at least the Beeb is now represented… so I was thinking, we could do some atmospheric shots. Why don't you give me the thruppenny tour?' Caudwell seemed to notice other people milling nearby. 'Maybe some local… characters. And then we could do an interview or something like that.'

'Sounds good. In fact, we have a little something lined up which you might like.'

'Which is?'

'Come and see, it's just across the square here. Bring your cameraman.'

A woman came over and offered her hand to Caudwell. 'Hi, I'm Lexy Donoghue.'

Harry shook it. 'Oh yes, the ah… blogger? Sure, I read your feed. Great stuff!'

Lexy gave him a feline smile. 'Thanks, but it's an amazingly interesting story.'

'It sure is, and it needs to be recognised, which is why I've come here. Did you know that I had Welsh ancestry? Used to get a heck of a ribbing about it at Winchester, but it was a cross I was proud to bear. I'm related to Frances Lewis of Llandaff, you see.' He noted that Lexy looked blank. 'One of the signatories of the American Declaration of Independence… as you'll know.'

'Yes, of course. Listen, I'm embedded here for the next few days, so perhaps you might like to get a few minutes with me after you've spoken with Meic.'

'Sure thing.' He turned to Davies. 'Well, lead on, MacDuff!'

Meic smiled and led them across the square, past the carcass of the overturned police van, to a rough stone wall where a group of his followers clustered around a green cast-iron plaque with silver lettering.

This plaque marks the spot where King Edward I and his victorious army, made camp en route to battle in 1294.

"MALLEUS SCOTORUM"

Paid for by public subscription And erected by the Historic Society of Wales. Unveiled by John Shankworth M.P., 23rd April 1927.

Harry took a look at the lettering. 'The design is very much of its time. I've seen quite a few of these types. I hadn't realised that there was a royal connection… Edward, the Hammer of the Scots, that's what the Latin is…'

Meic coughed gently. 'Yes, but the point is, that Edward I conquered Wales and that now this plaque, which we have to walk past every day, symbolises that conquest. And that's just wrong.'

'Okaeeee…'

'So we're going to take this plaque down. Right now.'

'I seeee…'

'And that might be something which might be good for your report. You can capture it on film. What do you think?'

Harry frowned. 'Got it, got it. But can you, you know, jazz it up a bit?'

Meic smirked. 'I think that we can manage that.'

Lexy stood by the BBC cameraman, who was now focusing in on the scene, and held up her phone.

'Well, let's roll then!'

Meic gestured to Gwyn Phillips, who was carrying a crowbar. 'Let's have it off the wall. And really lay into it.'

As Gwyn started levering the plaque off, Meic gestured to the group to shout. 'C'mon everyone, show them who is in charge now! Show them what Wales means!'

The crowd, which had quickly built as news of Harry's appearance spread, started to chant and shout. Gwyn managed to dislodge one side from the wall but, much to his embarrassment, was labouring with the struggle and sweat patches had streamed into the armpits of his T-shirt.

Harry had seen enough faffing around. 'Give it to me.' He gestured for the crowbar, which a panting Gwyn handed to him. The presenter then set about the plaque himself, managing to quickly lever the other side off the wall, and raising the crowbar slowly above his head in victory, to acclaim from the crowd. 'That's how to do it. With a little help from your friends!'

Lexy looked on, holding her phone steady on Caudwell's triumphant face, wondering whether his film would see the light of day, given that it appeared to breach the broadcaster's impartiality rules. Meanwhile, the crowd were stamping on the grounded plaque, whooping at their conquest, and she noticed that the cameraman was now focusing entirely on them, cutting Harry out of the picture.

Meic turned to Harry. 'That was brilliant from you. I never expected anything less.'

'You don't think I went too far?'

'No, it was great television. But then I'm not a professional like you, so wouldn't know, would I?'

'My viewers will love it. I've always had a natural aptitude for the small screen.'

Meic caught Lexy's eye and smiled, one player to another.

'So perhaps now time for a short interview?'

Harry let the crowbar drop to the ground and wiped his forehead. 'Sure, how about over by the harbour? It would give it a nice backdrop with those pastel houses behind you.'

A few minutes later, Harry faced Meic, and started the interview with a piece to camera. 'You'll know me for my award-winning documentary programmes, but today I'm investigating something different. I'm here in the village of Llanawch, which, as you'll know by now, is a village… a village under siege. I just happened to be in the area when the problems here kicked off and, acting on my initiative, I decided to dig down to the heart of the matter here and find out more. So here am I, after a long speedboat ride on pretty rough seas, with Meic Davies, who is one of the community leaders here.'

He turned to Davies. 'Meic, tell me about what's been going on over the last day. Why are you protesting?'

'First of all, thanks for coming to talk with us. It means a lot, when someone important, like you, allows us to tell our side of the story. The police obviously want to censor us and all of us in the community appreciate the BBC's support for freedom of speech.'

'That's my job. So, I had to visit you today by sea; why did you close the roads?'

'We very reluctantly blocked access to the village because we were faced with no other choice. It is not something that any of us here has done lightly. Our village is slowly dying, it is being taken over by outsiders who just don't want to integrate, and the government, who aren't helping either.'

'And why's that?'

'Well, it's quite simple really. They are denying our children and young people a fair chance in life. Local homes are being bought to become holiday cottages for a fortnight a year. Or people are coming here to retire, give nothing to the community but in fact become a burden on our already strained public services. You see, unless we did something, no one was going to listen…' Meic shrugged his shoulders.

'Yeah but isn't this just the free market in operation? What's wrong with that?'

'Free markets are a lazy argument because free markets don't work in all situations. Free markets don't think about the society as a whole, that's why we have regulators in certain situations to make sure they work for all. Think about healthcare and the environment for example. Without them, it would be the Wild West ruled by the rich and poweful with the rest of us at the bottom.'

'You talk about outsiders not mucking in, but aren't you now excluding them?'

Meic smiled and shook his head. 'We are inclusive. We're not against those that seek to become part of our community and our way of life. By that I mean a traditional community-based, Welsh-speaking way of life. But we are upset by those who deprive us of our very soul. Those that refuse to acknowledge that they live in a different country. How would any of your viewers like it, if someone came into their home and started telling them how to live their lives? We have human rights, even a moral right, to live as we want in our own home place. We're being bullied and ignored by people more powerful than us. The same people who always think they can get away with it.'

'Bullied?'

'Yes, bullied. There is no other word for it.'

Harry mugged puzzlement. 'Okay. But why protest in this way? We live in a democracy, after all. Can't you go through those channels?'

'Of course, we believe in our democracy. But we've tried so hard with councillors and MPs and the like, and no one has listened to us. Nothing has changed. Just because we're not a big city, it doesn't mean that our rights and our voice can be ignored.'

'I get what you're saying but what about—'

There was a sudden commotion just behind Meic, who saw the source of the noise. Bethan Evans, standing with some of the other mothers and a small group of schoolchildren, started chanting, 'Save our school, save our school!'

Harry gestured to the cameraman to take in the women. 'Hey there, what's this about? You protesting as well?'

Bethan craned her head up at him. 'We're protesting against the closure of our village school.'

'Sure.'

'Tell me about it.'

'It's simple. The council are closing down our school to save money. Our kids will have to be bussed to a school a long way away and that's tiring for them. The school is like the heartbeat of our community. You can't take it away. And we are the mothers who want the council to reverse its decision and give our kids a fair chance.'

'I can see that.'

'Good!'

Meic edged himself awkwardly into the picture, slightly thrown for a second. 'I was about to say, yes, well the school is being shut and that's a problem.' He regained momentum. 'You know that there are other communities like us out there who feel equally forgotten and... just go fifty miles up or down this coastline and you'll see—'

'As I did today! And quite the journey it was!'

Meic nodded. 'As you did indeed, and you'll find many villages just like us. And it isn't just this part of Wales. Think about Cumbria, the ghost villages in the Lake District, or Devon and Cornwall. Ask those places what they think about incomers. They'll tell you just the same as us. All of us are treated like living museums for those wealthy people who can afford second homes. The rich who scuttled down here at the first sign of trouble and infected us all with Coronavirus.'

'Yes, I holidayed in Padstow last year, so I'm absolutely up to speed with the issues.'

'Right, so you'll understand that one in four people of working age around here doesn't work. That's because there are no jobs. For those that are lucky enough to have one, wages are around seventy per cent of the UK average – the second lowest average wage in the UK. And I'll tell you something else, these public service cuts are having a massive impact. We're not London with its citizens of nowhere with all their money hidden away in tax havens. Over thirty per cent of people in this country are employed by the public sector, so we've got lots of low-paid council workers, teachers, and nurses. The people you relied on during the crisis and they're not getting six-figure bonuses.'

'No. Okay, I understand. Who doesn't love the NHS? Yet I was reading earlier today that there was some violence last night.'

'If you push a dog into a corner and poke it with a stick, what do you expect? The police provoked us into a reaction. I mean who can blame us for wanting to take our future into our own hands? And please don't blame us for wanting our children to grow up with prospects and hope. As Bethan was saying, even our brightest kids start life with one hand tied behind their backs. The system is rigged for the rich – they take all the opportunities and all the money.'

'I see. Well, that's been an education.' He winked at Bethan. The camera swivelled to focus on Harry's face. 'There seems to be a lot of anger here in Llanawch and, while some might say that this is a storm in a teacup, others might see this as part of a broader process, a new era in which we're living. I wish all the people here all the best. Thank you, Meic. And thank you, mums!' He gave it a nice positive note on which to end.

Harry waited for a few seconds before the camera's light went out, then turned to Meic. 'Thanks for that, really, really good. Some of those stats were pretty shocking.'

Meic nodded his head in the direction of Lexy, who was standing there with her phone. 'We thought that we'd record the interview ourselves, to put on our website, just so there's a permanent record. You know, so everyone gets full disclosure rather than just a soundbite edited to tell a different story in future news bulletins. I thought we could put it on the site next to the live webcam from the barricades.'

'Okay,' Caudwell rubbed his chin, 'I'll mention it to my producer.'

Bethan piped up, 'Yeah, keep the coverage factual, we're not a bunch of yokels for you to parade around. This isn't bloody prime-time entertainment, this is real life for some of us.'

Harry laughed and patted her on the shoulder. 'Of course it is, of course it is.'

Meic shook his head and, ignoring Lexy's attempts to talk to Caudwell, guided the BBC man by the elbow back to his boat. 'Of course, I'm not saying that you'll do anything else but please make sure that if you use soundbites, they reflect the overall interview.'

'Don't worry, Meic, I believe that we're on the same wavelength.' He wondered how quickly they could get an edit turned around.

'You really had me on the ropes there at one point.'

'Really? Yeah, I guess I did. Probably runs in the family. This will show that *Newsnight* clique back in Broadcasting House. They're always looking down their nose at factual programming.'

'Well, I'll let you crack on then with getting this on air. I look forward to seeing the reaction to the interview, I really do.'

Harry allowed his cameraman to clamber down the ladder first – officers should always look after the men – before hopping into the boat. Meic and Sion waved him off, receiving a salute in response.

Across the square, behind a pair of handcrafted Swedish net curtains, Frankie fumed. After all, she'd organised the interior design of Harry Caudwell's apartment on the Thames just a few years previously. And he hadn't even bothered to drop by – such ingratitude. Surely, he would know that she lived here. Nevertheless, she decided that she would email him with her considered appreciation of the situation. She might even suggest that they could do a phone interview.

Twenty-Eight

The next morning in Cardiff, Rachel Rees, acting First Minister, wilted at sight of the briefing papers stacked on her desk, all awaiting her signature. In the age of the iPad the civil service machine still worked in A4 format. Each day, as she strolled into work, she'd always tick off what should be on her agenda, but within five minutes of getting to her desk, she was rolling with the punches. Her day was divided into precise quarter-hour slots, none of which were ever allowed to be free. And she wasn't alone in her office, being accompanied by the lurking after-effects of last night's social with her constituency workers. From experience, the brain-ache would peak around mid-morning and then it would be a long drag of a day until six, when she might be able to sidle off into the folds of her small, thin-walled apartment overlooking one of the nearby old docks. Rachel felt guilty about her state, and checked her social media, scrolling through the daily torrent of keyboard warrior abuse – *corrupt whore, remoaner dyke, socialist bitch* – to get to the serious direct messages from Labour Party headquarters and her constituents. Distracted, she raised her eyes to the sun-bleached view of the redbrick building opposite her office window and waited for the paracetamol to fully kick in.

Given her position, even if it was temporary, Rachel would have expected a more spectacular vista, perhaps of the kind enjoyed by Lewis, one of the Directors in the Welsh civil service, who currently sat across her desk. She'd only inadvertently discovered that this official – and not even a permanent secretary either – enjoyed a high-ceilinged grand room with a view of Cathays Park, when she had visited yesterday to get his sign-off for a press release. A sign-off performed via a fountain pen on his sizeable desk. She'd stormed back to her meagre quarters in her official Prius and silently screamed at the unfairness. Rachel was a democratically elected member of the Senedd, the ranking politician currently on duty in Wales, while he was just a taxpayer-subsidised lackey with an OBE awaiting him on retirement. He was supposed to serve her, yet he was given the bigger office. Typical; the establishment always looks after its own. She imagined that he would be a member of the same clubs as all the other boys and girls in the scratch-my-back Cardiff establishment. Corrupt buggers they were – making their back-room decisions. And mostly white males at that. As per bloody usual.

Initially, Rachel had been excited about the idea of being in charge, but it soon became clear that a truce on decision-making had been called in the actual First Minister's absence. He was on holiday, hiking in New Zealand, and with the next five ministers down the list also either vacationing, or in one case discreetly attending a drying-out clinic, she'd been all that was left to cover for the cabinet. The Minister wrapped some strands of hair around her finger as she tried to refocus on the super boring document laid before her on the desk. Lewis wanted a decision from her.

'Well, what you're saying is that we may have to cancel the Pillars of Light project?'

'Correct,' clucked Lewis.

Rachel sniffed. 'I thought that it was supposed to be iconic for us. The mocked-up photos looked fab. Every border crossing into our nation with light beams shooting up into the heavens. "A small vibrant country with big ambitions." We talked about it in cabinet last year. What's not to like?'

The civil servant cast his eyes downwards as he considered his response. 'I'm afraid we can no longer afford it. With the new spending commitments announced by ministers last month, and the loss of the European financing package, we simply don't have the funds available for what is in reality a large and expensive work of public art, however *iconic*. Unfortunately, the Treasury want immediate cashable savings as well as the planned capital expenditure savings.'

'London again. When are they going to replace our EU funds, that's what I want to know? It is a disgrace; the London Tories called the referendum and now they refuse to take the consequences. Just another example of their hypocrisy; they've stolen our coal and our jobs, and now they take the food out of our mouths. Her so-called Majesty's bloody Treasury, what do they know about anything... these London senior official types have no heart and that what is needed, some *hwyl* not just silly facts. You could prove anything with them. Everyone knows that. They don't understand the people. But we are passionate about the people. Tirelessly passionate.'

'Competence has also been found to be useful, Minister.'

'The kind of competence that agreed that £37 million subsidy for those indoor snow resort swindlers over in Ammanford?' She smirked.

A small blue vein twitched at Lewis' temple. 'The enquiry didn't find any evidence of wrongdoing – the consultants told us that it was a potential game-changer for the valleys…' The words hung in the air.

He decided not to mention that he'd signed off on the grant. Such a mistake transferring down here: thrashing around in this paddling pool, rather than swimming in the seas of real power. But with the kids in school, his wife refused to contemplate a move. Still, he reflected, it meant that he'd progressed further in grade than he might have anticipated in the more competitive world of Whitehall. In any case, Wales didn't need those Whitehall or private sector types coming down here, upsetting things with their misplaced ambition. Those people simply didn't understand how hard he and his colleagues had struggled to calibrate a balanced system of public administration. He returned his thoughts to the room, catching the end of one of the Minister's inane thoughts.

'… tell me, what exactly does this cashable savings crap mean for our social equality agenda?'

Lewis retained his customary tactful face. 'We'll have to postpone the new mutual enterprise start-up workshop programme, discontinue the free hospital car parking scheme and most likely halt the primary schools repair programme.'

Rees put down her biro. What a vote-winner, cutting stuff which was good for the unemployed, good for the sick, and good for children. In fact, not to put too fine a point on it, the actual opposite of the reasons she always gave for entering politics. She rolled her eyes and emitted a long yawn. She didn't care what this bloody man thought. I bet he went to Oxbridge; he was always wearing those posh cufflinks with the little crests on them. They all did, the real or wannabe public schoolboys. Not open to the likes of me though. Rachel wondered if she still had the crumpled rejection letter in a box in her attic. Didn't even give me an interview, not posh enough for the bastards, not even with my dad a sitting M.P. Nothing wrong with politics at Swansea University though and it hadn't held her back, even though *they* had tried. From equal rights organiser on campus, to president of the youth wing of her party, then deputy director for a national equality campaign culminating in election to the then-Assembly via the regional list.

Perhaps things hadn't since gone quite as well during her first term in office. Rachel knew that for the old guard in the party, she was the wrong type – not *one of The Boys*. She'd beaten a couple of long-serving councillors to get her seat and they'd been waiting for her to fail ever since. Too young – not clever enough – no experience outside politics – no mainstream appeal. Rachel knew where that last dig came from, because *The Boys* were unreconstructed misogynists and full-on homophobes at heart. But if she was shacked up with Clare Balding or Jodie Foster, they'd all be inviting themselves over to dinner like the pervie hypocrites they were. Yet despite the hate, she'd finally wrenched a portfolio out of the party leadership, becoming the youngest minister in government. And definitely the one with the highest profile, she thought with pride. With all those television appearances, articles for the local papers and social media presence, some of *The Boys* called it self-publicising, but nowadays that was the art of being a contemporary politician. Getting yourself out there. Showing up opponents and winning the game.

While expressing your political philosophy, of course.

If only the party, following a disastrous series of by-elections, hadn't opted to go into coalition. As she'd explained at last year's national conference in the sodden concrete wilderness of Birmingham, Wales wasn't England. Placating the middle classes wasn't a priority in Wales, even for the Welsh middle classes. The country was socialist to its South Wales bedrock – win the valleys and you win the nation. But having to share power with these other *elements* was a pain in the proverbial. Particularly as they were the usual nationalist dreamers, running on a boost from the Scottish and Brexit madness with all the forces it had unleashed. Even the Greens, with their save-the-planet panicking, would be preferable to these nationalist idiots. Every week, she had to restrain herself from tweeting about some totally stupid political idea from their coalition *partners*. Every other cabinet meeting she'd be forced to sit through the latest half-cocked proposal to make Welsh learning mandatory, or to build a motorway from Cardiff to Holyhead, or put a Welsh person on Mars. Anything but deal with the real issues of the day, and none of them liked rugby – they were all football up there – typical.

Christ, her head was still throbbing, and her mouth remained parched. When was this bloody paracetamol going to kick in?

The official gave a small cough. 'Minister?'

Rees picked up her smartphone and fiddled with it. 'Well, I could possibly live with the Pillars of Light thing going, that's the Culture Minister's idea anyway. But I think scrapping the free car parking would be a mistake, especially for medical staff given everything, unless…' She glanced up. 'No chance we could organise an exemption for former mining communities?'

The civil servant looked up from his briefing papers. 'Um, this conversation is more along the lines of informing you.'

'So I don't actually need to do anything?' The politician leaned back in her chair.

'Well, would you like a discussion paper prepared for the First Minister?'

'Yes, let's do that for the autumn if possible.'

Lewis nodded, unsurprised at the outcome: always a discussion paper, never a decision even in the unlikely event of one being requested. He looked at the woman, girl really, in front of him. She couldn't be more a cliché if she sported dungarees and Doc Martens. She wore bright red hair in a man's cut – the shock of the colour only emphasising the plainness of the double-chinned canvas it framed. It struck him that the hair was her sole feature of note: indeed, she had mistaken a physical characteristic for a personality. And that wasn't enough even accounting for her youth. He hated the way the local politicians evoked elitist feeling within him, but they were all useless to a woman. The men weren't much better – some of them going so far as to affect the top-button-undone, tie-skewed look like faded further education college lecturers.

Rachel watched the official in front of her who now bore the ghost of a human smile upon his smug, privileged face. Inwardly, she recoiled; he was just another mid-life cyclist type, the lycra outfit doubtless matching his skeletal face. Middle-aged men never looked good without a bit of weight to them, just looked like they were trying too hard otherwise. And civil servants like him were hopeless at understanding the people's needs, and what was really important, like a living wage, a proud health service and building social opportunity. They never supported elected ministers in achieving anything; you had to fight these bureaucrats to get anything changed. She took a large draw of water from her bottle and fumbled with the cap. 'So, I've got stuff on my plate here, even if you haven't. Is that it?'

Lewis dropped the smile. 'Yes. But sadly, we have one more item to deal with. A matter of urgency.'

With a loud tut Rees moved on to the next paper in front of her. 'Llanawch? Yeah, I saw some of this on the breakfast telly. What's going on up there then?'

'There have been some developments overnight. At the moment the police are holding off from any further initiatives until some fundamental issues have been clarified.'

'What do you mean by that?'

'There are *some people* from London here to talk to you.' The civil servant gave her a knowing stare.

Rachel looked at him bemused as Lewis walked over to the frosted glass door, opened it and spoke to the people waiting outside. 'The Minister is ready to see you now.'

Two men and a woman, all dressed in dark business suits, walked into the room and without waiting to be asked, took seats at the conference table in the corner. They didn't say anything as Lewis sat across the table from them. The Minister pulled a face, then got up from her desk and took her seat at the table. She noted that the younger man and woman looked tanned and physically in shape.

She was aware of the three of them evaluating her and this only served to increase her irritation with this sudden interruption. Rachel hoped that her breath was okay, as she'd run out of mints.

'So, from London, are you? Well, aren't we the lucky ones?'

The older man, sporting a pale complexion and cropped haircut, leaned forward and fixed a sharp blue-eyed stare upon her. 'My name is Pedersen and I'm from the Home Office. The gentleman to my left is Phil Sparkes from the Downing Street media unit, and the lady to my right is attached to the Home Office to deal with, ah... ad hoc security matters. You can call her Joan.'

'Well, that's very nice. Welcome to Wales. So why are you visiting us?'

Lewis leaned into the table as if to speak, but Pedersen answered, 'We're part of the emergency response team for the incidents at Lan... ouch?' He shrugged.

'Llanawch.' Rachel emphasised the pronunciation which she'd heard earlier on the news. 'Some protestors have pushed it a little too far from what I can see. They'll soon settle down, if I'm the judge of anything. And I've instructed my officials to stay on top of it.' She quickly glanced at Lewis, seeking confirmation, but for once receiving no eye contact. 'Which they are.'

Pedersen exchanged a look with the woman named Joan. 'Really? You may not be aware of the full facts, Ms Rees. Firstly, the new field commander has informed us that she believes that the local police force is no longer in a position to effectively resolve this incident. Secondly, we have the start of contagion. A copycat hijacking of an English removals van took place near...' he paused to recall the name, 'Saint David's in the west of the country two hours ago. Did you know that?'

'No.'

'That's because we've had to place a D-notice on it. Several people were arrested at the scene so there's no leakage yet, but with social media it's only a matter of time.' He paused and looked out of the window. 'However, there is significant concern in government that these issues will quickly spread and will impact national security. Simply put, we cannot allow citizens to go to war with the police.'

'I don't understand. What about the First Minister?' Lewis noticed a strained tone in Ree's voice.

At that moment the man's mobile phone rang. He held a finger up to the minister and answered, 'Pedersen… Yes, with them now… About ten minutes… When? How bad is it? Yes, use Avon police… Clear it immediately… They what? Already?'

He ended his call and stared directly at Rees. 'I'm afraid we've run out of time for the niceties. Your First Minister was called by the Home Secretary a quarter of an hour ago and I am now officially informing you that we are taking over operational command of the situation.'

Lewis sat upright. 'What? I hadn't been informed about this.'

Rachel slammed her palm on the table-top, rattling her bracelets. 'Just wait a minute now. Coming in here, trying to call the shots. Who do you people think you are? We're not some bloody colony, you know.'

Pedersen scratched the back of his head. 'I'm afraid the situation in this village has got out of hand and we've been designated by No.10 to quarantine the incident. We are ordered to bring matters to a satisfactory conclusion.

You already showed during Covid that you're unable to control your borders. Or did I miss something?' He looked over at her. 'I didn't think so. Given this we will be assuming control of security at this end. The one person missing from this room is Commander McArdle from the Metropolitan Police, who has just been appointed as the senior officer in the field at Llan… awch.' He smiled thinly over the last word.

'The Metropolitan Police?' Rachel's head was really starting to pound.

'That's right. You should work on the assumption that we will be bringing in external policing elements. I am required by law to inform the most senior local political authority of our assumption of incident control under the Public Security (Prevention of Disorder) Act 2021, a copy of which I am now serving to you as witnessed by your designated senior official.'

He slid the document across the table to Lewis, who began to skim-read it. The Minister seethed. 'You can't just take over my country. We're a devolved democracy.'

'Ms Rees, I am empowered by an Act of Parliament to take control for matters of national security. Read the legislation, your own party tabled it back in the day. Our powers are merely to bring this security situation to a swift end before it goes viral.'

Lewis spoke up from the document, his voice calm. 'Minister, from what I've read here, they have the authority to do this. We should really get our own legal counsel to check this though, which I'll do with your permission.' He looked at the Minister.

'Fine.' Rachel stared hard at the conference phone pod on the desk.

Pedersen nodded to himself. 'The phone call I just took was about the Severn crossing. It appears that a group of drivers have abandoned their cars in the middle of the bridge, blocking it in both directions, so the M4 into Wales is closed. There is no way we can keep the lid on that.'

Phil Sparkes piped up, 'It's already broken. It's on the protest feed and getting retweeted.'

The older man resumed, 'Looks as if we're dealing with some very savvy people here and losing the ground and media war. We need to resolve this asap or else we'll face problems elsewhere. It doesn't take much to start a fire when there's so much dry wood to hand.'

His phone rang again. 'Pedersen. What? Oh no... Right, this is serious, I'm on my way.' He slipped his phone into his jacket and rose from his seat. 'We have to leave. We'll be based at police headquarters in Cardiff for the duration. If you have any questions, your officials can contact us there or on my mobile.' He slid a card across the table to Lewis.

The Minister looked up at him. 'Tell me, that call sounded bad. What's just happened?'

'Trouble.'

'What kind?'

'The Sky News helicopter is now flying over the protest. It will be 24/7 wall to wall coverage from now on. I suggest that you fire up your media operation to work under Phil here.'

Rachel instantly reacted, 'Our media operation? Right, I'll call her after this. If that's okay with you.'

'Good, connect them to Phil. I'll assume that you can handle the local politicians in the Assembly.'

'It's called the Senedd now. That's Welsh for Parliament.'

'Is it? Didn't know that.'

'Well, it is.' Rachel's eyes burnt.

'One quick question, if I may.' Lewis leaned forward conspiratorially. 'Is this a COBRA situation yet?'

The woman known as Joan quietly spoke, 'Not officially. But the red team in the Contingencies Unit has been activated. Read what you will into that.'

'I see.' Lewis pursed his lips.

Pedersen stood up along with his colleagues. 'We'll be in touch as needed. Thank you, Minister.'

The three officials rose quickly, the balance of power now clarified. Lewis, caught by surprise, stood off-balanced at the table, his chair tilting back, and he attempted a damp-handed shake with Pedersen, who then swept out of the room in the wake of his already-departed colleagues.

'Well, I must say that those London people don't seem to understand the realities of devolution. They still believe that they can boss everyone around like we're some colony.' Rees folded her hands.

Lewis turned to look down at the Minister. 'Legally that's exactly what we are. In any case, you didn't oppose them.'

'Well, not my place is it? First Minister's job,' she emitted a long sigh. 'Did you see how that woman was dressed? Like some little power-suited Thatcher disciple. Her type wouldn't last five minutes down the Treherbert Working Man's Club. They'd tear her apart… her and her James Bond buddies.'

'I suspect, Minister, that she is the one actually representing the security service.'

The official retook his seat and groaned inwardly. To him, it had long been clear that some of the politicians he was forced to mollycoddle had little understanding of how to govern effectively. It was all pork-barrel politics, virtue signalling and blaming Westminster. But now they had a crisis and still, here he was again, listening politely as these fools banged on about the betrayal of the miners' strike; the need for a Welsh way; and the holy grail that was Nye bloody Bevan.

And for that matter, all the rest of the cultural ragbag which had been bundled together sometime in the seventies and now passed for a national character: Dylan Thomas, Tom Jones, rugby, Shirley Bassey, male voice choirs, Richard Burton, rugby, hard men from the deep mines, tough women from the valleys, rugby, rugby, bleedin' rugby. This hand-me-down wisdom, which raged against the privately educated English elite creaming off the best jobs, yet put the children of politicians into power and gave a fawning public platform to the actors, celebrities and sportsmen. God, how he missed the intellectual cut and thrust of the Treasury. How he wished he'd stayed put instead of transferring to the Welsh Office on some misty-eyed pilgrimage.

The minister and the civil servant sat side by side at the conference table, staring mournfully at the cheap print of *Old Penarth* on the wall opposite.

Twenty-Nine

Commander Kate McArdle clicked off her mobile and gazed at the helicopter above. 'That's not such a bad idea. What air assets do you have locally?'

His arms folded, Superintendent Lewlowicz scuffed up a bit of dirt from the road and examined his colleague, newly arrived from London. The woman was trim, of his age and wielded her words carefully. She was dressed in full uniform with the kind of metalwork on her epaulettes that he was never going to achieve. Maybe she was just another fast-tracker to meet the gender quota, but he felt some granite there behind the lipstick. 'One chopper. Given the size of the area we cover, our force needs it. Quite a bit larger than your patch, in case you hadn't noticed,' he drawled.

'Four times the size. Or so my briefing notes said.' McArdle held his gaze. 'But then you do have a much smaller population of course. And a much lower crime rate. We in the Met have to police a high-density, crime-intense city, which means we have a lot of experience in handling situations like this.' McArdle smiled at Inspector Melrose who was standing next to them. 'Right, let's get it up there, carry out some surveillance, collect some intelligence. Do you have any drones?'

'Drones? Like Amazon, you mean?'

She started typing on her smartphone. 'I was thinking more the surveillance kind, rather than the ones that bring you your next box set.'

'No. We don't have any of those. Of either type.'

'No problem, I'll put in a request to London. The RAF may be able to help us out if they have a spare knocking about. We can get one flown over here. They can stay on station for extended periods.'

The Superintendent rocked back on his heels. 'They will be unarmed?'

McArdle sent her message and looked up from her screen, smiling. 'Possibly… probably.'

'Okay, so a stupid question. I'm just a uniform from the sticks, I know that. But what about this blooming news chopper? I suggest that we close the airspace and get it out of here so we can get on with it.'

The Commander shook her head. 'Let's not alienate the media any more than you've already managed.'

Lewlowicz puffed his chest out. 'With all due respect, ma'am, you were not on the scene at the time to be able to criticise my decision. You simply weren't there.'

'That's true.' She fixed him with a stare. 'But I'm here now and I've been given command because you were not able to deal adequately with the situation. And just in case you were wondering, six years with the RUC and twenty with the Met says that I'm likely to have *relevant* experience on my side. So how about them apples?'

'Apples? What in God's name does that mean?'

'Oh, it's just a phrase I picked up on my year seconded

to the Boston Police Department. Boston in America, that is.'

Superintendent Lewlowicz placed his hands on his hips. 'You know, I did spend some years in Southampton. I'm not some bumpkin that you can talk down to. But if I'm no longer required here, then maybe I should return to headquarters and speak with my superiors.'

McArdle made an obligatory attempt to be polite. 'My apologies if I spoke harshly, but I've been tasked to resolve this problem as quickly as possible. Personally, I don't think your… many talents are best used here on the front line at this point. Your Deputy Chief Constable agrees, but I would very much appreciate the Inspector here,' she nodded at Melrose, who was observing the scene with a raised eyebrow, 'staying on as liaison for me and to share some of his local knowledge. I hope that's acceptable to you.' She paused briefly to drag up a smile from the depths. 'But do tell me if I've been misinformed about your role.'

Lewlowicz took a step back. 'I see. Very well, Commander, I'm formally handing over tactical control of the operation to you. Melrose, keep me informed.'

McArdle and Melrose silently watched the Superintendent get in the back seat of his car and, as he was driven off, pointedly ignore the pair of them.

'One less problem. Melrose was it?' The Inspector nodded. 'Good, I hope that hasn't put you in the doghouse.'

'I'll live.'

'I'm sure. When we're finished here, I want you to get the helicopter on scene – let them know that they won't be alone. But first, I want your appraisal of the situation.'

They wandered closer to the barricade until they stood about fifty yards away. Melrose pointed at the blockage ahead of them. 'As you can see, ma'am, at first it was a pretty rudimentary barricade, which they built overnight. However, in the last twenty-four hours they've been reinforcing it using a JCB. So now we'll need some earth-moving machines to clear it.'

'We can obtain those within six hours. My colleagues have the Royal Engineers on standby to support.'

'We're bringing the Army in? I'm not sure the local council are going to like that.'

'Just a couple of assault bulldozers to clear this mess. We're repainting them for a less threatening look.' McArdle remembered how the old battleship-grey RUC Land Rovers had been repainted white with a red stripe in an attempt to normalise their appearance when they'd turned into the Police Service of Northern Ireland. A little bit of rebranding could be powerful.

Melrose blinked. 'I see. Um, the next issue is the protestors themselves. Overall, we're assuming that the whole village is in on this carnival.'

'Oh really? Why do we think that?'

'Intelligence… but as I was saying, the defenders on the barricades are a mix of fit young guys, and more vulnerable people.'

'More vulnerable?'

'For example, the trouble yesterday was caused when they put women in front of the barricade. That stopped some of the men in their tracks.'

McArdle scoffed, 'Oh come on, Melrose. Stop pussyfooting around, they're just women. We've got equality now and that includes the responsibility to behave yourself or be arrested for public disorder. We even have the power to enforce public order cases – like me. Imagine that.'

'Okay. Well today, it looks as if they've got some children standing up there. Makes it difficult for us to move in without the risk of injury.'

'We're not from the health and safety, are we, Inspector? These women and children. Are they behaving provocatively? Displaying threatening behaviour, throwing missiles?'

'No, they're just being used as a human shield.'

'Smart move. But I dealt with worse in Ulster. When the time comes, we'll designate female officers to crowd control any kids who get in the way. It just looks better.'

'Do you want to know about their leader – Meic Davies?'

'I've talked to Special Branch and our other friends about him. Quite a thin file. So I'm interested in your impressions. I understand that you've met him face to face.'

Melrose paused; he could feel a slight clamminess gathering at his temples. 'Not your run of the mill chancer. Pretty clever and maybe, kind of charismatic in a way, I'd say. I must admit that I underestimated him. So be wary, ma'am.'

'Uh-huh. It looks very well planned to me, not your usual boyos out for a casual Saturday night drink and a bit of ultra-violence. Though I can't say that I've yet come across a mainland village going to war with the police.' McArdle pulled out a pair of sunglasses from her top pocket as she squinted at those manning the barricade. 'And what about this Lloyd Parry guy? Your man on the inside.'

'I wouldn't call him that,' the Inspector snorted. 'He missed all the signs in the run-up to this. Gave us absolutely zero warning on all this shit. Excuse my language, ma'am.'

'Hmm, I hear he performed pretty well during the

action yesterday – stopped a nasty situation from getting worse.'

Melrose remained silent.

She turned to face him. 'Well, he's your guy, not mine. Now your men, can they maintain a watch for the rest of the day?'

'Certainly. But, as the Superintendent might have told you, I don't think they're in the mood to disperse the protestors.'

'No, we've received that message already. Loud and very clear. I just need them to maintain the blockade here and on the coast road. Can they possibly manage that? I'm expecting reinforcements by evening.'

'I don't understand. Where from?' Melrose looked confused. 'The DCC said that we were already at full stretch. We'll have to call people back from their holidays.'

McArdle stopped her review of the barricade and turned to Melrose. 'Now we can't expect other Welsh constabularies to tread where your lot won't. We've activated the national civil disorder plan and we've been allocated tactical support groups from the Met, Nottingham, South Yorkshire and Greater Manchester forces, plus one or two other units. Firearms, horses, the usual roll-call.'

'I thought we could deal with this quietly.'

'They've left us with few options.' McArdle started to walk back towards her new command post. 'You saw what happened in the cities with the riots. We had a near complete breakdown of order in London. We were stretched to the limit, beyond it for a few nights. What if other villages in Wales or in Scotland follow suit? Or other groups who may have a different agenda? Pandemonium will ensue. Therefore, we need to grip the situation, go in quick and hard here, and be seen to restore complete control. Ensure that the message gets out and that is why we need the media. And I'm afraid that, after yesterday's performance, whatever the rights and wrongs, your guys just aren't considered up to it. You do understand, Inspector?'

Melrose took a long intake of breath. 'Yes, ma'am.'

'That's why I'm focused on this blockage rather than the coastal approach road to the west. The media are here, not there. So make it clear to your men that theirs is a holding operation and they'd better not fuck up… excuse my language, Inspector.'

'One question, ma'am. With all these reinforcements, how are we going to house and feed them all?

'Arrangements are in hand. I'm told that there's an Army training camp nearby.'

'If, by nearby, you mean twenty miles away.'

'Nearby enough. Listen Melrose, I'm sure that you have ambitions like any other middle-ranking officer, so my strong advice to you is to follow orders as efficiently as possible. Understand?'

'Yes ma'am.' He unconsciously dropped back to a step behind her as they walked.

They reached the command post. 'By the way, I'd be grateful if you kept our plan under your hat until your men are relieved. Agreed?'

'Yes ma'am.'

McArdle halted. 'Now, two final things. The media, where are they?'

'We have them penned at the holding barrier up the road. There are quite a few more of them than yesterday.'

'Don't act surprised. You're a clever guy. Tomorrow's papers will all lead with stories about state censorship if we keep them there. Remember, Melrose, we need them on our side, reporting our response in the best possible light. Do bring them forward with my compliments but keep them away from the immediate front line. And inform them that I'll give a press conference at five-thirty this evening. In time for the evening news.'

'Right ma'am.' Melrose began to head to the nearest radio.

She called after him, 'And I want to speak to this Lloyd Parry guy. As soon as possible.'

'We'll get him on the line for you, ma'am.'

Thirty

Lloyd sat on a low stone wall a few yards behind the barricade. In rolled-up shirt sleeves, he held up his tunic in front of him and ineffectually brushed the dust patches that seemed embedded in the wool. They'd need a damp cloth. He wondered how long this whole stupid business was going on for. He'd endured a sleepless night back at home – the bed felt like a void opening up on him, so he'd transferred himself and his night sweats to the single in the spare room for a second night. Then this morning at the station, Roy had asked if he could take some holiday, starting immediately. What could Lloyd do about it? Roy had grown up here, all his friends were from the village, so he'd signed off on it. No point both of them getting the push. He took a swig from a can of orangeade, bought this morning from the village shop, and watched a few of the protestors chatting away. A small group of children played football on the road directly in front of him. Bethan Evans looked on, having encouraged the kids to play near the barricade – whether as a reminder of the closing school, or to put off further police action, only she knew. Up on the barricade, he could see Gwyn Phillips and a couple of his gang huddled together, observing the police beyond. They'd blanked him all morning. Not that Lloyd expected anything different. Naturally he was persona non grata at present. He wondered what Ruth was up to.

Duty – that's what he had to remember right now. His call to duty.

Suddenly the football bounced towards him and over the wall. The kids tentatively approached him. 'Hey, Sergeant Parry, can we have our ball back please…'

Lloyd reached back behind the wall to scoop up their ball. He picked it up and took a look at the worn face of Lionel Messi, surrounded by stars on its surface, and smiled; down south back in his day, it had been Gareth Edwards or bust. He strolled over to them, tossing the ball up in his hands. 'Well then kids, who's playing here then?'

They stared at him blankly, before one of the older boys spoke up, 'Liverpool against Barcelona.'

'Nice. Two top sides there…'

'Barcelona are better.'

A shriek from a girl in blue, Lloyd recognised her as Maggie John's youngest, 'No they ain't!'

'So, you all like footie then?'

The tall boy had a small scar on his cheek and spoke again. 'I'm going to be a pro footballer, play in the premiership.'

Lloyd smiled. 'Good for you. Hard to get into those clubs mind, but good for you.' He looked at the girl. 'And you, what do you want to grow up to be?'

'On the *X Factor*.'

'Oh, right.'

'You can't just go on the *X Factor*,' another boy sneered.

'Yes I can.'

'No you can't, you have to do the auditions first.'

'I know that, I'm not stupid!'

Lloyd tried to calm their spat. 'When I was your age, I wanted to be an astronaut.'

This statement met with incomprehension, then two of the boys looked at each other and sniggered. A little girl, who had been put in goal during the game, whispered something to the older girl standing by her.

Lloyd squatted down, balancing on his knees. 'What's she saying?'

The older girl looked embarrassed. 'She said that her mam said that she wasn't to talk with you…'

'Oh.'

The tall boy looked at Lloyd. 'My dad said that you weren't to be trusted… so can we have our ball back?'

'Yeah, sure. Here you go.' Lloyd stood up, feeling his knee play up again, and tossed the boy his football. The kids ran off to resume their game. The whispering girl looked back at him, then quickly away. So that was it: the men thought he was a traitor, the women a marriage-breaker, and now the kids were banned from talking to him. The day just got better and better. He crushed his empty can and wandered over to where his Land Rover was parked under the shade of the trees. As he reached it, his mobile phone rang. Lloyd saw who was calling and answered, knowing that he couldn't really avoid this one.

'Just what do you think you were doing, Dad?' Hywel shouted down the phone at him. 'Mam is really, really upset.'

Lloyd winced, what could he say? 'You've a right to be angry.'

'Don't patronise me, you selfish old so and so. Didn't you think about Mam, about your family?'

'Of course I did!' Lloyd saw the children look up from their game. Lowering his voice, 'Yes, I did, but these things happen.'

'These things don't happen unless you want them to… what about your grandchildren eh? They'll be born into a family at war with itself.'

'No one is saying that's going to happen… we're just spending some time apart, that's all. Think things through.'

'Bollocks. You obviously didn't listen to Mam. She is off the charts. Did you know that she's already been to see the solicitors in town?'

Lloyd was stunned. 'No. I thought…'

'What did you think? You can't do that to somebody, and think it's going to be fine in the morning.'

His father swallowed. 'Have you spoken to your brother?'

A big sigh; Hywel had slowly calmed down since the explosion at the start of the call. 'Yes. Arwel's about as impressed as I am.'

'Do you think he'd speak to me?'

'I dunno. You know him and Mam have always been really close. I'd let him cool off a bit first. But I'll tell you something, he can't be more tamping about this than me. You've let us down.'

Lloyd heard the phone beeping with another call and checked the display to see who it was. Shit, great timing. 'Sorry Hywel, I've got another call coming through from headquarters. I have to take this; you know how it is.'

'What? I see, that's how it is. Well, I'm so sorry to keep you from your bloody important call.' He rang off.

Lloyd took a deep breath and took the other line. He answered in a level tone, 'Sergeant Parry here.'

'Sergeant, this is Commander Katherine McArdle from the Metropolitan Police. I've assumed command of the incident.'

'What about the Superintendent?'

'He's been reassigned to other duties.'

'All right then. What do you want me to do?'

'Where are you now?'

'Parked up behind the barricade. Are you on scene here?'

'Yes, I am. I'm looking at the barricade right now. You still on our team, Parry?'

'Yes. Don't think anyone around here wants me playing for them anyhow.'

'Have you got freedom of movement?'

'Sure.'

'Could you get through the barricade?'

'I think so.'

'Then meet me on the police side in two minutes, I want to talk to you.'

Lloyd started to button up his tunic and ran his hands through his hair – his curls were out of control – as usual. No idea what branch of the family he inherited that trait from. As he started to clamber over the barrier, one of the rugby club lads called over to him, 'Oi! Where do you think you're going?'

'Out there, sunshine. And I'll be coming back as well. Do we have a problem?' Lloyd glared at him.

Gwyn Phillips called over to his mate, 'Let him be, Chris. Meic says to let him be.'

Lloyd dropped down to the other side and walked towards the two figures standing between the barrier and police encampment. He recognised Melrose, who looked even more unimpressed than usual.

'Inspector.' He turned to face the woman, 'Ma'am.'

He saw the senior officer's eyes flick up and down him. 'Sergeant, I'm Kate McArdle.' She held out her hand.

He shook it gently. 'Lloyd Parry.'

'What's the mood inside the village?'

'Hard to sum up really—'

Melrose butted in, 'Well give it a try for once, Parry.'

Lloyd raised his eyebrows but ignored the interruption. 'I'm not exactly flavour of the month back there, but I'd say that we have a large-ish bunch of younger activists, led by a very determined guy in that Meic Davies. He's more of a zealot really. And the rest of the village seem to have mostly fallen in behind them. I say mostly, because I would say that there are a few people not really on board with all this – mainly some of the more recent incomers – but my guy tells me that some of the locals are just going along with it at the moment.'

'So, a collective action, you'd say? But maybe with a few cracks?'

'Maybe. I mean Davies has recruited his own private army, a mix of your usual nationalist types but also a group of local youth. They're enforcing control within the village, nothing physical, just a bit of old-fashioned intimidation.'

'Such as?'

'Well, one example – the local Spar has a couple of the rugby club boys kicking around outside, not stopping anyone going in, but as a kind of reminder of who's in charge.'

'Sounds like a nasty little operation.'

'Not that exactly, but well-planned, I'd say.'

'But any violence or overt harassment? Anything we could nail this Davies on?'

'I've haven't seen any more serious stuff since it all kicked off. Some of the boys seem to enjoy throwing their weight around, but that's young men for you. Generally, it's all pretty quiet. Compared to the other night that is…'

McArdle smiled. 'Quite. You mentioned the village shop. Any panic buying?'

'No, I was just thinking about that. They seem to have lots of supplies and there was an orderly queue, not much busier than usual. No panic or anything. Only thing different was that with them not being able to take cards, no one seemed to be using cash, everything was on a tab. Apart from me, that is.'

'We cut off the payments system for all the shops. But you say there are no problems with food supplies right now? And you were the only one paying in cash?'

'Looked like it. As I said, wouldn't win any popularity contests.'

'Right. What we can deduce is that there is either a huge amount of trust that the bills will be settled, or the knowledge that they definitely will be. After all, shopkeepers aren't known for their benevolence.'

'That's what I was thinking.'

'And what about you. How are things going, are you short of food?'

He stuck his tongue into his cheek. 'I'm okay on food, I can work through the freezer at home. But I'm running a bit short on cash to be honest.'

Melrose snorted, but McArdle seemed to weigh Lloyd up, then turned to the Inspector. 'Give him some cash.'

Her Inspector looked bemused. 'Cash?'

'Yes, money. £40 should do it.' She saw that Melrose didn't understand her. 'Well, I don't go into an operational area toting a Chanel handbag, do I? It doesn't match my stab-proof vest for one thing.'

'Right.' Melrose reluctantly reached for his wallet and pulled out a pair of twenties. Without moving from his spot, he raised his arm to the perpendicular. 'Sergeant, there's forty there.'

Lloyd didn't really need the money, but he liked to see Melrose made to feel awkward, so stepped forward to take the proffered notes, and mumbled, 'I'll pay you back when I can get to a cash machine.'

'Yes, yes you will, Sergeant.'

McArdle shot a look at Melrose while talking to Lloyd. 'Anything else of interest?'

He considered for a moment. 'Well… I believe that it's open house on our communications. They have the radio from Blunt's van from the other evening. That I know for a fact, so I imagine that they monitored all your operations yesterday.'

'Now that is useful information. We can work with that – our apparent operations being eavesdropped. Don't let onto them that we know this. From now on, we'll contact you only via mobile,' she lingered on the dust patch on his uniform, 'so remember to keep it charged. Melrose, we'll need to use emergency procedure from this evening onwards. But we should still provide some plausible *traffic* on the main band.'

'I also know that they're using texts to communicate.'

'We may be aware of that but thanks for confirming.' She folded her arms. 'Now, the situation has changed on this side. The village will be fully secured through reinforcements coming in from England. England because there will be no local ties to worry about, so no hesitation when it comes to carrying out orders. You understand what that means?'

Lloyd cast his eyes downwards. 'I remember the strike. I know the score.'

'Yes, everything clearcut. No easing up when action is needed. No issues around local retribution afterwards.'

'So when are you going to be coming in?'

'To be decided, Sergeant. I've been given full discretion on that. But come in we will. And hard if necessary.'

'Commander, there are kids back there.'

'So I see – a lot of big kids.'

'No ma'am, real kids, eight or nine-year-old kids. Christ knows who else they'll put on the barricades. If we had a village paralympic team, Davies would probably have got them up there as well. You can't come in too hard.'

A tone came into McArdle's voice, a razor blade dipped in honey. 'I know my job, Sergeant. Believe me, if we can avoid injuries that is always going to be my preferred option, but we cannot allow this situation to drag on. It will only get worse.'

'You know, there's a lot of resentment and anger that's built up here. They feel like they've had a raw deal.'

She sighed. 'Everyone has problems. The whole country is seething about something – climate, poverty, immigration, class, vaccines. But it isn't our job to solve the problem, that's for the politicians. We're just here to uphold the law.'

'Keep everyone in line.'

Her eyes narrowed, no honey now. 'If need be. If that's what we have to do.' She looked at him. 'Listen, I need you to be my eyes and ears inside the village. We're putting an air asset on the case, but you can't beat human intelligence.

I want you to remain in contact with me at regular intervals on my direct line, let me know what's going on… can you do that for me, Sergeant?'

He looked around with a shrug. 'I can do that. That's my duty, isn't it?'

'Exactly. We all have to do our job, regardless of how we may feel. I really need your help here. I need you to hold things together in there, help the people who don't want to join the party. It is down to you now. You good with that?'

Lloyd grimaced. 'You can rely on me.'

The commander reached up to place a hand on his upper arm. 'That's what I thought.' She gave him a smile, which Lloyd found slightly disconcerting in so senior an officer. 'You'd best be off, and Sergeant…'

'Yes ma'am?'

'Remember what I said. Uphold the rule of law. That's our job. Nothing else.'

Lloyd nodded and walked back to the barricade, thinking for some reason of his dead sister. Climbing back over, he could see the beginnings of a party atmosphere. Beers and wines had replaced the coffee and tea at the stand, people were laughing and standing together. As he passed in between them, mostly ignored, he could sense a feeling of joy almost as if the village had been lifted by rediscovering itself. Even Lloyd in his depths of isolation could sense the place as more than a collection of paint-chipped streets leading to a battered pub. It was more than a collection of holiday-home dreams and the whims of others. And more than a destiny already written in the stars.

Thirty-One

Lloyd drove down into the village square, and parked his vehicle. He got out, and reached inside for his cap, which nestled on the passenger's seat. Suitably attired, he strode toward the Pimlotts' home. A few of the boys stood in singlets and jeans near the wrecked police van. They watched him curiously as he crossed the cobbled square; one of them called out a single 'Traitor!' Lloyd rapped on the door knocker then stood back from the doorway so that he could be clearly seen from the house's bay windows. Sure enough above to his left, a net curtain parted an inch, and he heard footsteps descending the stairs inside. The door opened; it was Frankie Pimlott.

'Sergeant.'

'Ms Pimlott.'

'To what do we owe this pleasure, this royal visit from our local law enforcement officer? Are you here to inform us that we're being turfed from our homes for not being Welsh? I for one would not be surprised, anyone with a half a brain cell can see that we're being forced out of our own property.' The sarcasm was being laid on with a polished shovel.

'No, madam, I'm just checking on some of the households to see if you're okay…'

'Have you checked on the Milton-Greenes? Y'know, the poor saps across the harbour who were foolish enough to invest in a house here? Who spend a pile of money in this place every time they come up? It looks like they're leaving today.'

'No, I didn't know that.'

'On the ball as always, I see. Of course, you do appreciate that if you'd allowed me to prosecute this Meic Davies individual when he physically assaulted me, as I wished, then none of this would have taken place. He'd be in prison, just where people like him should be. But I deferred to your judgement and behold the consequences. Civilisation drowned by the rule of the mob.'

Lloyd shook his head. 'Now no one could have foreseen this.'

'You realise that the hooligan didn't even repay me for the dry cleaning to my suit?'

'No madam. I can understand why you're so angry.'

'Are you trying to be funny? Are you?' Frankie glowered. 'I suggest that you're the very last person who should be poking fun at me.'

Lloyd ignored the comment as he could see Ruth appear over her partner's shoulder. 'Sergeant Parry, is everything okay?'

'I'm just doing my rounds, checking that some of the *newer* residents here know that the village shop is still open. Maybe you're running low on milk or something…'

Ruth looked into his eyes, recovering herself before Frankie could notice. 'Milk? Yes, I think we're running short. But my partner…'

'You mean your wife,' Frankie shot the phrase out.

'... my partner didn't want me to go out in case there was trouble.'

'Well, no problem now. I'm happy to escort you to the shop and back.' Lloyd flushed. 'If you need milk, that is.'

Ruth turned to Frankie. 'What a kind offer. Wait one moment, I'll just get some money.'

She left the pair while she fetched her purse in the kitchen. Waiting for her, Lloyd examined an abstract painting hanging in their hallway, while Frankie took an intense interest in the view of the boats in the harbour. The over-sized sound of an over-sized clock grew louder from the open door of their front room.

'Here we are. Shall we go? Won't be more than twenty minutes, Frankie.' Ruth looked at her partner, who was in full uncomprehending mode, mouth slightly agape, probably in need of a reboot.

Frankie recovered herself. 'For milk? Really, I mean, make an effort to hide it at least.'

'Oh, zip it for once, woman.' Ruth breezed out of her home and Lloyd jogged after her to catch up.

'Sorry, I wanted to see you.'

'So did I. How is it going out here in 1775? Any tea tipped into the harbour yet? I saw that we even had a technical advisor on that here yesterday evening.'

Lloyd looked blank. 'Not great to be honest.'

'I tried to contact you. Did you get the note?'

'Yes, thanks. It meant a lot.'

'I wanted to call, but I'm currently being trailed from room to room by you-know-who. That's when she isn't surveying everyone from the bedroom window.' Ruth inclined her head back to where she'd come from and slowed her pace. 'So what are we going to do?'

'Don't know, Ruth. But we need to find some place where we can talk properly.' Lloyd came to a halt. 'Catrin left me.'

'Yes, I overheard two of the fishwives chatting at full volume as I walked past them. I'm sorry.'

'No, you don't need to be. It's been a long time coming. But I don't think you should stray too far from your home. It may get a bit funny about here from now on.'

'As if it isn't already?' They began walking again. The sun beat down like a firing squad.

'Well, I spoke with my colleagues. They don't sound as if they're going to let this go on for too much longer. That means aggro. Ah, here we are.' He looked at Sion and Graham loitering outside the Spar. 'With two of Meic's little helpers to make sure we don't trip over the step.'

They entered the shop – Lloyd noted that the tinned goods shelves showed little sign of depletion. Rich Hughes looked up. 'All right Lloyd, back so soon?'

Two women already there froze, their eyes laser-guiding in on the spectacle of the policeman together with Ruth, before they turned away to examine the stale remains of the bakery section. Ruth had experienced this reaction before, though usually in an office setting, so felt unperturbed as she walked over to the chiller cabinet and removed a two-pint carton of milk from the shelf. Smiling at Lloyd she wandered over to the freezer chest, opened it, pulled out two ice lollies and carried her purchases over to the till. Lewis was just about to punch in the numbers, when his wife, grey hair bobbing, appeared from the storeroom behind the counter and elbowed her husband aside. 'I'll take care of this, dear.'

Mrs Hughes picked up the milk and scanned it. 'Bag?'

Ruth shook her head.

The older woman appeared to look more closely at the label. 'Oh yes, full creamy head. Just right for your tastes.'

Lloyd spoke quietly, 'Let's just have the minimum of fuss here, eh?'

'Well, Sergeant, how's your wife then. I heard that she's moved out. Was in school with her I was.' Mrs Hughes scanned the two ice lollies and then threw them onto the counter.

Ruth looked up sharply. Mrs Hughes dead-panned, 'Oh, don't tell me he hasn't said anything? No? Well that's the sergeant for you. Likes to have his little secrets. Catrin – Mrs Parry – left, oh let's see, two whole days ago now. Took her youngest with her. That's £2.97. Cash only if you please.'

Lloyd sighed. 'Let's go, Ruth.'

Ruth stared at the shopkeeper for a moment before she dropped a five-pound note onto the lollies.

'Thank you, Ms Pimlott, two pounds and three of your English pence. All present and correct. Wouldn't do to short-change you now, would it. Not as the master race.'

'You're quite happy to accept those *English pence* you racist cow.' Ruth pronounced the words slowly, then spun on her heel.

Mrs Hughes took a backward step, her mouth open. 'How dare you, I'm not one of those. If you decide to live here, try learning our language first before you judge us, you little slag.' She leant over the counter, haranguing at Ruth's retreating back, before turning to the policeman. 'And you're no better, Lloyd Parry, call yourself Welsh. How long have you been here, haven't made a blind bit of effort to fit in!'

Lloyd picked up the ice-lollies and half-jogged after Ruth, trying not to make it too obvious, even though he knew that it was pointless given they were obviously village gossip. He sped up. 'Ruth!'

Meic's two goons laughed as he ran past them, catching her just over the road. She stopped and stared into space ahead. 'That bloody fat old spiteful cow!'

'Oh come on, Ruthie, it's not that big a deal, is it? She's just one of the chapel squad. If you have sex for anything other than procreation, they summon down the hellfire.'

'I know.'

Lloyd took her hand – fuck the whole lot of gossips. 'What's the matter?'

She sighed. 'I don't know what I'm thinking. Not anymore. Everyone knows about us. This changes things for us. It has all become real.'

Lloyd couldn't find any words that seemed right; he tried to say something but stumbled.

She examined his face, touched his cheek with her hand. 'You're right, we should talk, but not now. Let things calm down over the next couple of days, then we can meet. Your wife and kids, Frankie… I don't know, this isn't quite how I thought it would be. I just need some space to think. Sorry, Lloyd.'

'But—'

'No, Lloyd, don't say a thing. Please understand.'

Graham had slumped over from his position outside the shop, swigging from a lager can, laughing, amused by seeing the confirmation of what he'd heard in the pub. 'Eh Lloydie, getting a bit of jigga-jigga action there…'

Lloyd swung round at them, but it was Ruth who came striding back and answered, 'If you have got anything to say, come over here and say it to my face. And then we'll see how small your cock is, before I fucking rip it off!'

Graham stared at her. Ruth forced him to break her gaze and he retreated. 'Fuckin' dirty bitch.' Sion looked scarlet as his mate sat back down, much to Graham's delight.

Lloyd made to walk towards them, but Ruth grabbed his arm. 'Forget it, he's just a small boy.' She took a deep breath. 'But what I said was true, we both need to think about this.'

'Yeah, I guess.'

'It's funny, isn't it?'

'What?'

'Those idiots, swaggering around like Gestapo. They can dress it up any way you like, but it's just inadequate little boys at play.'

He watched her walk slowly to her front door and close it behind her. Heard the double click of the locks. Boats in the harbour rode the tide, dumb to the scene.

Lloyd felt a sudden chill in his hands: the lollipops. He unwrapped one, and bit into the raspberry-flavoured ice. The other he placed on top of the Pimlotts' front garden wall. Then he walked back to his Land Rover and drove one-handed to the opposite side of the harbour, taking his time in order to finish the ice-lolly. As he approached, he could see the Milton-Greenes carrying luggage to their jet-black Range Rover. Meic Davies was also in attendance, talking to them as they brushed by him carrying luggage. Bit of a turn-up.

Lloyd pulled into the kerb and wound his window down.

'What's going on here, Meic? What are you doing?'

Meic held up his hands. 'Believe it or not, Sergeant, I'm trying to encourage these good people to stay in their home.'

Lloyd looked at Jolyon Milton-Greene. 'Is this true?'

The Englishman slammed the boot of his 4x4. 'Yes, true to a point. But then we wouldn't even be thinking about leaving early if we hadn't been forced to live in Gulag Gogogoch. By him.' He pointed at Davies.

Lloyd remonstrated, 'Mr Milton-Greene, no one is making you go. This is your village as much as his.'

He looked at Meic, expecting a quick retort, but the young man's face remained impassive. 'I've told them, Sergeant, it's only the new incomers and interferers that we don't want. If they are already here and integrate properly, then we'll tolerate them.'

Milton-Greene threw a bag into the back seat and slammed the car door. 'Neither my wife nor I wish to be *tolerated*, chum. One of your local heroes sold me this house for a great deal of money. They didn't object at the time to us using this place for our holidays and no one forced them to accept my offer. In fact, as we remember it, they were very happy about the premium they received and being able to retire to Costa Del Sol or wherever.'

'But what choice did they have?' Meic checked himself. 'Look, if you want to leave do it, but it is not the official position of this community to force people out.'

Lloyd opened the door of his Land Rover. 'In any case sir, you won't be able to drive out. Both exits from the village are blocked.'

'So how the hell do I get out? We both have work on Monday morning, back in the real world.' Milton-Greene glowered at Meic. 'Some of us have to live in the real world in order to pay our taxes in order to subsidise *you people*. Have you thought about that?'

Meic spat on the grass bordering the street. 'Listen, I've tried to be reasonable, but people like you,' he took a deep breath, 'people like you just want us to bow and scrape and return to an age when you were the big mine-owners and we were the serfs. Fine, but it won't be happening here. Your lordship can royally piss off and with my blessing!'

'How dare you! I've invested in this place.'

'You've invested in an asset for yourself. And you did it through a company. I know, I've seen the Land Registry. And why's that? To avoid paying taxes.'

'You have no right to—'

'It's public information. And you know what else you can find on the internet? That during the crisis, because this house was registered as a business, you claimed for £10,000 from the Welsh Government out of the emergency Covid fund. That's how much you wanted to be part of the community. Take cash out and use services which you won't pay for.'

Jolyon Milton-Greene whitened and deployed "the accent" as his last line of defence: received pronunciation usually worked in cutting these people down to size. 'My financial affairs are none of your business. In any case, there was a good explanation for that.'

Meic was already walking off. 'I don't think so, you fucking parasite. See you up at the barricade, twat.'

Lloyd sniffed and turned to the Milton-Greenes, who were exchanging a look. 'Okay then. I'll tell you what, I'll drive you up to the barricade and we'll get some of my colleagues on the other side to give you a lift to the nearest rail station.'

Jolyon Milton-Greene raised his hands to the gods, his signet ring flashing in the sun. 'Get a train? You all told us to bugger off when Covid was around, then couldn't wait to get us back a few month later when you need the cash. And now this, unbelievable! These people…'

From her home across the harbour, Frankie watched the scene through her Czech-made binoculars, as the Milton-Greenes transferred their luggage to Lloyd's car. She uttered a small sigh over the thought that Sophie Milton-Greene would no longer be around to share a glass of fine red and compare notes on Chekhov. Such a sophisticated, well-put-together woman and a decent bridge player as well. Chalk up another victim to this pogrom.

It appeared to Frankie as if the oaks were falling one by one. These small-minded nationalists were getting their own way and the police were helping them. This was nothing other than tyranny, just with a different face. Ruth was nearly as bad, consorting with *that* man. She knew nothing about the police guy. Nor did she know about her own wife either, so wrapped up as Ruth was in her latest quest for *personal fulfilment*. Did she know that Frankie's father had been a designer at the huge British Leyland plant in Longbridge? His vehicles, it could be said with hindsight, admittedly hadn't set the world aflame with their beauty, performance, or reliability. Still, it was something tangible. But when had Ruth ever bothered to show an interest in Frankie's family? When she was younger Frankie had wanted to surpass her father and build things that people could touch and admire. That's why she'd been drawn to architecture, even if it had turned out to be not quite as glamorous a profession as Norman Foster and Ayn Rand had portrayed. But in the past decade it seemed all she had built was a reputation for having an educated view on the best-looking juicer or the hippest opening night to attend. Some people, such as her father, might consider that outcome a disappointment.

But now here she was, in a position to change things for the better. Meic Davies wasn't the only so-called person of destiny around here and it was up to her to stop the fascist scum in his tracks. Frankie returned her attention to the laptop and the email she was composing to her new editor.

To: andypallister@dailygazette.com
From: styleguru101@pimlottassociates.com

Andrew,

I enclose my first short piece from inside the village per our phone discussion. You may note a change of tone from my usual prose, possibly more suited to a leader article? I'll continue to send you regular updates on events as they transpire.

You should also be aware that Sky News has been in touch for a live interview for their bulletin, so that should increase the readership.

Yours,

Frankie.

Llanawch – A village on the edge

By Frankie Pimlott

Germany 1939, Bosnia 1993, now Wales can be added to the infamous list of countries which have experienced the shame of ethnic cleansing. Within the last hour I've witnessed at first hand the expulsion of an ordinary English family from their home. Not just at the hands of the local bully boys, but aided and abetted by the local police, who seem intent on cowering to the will of these criminals rather than enforcing the rule of law. Not even in Scotland at the height of the civic nationalist campaign, nor outside the Supreme Court after the Referendum, did I witness such outrageous intimidation of fellow citizens.

Our ancestors fought and died to make this country free and safe from fascism, and sixty million people in the rest of the United Kingdom subscribe to the so-called *old-fashioned* values of democracy. Yet this means nothing to the small band of rabid nationalists who have held this village hostage. The saddest thing about this situation is the docility of the local populace, the passive acceptance of this self-appointed regime. Hasn't anyone read the dictum that it only takes good men to do nothing for evil to prosper? Doesn't anyone remember the events of a few years past? It is no good being opposed to something, if you aren't going to do anything about it.

My hope in coming to Llanawch was to help change it in a positive way, to give people a better place to live in, and to halt the seemingly terminal decline which this place, like so many others, is experiencing. But much bitterness on the part of those unwilling to accept the inevitability of change has flowed under the bridge since then.

There are countless places – inner cities, county towns, country villages – which are desperately in search of a hopeful future, because they have remained too long in the past. However, building that future requires a new mind-set and fresh energy; often – as we have seen in the case of Stratford and the Olympics – it requires a spur to make change happen.

I have laboured hard, almost single-handedly it has to be said, to be the catalyst for better times for this small village. But it seems the mediaeval outlook of some elements in this community cannot get over ancient history and would rather cut themselves off from the modern world. The majority must fight their myopia and build for the future, just as we are rebuilding a better, fairer, less bigoted Britain in the wake of our 2020 nadir.

Perhaps it will be my turn tomorrow to hear the harsh knock on the door of the local terrorists. Perhaps they will come to visit me in the night, and I will be ethnically cleansed, and I will give you no guesses for wondering what ethnic background appears to cause such distress.

But until the forces of right and law reclaim this place, I am remaining. I will not tolerate these people any longer. This country of ours was not built upon those who would cede power to undemocratic bullyboys, and neither will I.

Frankie scanned once more through the piece. Was it too angry or just direct? Notwithstanding, it was a powerful polemic which spoke truth, and she was one with Cicero in that there was no dignity without honesty. Not to add that a little controversy might draw in more readers – a columnist lived on generating a reaction, any reaction.

She made herself click on send and without thinking walked over to the window to survey the square. Those people out there, good honest people on the face of it, she supposed, but with such limited horizons, and who could deny that? Even so how could they be duped by such a charlatan? That Ruth appeared sympathetic to the villagers and that stupid, lazy policeman was quite beyond her comprehension. That they were growing apart by the day had become obvious; what to do about it was unknown. Maybe she should tell her about her illness, even if the sea air seemed to have done her much good. No, not her business; Frankie was not in the business of becoming some charity case dependent on Ruth's affections. And if that silly girl thought she held the whip hand she was mistaken.

In London, Frankie had sensed that there might have been other temptations for Ruth, but this one was different, and a man at that. What her wife failed to realise was that two could play at that game. Frankie knew that she wasn't without her own admirers in their circles in London. She looked at the photo of them together on holiday in Sardinia which was perched on her desk. She softly drew a finger along the glass and examined the grey residue collected on her fingertip. Damn it all, this place was so dusty. They had employed a daily cleaner in London, but Ruth was neglecting her duties up here as the non-working partner; she should be keeping the house tidy and free of this disgusting squalor. Frankie sniff gave her eye a quick rub to clear it of the irritation.

Thirty-Two

Meic watched as the last of the guests from the hotel scrambled over the barricade and, trailing their roller suitcases, sought the protection of the police lines like war refugees seeking sanctuary. Even from this distance he could hear the hungry clicks of cameras and rapacious shouts as the media pride feasted on the latest twist in the story. Hovering above the scene, the police helicopter was ordered to return to base, ostensibly for refuelling, but actually to make way for the Sky and BBC news choppers to dogfight for position. McArdle knew the power of the live image in garnering public support, and as such she'd placed several women constables prominently on the front line – editors loved a photo of a blonde woman officer (preferably looking suitably vulnerable as well) bravely holding back the massed hordes and protecting civilisation.

The exodus of holidaymakers trapped inside the cordon was the one element which Meic had not anticipated and he berated himself for his lack of foresight. Even though the protest was partly about holiday homes, he hadn't figured the occupants of those homes into his calculations. Stupid.

Spun the wrong way, this was going to look very bad for his protest. He felt a grip on his upper arm.

'So, what have you got to say about this then?'

It was Alex, the hotel's manager.

Meic flicked the pudgy hand away. 'They're getting their knickers in a twist, that's all.'

'That is my trade walking off down the road. We're almost empty and our restaurant bookings are cancelling by the minute. It's going to take me months to catch up on lost business. That's if I can.'

'Yeah, sorry about that. No, don't be like that, I honestly am.'

'Sorry is not going to pay staff wages. Don't you understand?'

'Well, I can't pay them; we don't have the funds. That's all there is to it.'

The manager ran his fingers through the remnants of hair on his head. 'I'm not asking you to. But you can call this stupid protest off. Some of us have businesses to run.'

Meic placed his hands on his hips. 'Look, we all knew that there would be some hiccups, but the village together signed up for this, including the businesses.'

'Businesses? Oh, you mean Hughes, down at Spar? Well, his shop isn't going down the tubes, is it now? Everyone needs food, but my customers don't live here. They can't get to me for a bed for the night. This is high season mind; this pays for the rest of the year, doesn't it! And you know the shitty seasons we've struggled through since all that Covid performance. High season? It's been more like a succession of autumns.'

Meic held his hands up. 'I understand, but we can't turn back now.'

'I didn't agree to this,' he gestured at the departing tourists, 'we're not all behind you, Davies. What you and your boys don't seem to get is that many of us didn't sign up for an independence movement. We just wanted the council to do something.'

'Oh for Christ's sake, Alex! In case you hadn't noticed, protesting is what we're doing. Don't you think that there's any other way to get London's attention. And we have, and now we've got them panicking.'

'Panicking? Are you bloody crazy? That's total crap. They have got us nice and bottled up on this side and I don't see any panic over there,' Alex gestured over at the police. 'Do you know what I have to do now? I have to call the hotel's owners and ask them permission to keep the staff on and pay them. This isn't bloody furlough, there's no government bailout this time, you moron. People could lose their livelihoods. And you're not the one who will have to tell them to their faces!'

'Well, that's your job. So why don't you do it?'

'Don't you realise what's going here? We were betting on this year to balance the books and now you pull this stroke. You're fucking up any chance of us staying in business. And I can't be the only business in the red…'

The manager threw up his arms and shambled back down the road to make for the bar of his near-empty business, but the rising volume of the exchange had attracted the attention of those manning the barricades. Noticing this, Meic turned to them to laugh it off. 'Okay, okay. We all knew that some of the weaker ones among us would crack. But we're not like Alex, we are *the strong*. We have to carry the rest through until the government listens. Now ignore the whining and the crocodile tears and a few of the plague-carriers pissing off back to London, and let's all do the right thing, which is to send a loud message to everyone out there. That Wales is not for sale and we are not for turning!'

With his barricade crew returning to their positions, Meic climbed up onto the back of his 4x4 where his lieutenant, Sion, was looking over at the opposing lines. He could see a woman police officer standing in front of a group of press.

'What's happening?'

'See that woman. I think she's in charge – she's been bossing the men around for most of the day. Come to think of it, you two have a lot in common.'

'Very funny. What's she saying?'

'Can't make it out through this breeze.'

'I can tell you.' A woman's voice from behind the front cab.

Meic looked down at Lexy, who was holding her laptop. 'Bring it up here.'

Meic held out a hand to pull her up, which Lexy ignored. She set the laptop on the roof of the driver's cabin once more. 'Live coverage from the BBC News website. Check it out.' She lit up a cigarette as they watched the news conference.

'Hey look, you can see us in the background.' Sion pointed at the video stream. 'Hey, world, have some of that!' He stuck two fingers up in the air, watching himself several seconds later on the screen.

'Stop that you twat, we're not a bunch of yobs, but do that and that's what they'll think.' Meic gave Sion a hard punch on the arm, not seeing the look of pain on his friend's face. 'Turn up the volume, then.'

Lexy adjusted the controls and moved her position slightly so the on-looking camera had a clearer view of her. She tossed her hair, seeing the BBC camera steady and then focus in on her. Yeah, lap it up boys. That would get them wondering who that mystery woman was. She held her cigarette at what she thought was a suitably seductive angle, and saw her delayed action reproduced on the laptop's screen. Her life had become a digital reality; all those people watching her online, it was intoxicating.

A red banner, running along the bottom of the video-stream read, "LIVE: Llanawch Siege. Police press conference with Commander Kate McArdle."

'...taking so long?'

'Now is not the time to make hasty decisions. We in the police service are very aware that vulnerable people – young children, pensioners – have been placed on the barricades by the ringleaders. We are not sure if there was an element of coercion here or not. In any case, we will carry out our duties in a careful and most of all, responsible, manner to take account of the people that have been caught up in this.'

'We've been told by sources in Cardiff that you've been forced to call in police from outside the area because there's been a mutiny by local officers. Can you confirm whether this is true?'

'This is a delicate situation, so under previously agreed arrangements we have called in specialist policing units, who are best able to efficiently and carefully resolve such matters.'

'So why the reports that the Army has been placed on standby? Why the firearms squads?'

'The Army has not been placed on standby. They are just helping us with some logistical issues, that's all. We've borrowed some construction vehicles from the Royal Engineers and brought them here because they were the nearest machines available suited to road clearance. We need to widen this area where we stand as it's all a bit of a squeeze in here.'

'And the firearms squads?'

'We have received reports of firearms being in the possession of a faction of the protestors. My experience is that it is best to be prudent in these matters as it will minimise danger to the public. I think I have time to take one more question… ah, Brian.'

'You were applauded for your leadership during the *Financial Times* climate protest siege in London last year. That ended peacefully. Do you expect the same here?'

'A peaceful end to the protest here is obviously our over-riding aim and we are working tirelessly towards that. I think that if the protestors behave reasonably, we have every chance of a successful resolution. However, we as police officers have a duty of care towards the safety of those in village who don't agree with the protest and are not in a position to leave, or as we just saw, be expelled. While we will avoid the use of physical force, if we feel that the public's lives are being placed in danger, then we have absolutely no option under law but to act in the interests of public safety. Thank you, ladies and gentlemen.'

Meic looked at Lexy. 'Well?'

She took a drag of her cigarette. 'She's good. I think that she may have played this game before.'

'I can't believe that they've called the Army in. It's like

they've declared martial law in our little bit of Wales.'

'That's not how it came across. No one mentioned any troops being called up, just a couple of diggers.'

'Well… still, London has got to be running scared, what do you think? You wait until people see those tanks, then they'll realise what kind of country they live in.'

'Maybe, but you've got to keep putting the word out. Listen, can I get an interview with you? CNN have called me for a *human interest* piece.'

'Human interest? They do realise that this isn't *Passport to Pimlico*? These are people's lives.'

'Meic, they're Americans. They wouldn't have seen *Passport to Pimlico*, the body count in it is too low for their tastes… relax, I'm joking. I'll make sure you get your point across.'

'This isn't funny.'

Lexy bristled. 'Hey, you of all people should remember the power of media, mainstream or social. Who is getting Wikileaks to dump a batch of MI5 papers on Welsh nationalists onto its site? Me, that's who. I didn't see you come up with that one.'

Meic nodded; he'd have to go along with her as long as she was useful to him. 'Okay, fair play. But I was the one who had the idea for vloggers to publicise us. And bankrolled it.'

Lexy stepped back and saw how his eyes had once more flicked downwards. 'Fine. But it's CNN, which means global coverage. So when can I get some sound bites and video from you to post?'

'Give me five minutes, Sion's asked for a quick word.'

Lexy looked from Meic's face to Sion's and smiled knowingly; she had picked up the vibes even if Meic was blinkered to everything but the protest and her chest. She stubbed out her cigarette and pretended to fiddle with her phone as Meic and Sion walked to the water's edge. She watched the discussion which quickly became animated. Lexy pointed her phone at them and, under the guise of adjusting the controls, took a few photos, just in case. Hell, why bother to disguise it, they weren't noticing anything anyway. She watched as Sion pulled something – *was it wrapped?* – out of his pocket and handed it over to Meic. Meic examined the package, looking puzzled. Some more words were exchanged. Sion looked agitated, and so did Meic, for that matter. And then Sion placed his hand on Meic's forearm, only for it to be violently slung off and for Meic to shove him back, stumbling onto the ground. Sion look stunned, then got to his feet and ran off. Lexy could see the anger suddenly etched into his face.

As she mused later that evening, knocking off three hundred words on the scene for *The Telegraph*, the story wrote itself. That she had bothered to write it at all was a sign of her boredom. The hotel bar was empty, and she'd been rash enough to fruitlessly try it on with the young Spanish barman on her second night there, when keeping him in reserve would have been a smarter option. It had been a long time since she was hottest-to-trottest at college and his disdain only made her feel the age gap. She picked up her mobile to see if there was any Tinder action going but put it smartly back down as she realised that all communications from the village would doubtless now be monitored. Lexy wasn't about to give the listening authorities any leverage over her for future use. Bored, she picked up her laptop from the room's writing desk and slumped onto her double bed with its spread of pillows. The mouse cursor hovered over her Favourites menu, before she clicked on the official protest website with its twitter feed. Always entertaining to waste a few minutes checking out the random thoughts that people felt comfortable transferring directly from their mind to the public domain without any filtering standing in the way… now what's been posted onto the *Walesfightsback* hash tag in the last hour?

> *@boyosfromblackstuff* Meic we support you for evermore #fairplaycymru sign our petition and support your country!

> *@saveshermouthuponlee* Not just Lanawch. Mega supermarket has been given planning to open outside our town in Dorset – goodbye High Street #fightthechains

> *@meibbeginner* so proud that some Welshmen stand 4 what is right #cymruambyth

Lexy rolled her eyes. So far, so predictable.

> *@comedyhousexeter* Do you think the welsh stasi beat protestors with leeks?!! #JackieHarrisTourUK2023

Oh Jesus, who was going to buy a ticket to a gig with gags like that, still at least he hadn't worked in a cripple joke which was his usual shtick. She read on, looking at later entries.

> *@manobeer* why is Cardiff letting London call the shots its our country. Typical kowtowing from so called ministers in the Bay!

@tmgoddard All this talk about the young, what about pensioners? the cost of cigarettes and beer keeps rising and they are now after our free tv licences

@bronwynww that *@MeicDavies* is hot wud do him anytime anyplace tweet me meic!

Been there, didn't do that.

@colonelsensibleUK why are we wasting money on police for this protest when our own schools underfunded?? We have all this debt to repay and they are just adding to the pile. Leave the taffs to it. #Englishindependencenow

@saltireoftruth Your Celtic brothers are behind you all the way. Politicians talk of being in this together but they keep dumping on us. Get the message that we've had enough and we're not the only ones! #ScotlandDecides

@threelionsandproud I'm English living in Wales. Looking forward to the Welsh Government paying me a relocation allowance!! #notwantedhere

@concernedcitizen Did someone misplace the rule of law? Too many special interests and minorities telling us how we can think. End it now.

@DomDavies News has reached Hollywood! Go Wales! Sorry can't be with you right now but

thinking of you all. My new film is released next week so busy! #LegendoftheSpaceVikings2

Make a note, contact his agent to set up a phone interview, get his views on what this means for his homeland. You're full of ideas today girl!

@Bluedefender89 More media bias, establishment close ranks to protect the so-called union again. #Yes

@mrsocialenterprise Has someone told these guys they may do better creating some community business? SMEs are bedrock of jobs creation. Better off redirecting their energy to business start-ups. http//ruralbusinessaction.com

Yada, yada, yada. Save the advertising for the *Nowheresville Times*.

@LuckhamRules Protesting is fine, but the Southeast don't want to pay for a new Greece Ireland Portugal. Already enough for us to bail out!!! #charitycases

@mrspaFrankieaharris Hubbie is a policeman on front line up there and I'm worried about his safety. Sadly he doesn't get same rights as the law breakers who put him in danger.

That could be a nice angle to work. Lexy made a note of the woman's name on her bedside pad underneath the film star's.

> *@Longmemories86* Surely not the same Michael Davies as at my school. Oh dear. Once an idiot, always an idiot. Ask him about not becoming Head Boy and watch the steam come out of his ears!

Pissing shit ants. That was supposed to be her exclusive. But she was kind of trapped, unable to publish it until the siege ended. Let's hope it didn't excite attention.

> *@TechJack1* Protestors need to get real. The world has changed. I grew up in a place like this but moved to where the jobs were and built my business from there. Too many politicians talk but have no idea about job creation. #HendersonTechnology
>
> > *@OneSocietyLeeds* How's Monaco? Still dodging the taxes? If you don't live here and don't pay tax here, don't lecture us from your billionaires bolthole.
> >
> > *@SaturdayComes1100* Enjoyed losing my job when you shut the Leicester factory. Still looking for work. Hope the low-paid workers in Myanmar are enjoying producing your latest over-priced designer shit.
>
> *@younggungoes* thanks welsh protestors this will wake up country to shattered dreams of young people in uk today #lostgeneration
>
> *@peterkevensam* While my heart goes out to people of Llanawch, this is all down to bungling & brutal government cuts #VoteEvans4Senedd2026

@UnionJack51 Hehe. Britannia no longer rule the world. So wrong on Iraq, Brexit and Hong Kong. Wales should go independence. They should learn from Chinese Dream to see real success story.

@JoshuaHaynes-Willis MidWales Green Collective salutes you and we'll hold a minutes thought at our committee meeting tonight.

@SirMarkWareham Pictures of ethnic cleansing in a Commonwealth country truly sickening. The government must intervene at once or face more puerile calls for the breakup of the once-proud Great Britain. #dailygazettecomment #BackingBritain #GlobalBritain

Lexy felt a chill as she read the final comment. For all the expensive public inquiries, the media owners still ruled the roost and Sir Mark was one South African magnate it was foolish to cross, it didn't matter if you were the Prime Minister or a freelance Irish journalist with an appetite for sexually dubious men. Perhaps it was time to switch sides; being friends with Gazette Group Corporation could be a less limiting career move. She weighed this up against her loyalty to Meic, who had, after all, given her the means to get her by-line onto the front pages. But business was business. Lexy searched through her contact list and emailed a features sub-editor she knew who still worked at the Gazette: *Let me know if you need some colour from inside the protests. Yr call darling. Lexy.*

Thirty-Three

The twin-prop aircraft reached the coast near Aberystwyth and turned north to follow its line. The pilot's voice was clear over the headphones given to the two passengers at the start of its flight from Cardiff. 'Ten minutes to Llanbedr Airfield.'

The woman called Joan pulled down her microphone and replied, 'Take us via a clockwise loop over Llanawch. I want to see the geographic layout.'

'Wilco.'

Crammed next to her in the back section of the plane sat Lewis. He wasn't happy with being diverted from his important duties in his office, but the Minister had insisted that someone senior from the Welsh Government was on scene. Given his travelling companion he sincerely doubted that his presence would have any impact at all on decision-making. It was the typical Whitehall stitch-up, the slightest sign of something important and suddenly Cardiff was side-lined. All the more reason why he should move. He looked across Joan to the view of long deserted beaches, suddenly replaced by rapidly rising cliffs passing below them and touched her shoulder. 'Pretty beautiful scenery isn't it,' he shouted over the engine noise.

She nodded, slightly detached, and returned her gaze to the window as the plane started to bank in a lazy circle over the mouth of the estuary. Lewis tried again. 'So small, it's just a pin prick.'

'Yes. But pin pricks can infect a whole body. So we're treating this one now.' The circle completed, the plane straightened up and began to descend. The pilot's voice cut in, 'Two minutes to landing, make sure that you're buckled in.'

Lewis listened to the tone of the engines drop, and from his window he saw the ground rush to meet them, over the airfield perimeter fence and then they were down and taxiing towards a hanger.

The propellers jerked to a halt and one of the pilots appeared from the cockpit to open the exit and deploy the small steps to the ground. 'Okay, looks like there's a car organised to meet you just out there.' He smiled as they walked past. 'We know you have a choice, so we thank you for choosing the Royal Air Force.'

Lewis saw Joan smile for the first time. 'Not sure about the meal service!'

They stepped down from the craft and walked towards the waiting police car. The civil servant looked around. 'I'd forgotten that this place was up here.'

'Have you never been? After all it is your country.'

'At my level you don't generally get out of Cardiff that much.'

'It's an old wartime airfield which we kept going during the Cold War. At one point, it was designated one of the dispersal sites for the V-bombers in case things became hot.'

'So top secret then?'

‘Oh, I should think that everyone around here knew at the time. It’s quite difficult to disguise a Vulcan bomber howling overhead. But of course, they didn’t have Instagram then to tell the world and the Soviets.’

A policewoman was waiting for them at the car. ‘I’m Kate McArdle and you must be Joan.’

‘Present and correct, Commander.’ They shook hands. ‘And this is Lewis our, I guess, “minder” from Cathays Park.’

Lewis who was putting on his jacket, asked, ‘So I could do with a full briefing then. For instance, I’d like to know what your strategy is to get this sorted.’

McArdle exchanged knowing glances with Joan. ‘Well, we enter the village and re-establish order…’

‘Well, that’s obvious.’

‘And then we buy them off.’ Joan looked at Lewis. ‘Don’t worry, we’ll use the Treasury’s contingency fund, it won’t hit your budget.’

The Commander held open the front passenger door for Lewis. ‘We should get going, it’s quite a way over the mountain to reach our command post on the other side.’

Lewis took off his jacket and sat down, sensitive to the quiet exchanges of the two women who took the seats behind him as the car moved off.

Judge Heywood looked up at the plane circling over the village, raised his cup of tea, blew on its surface and took a tentative sip. ‘I see that it’s another hot one today. Forecast is for late-twenties in a couple of hours.’

Lloyd lowered his binoculars. They were standing in the open dormer window of Heywood’s attic, from where the barricade could be clearly viewed. 'I'm sure there's a link between stuff like this and the weather. I mean, nobody kicks off in the middle of a monsoon.'

The Judge sniffed his agreement. 'Anything happening? It was all quiet last night.'

Lloyd carefully placed the binoculars on the windowsill. 'The usual stand-off. We've got Gwyn Phillips and his mob hanging around the barricade. But nothing doing from my about to be ex-colleagues.'

'What do you mean?'

'Just they won't want me around after this. I can easily imagine being surplus to requirements.'

'Don't be too harsh on yourself. You'd be surprised at what sensible people will want.'

The Sergeant checked the time. 'I need to contact headquarters.'

They made their way downstairs. Lloyd looked around at the hallway paintings with their vibrant strokes of blues, purples and reds. He'd only visited Heywood's home on a couple of occasions before but had always been impressed. It was how he imagined someone like the Judge, those well-off and educated types, should live. 'It's a very nice house you have here – nice paintings.'

'Thank you. My late wife's work. Unlike me, she was very creative, she loved to paint.'

'How many years has it been now?'

'Oh, not that long, but going on an eternity…'

There was a silence; Lloyd didn't know how to reply. The Judge looked at him. 'Sorry, that was maudlin,' he guided Lloyd to the door. 'You know, when I was young, I'd always dreamt about owning a place like this. Specifically, this place. Even when I had a big practice and was pushing for silk in London, this house was always at the back of my mind. When I was growing up around here, it was the best house in the village, apart from the rectory of course, and was owned by the local solicitor. I thought to myself, growing up in a tiny, terraced house, Harlech Street you know, I thought, I fancy a bit of that. Probably why I went into the law in the first place. And then I met Judith, and we had the kids, and got on with life in the city. But then it was time to come home, and we'd planned a lovely retirement here. And then…' his eyes wandered, 'well, you can't plan for cancer, can you?'

Lloyd grimaced in sympathy. 'No you can't.'

The Judge gave a slight cough. 'Do let me know if I can be of assistance with this mess.'

On the doorstep Lloyd paused. 'Thanks, Judge. You know, I just can't understand this. It seems just so – I don't know – like a big own goal. I can't see what the village is going to get out of any of this. I know Bethan and everyone else is hacked off about the school and bloody Frankie Pimlott, but surely there's a better way to get things done. It just feels like King Canute trying to turn back the tide.'

'You shouldn't be surprised, Lloyd. People sometimes need to believe in a hope, and they suspend reality. These are tough times for Llanawch and they are looking for someone with answers. Young Meic Davies, it would appear, is just the man for a crisis. But you and I both know that things can change rather quickly.'

The Judge selected an umbrella from the stand and started to mimic forward-defensive cricket strokes. 'Used to play for my college. Long time ago of course. Never quite got round to joining the cricket club here. Which is greatly to my shame.'

'What do you mean by change?'

Heywood looked up. 'You see Lloyd, how can I put it? Um, try this – what Meic Davies hasn't taken into account is the intrinsic fickleness of human beings.'

'I don't follow?'

'What is gold today may become lead tomorrow. Transmogrification or reverse alchemy, you see. It's the psychology of crowds.'

'I don't follow.'

The Judge replaced the umbrella and walked out onto his drive. 'It strikes me that we have a group of people here, all currently on the same emotional arc. They're happy, they're elated, excited, the outside world is noticing them for the first time, the village is in the papers, on the television. This has become a place to be and so they are finally someone. But attention will move on, time will pass, and all too quickly. Thus the issue becomes: what happens next? And people will start to think about this and that's when there'll be a problem.'

'Because there isn't a next...'

'Exactly. There is no way out of this situation. The authorities are not going to let one small village cock a snook at them. One way or the other, they are going to restore law and order here. They cannot afford to do anything else. Even the Scots haven't pulled this trick.'

'I agree. It's just everyone's in total denial.'

'Not everyone, Lloyd.' He examined the policeman's face. 'Davies is too intelligent to venture up a dead end. I suspect that he has another agenda here. One which stretches beyond the confines of our village. Have you noticed that it's always Davies to the forefront when it comes to the media? Never anyone else. My instinct is that the village is being used by him for self-promotion.'

'But aren't there easier ways to become famous?'

'Maybe. He could write a book perhaps or makes some speeches. But that is terribly tedious, don't you think? After all, he'd be one of hundreds doing the same. Yet, because of this siege, I'd fancy that people will remember his name in several years' time. No politician can buy that treasure.'

'So, this is politics?'

'Yes of course, isn't it obvious? It should be, but I fear that everyone has allowed themselves to become caught up in the emotion of the act itself. It's seductive to be out on the street shouting at authority. I've seen that in my courtroom on a number of occasions. But at some point, people are going to begin to understand what's really going on.'

'And then?'

'Davies has a big problem.' Heywood looked at the estuary. 'My God, it is stunning out there. You know, every morning I feel that returning home was the second-best decision I made.'

'Second-best?'

'Marrying Judith. Naturally,' a wisp of a smile on his lips.

'She was a good woman.'

There followed a brief silence, broken by Lloyd clearing his throat with a cough. 'Just thinking about what you said. What if the villagers had a bit of a, er… education about Davies?'

'What, show them the real man, as it were?'

The Judge took a packet of tobacco out of his trouser pocket and started to fill his pipe. 'One of the better things about this ludicrous situation is that currently I can smoke where I wish, even in the pub. But I'd be more than happy to lose that benefit.'

Lloyd opened the door of his Land Rover. 'Thanks for the advice, Judge.'

'Before you go, just two things to bear in mind. A touch more psychology, I'm afraid.' He lit his pipe, puffing to help it catch. 'People don't like finding out they've been misled. And messengers often get shot.'

'I'm already carrying a wound; another won't make a difference.'

'Yes, I heard about that.'

'News even reached you?'

'Even out here in Siberia. Our friend Stevie at the pub may pull a fine pint, but he isn't exactly the soul of discretion. You know, Judith and I separated once, not for long, when I became fixated on my job. We got back together again, and it all worked out for us, but it's not always for the best… Tell you what, I'll buy you a drink tonight at the pub. You look as it you could do with one. Say about eight-thirty?'

'You've got a deal, Judge.'

'Goronwy, please.'

'Right then. I've got something to do a little later but count on me being there.'

Lloyd carefully eased his vehicle out through the gateway and parked a short distance away from the barricade. He could see Meic busy giving orders to the protestors manning the defences. As Lloyd neared them, he noticed that several pensioners from the village were sitting on deckchairs in the shade of a tree, ready no doubt to be positioned on the front line in case the police made a move. Meic turned to clock him, but they were both suddenly distracted by a car horn from the police lines.

A number of coaches had halted and were discharging police officers in riot gear who collected shields from a pile at the side of the road and without fuss formed into several lines. A section of mounted officers in hi-visibility jackets trotted past the coaches; plastic protective visors covered the horses' eyes. The new squads looked purposeful, and Lloyd could tell from the way that they deployed that they were professional and well-practised, quite different from his colleagues in the local force. The reinforcements were here.

An hour later, the party from the airfield had arrived at the mobile police command post and stood inside, examining a wall-screen showing an aerial view of the village. McArdle's hand swept over the screen as she set out her plan of action. 'We've sealed off the village, both road exits are covered, with the main force assembling here, just outside. And following that television report on *Newsnight*, we've commandeered a fishing boat and have it blocking any further contact from the sea.'

Joan spoke. 'No Navy?'

'They're a bit short given the current pressures in the Channel.'

'Of course. Carry on.'

'Right, so we've physically isolated the village. The next step is to cut off other contact. So, tonight we'll cut the power, and the same will happen to the mobile signal – outside the village, that is.'

'Why the stagger?' Lewis spoke up, trying to conceal his irritation at the female tag team.

McArdle frowned. 'So that we can monitor how they're responding to the power cut. They're using encrypted messaging but we're still able to follow their communications. Or at least Joan's team is. We'll let them use mobile comms in the village but cut off the ability to communicate with the outside world, so controlling any media pressure.'

Lewis wondered whether the telephone intercepts had extended to his own phone.

'And once we're certain of their plans, we know how to proceed at dawn.'

Joan again. 'Which is when you go in?'

'Correct. We'll hold the coast road, and the main push will be from here. They shouldn't have many people on the barricade then, so less chance of casualties. We'll send officers on foot over the barricade to arrest whoever is there, and then we'll bulldoze the barricade so that we can send a convoy with a squad down to the town square... here. And another squad up to the ringleader's home... that's here.'

'How long do you expect it to take?' Joan brushed a speck from her jacket lapel.

'Five to ten minutes from start to officers deploying in the village. Fifteen minutes until Meic Davies is arrested and en route to police headquarters for questioning. Within twenty-five minutes we'll have set up several control points through the village.'

'Your people are ready?'

'We'll brief them later. You're both welcome to attend, or you can get some rest at the B&B we've booked for you in town. We've brought all the reinforcements to the barricade today so they can get a feel for the area, but most of them will be heading back to camp now.'

'Sensible.'

A noise came from outside. 'Ah, the special equipment. Shall we take a look?'

McArdle led the way, followed by Joan, then Lewis. They joined Inspector Melrose and watched as the Army bulldozers were carefully reversed off their transporters. There were two of them, with a handful of troops wearing desert combat fatigues in support. The thing that most surprised Lewis was that instead of their traditional olive-green camouflage, the vehicles were painted in white livery, with the letters 'UN' on the side. Why they couldn't have hired a JCB from a local builder he didn't know. It all seemed just so provocative.

Melrose was of a similar view, typical flash when they could have walked into the village by now with all the new officers on scene. His counterpart in the newly arrived firearms unit stood next to him, overseeing his own squad of policemen performing a weapons check.

'Don't you think we may be in danger of overkill?'

The firearms officer stood next to him. 'In Nottingham, my guys are called out daily. You're just not used to gun crime, that's all.'

'I'm not saying that we don't need you guys. It's just with the Army and the horses and the helicopter and more riot gear than I've ever witnessed… just wondering, that's all.'

'They may be armed. And if they are, they'll soon wish they weren't.'

Melrose folded his arms. 'You ever heard of the Chartists, in Newport?'

'Who?'

A pause. 'Just make sure your men don't get too trigger-happy. These are taxpayers not terrorists.'

The man lowered his voice, so it didn't carry to the senior officers standing a few yards away. 'They should fucking act like it, then. My men didn't ask to be here picking up the pieces of your fuck-up. A couple of my guys have had leave cancelled. Let us do the hard stuff and then you can go back to catching sheep rustlers.'

Melrose pursed his lips. 'Nice. I'll just check up on Her Maj – see if she needs anything.'

He walked over to McArdle. 'So how are you getting on with your new colleagues, Inspector?'

Melrose shrugged. 'They're okay.'

'Well play nice.'

'Ma'am, these Army bulldozers. Seems like they've just returned straight from peacekeeping duties with the United Nations.'

She smiled. 'You mean the lick of paint? Yes, it would give that impression, wouldn't it. I'm calling a commander's briefing for 16.00 hours at camp, make sure the new arrivals know. Rank of sergeant and above. The Deputy Chief Constable will also be there.'

Rachel Rees took a draw from her glass of water, replacing it with a shake on her desk as she listened to Pedersen drone on in his manicured accent. In the corner of her office, a small television screen showed news pictures of the police deploying opposite the barricade.

'So, Minister, we will shortly be in a position to reopen the road.'

'You mean you're going to go in?'

'I've spoken to Commander McArdle and she confirms that they will be ready to move by early afternoon. The police are inclined to wait until the morning for operational and safety reasons, otherwise we'd be making a move now. We both think it best that we clear up this problem as soon as possible to limit copycat protestors. You heard, of course, what happened on the border last night?'

The Minister nodded. 'I saw the briefing this morning. Can we really stop people's movement like that?'

'I think that I recall that you have some experience of closing the border during the Covid-19 lockdown. As you'll know from that, you can control movement if necessary. These were protestors coming in from Scotland and Cornwall on the way to Llanawch. Busloads of them, just like old-school flying pickets. But we intercepted them before they entered the region and we've impounded the vehicles.' He smirked. 'They face a long walk back.'

'You seem to have my country sewn up tight.'

Pedersen ignored her tone. 'We developed a robust contingency plan a number of years ago to deal with a foot and mouth outbreak, and more recently following the pandemic.'

'And that worked well.'

He grimaced. 'So all we've done is merely transpose it to this situation.'

'Are you sure that this can't be settled without resorting to force?'

Pedersen closed his file and slipped it into the leather laptop case resting on the desk. 'That would be clearly our preference. But we are facing a hostile crowd and we've detected no sign of the leadership inside the village softening their stance, quite the reverse, in fact. Our man on the inside has reported that the protestors have collected stockpiles of stones ready to use as missiles against us. So, I would say that our response is proportionate and prudent. And of course, that is the line that we will be sticking to with the media for the next forty-eight hours; you'll find it in your briefing notes.'

'It's just,' Rees searched for the right phrase, but came

up short, 'I hoped that we could just hold off until they got bored or something.'

'Minister, we've discussed this before. London has decided that we need to be seen by the wider public to actively manage this situation. We tried to hold off, but COBRA has now been officially activated by the Prime Minister. And that means we have to resolve this; we cannot afford to look weak in the face of intimidation.'

'But this just feels all wrong.'

'We're not acting on feelings; we're acting on reality. And the reality is that a small group of thugs are flaunting the law and imposing their will on other citizens. We let this go on, and we send out all the wrong signals. Our long-standing policy is to move quickly on these problems.'

She looked at the ceiling, finding a cobweb tucked in the far corner. 'So there's no room for compromise, we just go with your standard playbook?'

'At moments like these, one would do well to remember that security policy is generally well thought through. Policy is not like trying on different pairs of shoes. There are consequences of a bad choice beyond bunions.' Pedersen saw Rees grimace at the comment, and he adopted a more conciliatory tone. 'Do bear in mind that it is not definite that we'll need to use all our bells and whistles, we do have other options to help persuade the villagers that their best interests lie in compliance. However, we simply have to give the commander on the scene the ultimate discretion in this matter. We cannot second-guess her.'

'Does the Welsh Government have a choice in the matter?'

He smiled gently. All this consultation with the provincial folks was for show anyway and to cover political backs. Once the police had gone in, the local politicians could bask in their press conference with the Home Secretary or PM, but right now Pedersen had no intention of devolving any of the decision making on what was, after all, an internal UK security matter.

The ticking of the clock seemed louder than ever.

Thirty-Four

Lloyd had returned to the police station and was in the midst of splashing water over his face, when the landline rang with an electronic warble. He slowly made his way over to the desk and stared at the phone; no calls had come through on the line since that first night of the troubles. The ringing continued and finally he picked up. 'Hello?'

'Sergeant Parry?'

'Speaking.'

'I have some information which will be of great interest to you. Meet me at Meic's house in half an hour.'

'Who is this?'

'If you want something on Meic, just be there in thirty minutes.' The line went dead.

Lloyd stared at his phone, before slipping it into his tunic pocket. The voice was familiar, but he couldn't place it. Maybe he was being set up, but… it was an opportunity. No more safety first, it was time to make things happen. He grabbed his car keys and charging mobile from the desk and was just heading out when it vibrated in his hand, a text which read: *Can we meet?*

Y, his big thumb straining to hit the right button.

Where?

Am heading out the door now your call.

Cud meet at our wood?

OK when?

Cud do now?

OK 15mins will wait there.

Lloyd parked the Land Rover in a clearing a little way into the woods, well-hidden from any passing traffic on the coast road. He got out and rolled his sleeves up as sparrow-song fluted through the cool pines and he whistled a few notes in answer. It felt peaceful here; not many from the village would come up this way, just foresters and the occasional rutting couple. Speaking of which, he could hear the footsteps of someone nearing his position, and a minute later Ruth appeared, picking her way between the hardened ruts in the track. She was wearing a light cotton top, shorts and pale blue sneakers.

She uncrossed her arms as she walked towards him. 'Have you been waiting long?'

They stood awkwardly facing each other.

'No, just listening to the birds in the sky, the wind in the trees. The usual.'

She smiled and leaned in to kiss him on the cheek. 'So some peace at last.'

'Yes, the last few days have been a bit much.' He shut the door of his car carefully.

'I can imagine.' With one foot she dragged at a twig lying on the ground. 'I just thought it would be good to meet. We do need to talk. This whole thing has gotten out of hand.'

'The village? Us?'

'Both.' She looked around at the trees. 'Why are we meeting up here anyway? You didn't expect…'

Lloyd shook his head, 'No, not that. I wouldn't expect anything right now. To be honest I was coming up here anyway.'

She cocked her head. 'What for?'

'I'm meeting someone over at Meic Davies' place, and I don't want to go in the front entrance. I just need to check it out first.'

'Oh, right.'

'These woods run to the back of his property, so I thought I'd go in that way.'

'Do girls get to come on your secret missions?'

Ruth saw his uncertainty. 'We can talk on the way?'

'Okay then.'

They set off on a rough path leading from the clearing. The light slipped through the branches above, casting bleached strips across their route. Their path was buoyed by the spring of layers of browned pine needles underfoot. The silence was charged, interrupted only by the occasional crack underfoot causing a reaction of warning birdsong.

'Watch out for those nettles.'

Ruth swerved a bush, suddenly aware of her bare legs. She looked at Lloyd's back as he trekked ahead of her. 'I've been thinking about us, Lloyd.'

He grunted.

She waited for a proper response.

He looked over his shoulder at her. 'What have you thought?'

'I've loved our time together.'

'So have I. Even if I'm not good at saying it.'

'But I need to think this through. I just don't know what

I want, that should be obvious. I don't know if I want to stay with Frankie or leave her. I've been an attachment to someone all my life, her or my parents or the marrieds I've briefly known. There hasn't been a gap year for me. It might be time to lead my own life, not simply go along with what others want.'

'I see.'

She heard the neutral tone in his voice. 'And if I do leave her, I don't know that you're the right answer, or if any man is. I've spent my adult years with Frankie for better or worse and I haven't craved an emotional connection with any man since I was a schoolgirl. Sex maybe, no, definitely. But not intimacy. Does that shock you?'

Lloyd paced on, silent.

'You should know that you're the first man that I've gone for in a big way in my adult life. And I don't understand why.'

He laughed quickly. 'Maybe it's the uniform.'

'I'm being serious.'

He felt the silence bear down on him. 'Look, sorry. It's just difficult to… everything has happened all at once. I didn't plan it.'

'But you've had affairs before? You told me that second time.'

'Yes, I remember. But what I mean is that I don't go around looking for them. It just felt right. And Catrin had become just distant.' He fell mute for a few painful yards. 'What about your, er, wife?'

'My wife? You mean Frankie. She isn't, we're not married, in a civil partnership – she couldn't wait to do that and invite all her friends to the party, but I always refused to get married.'

'I see.'

'But she does like to pretend, thinks it gives her more legitimacy, especially with you simple country folk.'

'Hmmm, I must remember to be chewing on a piece of straw the next time we meet.'

'Yeah, right. But I don't want to become some fifties-style housewife. I've tried it and I hate it. I know myself now and that is not me. But that's exactly what she wants – me under control, under her thumb, micro-managed.'

'She has quite a strong character, that's for sure.'

'It's all show. She just doesn't like being challenged, that's all. That was part of my attraction in the first place I think, with hindsight. First-timer, overawed by it all, easily manipulated. No threat. But then I grew up.'

'She doesn't seem to like people much.'

'Oh, you mean her manner? I've seen it before. Whenever Frankie is going through a tough period, when she feels that things aren't going quite her way, she becomes very critical of others.'

'Oh, like distraction tactics?'

She smiled. 'Perhaps close to that. She substitutes snobbery for success. And then things usually pick up again and she becomes a little more bearable. But not by much.'

'Let's not talk about her.' He trudged onwards. 'What about me and you?'

'I don't know, Lloyd.'

'You do know that I didn't mean to make things hard for you. Cause trouble.'

'You didn't, this had been coming anyway.' They passed over a section of collapsed stone wall, moss covering the fallen stones. 'Can you bear with me? I just need to get my head right and make some decisions.'

'Right.'

'I know I'm asking a lot. Especially with your own situation.'

Lloyd slowed down. 'Well, as you said, it's been coming a while.' He stopped and turned round to face her. 'Listen, I'm a middle-aged man about to be divorced, and badly, with no career prospects and living at the ends of the earth. Now some women might think that I'm not exactly the catch of the century. And I realise that we come from two different worlds, but… you know, well, it was good. I like, you know, being with you.'

She looked into his eyes; it was a moment. 'I know that, and I wanted to be with you but it's too much right now with everything… I just don't want to make the wrong decision. I can't just suddenly flick a switch. I just need some space to think.'

'I can wait for you. I can manage that.'

'Thank you. I'm just sorry I can't…'

'If I know one thing from the last week, it's there's no point being too proud. I can wait, OK?'

They resumed their journey and Lloyd sensed the intensity of the light increasing as the trees thinned out. 'By the by, does she know where you've gone?'

'She didn't follow me, if that's what you're worried about. She's treating the siege like the Covid-19 lockdown. Never goes out.'

They came to the edge of the wood and halted. 'Well, many are. That's why we need to end this, give people back their streets. Llanawch isn't just a playground for young Mussolini Davies to swagger around like he owns the place.'

Lloyd slowly scanned the back of the Meic Davies house, looking for signing of life. All windows closed and no noise. He whispered to Ruth, 'Wait here a moment.'

He stalked the short distance from the treeline over a grassy field to the low wooden fence, climbed over, and waded through the overgrown garden to the back door. There he paused, listening for sounds inside. Nothing. He tried the door handle, but it was locked. He stealthily followed the concrete path that ran around the house to the front drive, with the big stone barn on his right. He came to the corner, his heart beating fast; he found that he'd drawn his baton. If this was an ambush, here's where it would be, out front where a group of them would have the space to take him.

Lloyd took a breath and stepped firmly out into the driveway.

'Oh, hello, Sergeant.' Sion looked up from his mobile. 'Thanks for coming.'

'It's just you then?'

'Yeah, all the boys are up at the barricade… or shagging their females.' Sion slid the phone into the back pocket of his jeans. 'Why, were you expecting someone else?'

He shook his head, looking the lad up and down. 'So why are we meeting here then, Sion? What do you want to speak about?'

'Got something to show you.'

'And what's that?'

'Something that will be very interesting to you.'

'Mind if I bring someone else to see?'

'Who?'

'Me.'

Both men looked around as Ruth strolled around the corner. 'Well, there was some kind of creature scurrying about quite close by, so I didn't want to hang about.'

Sion bit his lip. 'Sorry about the other day at the supermarket.'

Ruth gave him a withering look. 'Not feeling so tough now?'

'Not feeling like any more of this crap.'

Lloyd put the baton back in its holder. 'Well, we're all introduced. Show us what you've got to show us.'

'I will, but before I do, I want you to promise me that you never saw me here. I have nothing to do with this.'

'You have my word.'

'And you, lady?'

Ruth sighed. 'Yes, whatever.'

Sion seemed satisfied. 'Good. Then come over here, to the barn.'

Lloyd and Ruth exchanged a look before following him over to the large wooden barn doors. The younger man picked up a rusted metal bar lying nearby, pushed it between the door and the padlock and efficiently levered the lock off.

'Hey, you can't do that, it's breaking and entering.'

Sion laughed. 'Who cares? I don't anymore. Anyway, you were just passing by and saw the doors open, so you investigated.' He swung open the door, its bottom scraping on the gravel driveway. 'Behold, more riches than Bill Gates.'

Lloyd tentatively looked inside and walked past Sion. The light was dim, due to the newspaper pasted over the windows. But as his eyes adjusted, he could see crates of tinned food and bottled water stacked up on one side of the barn. Yet that wasn't what caught his attention. Parked at the end of the barn were two quad bikes, and the number plates rang a bell with the crime report forms he'd filled out just a couple of weeks ago. It slowly dawned on him that Meic was in possession of stolen goods. He looked around, bags of fertiliser, a mini-digger parked next to the bikes, a seeder, a bailer, and a few other implements – the brand names displaying New Holland, John Deere, Massey Ferguson. From what he'd picked up from Hywel's chat about his job, there'd be about ten thousand pounds worth of gear here. At least. Davies may have bought a farmhouse and this barn, but the land itself had long been swallowed up by neighbouring farms, so there was no reason for him to have any of this stuff.

He shook his head. 'Unbelievable.'

Sion stuck his hands in his hoodie pocket. 'Isn't it.'

'I just don't understand, why? Didn't he have a big inheritance or something?'

'Yeah, but I got the impression that he needed more.'

'But how did he…?'

'I've said enough. You're the policeman. You solve it.'

Lloyd paced around the barn, taking it all in. He was puzzled about something else. 'Why did you show me this?' He turned round to get an answer from Sion, but he had slipped away. He glanced over at Ruth. 'Right, well then. Now we know who has been behind this mini-crime wave.'

She looked blank. 'What, you mean the protests?'

'No. Before the protests I'd been spending my time on farm thefts.'

'Oh right.'

'May not seem a big deal to you, but for the farmers it could be the end of their business. So it's bloody important. And this scumbag is up to his neck in it.'

Ruth looked about her. 'Soooo, this is your evidence then?'

'Yes. Got him.'

'What if he moves all this before the cavalry arrive?'

'Where's he going to move it to? The village is bottled up.'

'Still. Better to be safe than sorry.' She pulled out her mobile and started to video the interior. This prompted Lloyd to dig his own phone out, with which he took photos of the quadbikes' plates. It was he thought, pretty sloppy work to leave the plates on, as he took a few more pictures. Ruth continued to video and then walked outside, still filming, to confirm the location of the barn in one take. After making a few notes, he closed the barn door behind him – the lock was smashed, and it would be obvious to Meic that someone had been there. Time was of the essence in cross-referencing the bike numbers with his crime reports back at the station and then informing headquarters.

'The light is starting to fade. Let's get back to my car, I can drop you off somewhere nearer your house. And then I need to call this in.'

They retraced their steps over the garden, and back through the wood. Around them they heard the chatter of birds bedding down for night growing sparser as they progressed. The clearing and Land Rover came into view.

'Where do you want me to take you?'

McArdle dropped the call on her mobile and looked at the screen. 'Well, that's interesting. Do you have a D.I. Danny Collins on your team?'

Melrose was standing nearby, thumbs looped in his stab-vest and gazing over the lines of barracks at the military camp. He turned his head towards her. 'Why?'

'That was Parry.'

'What did he have to say for himself then?'

'It looks like he's cracked the case.'

Melrose looked quizzical and walked over.

'From what our friend says, Meic Davies has been running a nice little sideline in handling stolen goods, possibly even theft.'

'You're joking. How does Parry make that out?'

'He's just come from where Davies stores the loot. Wanted me to inform D.I. Collins.'

'Has he arrested Davies?'

'Not yet.'

'Good. He'd just mess it up. Do you want me to tell him to wait for the professionals to make the collar?'

McArdle smiled. 'You don't have much faith in your man, do you? I wonder how you'd feel if your boss didn't trust you.'

Melrose stiffened.

'No, we're going to leave Parry to do his job. And if he doesn't, then we'll do it.' She looked at her watch. 'Right, Inspector, bring the squad commanders together again for another briefing.'

'You've only just spoken to them.'

'Yeah, I'm aware of that, but if Parry plays his cards right, we may be able to go in unopposed. In the meantime, they could do with a nudge. We'll cut the supplies at 21.00 hours tonight. Let's see how they like a few hours without their home comforts.'

'Are you sure?'

'Positive. Come on Melrose, chop-chop. I need to call my superiors.'

An hour later and still in uniform, Lloyd strolled into the pub on the harbour front. The hubbub dropped down a little as he entered, but, adjusted to his new pariah status, he shrugged off the hostile looks from the younger members of the crowd. He waved to the Judge already sitting at his corner table and walked over to him.

Heywood appraised him. 'Well, here's a man looking pleased with himself. Which leads me to wonder why… But first things first, what will you have?'

'Make mine a large pint of bitterness.'

The Judge smiled. 'I think that's on tap tonight, I heard that young Meic Davies had Stevie get a keg in just for this week.'

Lloyd stared at the brasses hanging around the cold fireplace; he'd been in this place on a thousand and one nights but never really taken them in before now. He felt a warm glow come over him. It felt good to be back in the pub again, even if circumstances weren't that great. He looked around and clocked one of his friends across the room and tried to make eye contact, but his mate was pulled away and out of the pub by his wife, who gave Lloyd a sharp glare. These were sad days.

Heywood came back with a pint and a whisky for himself. 'Cheers.'

'Iechyd da.'

They took a moment to savour the drinks. 'So why were you so happy?'

'I think I've found us a way out of this impasse.'

'Oh really, I'm intrigued.'

Lloyd took another swallow of his beer.

'Well, do tell…'

'I'm afraid I can't, not quite yet. Sorry.'

The Judge swilled his whisky and took a sip, a light smile playing on his face. 'I was thinking about your son this afternoon. The younger one, that is.'

'Why's that?'

'I was musing that he's going off to university in England just as I did.'

'Fingers crossed.'

'Yes, of course. But it may well be that the next time he comes back to Wales, if he ever comes back, will be to retire. Just like me.'

'Knowing Arwel I think that's more than likely. He developed this wanderlust, I guess.'

'But it crossed my mind, and not for the first time, that Wales can't afford to lose bright young people like him. But they go, for obvious reasons, they want to live, to seize the chance of an exciting life. Yet they never return – perhaps they aren't encouraged to return – when they could still make a difference. So, we're left at the opportunist mercy of the likes of Meic Davies and the columnist lady across the square.'

'You mean Frankie?'

'Yes, quite. But I feel that I haven't done my bit. I left home, I stayed in England and made a career in the English legal system. And in all these years, I never contributed to my home beyond drawing a pension here and breathing the air. And that fact I am likely to dwell on long after this mess is over.'

'Don't be so hard on yourself.'

'Where I think I'm coming out on this whole situation is that we've got to find a way of giving young people the opportunities here, so they'll stay and use their talents in this land. And we should try to bring those who have left back home. Those that want to, of course. Ah, I think that we're about to be joined…'

Lloyd smelt the scent of a woman's soap close by and he turned around to see Bethan standing behind him. He nodded; she made no disguise of her contempt. 'Not speaking to you, Sergeant, the Judge is who I want.'

He shrugged his shoulders, fuck her and her small-minded clan – they'd soon see. The Judge looked up. 'And what can I do for you, then?'

'Can we speak?' She gestured at Lloyd. 'In private?'

'You can speak in front of my friend here.' He folded his arms. 'Take a seat.'

She made a face but sat down between them, angling her body towards Heywood. 'Look, I know that we haven't spoken much before…'

'True enough.'

'… but I need your help.'

The Judge looked neutral. 'What kind of help?'

'Well, advice really.' She seemed to take a deeper breath before continuing, 'I just don't believe that the protest is getting anywhere.'

'I see, and why is that?'

She shrugged. 'I dunno. It's a lot of noise and we had the TV cameras in and the stuff on the internet and everything, but… where's it getting us? We're supposed to be out there saving the school and making a better life for us here,' she banged the table with her finger, 'but all bloody Meic wants to talk about is what he wants and it's all about him and it's like he doesn't really care about what we care about, he just loves the spotlight. Drunk on a bit of power he is.'

'That hadn't passed my notice.'

'It feels like he's hijacked our protests against closing the school and then forgotten about us. I mean all the mothers just want the school kept open but every time we try to get something done, he pulls it onto talk about independence and "not taking it anymore" and all that shit, excuse my language, but we're not interested in that, we just want a good community for families to live in.'

Heywood leaned back in his chair. 'It strikes me that you can protest for something or against something and that can be equally powerful. But I suggest that you have to be clear about what you want. Sadly, I can't discern any clarity in the aims of this protest beyond being angry about holiday homes, London and so forth. And what can the government do about that? I know these types of people. I used to drink with them in my London club, and they won't be pushed around on the big issues. What you need, is to give them something manageable to respond to, something which they can afford and makes them look munificent, generous, kind.'

Bethan bit her lip as she considered this. 'Like the school?'

'Exactly. Independence isn't going to happen unless it's through the ballot box. You can raise awareness, of course, with protests, but you won't force London into it this way. But a million pounds to keep a school open? Well, that might be acceptable.'

'So how do we go about it?'

'I have some ideas.'

'Will you help us then? Please?'

Heywood pondered the question and looked at Lloyd. 'I see that you've almost finished your pint. Perhaps you can buy me a wee dram… tomorrow? It might be best if you weren't party to this conversation. For your own sake.' He indicated the woman.

Lloyd drained the last of his beer and got up. 'See you about, Judge. You too, Bethan.'

'Thanks for being understanding. Why not come round the house when you can tell me your news. I have a bottle or two of some very good wines which I could open.'

Lloyd smiled. 'That's a deal.' He made his way out of the pub.

Thirty-Five

At nine o'clock, a few minutes after the sun had dipped below the western horizon, the lights went out. Kettles clicked-off in mid-boil, fridges ceased their hum, television screens went blank. Older villagers picked up the landline phones to find them toneless. Their children found that mobiles still worked, even if they couldn't get the internet. There was little panic – power cuts happened some winters with the snows. Candles were dug out from the backs of cupboards, small picnic stoves were lit in houses to boil water, and farmers made their way out to sheds where their back-up generators were stored.

Meic was still at the barricade, keeping an eye on the new police arrivals, when the streetlamps went down, and the texts started stacking up from his boys in the pubs. He had anticipated this move and within a quarter of an hour, his car was being driven through the streets of Llanawch as he shouted to villagers to gather by torchlight on the square at ten. Those that ventured out into the night and picked their way down to the harbour found Meic standing on the bench outside the pub, flanked by gas-powered lamps and cronies.

As the church bells finished chiming, he began, 'First of all, thanks to you all for coming down. They've cut our power, but we have food, water, and most of all we have each other! London can't beat us, no matter what they try to do!'

As some of the crowd shouted out their approval, Judge Heywood and Bethan wandered out of the pub, spilling its flickering light from the doorway. At the back of the crowd, by the shop, Lloyd jumped onto a low wall to give himself a view of Meic. His face darkened as he listened to the little speech. There was something that left a bad taste in his mouth about the man, even more so since his discovery of a few hours earlier. He noticed the door of Ruth's home open and her slip out to take up position in her garden behind the walls, an iPhone held in front of her face, recording the scene. The Sergeant looked about, but it seemed that no one else had noticed.

Meic held up his hands in appreciation. 'Thank you, friends. We're on an immense journey together and this is part of a long march for our nation.' He dropped his voice. 'I know that there are some of you who may not believe that we are getting anywhere and it's time to give up,' Meic paused and then raised his voice high, 'but think of this as our Arab Spring! Our Berlin Wall! Think what we can do by staying strong and continuing our fight!'

There were male whoops from the boys in the crowd.

'All Wales is looking on at us. Proud!'

More cheers on demand.

'They are trying to take our country from us, centuries of oppression. Are we going to let them?'

'No!' the rugby boys answered.

'They are taking our children's futures. Are we going to let them?'

'No!' A few more women's voices this time.

Lloyd couldn't help but release a pent-up shout. 'Christ! Do we have to go through this all over again?' He had stomached enough of this rubbish.

Some heads in the crowd swung around at him, and he pushed his way forward through them to stand opposite Meic. 'I don't know about anyone else, but I'm just so bloody bored at hearing this routine time and time again.'

Gwyn Phillips' contribution was focused: 'Wanker!' A few of his former gang joined in along similar lines for old times' sake.

The policeman laughed. 'Jeer all you like, but I'll tell you what, all this moaning about six-hundred-year-old grievances won't change one bloody thing. We ain't got the votes to be even tossed a bone. I lived in Leeds before I came here. And you know what they think about us there? Nothing. Bugger all. We don't even register.'

Meic laughed. 'Who cares what they think?'

'Good God man, you think we're the only place to have problems? We're not the centre of the universe. I mean, I grew up in a mining community, but how much longer do I have to hear about the bloody miners' strike, like it's some kind of religion?'

The younger man stepped down from the bench and squared up to Lloyd. 'This country was the centre of world industry. And Thatcher took it away from us. And they've taken our water. And our people – London creams off the best.' He raised his voice. 'Wales deserves better than that. They've stolen from us, brutalised us and now owe us big-time.'

'Thatcher? Were you even born then? And who's *they*? The English? The Tories? Why the hell are we still fighting the last war? Can't we move on to the world today? Or shock horror, tomorrow?' Lloyd swung around to face the crowd. 'This man talks of Wales? What kind of Wales then? A land where you can be born but if you don't speak the language then you're half-Welsh? A land where anyone coming into a community has to toe the line so that things remain the same as they've always been? Somewhere you avoid facing the future, because it's easier to be a victim of the past? Where everything revolves around how shit the neighbours are, rather than how good we could be ourselves?' He surprised himself as the long-suppressed thoughts tumbled out.

He turned to face Meic with a steady gaze. 'That's not my country. And I don't think it's the country that most of us want to live in either. What about hope, eh? What about a bit of bloody vision and energy? You talk and act as if the country's dead and buried, rather than trying to get back on its feet. Why don't you do something positive rather than just shouting at people? Something practical which will help?' Lloyd shook his head. 'I don't think you want to do anything good or different, because that doesn't suit you. You want to stay stuck in the past by telling people that the future has been taken away. What a message of despair…'

Meic spoke over the policeman's head. 'Just what does this prime-time idiot think we're all doing here then? Having a picnic? We're taking direct action. This is a revolution!' He whispered down at Lloyd, 'Keep going, dickhead, keep digging your own grave.'

Lloyd ignored the sentiment. 'A revolution? For what purpose? Just so you can be the man of the moment? Just so we can all get angry and hate anyone not from here?

Anything but doing something constructive, because we don't like change, do we?'

'I let you go on with your pathetic speech just to show everyone your true colours. You're red, white and blue all the way through,' Meic sneered, and turned to the watching crowd for support, before screaming, 'this man's a traitor to us!'

As if on cue, Gwyn moved forward. 'Fuck off, Lloyd, we don't need your kind here. Why don't you piss off, and join your mates behind their riot shields before I sort you out?'

Lloyd eyeballed Gwyn. 'Take one step closer and I'll bloody drop you on the spot. Witnesses or not.'

Gwyn faltered at the unexpected threat and glanced up at Meic for instructions, but none seemed forthcoming. The murmuring in the crowd grew louder. Lloyd knew that it was now or never; he hopped up onto the bench. 'And you lot, before you decide to burn me at the stake, I've got some news for you. As Gwyn pointed out, I'm a police officer. And I did some policing today. A couple of hours ago I was up at Meic's house.'

A shout from the crowd, 'So what?'

'I had a look around. I had a look in his big shed in particular.' Out of the corner of his eye he could see Ruth run back into her house.

Meic looked across at Lloyd.

'Some of you have heard about the thefts from farms in the area. Well, funnily enough, it turns out that some of the stolen items are stored up in Meic here's barn. I saw them with my own eyes. Anyone doesn't believe me, go and have a look,' he could sense confusion in the crowd, and pressed home, 'and I was wondering whether some of John

Roberts' gear had ended up in your shed. Remember him, Meic, the old man who killed himself back in April?'

Meic remained silent.

'John Roberts couldn't afford to replace the machinery that was stolen from him because he had no insurance. You must remember. Because I do recall you mouthing off about it at the time. Gwyn was there, weren't you, Gwyn? Sion as well. What have you got to say to that then?'

Meic looked over to where Sion was standing, but he saw no pillar of support there, just a short-arsed poof wearing a sneer on his mouth. Now Davies sounded slightly less sure of himself. 'Did you have a search warrant?'

'Oh, I thought we'd all agreed that the law had been suspended around here. Well then, explain the stolen goods.'

'Don't pay any attention to that traitor. This is a fit-up. He's trying to frame me, it's a typical MI5 job. They've done it before to other Welsh patriots.'

One of the female groupies from Meic's goon squad spoke up. 'Why the fuck should we believe you? Your own wife can't trust you to keep it zipped, so for all we know this is just another lie!' She laughed, and a ripple of amusement went through the crowd.

'Hey over here! Look over here!'

People turned around to see Ruth waving at them with both arms as if she was guiding in a rescue helicopter. 'Over here! Now, look at this!'

The whitewashed walls of Frankie's cottage became a mass of colours, colours which formed a picture; pictures which were a video of the interior of Meic's barn. Using the smartphone projector Frankie had left discarded on a shelf in her study, Ruth could show the crowd evidence from her little expedition earlier that evening. She set the video to run on a loop and stood out of the sightline.

'Turn off your torches, everyone, you can see it better.' And one by one, as the light from the torches dimmed, people saw the pictures of the machinery and her walk outside to a frontal view of Meic's house, to connect the interior of the barn with its host.

The crowd had fallen silent, the light from the projection casting a pale glow over their resentful faces, unsure now, searching for the right response.

A deep voice exclaimed, 'Hey, that's my quad bike! Recognise it anywhere. The thieving bastard.'

Meic snarled at Lloyd, 'You fucker. You can't do this.' He stepped forward and took a swing, connecting with the Sergeant's cheek. Lloyd staggered off the bench into the front line of the crowd, who helped him back onto his feet. He could feel a trickle down his cheek, he hoped that it was blood rather than tears.

'Well then, piggy. What are you going to do about that then?' Meic sneered. 'C'mon Gwyn, fill your boots on Lloyd here. Doesn't have his Saes mates to protect him now.'

Gwyn started to move forward to take down Lloyd but felt a powerful hand from behind restrain him. A voice attached to the arm murmured, 'Not now, Gwyn bach, not if you want to keep looking pretty.' The farmer who had stepped in at the pub to defend Hywel a few weeks earlier eyeballed Gwyn, who in turn backed off.

The farmer turned to Meic. 'So is this true? You've been nicking our machines then?'

Meic swallowed. 'It's not as bad as that bastard makes out.'

'Not as bad? I reckon that this is about as bad as it gets.'

'I did it for you guys. How do you think all this has been funded? Someone has to pay the bills at the end of the day.'

The farmer nodded and looked about at his fellow villagers. 'So, I can't speak for anyone else. But my dad had a bailer stolen a few months back. Was that you?'

Meic's face showed anger, then resignation; he shrugged his shoulders.

'Fucking hell, who do you think we are – a bunch of idiots to be played with?'

Meic tried to talk over the hubbub. 'People, this is a distraction. We're still making a point here. The world is listening to us. They are raping Wales, and we have to forget about these silly distractions and focus on the main game—'

Lloyd cut across him. 'That's enough for one day. Meic Davies, as soon as this is all over, I can guarantee you will be placed under arrest and charged with theft.'

Gwyn put his hands behind his head. 'Can someone tell me what's going on here?'

Lloyd sighed. 'Gwyn, you guys as well, you've let yourselves believe an egotist who thinks only of himself, not of the repercussions for all of you. What do they say? Beware of worshipping false idols…'

'Eh?'

Lloyd gestured to the crowd to calm down. 'Listen everyone. Look around you. The power has been cut; so have the phone lines. Can you hear that sound above us?' A few heads tilted upwards. 'That's a military drone monitoring us all with its cameras ahead of the main event tomorrow, because that's when they are simply going to come through the barricades, and nobody is going to stop them this time. They're not messing around. You have to think about our future, not about big empty gestures. Your businesses are losing money, and this village is getting itself a bad name. It is time to end it.'

Judge Heywood, who had stepped forward, now spoke up. 'You know me, and you know my background. What Lloyd says is true. I've seen the police up there this evening, there's more of them than ever. We are faced with two options here. We can either bring this episode to a close with some dignity or we can continue to follow this fool here who has stolen from us and is pursuing his own selfish agenda.'

Bethan climbed up onto the bench, puffing a little at the effort. 'We've made our protest and now the eyes of the country are upon us. Meic's given us that at least. But the food will run out and probably people's attention. So now we need to start talking to get what we want.'

A woman's voice shouted out, 'So what do we want?'

'How about this, first we get the school reopened. Then we get some funding up here to create some jobs. And then, we talk about limiting holiday homes, but only after we've got the school sorted.'

'What if they won't listen to us?'

'They may not listen to you or me, but they'll listen to him.' She thumbed at the Judge. 'Why don't a few of us go up there and talk to the police and try and get something out of it? Mr Heywood here has offered to lead a negotiation on our behalf.'

Now Sion shouted from the edges of the crowd, 'Hey listen. We've been betrayed, that's true enough and some of us more personally. But I think what Bethan is saying is right. We've got to start talking. Let's just get this stupid siege lifted and get the school reopened.'

Lloyd waited on the villagers. He could see that some of those who had been hanging about at the back had begun to drift away, their torches bobbing in the darkness like flotsam from a sunken ship. A net curtain stirred from the top floor of the Pimlotts' home; below on the front lawn he could Ruth's face looking at him. He tried to move towards her, but he was distracted by Gwyn Phillips, who walked up to Meic and quietly said, 'We're going to have you for this, fucker. No one uses me and the boys and gets away with it.'

'Leave him, Gwyn. Now go home. Go on, bugger off.' Lloyd watched him wander off in the direction of another pub. Meic looked at the policeman and then he faded away as well, torch-less into the night, observed only by three pairs of eyes. 'Ever feel like you've been cheated…'

The torches went on their way, a rope of fire fraying street by street, step by step, until not even the glow from a lone strand could be seen.

Thirty-Six

Just after five the next morning, Meic found himself slumped on the sofa in his living room, an empty bottle of wine nestled next to him. He sat upright, tentative in his movements given the slight blurring of vision and thickness of head. Memories of the previous evening began to trickle through his consciousness, and he frowned. Being a leader was isolating and, as he'd found out, thankless. He'd spoken all the words that were expected of his role, acted out the part for the television and directed the community. And they hadn't bothered to stay for the second act. A small gas lamp sat on his coffee table, which he turned off, so making the view to the dark mountain moorlands clearer without the reflection from the windowpanes. He clawed at his scalp roughly, feeling his thirst, wondering if there was still a bottle of Evian in the fridge. All that planning, all that hard work and he'd been undercut by his own egotistical mistake. Meic shook his head in disgust. When the money had started to run out, he'd been desperate for another source of income, anything just to keep his important work here going. It was a chance encounter in a Cardiff bar, him shooting his mouth off about the rich farmers back home to some guy in a shiny suit, which led to another conversation in a quieter bar, which led to a business proposition.

It had been that Albanian bastard who'd helped to get him into this mess, he mulled. That two hundred pounds of short-barrelled flesh and sinew who had appointed Meic as his man in the north, offered him temptation. And Meic was flattered, he knew that he'd been played but couldn't help himself. They'd stumped some money upfront, a sum large enough to pay for a few months of expenses, and so he'd cased a farm ten miles down the road, trying not to shit on his own doorstep. Worked out the farmer's patterns and took a note of equipment, then called the Cardiff boys up when the moment was right. They'd done all the heavy lifting and got the tractor out of the area on the back of a low-loader truck.

That was the pattern for the other thefts, until the last month, when they'd started storing the stolen quadbikes and machinery in Meic's barn. Too many police around, they said. Would get the goods out on their next swing by, the Albanian said. It had been the first and only time he'd taken the risk of keeping the gear on his property. And now that bastard pig had discovered it. A stroke of fortune for Parry and bad luck for Meic. The plan had always been to rely on political and media influence to keep him out of jail when the barricades came down, or at least minimise the sentence. And in any case, being jailed for a short time could be spun as positive for his career. Look at Gandhi or Mandela. Closer to home there was Saunders Lewis, that old right-wing elitist turned into a folk hero by a few months in the Scrubs. But theft was different. The media would portray him as a common criminal and ignore his greater achievements.

No-no-no. No Meic! Bad thoughts. Negative, stupid thoughts. Pull yourself together. You can't let a nobody like Parry fuck you over. There had to be a way to turn this around. He sat up, elbows on his knees, as he leaned forward to look at the Glock pistol which lay on the coffee table. He'd picked it up from where that Special Branch twat had dropped it on the square. The magazine held seven more bullets, but one would be enough for his purposes. He felt the weight of the weapon in his hand and checked the safety catch. He wasn't going to run away from this.

Meic took a final gulp of warm coffee, before he rose, opened a dresser drawer and pulled out a plastic bag, which contained an old T-shirt of Kerry's he'd meant to return but had never got round to. He lifted the T-shirt to his nostrils; he could still smell a trace of her, then dropped it back into the bag with the gun. He walked outside and drove his pick-up to the end of the drive. Getting out, he returned to the barn, feeling static in the air as he opened its door, grimly noting the broken lock which had been levered off the previous evening, probably by that policeman. Just inside, in the corner, he picked up one of the red plastic fuel containers. He then placed some flattened cardboard packing cases underneath each quad bike and proceeded to pour petrol all over them. Meic pulled out the T-shirt from the bag, before replacing the bag and gun in his pocket. He ripped the shirt into two pieces. One piece he chucked outside the door of the barn, the other he carefully dipped into the petrol container to form a simple incendiary device. He lit the lit the rag and ran out of the barn. He waited by his truck and then, with a large whoosh, heard the bang. Meic saw a fireball shoot upwards to the roof of the barn, engulfing the quad bikes. He turned his back on the rapidly burning evidence and got back into his car. The sound of another explosion told him that the fire had reached the rest of the spare petrol. He drove slowly towards the village.

A few moments later as he crested the hill, Meic looked out to sea, and looked down at the boat the police had commandeered to blockade the harbour. What a waste of money. It was pathetic the lengths these people would go to assert their authority. It just confirmed everything he thought about the elites who ran this police state. How his father had managed to work amongst those types for so long was hard to understand. But he guessed that one does what one has to, simply to get by. And to this end, Meic had one drop-off to make in a field, before he arrived at the barricade.

As he stalked over the rough ground, the less manicured the better in his eyes, he felt a connection with his forefathers. This was the ageless moorland of *The Mabinogion*, R.S. Thomas, Kyffin Williams in all its natural beauty. Those who came before would walk miles to work over the mountains to earn the pittance that would barely let them survive. He'd tried to uncover similar feelings from the villagers, that same yearning to draw on the strengths of the past, but most of them were immune to their own genes, to any thought beyond today and the next. Sion had been an exception; he understood the intertwining of language and the culture, and how it had kept the Welsh heart alive through centuries of oppression, but he was flawed in other ways. Yet when a people let themselves be cut off from their own history, became detached from their roots, it was easier for them be blown away as grains of wheat in the wind. And a storm was coming. He cursed his own kind and their weakness for the soft life.

Surprisingly, after the excitement of the square, Lloyd had managed to get a few hours' uninterrupted sleep, but awoke early, as was his habit in summer. After a quick shave, he put on his last clean uniform shirt and trousers and set off in his Land Rover. His equipment belt still lay on the passenger seat, where he'd tossed it the night before, and he checked that the handcuffs were still there. Lloyd felt that it hadn't been the right time to arrest Davies; it might have soured the mood and provoked some in the crowd. But now it was time for Lloyd to do his duty and bring the fallen idol in. He steered in the direction of Meic's place, but just as he passed through the square saw a slender wisp of dark smoke curl up above the treeline. Lloyd pressed the accelerator and within two minutes he was pulling into the entrance to see flames licking around the shattered windows of the barn.

He hunched over his steering wheel as he skidded to an emergency stop on the gravel. He jumped out of the car and ran towards the house, banging on the front door. 'Wake up! There's a fire in your barn! Meic, get out of bed!'

No answer. Lloyd ran back to his car, slid the baton out of the belt and sprinted towards the nearest window. He was worried about the fire spreading and people getting caught inside. Just as he was about to smash the glass in order to gain entry, he paused and then jogged to the front door and tried its handle – it was unlocked. Two minutes later, finding no one in the house, the Sergeant was back at his car and calling the fire in to headquarters, requesting an appliance urgently. It was, to him, pretty clear what had happened. Meic had decided to make a sharp exit without leaving any evidence of his wrongdoing behind. There were only two ways out of the village by road, but both were covered by his colleagues, unless Davies was hiking out over the hills – but even then, he'd be tracked by the aerial surveillance. Lloyd started his engine. There was nothing further he could do here with the barn too far gone for a garden hose to make any difference. He reversed out of the drive, as he didn't want to get caught by the flames and set off towards the village.

About a mile down the narrow lane, he had to brake sharply as Meic's utility vehicle pulled out of an entrance to a field thirty yards ahead of him. The Sergeant switched on his blue lights to pull Meic over. He saw Meic's eyes clock him in his rear-view mirror, then waved his hand in acknowledgement, just before he accelerated away in the direction of the village. Lloyd turned on his siren and sped after him; where the heck did Davies think he was going? Unless he was planning to crash through the police cordon, he wasn't heading anywhere. The cars sped downhill, now through the village, and Lloyd eased off a little for fear of any early morning pedestrians. Meic's vehicle started to pull away as it punched through into the square and pulled uphill. Lloyd kept him in sight but slowed down to the speed limit as there were no other routes out; all the turn-offs from where Meic was on the road ended in cul-de-sacs of bungalows. As he went through the narrow part of the road by the bakery, he caught a glimpse of Davies still ahead, making for the barricade. As they approached it, he saw Davies indicate that he was pulling over and then calmly park his car in the lay-by a few yards down from Heywood's entrance.

Turning his siren off, Lloyd pulled into the lay-by behind Meic's utility. He could make out several squads of riot police up in the woods directly above the road, ready for a flanking move. It was overkill, but he supposed it was to be expected. After the confrontation in the square, Lloyd had called McArdle from his car radio to update her on events and had been told that the barricades would be cleared first thing in the morning. Maybe someone was listening, but it didn't matter; the village no longer wanted to fight for a foolish cause.

Lloyd exited his Land Rover and walked towards a smiling Meic Davies. The younger man chucked his car keys at Lloyd, who caught them one-handed.

'Come to hand myself in, Sergeant.'

Lloyd looked him up and down. 'Co-operating at last, are we?'

'Whatever you'd like to believe…'

Lloyd straightened his cap. 'Before you decide to hop onto your bloody soap box best to get going. I said my piece last night.'

'Indeed you did. You surprised me, Sergeant.'

Lloyd glanced at him. 'Let's do this without trouble.'

Meic laughed. 'You mean we're not going to have a big cathartic display, some manly chest-beating, a touch of gun play, followed by a satisfying ending?'

'Not interested, it's too early. Right then. Turn around, hands behind your back.' He placed handcuffs on Meic and quickly patted him down. He was clear.

'I suppose that this is the point where I ask if that's really necessary.'

'And I suppose that this is the point where I reply, shift your backside.'

They walked to the abandoned barrier side by side and climbed onto the top of it, seeing the squads of riot police arrayed before them.

'You seem very calm for a man about to go down for a long time.'

Meic smirked, 'We shall see.'

Lloyd raised his eyebrows and guided his prisoner down from the top of the barricade. They slowly walked towards the first line of police. A whistle blew, and suddenly the police ran towards them, parting slightly as they let Lloyd and Meic pass through their rank. Lloyd glanced behind, seeing his fellow officers easily surmount the barricade. This time there was no one there to get in their way.

A loud crack was heard above them, then a few seconds later the first spots of rain splashed onto the tarmac. Suddenly the rain was coming down in great bursts, thick and tropical.

'Well, that's that then. Let's get you booked in before we get soaked.'

'You really think it's all over?'

'Yep. C'mon, get a shift on, it's bloody wet.'

'You know, Parry, you confuse the man with the message. Even when I'm out of here, the problems will remain. Your kids may have left but other children will need an education, good jobs, a chance to buy an affordable home and raise a family without migrating.'

'I don't think I've confused anything.'

'So, think on this: what did you do when your country needed you? Hid behind your uniform, that's what.' Meic watched the Sergeant's face and knew he'd scored a hit. 'You think that you've won today, but I'm just one man. Your sort hasn't won anything. Tomorrow will be a different story and history won't be kind to you.'

Lloyd came to a halt in front of McArdle and his own Deputy Chief Constable, who were standing in the shelter of a tree.

'Sir. Ma'am. Sergeant Parry bringing suspect Meic Davies into custody, charged with multiple public order offences. Assault on a police officer, namely me. And of course, handling stolen goods.'

He saw the DCC's knuckles blanch. 'Very good. We'll take it from here.' The senior officer nodded to Inspector Melrose. 'Take him up to headquarters – I'll personally interview him there.'

Lloyd let go of Meic's arm as Melrose yanked him away.

'See ya, Sergeant,' Meic called back as he was pushed into a waiting police van.

'That will be in court, Davies.'

The DCC looked at Lloyd. 'So that's that. You can take a few days off, Parry. We'll cover policing in Llanawch for the moment while matters settle down. My office will in touch with you in due course.' He nodded at Commander McArdle and walked briskly to his car. No rain, not matter how heavy, was going to impinge on his dignity.

She smiled at the Sergeant, seeing the rain stream down his face. 'It may be too late, but why don't you come under my umbrella.'

'Thank you, ma'am.'

She looked at the scene as the bulldozer began to rumble forward, its caterpillar tracks clanking. 'I sense disappointment. What did you expect from him? A medal?'

Lloyd wiped some rain away from his forehead. 'Nah. I got about what I thought I would.'

They watched the two machines swat through the blockage, scattering a day's heavy labour to the roadside to the sound of shrieking metal and scraping stone. As their work was completed, the noise was replaced by a chorus of petrol engines igniting. From the time the police had launched their assault to the road being opened had taken no more than sixty seconds, and now a convoy of police vans slowly transited the broad gap, before zipping off as they headed for the village square and other planned checkpoints. Life in Llanawch was about to be forcibly placed on a path back to move-along-nothing-to-see-here normality. A pair of police cars followed, escorting two fire engines, as they headed for the source of the expanding pall of smoke hanging over the far western end of the village.

'Well, there we are. The highway is reopened, and Davies is in custody.'

McArdle smiled. 'My job here is done.'

'Not quite, with respect, ma'am. I need to introduce you to a couple of people, and one of them lives just over there.' Lloyd pointed at Heywood's house.

'Who are they?'

'They want to talk to someone in charge. They're going to represent the community, the sensible faction, that is.'

'Sorry but that won't be my area. I can introduce them to the right people though. Perhaps Mr Lewis from your government over there might be a helpful start.' She indicated the morose-looking individual standing alone under a nearby tree, sipping from a plastic coffee cup.

'Oh right. Didn't know they were involved.' Lloyd

watched a camera crew load themselves up into a police van. 'Not arresting the TV people, are you?'

McArdle looked at her watch. 'No, that's the BBC. Word from above, they have to be first into the village or else the sky will fall in. Desperate for a watercooler moment no doubt. Who would have thought a public institution could be so emotionally needy.'

Lloyd smiled blankly, mystified by the comment.

'I didn't say that, by the way.'

'No, ma'am.'

'Right, Sergeant, that's enough social observation for one morning. You have one final duty. Give me a lift to the village centre.'

Thirty-Seven

Lloyd drove carefully back, through the outskirts of the village and down to the square, passing through a newly set up police checkpoint en route. He trundled past a squad of police officers in riot gear rolling to a halt in front of the village shop where Rich Hughes, sensing a new customer base for his long-life pasties and energy drinks, was opening up ahead of the usual time.

'Time to review the troops.' McArdle held out her hand, which Lloyd shook once. 'Thank you for the lift, and best of luck. You've been very helpful.' He watched her stride across the square to get a report from the Inspector who'd been directing operations.

Lloyd got out of the Land Rover, leaned against the bonnet and surveyed the square. A police photographer was busy taking pictures of the upturned van, while a scene of crimes officer in his white plastic onesie dusted for prints in the interior. A couple of residents hovered uncertainly at the edge of the square. None of Meic's former gang were anywhere to be seen. He heard footsteps approaching him and snapped out of his thoughts. Someone in a white linen suit.

'Ms Pimlott.'

'Sergeant Parry.'

They looked at each other.

'So you survived it then.'

Frankie picked an invisible hair from her jacket and sighed. 'Mostly.'

'What brings you out so early?'

'To welcome our glorious liberators to the village. The yoke of minor despotism has been lifted. And about time too.'

Lloyd could feel himself talking a little more quickly. 'Material for one of your well-timed and in no way inflaming-the-situation newspaper columns, I suppose.'

'Quite so.'

Her voice seemed a little distracted to Lloyd. 'Are you going to stay in the village when everything's back to normal?'

'I doubt it.'

'Oh.'

Frankie took a few photographs of the police setting up their positions on her phone. 'So, will you miss me, Sergeant?'

'Well...'

'Or will it be Ruth that you'll miss?'

Lloyd rubbed his chin, before folding his arms. 'Ah, I see.'

'I know you two are fond of each other.'

'Well, she's a nice lady.'

'I use *fond* as a euphemism, of course.'

'Right.'

'I realise that I have just been relegated to only the *second* most hated person in your wonderful and welcoming village, but when I was still public enemy number one, someone was kind enough to drop an anonymous note through my door. It was extraordinarily descriptive and quite believable. In fact, it confirmed my prior suspicions.'

'Now before you start,' Lloyd held up one palm.

'No, no, no. This is actually where I get to speak. As the wronged wife, I believe that traditionally, I say my piece, and you listen to it, preferably sheepishly.'

Lloyd nodded slowly.

'Of course, when I say *I believe*, I am actually being a tad misleading. I actually know. Because I've had to make this speech once or twice before. Can you believe that?' Frankie started to pace. 'I've actually had to go and tell strangers that I know that they're having an affair with the woman I'm married to, and it would be awfully good manners to stop it.'

'I see.'

'But perhaps you don't, so for the sake of clarity: you are just another squib of temporary excitement for my wife. I don't know what lies she's fed you about our relationship, lies which you obviously have swallowed, but the truth is that Ruth feels the need to stray from time to time, and so she sniffs out whatever amoral slab of meat of either gender is most convenient. You're simply the latest.'

'I didn't think I was the first.'

Frankie laughed, 'Don't mistake my civilised demeanour for weakness. Underneath, I'm seething. I certainly got you wrong. Had you down as a bit of an attendant lord, someone to start a scene or two,' she smiled at her literary allusion, even if it was wasted on Parry, 'but you're actually a scene-stealer. A bit of a thief in other ways as well.'

'Now, Frankie, listen…'

'Don't call me by my Christian name, you don't know me.' It was the one point at which Pimlott showed her anger. 'And I do not wish to listen to your improbable excuses, or wheedling apologies, or even promises to give up Ruth. Because I've reached the point where I don't really care what the silly little cow gets up to and so I don't really feel I need to take responsibility for her anymore, financially or emotionally. Of course, Sergeant, if you hadn't realised already, she is rather needy in both areas.'

Lloyd looked over her shoulder at the estuary.

'And you thought it was just physical need. Oh no, she demands more than that.'

Frankie looked back down the road at an approaching vehicle. 'Just so you're aware, I've decided to suspend my usual approach to resolving these matters amicably with as little fuss as possible, and on this occasion be rather vindictive. So, as I am clearly not the better of you physically, I'll have to use my intellectual talents and social status to seek retribution. You were supposed to be protecting us from wrongdoing, but instead you add to it, you abuse your position of trust to take other people's wives. You disgust me.'

Lloyd stared at her. 'Well thanks for that. To be honest, between you and me… I couldn't give a shit. Do what you have to do and stop bleating about it.'

'What an unpleasant set of individuals frequent this village, and to think I partly came to this hellhole for my health… still, a change is as good as a rest.'

She threw Lloyd a meaningful look, then strolled back towards her house, giving a brisk wave to Stevie who'd emerged from the pub to see what was going on and stood casually scratching his testicles underneath his towelling robe. Lloyd shook his head; he couldn't ignore the implications of Frankie's parting comments. It seemed pretty clear that she was set on making his life difficult. The thought occurred to him that he'd have preferred a straight bout of fisticuffs to settle this, but she was still a woman, of sorts.

Back in the Land Rover, en route to his own little station, he mulled over Davies' final words to him – they hurt, they were meant to. Meic was typical of his kind; if anyone disagreed with his view, they were just not Welsh enough. Lloyd really disliked people like him, the true believer squad who thought that they were the only ones who could ever be right. But what was worse was the bullying, the intimidation, the pile-on of anyone who dared to speak up. He couldn't stand that crowd's pinched, shop-worn version of patriotism – endlessly harking back to the past mythical glories while claiming modern victimhood. He'd been taught by a few of them down Swansea way at school. And this idea of independence, he couldn't believe that old chestnut was rearing its head yet again. Hadn't people had enough of this nationalist bollocks during Brexit?

But in his heart, he knew that this wasn't the real reason that Meic had scored a hit. Because what if he, Lloyd Parry, was on the wrong side of the argument on all of this? What if all he was doing was what he accused Davies of last night, of not wanting change, just defending the status quo however he wrapped it up in his duty as a police officer? What if he was the one that wasn't part of the times?

That couldn't be the case surely, but...

He parked outside the station, pausing hunched over the steering wheel, uneasy. He heard a bell begin to toll in the distance. Half a mile away within the moss-clad stones of the ancient church the Reverend Winter fought to keep his bell ringing, almost falling to his knees with the pain of each muscle-draining effort. Pain which only served to reinforce his faith in Meic and the power of renewal.

Thirty-Eight

Meic took his place at the table in the main interrogation room in Colwyn Bay police headquarters. Facing him were the Deputy Chief Constable and Inspector Melrose, with a constable stood behind them next to the door. Melrose started the recorder and confirmed who was present for the benefit of the transcript.

Meic leaned back in his chair, arms folded. 'Shouldn't I be in an orange boiler suit? Isn't that what the state gives political prisoners nowadays?'

Melrose leaned forward. 'Don't get cocky lad, you're just a common criminal.'

'I'm a freedom fighter for Welsh rights being persecuted by the English police state.'

'That's enough,' the DCC's words were delivered in a low, measured voice. 'Things will go more easily if we drop the posturing and get on with it. Your clothes will be returned to you as soon as they've dried, as well you know. Now, Inspector,' he turned to Melrose who started reading from a sheet of paper in front of him.

'Meic Davies, we will be charging you with offences under the Public Order Act 1986; the Serious Crime Act 2007; the Road Traffic Act 1988; and the Theft Act 1968.'

'Impressive.'

'And that's just what we've come up with so far. I'm sure we will be adding a few more charges once our investigations are complete.'

'I see the night school classes are coming along.'

The DCC interrupted, 'This is no matter for any levity. These are all serious offences. You're looking at ten years' imprisonment for some of the public order crimes alone.'

Meic sat upright, placed his hands on the table and looked directly at the senior officer. Now was the time when he had to play his hand. 'Switch it off.' He inclined his head at the tape recorder.

Melrose narrowed his eyes. 'Don't you tell us what to do, sunshine.'

Meic ignored him and responded calmly, 'Chief, listen to me. It is in your interest to turn it off and let me speak freely. Or else this interview, once my legal representation has arrived, will be a string of *no comment*, before it all comes out in court.'

The DCC nodded his assent. As soon as the machine was off, he gestured to Meic. 'The floor is yours. But try not to indulge yourself in another diatribe, eh?'

Meic cleared his throat. 'I'll come to the point. I'm sure that the letter of the law has been broken—'

'Well, you're right about that.'

'... but not the spirit. If you think of this as a protest with legitimate foundations and carried out by an entire community with multiple upstanding members of that community – priests, schoolteachers, shopkeepers – being complicit in that protest, then it is in no one's interest for that entire community to be labelled unlawful. Particularly when you may find gathering evidence might be, problematic.

And your political overlords may not want all those people, with whom many in the electorate agree, put in jail or even humiliated in court. It might be very counter-productive to future political hopes and for that matter community policing relations.'

'Go on.'

'And given that the protest was relatively peaceful.'

'We found bags of stones stored by the barricade.'

'To use in running repairs on the barricade, and *certainly not* for any other purpose.'

'People were expelled from the village.'

'They weren't expelled; they departed of their own free will. In fact, I tried to persuade them not to leave. Indeed, I have your own Sergeant Parry as a witness.'

'What are you saying?'

'Given all this, I don't think you really would feel able to pursue a case at the more extreme limits of justice…'

The DCC smiled. 'Nice try. Maybe, taking into account the bigger picture, we wouldn't be inclined to pursue legal proceedings against several hundred people, but one would do.'

'Yes, I was coming to my situation.'

'Now I thought you might be – I'm listening.'

'It would be greatly embarrassing to North Wales Police if it was to get out to the media, say, that an automatic pistol was lost by one of its officers and fell into hostile hands.'

Melrose tapped his biro on the desktop.

'It might not look so good in the eyes of the public. Or even in the eyes of promotion boards. I may be in a position to alleviate your potential embarrassment and career prospects.'

'How so?'

'I have the weapon. It is hidden right now, but I could be encouraged to find it.'

'Sorry Meic, can I get this straight, I take a little longer to catch on nowadays. I suppose it must be my age, but to be clear, are you trying to do a deal with us? Because you may not realise that it is the Crown Prosecution Service which decides whether to proceed with a case. Or not.'

'I'm well aware of that, Chief. You're not dealing with the usual pond life here. But I'm also aware that they only go forward on the evidence that you submit. So, with no evidence, there is no case.'

'It would take a lot to sweep this little mess under the carpet.'

'I appreciate that. I know that you'll need to charge me with something. But it's a case of charging me with an offence where, with good behaviour I'd be out of prison in a few months, as opposed to a decade.'

The DCC sniffed. 'Interesting.'

Melrose slammed his fist on the table and shouted, 'We still have you for theft. What about the contents of the barn? I've got the preliminary report here,' he picked up a slim folder on the table and waved it.

'What theft? Someone was obviously trying to blacken my name by storing these quad bikes in my barn without my knowledge. I only discovered this last night because Sergeant Parry told me and then falsely accused me of being responsible in public. And that same person has now cremated the evidence, so you can't get any incriminating fingerprints off these bikes. You know if you're really looking for suspects I'd try Parry if I was you. I mean it has been clear to many witnesses just how much he hated me, probably enough to try and fit me up. And if he was so sure about me being guilty, then don't you think it odd that he didn't arrest me on the spot?'

Melrose's face reddened and he was about to reply but felt a restraining hand on his arm. 'If I understand it correctly, you're contending that you didn't steal anything,' the DCC returned them to the point.

'Exactly.'

'And that given the nature of the protest we should err on the lenient side when we come to putting together any case for potential prosecution. Is that right?'

'Correct.'

'Because you have proof that we lost a firearm, which if it comes to light would cause the force and me considerable embarrassment? Is that what you're saying?'

'You said it.' Meic leaned forward. 'You see, if there's going to be a fall guy to save your face, it sure as hell isn't going to be me. I'm no Lee Harvey Oswald. I'll take some of the consequences, but only to a point, before I get bored and start talking to the press.'

Melrose swung round in his seat to talk to his superior. 'You not going to let this… little shit get away with it? After all he's done? He's trying to blackmail us.'

The Deputy Chief Constable leaned back in his chair and took off his spectacles to clean them with a cloth. 'Hmmm. Well, it is a tempting offer.'

'Oh, come on, sir, he is playing with us,' Melrose's voice had risen.

Meic smirked at the scene he had caused and tried to catch the Inspector's eye.

The DCC replaced his glasses. 'Tempting, but not as tempting as charging you, Meic, with attempting to pervert the course of justice, and attempted bribery of a police officer. Inspector Melrose, I take it that you witnessed this and can write up a statement this afternoon?'

'Er, yes, sir... Yes, I did witness that. All of it, sir.'

The older officer continued, 'And Melrose, on top of those new charges, and the existing charge sheet, would you be so good as to add possession of an illegal firearm.'

Meic banged the table. 'Now wait a minute, we're off the taping system here, you said we were off the record!'

'I didn't say anything of the sort.'

'Well, you'll have to find the bastard gun and link me to it before you can charge me for possession. How about that then?'

The DCC stood up. 'You know, when the Home Secretary decided to put the Met in charge of the siege, it really hacked us off up here in yokel-land. It was like telling us we couldn't do our job. But on the other hand, there were benefits. They brought with them access to this very useful bit of kit called a drone. Like in Afghanistan, but without the missiles. And this machine has had you under surveillance for the past couple of days. You can watch the tapes if you want. Now, guess what?'

Meic said nothing; he knew what was coming.

'Early this morning, the drone's camera sent us pictures of you burying something in a field near your home. You should see the pictures; you wouldn't believe the zoom power of those cameras they have – worth every penny of the taxpayers' money. So, after you'd been arrested, we sent a car up there to retrieve what you'd buried. And hey presto, it's our missing firearm. Right now, we're having it tested for prints, for DNA... for you. And there's your link. What have you got to say about that?'

'I want a solicitor.'

'Of course, that is your right. But, Mr Michael Davies, my only decision now is whether to save myself a little bit of embarrassment, or to chuck the book at you.' He leaned close to Meic's face. 'So why don't you bugger off back to your cell, and have a think about that? Constable, take this man back to the cells.'

Behind the one-way mirror, standing in the darkness, observing the scene, the woman called Joan allowed her lips to form in an upward curve.

As the officer approach him, Meic stood up and stared at the DCC. So he'd spend more time than he planned as a guest of the English Queen. He could take that. He wasn't going to break down in front of them – the dignity of Wales demanded that he kept his calm. In fact, the extra time might prove useful. He could do what so many prisoners of imperial regimes had done down the ages: write his political manifesto.

'Well that is excellent news, Sophie, from small acorns do mighty oaks grow... You can tell them that I'd be very happy to have lunch together, Monday would suit best. No, no, I've nothing on up here, it's all died down bar a couple of reporters sniffing around... well it has been a few weeks since... Just some generic gawkers and protest-tourists around, same types you'd see visiting the West Bank, yes, collecting dinner-party material... Quiet would be the word, they've even finally downsized the police presence... Now do make sure that these people book somewhere decent, I haven't enjoyed a sniff of a Michelin star for a few months... one is absolutely starved of decent eateries in these parts… Her? She's fine, been taking lots of *long* self-involved walks recently… Yes, I know, but I have tried my utmost… Indeed, I heard it on the *Today* programme this morning, fast-tracked onto the candidate shortlist despite being on bail… Hmm, I agree, incredible, one-way ticket to martyrdom is more like it… just another reason to skedaddle tout de suite… oh yes, while these guys seem keen about this, it may be opportune to put out some feelers about the book on the back of their interest… Insider view of the protest, problems of rural communities and so on… Very good… See you then.' Frankie finished the call and slipped her mobile into the pocket of her slacks.

She gazed out the window for a moment – *How one woman's vision ran headlong into twenty-first century Luddites?* – no, that was more of a subtitle. Then how about something along the lines of *Building Back: a radical blueprint for a sustainable small-town future*? Frankie began to make herself a cappuccino, thinking about new book titles as she monitored the coffee machine's pressure gauge. Or *A Great Seaside Adventure: how one woman gave a village back its future.* That might be more like it…

'You sound pleased with yourself. Ruth wandered into the kitchen.

'Yes, that was my agent.' Frankie's eyes followed Ruth as she skirted around the kitchen table. 'If you're interested.'

'Ah there they are.' Ruth picked up the car keys.

'Sophie called to pass on the news that *SkyArts* channel have been in touch with her. It seems that they loved my columns during the disturbances and want to set up a meeting…'

Ruth looked directly at her for the first time.

'… with a view of me hosting their new international

arts magazine programme. She said that they were going to call me before all of this trouble flared up as I'd been on their radar for a while.

Noting that the pressure had reached its correct level, Frankie concentrated on steaming the milk, talking over her shoulder at her wife. 'Apparently this new show will involve rather a bit of foreign travel, filming interviews with international cultural personalities and such. I hope that won't mean that I'll be away too often, but it might be unavoidable. In any case, I'll need to return to London on Sunday.' She saw that Ruth was looking at her nails.

'You know, you could show a bit of interest.'

'I'm listening, what more do you want?'

Frankie started to froth a small jug of milk. 'A bit of respect maybe. This show will keep a roof over your head. You should be grateful.'

'I did have a job, remember? But I had to give it up so you could come up here.'

'Oh, that job wasn't suited to you.' Frankie sighed; she felt a little annoyed about this latest petulant display. 'We talked this through at the time.'

'You talked *at me*, you mean.'

'It is always me, isn't it? I'm such a bad person, quite possibly evil in the way I repress you, and your natural needs…'

Ruth simmered.

'Well, in this case, my darling, I'm going to London. And you can choose to come with me, or you can stay here.'

'Really?'

'Yes, really. You've had your fun, now I'm going to have mine.' With a fast-reddening face, Frankie turned away to finish preparing her coffee.

Silence descended upon the kitchen like a theatre curtain at performance end. Ruth looked on, and for a moment she saw a younger Frankie before her. She felt the muscles around her eyes slightly relax as she remembered those early days together. Thought about how they'd sit towards the back of the Arts Theatre in Cambridge, holding hands in the dark, eyes fixed on the stage and Frankie's fingers dancing over her sensitive skin. Her touch felt so intense then. But, Ruth reflected, she'd been different herself – young, in thrall to an idea about love from teenage years vacuuming up Austen and the Bronte sisters. That pure form of love wasn't how she thought about it now, as a grown woman. Love was as messy as the people who yearned for it. She returned to the present, and the moment, along with her love for the woman before her, had passed.

'Do you expect me to wait at home for you?'

Frankie finished spooning the milk froth into her cup and glanced up. 'Don't use that tone. I'm not taking you for granted, but what else exactly are you going to do?'

There was no reply.

'I suppose you could take up a new interest or hobby? I'd be entirely supportive if you decided to become a mature student. The Open University is quite good in its way; one of my old assistants did a part-time MBA with them. Of course, that's really a bit pedestrian, she was that commercial type, but you could study for history of art or something a little more imaginative.'

'I see.'

'Or maybe, here's another idea, you could get a little part-time work, something temporary perhaps? It doesn't have to be around here, perhaps I could make some connections for you…'

'Thanks for the advice.'

At this point even Frankie sensed the chill in the air. 'I'm just trying to be helpful.'

'And what about, how did you describe them, my *natural needs*?'

Her partner took a sip of cappuccino. 'Him? Oh, I'll get over it. Upsetting as it was, I think the mature action on my part is to forgive you. A vulnerable woman in a strange place, and he clearly took advantage. In fact, Parry may have a more troublesome time coming up, especially after that letter of complaint that I've sent to the Chief Constable and the Office for Police Conduct.'

An unexpected laugh slipped out of Ruth's mouth. 'Well, nah-nah, nah-nah nah. Playground spite wasn't what I expected from you.'

'Let the punishment fit the crime. He should know that. In any case, we'll be moving from here so there are unlikely to be repercussions from that direction.'

'But we've only just arrived.'

'It is necessary, Ruth. We can't stay up here – it's Siberia for media work. I feel much better and with this television work, our lives will naturally be back in London. I've triggered the early-termination clause in the contract, and as soon as our tenants leave, we can move back into our townhouse. And life can carry on as it was before.'

'Lovely.'

'And we could always keep this place as a holiday home as we originally planned. In fact, I'll get onto the letting agents on Monday. Actually, that's another idea – you could manage this place from London, and I could pay you a fee via the company. It would give you a bit of pocket money. Just came up with that one, I'm on fire this morning!'

Frankie finished her coffee and stared into space, mulling this new thought.

Ruth fingered the car keys. She'd been educated at one of the best universities in the country and once had enjoyed a professional career. Yet all through that, she'd often felt herself too eager to please, too hungry for approval, like a good little schoolgirl hoping the teacher would say something nice to her. She hated herself for it, debasing herself for a bit of attention. No longer.

'Frankie?'

'Hmm?'

'Aren't you angry with me?'

She considered the question. 'At first yes, and you can be quite, quite… trying. But wouldn't being angry simply be a waste of energy? It wouldn't get us anywhere. In any case, the episode here is coming to a close. The sooner we get back to our old life, the better.'

Ruth didn't know whether she felt relief or release. 'I'm going now. I'm going for a long drive. I've packed a bag and I don't know when or if I'll be back.'

Frankie stared at her. She began to speak but held her tongue; her wife's emotional outburst would surely pass. She'd be back.

'One final thing: I'm taking the car, so you'll have to find your own way to London for your old life. Goodbye, Frankie.'

Thirty-Nine

The door of the stone cottage opened, and Lloyd stepped out into the uncertain sunlight. He carried a bottle of beer in his hand and wandered over to a pair of white plastic chairs which hung around the patio. Tipping one over to remove the pools of rainwater from that morning's shower, he wiped the seat with his hand, then sat down and stretched out his legs on the other chair. Looking around, he could see the lush green returning to the fields, making fast work of the dried grass left by the scorch of summer. The wind had dropped in the last hour, and there were fewer flecks of white foam thrown up by the waves out to sea. With the school holidays over and with all the trouble, the out-of-season bookings for the holiday cottage had dried up, so Eleri from the letting agency had rented it out to Lloyd at a discount. Hardly anyone was staying in the adjoining small caravan park, which wasn't great for local business but that was how Lloyd preferred it right now. A solitary figure walked a dog on the beach, and he watched them for a few minutes while he savoured his drink. The first beer from a chilled bottle always had a crisp feel that had disappeared by the dregs.

He reached into his fleece pocket and brought out a crumpled envelope. Lloyd re-read the letter, hand-delivered the previous day by a bike sent from headquarters.

❧

19th September

Dear Sergeant Parry,

Further to our communication dated 4th September which granted consent to your formal request for a month-long leave of absence, I am now writing to inform you that a complaint of a serious nature has been made against you. Therefore, as per Rule 11a of the Police (Conduct) Regulations 2008 you are suspended from duty effective immediately.

Full details of your rights and obligations during suspension can be found in the enclosed document. I confirm that during the suspension period you will be entitled to receive full pay, but no benefits. You may wish to appoint a legal representative to advise you. Additionally, I have today informed your local Police Federation representative of the situation, and they will contact you in due course as per Federation guidelines for officer support during internal investigations. The date of your hearing will be communicated to you pending inquiries into the allegations.

I am also making you officially aware that the Chief Constable has decided to hold an internal inquiry into the recent protest at Llanawch and the sequence of events leading up to it. The inquiry will take place during October. As a leading participant in the incident, you should anticipate being called as a witness on or shortly after Monday 7th October. The proceedings will be held in camera at Police Headquarters in Colwyn Bay.

If you have any questions about either matter, you should, in the first instance, direct them to your Police Federation representative.

Yours sincerely,

Stephen J. Sheridan
Deputy Chief Constable.

Lloyd held the bottle between his thighs to stop it from spilling and replaced the letter back in the envelope. There wasn't much he could do. He'd expected something like this as soon as they dropped most of the charges against Meic Davies and instead got him for low-level affray. That would be four months at most, maybe out earlier for good behaviour. Someone had got at the CPS, must have. So they'd now be looking for a scapegoat and Lloyd wasn't slow enough to know that he was next in line. If they were going to kick him out of the force, then let them – but he wasn't going to roll over for any of those buggers. They could bloody well pay him off for it. And he wasn't returning to Llanawch either, not after how his so-called friends had left him hanging. Life in that place was like looking in the rear-view mirror. The village and his old home were Catrin's, they had never really been his.

He'd heard from Hywel that his mother had returned to the house, been surprised to find that Lloyd had moved his things out. She'd expected to find him there, slumped in a mess of empty food trays and crumpled shirts. Two decades' worth of accumulated possessions were currently dumped in the second bedroom in the cottage, untouched since the day that he'd moved in. Catrin's solicitor had been in contact, and as far as Lloyd was concerned, that was fine as he had no plans to make proceedings drag out. It was time to make a clean break and start doing something else with his life. Arwel hadn't spoken to him, but hopefully the boy would come round. Maybe he could visit him after he returned from his first term at university. He might have grown up a bit by then, noticed that life wasn't black and white. He had to hope…

Lloyd stared at the grass a few feet in front of him, and then lifted his eyes further to watch the opaque Atlantic roll up and slam into the muted tones of the beach, churning the sand it into grey silt before subsiding. It very much looked like the only winners out of the whole mess were going to be the politicians, whether local or national. The Prime Minister, First Minister, and the Leader of the Council had all tramped through the village square, paid their dues in front of the cameras. They'd talked about how they were going to change things, how they were going to reopen the school and how money for jobs would follow. And then in a few months, young Meic Davies would be out of prison, assuming he was convicted, and standing for election to the Senedd with a big, green-washed rosette on his lapel. All while Lloyd looked for work and rebuilt his life. It was funny, he reflected, but after the same politicians make this grand song and dance about reconciling the divides that they'd created in the first place, it's the people like him that have to pay to clean up their messes and pretend everything is going to be fine again.

What lay ahead was change. Only the rhythm of the waves out at sea was unchanging. Lloyd felt comfortable here, away from people, with the view of the coast, the fresh winds, the chance to think events through. When he did sort everything out, he'd like to stay on the west coast. Maybe he'd head down to Pembrokeshire, or even try Devon or Cornwall. Yeah, Cornwall looked all right on the tele, they wouldn't have heard of him down there. And then there was always the Kiwi option, he'd read that they were always looking to recruit British police officers. If he wasn't already past it, that was, he'd need to check the age cut-off. Over forty and you were invisible in today's world.

He heard a car engine in the distance, approaching from behind him. He strained round in the chair and saw movement on the usually quiet road which passed the turn-off to the cottage. There was a car. And it was familiar to him. He watched it as it slowly traced its way towards the turning. It was slowing. He could see more closely now. Definitely could place the car. And its occupant.

The car slowed near the entrance, hesitated to a slow halt. Lloyd could hear its engine idling as snatches of birdsong resumed from the clump of trees off to his left.

He stood up. It hit him how much weight was carried in that car, how important what happened next would be. And then the thought crossed his mind that perhaps there would be no redemption. That there might not be enough time left to make some of those dreams come true.

That perhaps, his life would have no neat end.

Author's note

This is a work of fiction even if it deals with some contemporary issues. There is of course no Llanawch, but travel around the Welsh coast, or the West Country for example, and you'll come across many places like it.

This book has been some time, and many time-zones, in the writing so there are a few people to thank: the enthusiastic team at *Troubador Books* who helped me to get this on the bookshelves; Tony Whittome for his advice on an initial draft and for telling me that I was on the right track; J. Parker for getting behind an early version of the book; and my very favourite translator who double-checked my Welsh grammar.

Finally, I'd like to thank my wonderful wife, who kept me writing to the final page on a diet of encouragement, love and cheese sandwiches…

About the author

James Coeur grew up in a rural community in West Wales where his early jobs were in tourism. After school he moved across Offa's Dyke to study and now lives in London.

For more information see: jamescoeur.wordpress.com/

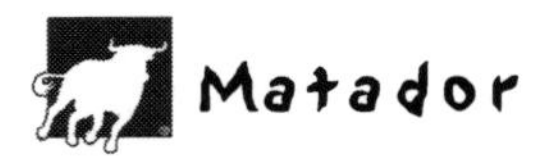
Matador